"Rare and wonderf...
An a...

Nationa...

JANE
FEATHER

"Ms. Feather is one of the best historical romance authors to date who knows the treasures of the heart and how to convey the messages."

The Paperback Forum

"Jane Feather is incomparable. Her stories shimmer with emotion and adventure, and her characters really do leap off the page into the reader's heart."

Affaire de Coeur

"Jane Feather expertly captures the era. She has a fine hand for merging historical detail with a tender love story and charms readers with her enchanting characters."

Romantic Times

"Spirited."

USA Today

"Delicious."

Detroit Free Press

Other Avon Books by
Jane Feather

BOLD DESTINY
THE EAGLE AND THE DOVE
SILVER NIGHTS

JANE FEATHER

Reckless Angel

AVON BOOKS NEW YORK

This is a work of fiction. Names, characters, places, and incidents either are the product of the author's imagination or are used fictitiously. Any resemblance to actual events, locales, organizations, or persons, living or dead, is entirely coincidental and beyond the intent of either the author or the publisher.

AVON BOOKS, INC.
1350 Avenue of the Americas
New York, New York 10019

Inside cover author photo by Peter Cutts Photography
Published by arrangement with the author
Library of Congress Catalog Card Number: 89-92980
ISBN: 0-380-75807-5
www.avonbooks.com/romance

First Avon Books Printing: September 1989

AVON TRADEMARK REG. U.S. PAT. OFF. AND IN OTHER COUNTRIES, MARCA REGISTRADA, HECHO EN U.S.A.

Printed in the U.S.A.

WCD 10 9 8 7 6 5

Reckless Angel

Chapter 1

"Odd's bones, Sir Daniel, I swear 'tis but a maid!" The trooper was on his knees beside a crumpled figure—just one crumpled figure among the many littering the field; some were silent, others shrieked their agonies to the night sky, yet others moaned their prayers for surcease with the helpless resignation of the vanquished.

Daniel Drummond swung down from his big black charger, whose head drooped listlessly in the August warmth. "How can that be, Tom?" He joined the trooper beside the inert body. "A maid in this charnel house?"

The body stirred, moaned, eyelashes fluttered upward, and Daniel found himself looking into a pair of enormous brown eyes now clouded with pain. "I want Will. Where's Will?" a small voice croaked, then the eyes closed again.

"Sweet heaven," muttered Daniel, unfastening her buff leather jerkin stained heavily with blood at the shoulder. Had there been any doubt as to the sex of this victim of the three-day battle of Preston, it was quickly resolved. Beneath the coarse linen shirt were outlined two unmistakably feminine hillocks. He had heard tell of the women who donned a trooper's britches and buff jacket, took up pike and halberd, and followed their men into battle, but he had never come face-to-face with the phenomenon before. This particular example seemed remarkably young for such devotion to love.

" 'Tis a pike thrust, I'd say," muttered Tom, peering at the ugly wound. "There'll be parties searching for the wounded soon enough; we'd best leave her to them and be on our way, else ye'll be languishing in a Roundhead prison."

"Aye." The Cavalier agreed absently, but he did not immediately straighten and get to his feet. His fingers were probing the wound. " 'Tis not excessively deep, I'd say, but there's no saying when she'll be discovered. She could bleed to death before a stretcher party arrives." He gestured expressively around the battlefield, its grim scene shrouded by the night, only occasionally brought into stark relief when the moon appeared fleetingly from behind the scudding clouds. Figures were moving among the bodies in a curious crouching run. They could be as easily robbing the dead and wounded as offering succor, Daniel thought with somber realism.

"We'll take her with us." He spoke with sudden decision, tearing off his sash. "She'll fare as well with us as leaving her here." He bound the wound as tightly as he could, and the deep blue of the sash darkened with ominous rapidity.

"We'll not make much speed," grumbled the trooper, looking anxiously around. "Not with a wounded maid on our hands. I don't mean no disrespect, sir, but if we're taken, you'll be as much service to her as a dead fish."

Despite his anxiety, Daniel smiled at his companion's customary lack of subtlety. "I'll not argue with ye on that score, Tom, but we're still taking her. She's no more than a child, not much older than little Lizzie."

Tom shrugged. The decisions were not his to make, although it did occur to him that if this girl in trooper's clothing were indeed little more than eight years old, matters had come to a fine pass in this land torn by civil strife. He took the still figure from his master while

Sir Daniel remounted, then handed her up before mounting his own sturdy cob. "Where to, sir?"

"We'd best keep off the roads . . . strike out across country," responded Sir Daniel. "They'll be looking to round up the runaways." A bitter smile twisted his lips. "As God is my witness, Tom, this is the last time I'll run from those foul, treasonous bastards." Prophetic words, but he was not to know that. He touched spur to his mount, and the charger seemed to summon up the last reserves of strength as he surged forward into the night, away from the ghastly field where agony and death hung like a miasma over the spectral shapes.

They rode for four hours, until dawn streaked the eastern sky and he could feel the beast beginning to founder beneath him. The body in his arms had stirred little, only an occasional whimpering cry indicating that she still lived. They came upon a small copse where a green-brown stream flowed sluggishly over flat stones, and Daniel reined in.

"We'll rest a while here, Tom. 'Tis secluded enough—a spot for cowherds and milkmaids, not soldiers."

" 'Tis to be hoped they're not cowherds and milkmaids in search of the reward to be won for a betrayed Cavalier," muttered Tom, dismounting to take his master's burden from him. He laid her on the bank of the stream and stood frowning down at her. "She bears no insignia; 'tis impossible to tell whether she fights for King or Parliament."

"Whether her lover does," corrected Daniel, removing his steel helmet with a sigh of relief. The rich, flowing locks of a Cavalier tumbled in dark profusion to the deep lace collar at the neck of his doublet. "I suspect 'tis love, not politics, that motivates this maid." He unfastened his breastplate and flexed his arms, stretching luxuriously. "Do you see to the horses and I will do what I may for her."

Kneeling down, he gently eased off the girl's leather jerkin. His sash was soaked and dark with blood. As he began to unfasten it, her eyes opened again. "I want Will," she said clearly. "Where is he?" She made a move as if to sit up.

"Easy now." He restrained her with little effort, but panic flared in her eyes.

"Leave me be. Who are you? What are you doing?" The panic edged a voice that he noted with interest was refined, bearing no trace of peasant dialect.

"I just wish to help you," he said. "Unless I much mistake, you have taken a pike through your shoulder." He drew aside the sash and took the torn edges of the shirt, ruthlessly ripping them apart to lay bare the wound where fresh blood still bubbled up to add another layer to the caked gash.

Her mouth opened on a cry of pain, but she closed her lips tightly, enduring his examination in stoic silence, although, when he washed the dried blood away with the sash soaked in the stream, tears squeezed out from beneath her closed eyelids, making tracks in the gunpowder dirt on her cheeks.

" 'Twould seem the bone is untouched," he said thoughtfully, "but I fear the muscle is torn. I will bind it tightly, and you must try not to move it at all."

"I do not wish to move it," she said, her voice clogged with tears. "It hurts so much."

"Y'are a brave girl," he said in encouraging approval. "How are you called?"

The look that crossed her face reminded him forcibly of little Lizzie trying to decide whether to fib her way out of a troublesome situation. "Harry," she said, closing her eyes.

"Mmmm," he murmured. "An unusual name for a maid, is it not?" There being no reply, he attempted another tack. "Who is Will?"

Her eyes opened again and the pain they showed this time was not simply physical. "I expect he is dead," she said. "I saw him fall just before this . . ." Her hand fluttered toward her shoulder. "Just before I felt this dreadful burning, then I don't remember anything else." There was a short silence while he bound up the wound, unable to offer reassurance and unwilling to lie. "Did we lose the day?" she asked finally.

"Parliament won the day," he answered her. "The king's army is no more. I do not know whether that means ye have won or lost."

"Lost," she said. "I am so thirsty."

So he had a fugitive Cavalier on his hands. Better that than the other, he decided. Attempting to restore the daughter of a stout Parliamentarian to her father could prove a mite awkward in his present position. He drew forth a tin cup from his knapsack, filled it with water from the stream, and held it to the girl's lips. She swallowed, choked, swallowed again. "Am I going to die?"

"I trust not."

"I do not mind if I do, now that Will is dead." Her lip trembled. "I wanted only to die at his side."

Daniel frowned at this romantic extravagance. "Far be it from me to deride the power of love, my child, but that is arrant foolishness. I trust your father will know what to do with you when you are returned to him."

A look of mulish obstinacy settled on the dirty face resting against his shoulder. "I am not going home."

Daniel did not trouble to take up the cudgels on this issue. It was hardly imperative at this point. "Try and rest a little." He laid her down on the ground again, fetched his cloak, and rolled it up to make a pillow. The cob was deprived of his horse blanket to provide covering for the invalid, and having made her as comfortable as circumstances permitted, Daniel lay down himself, his head resting on his saddle. "Wake me in two hours, Tom, and I'll stand watch while you sleep."

The sun was high in the sky, however, before Tom eventually woke his master. "I've seen no one, Sir Daniel, but the maid's in a bad way," he informed him. "Fever's high."

Daniel swore softly. "Take your rest, Tom. We'll start off again at sundown." He went over to the girl, who was thrashing on the ground, muttering incoherently, crying out in pain when her restlessness caused her to jar the injured shoulder. Her skin burned to the touch; the hectic flush on her cheeks and the lack of awareness in the brown eyes bespoke fever of an alarming height. He soaked his kerchief in the stream and bathed her face, holding her still as she tossed away from him with a violent protest.

There was little he could do as the day wore on and she roamed in the world of delirium. The wound was inflamed, the surrounding skin red and puffy, and the dread specter of mortification raised its inevitable head.

Daniel paced the little copse, while Tom slept and the horses grazed. It was obvious they could not continue their flight with the girl in her present state. But to seek help would be to court discovery. Could he leave her somewhere? Find a doorstep and abandon her in the dark of the night, hoping that she would find a succoring soul? Better to have left her on the battlefield at Preston. Moved by her plight, he had acted on an impulse that now struck him as foolishly chivalrous. But he must now live with the consequences of that impulse. Live with them or die with them, he thought with a humorless smile, under no illusions as to what betrayal and capture would mean: sequestration of all his lands and property, imprisonment, interrogation, and possibly execution. If he could reach home safely, avoid being taken as part of the spoils of battle, the worst he would face would be the crippling fines imposed on a Malignant.

Of course, there were as many for the king as for Parliament across this divided land in this year of our Lord, 1648, and his chances of finding a refuge with one of the former were as good as those of being betrayed by one of the latter.

An unearthly shriek filled the copse and Tom started up in alarm, shaking the sleep from his eyes. "Eh, what was that?" He stared around him. "Sounds like a banshee."

" 'Tis the maid," Daniel said over his shoulder as he tried to hold her still, to calm her with his touch and voice. "I must needs find a chirurgeon for her, Tom, but I'll not have you bear the risk with me. Make your own way into Kent. I'll follow when I am able."

"Nay, sir," Tom declared stoutly. "I'll not leave ye now, not after all that's passed between us." Bending over the stream, he splashed water on his face and head, shaking his head vigorously like a shaggy dog after a swim so that the drops flew in a fine spray.

"I appreciate your loyalty, friend, but there's no call for both of us to take the risk."

"Aye, there is," replied Tom, imperturbable. "Ye'll have need of a spare pair of 'ands, seems to me."

Daniel shrugged. "As you will." He held the cup to the girl's lips again, and she drank greedily, although she seemed not to be inhabiting the conscious world. "Let us eat before we start out. There's a morsel of bread and cheese left."

It was no more than a morsel and did little to satisfy the hunger of grown men. "We'd have to show ourselves soon enough anyway," Daniel remarked, saddling up his charger. "A man cannot live upon air and water."

Tom grunted his acquiescence, tightening the girths of the cob. "I'll hand the maid up to ye, sir, if'n y'are ready."

"As ready as I'll ever be." Daniel received the burden still wrapped in the horse blanket. For the moment she was still, although her sleep was uneasy, judging by the flickering eyelashes. He looked down at her face intently. Despite the knitted cap that hid her hair and the dirt and the hectic flush, high cheekbones, a slightly snub nose, and a prettily shaped mouth indicated a pleasing countenance. "I wonder who the devil she is, Tom. I'll swear she's gently bred . . . certainly has no business roaming the battlefield at the side of some young sprig she fancies herself in love with."

"Nay, should be plying her needle by the fireside," agreed Tom, "or minding her household tasks like any other proper damsel. A wild, hoity maid she must be!"

He tut-tutted in emphatic punctuation of this judgment, one with which Sir Daniel could not find fault.

They rode through the gloaming, keeping off the main thoroughfares. It was full night before Daniel saw what he had been looking for. A cottage, smoke curling from the chimney, candlelight in the lower windows, stood isolated beside a stream where a mill wheel turned ponderously. A small kitchen garden and a few apple trees were the only signs of domestic cultivation, but the wheat in the field beside the cottage was half harvested and it was to be presumed that the mill provided its owner with a reasonable living grinding his neighbors' crops.

"I'll sound 'em out, Sir Daniel," Tom said. " 'Tis hard to tell whether I be for King or Parliament, but if they sees ye first they'll be in no doubt."

Daniel nodded. Tom's yeoman's garb bore no distinguishing features, but he himself wore the lace, the sash, and the long hair of a Cavalier. "Have a care." He drew his horse into the shadow of a weeping willow beside the stream. The girl in his arms was babbling now, fighting the arms that held her, calling out for her Will. He clamped a hand over her mouth lest she betray them should the cottager turn out to be unfriendly to the king's cause.

Tom stood outlined in the square of yellow light filling the doorway, in earnest conversation with a round body in print gown and dimity cap. He gestured toward the weeping willow, and the woman's eyes followed his hand. Daniel heaved a sigh of relief. They must have struck lucky. He moved his horse out of concealment, trotting across to the cottage.

"Your pardon for disturbing you, goodwife, but I've need of a chirurgeon."

"Aye, so your man says." A pair of shrewd but faded blue eyes scrutinized his face for a long moment. Then, as if satisfied, the woman nodded briskly. "There's nobbut a leech in these parts, but he'll do as well as any, I daresay. Bring the lad within." She indicated his burden.

" 'Tis no lad, goodwife, but a maid," Daniel said, dismounting awkwardly. He followed his hostess into the kitchen, holding the now freely raving girl-who-called-herself-Harry.

"Lord a' mercy! I don't know what the world's coming to," exclaimed the goodwife, bustling to the foot of a narrow wooden staircase at the rear of the room. "His sainted Majesty locked up, the prince fled, and neighbor against neighbor. Now there's lasses on the battlefield! This-a-way, sir."

A small attic chamber was revealed at the head of the staircase. It contained a cot and a huge wooden chest of the kind used for storing household linens against the moth. The air was heavy with the scent of ripe apples laid carefully in rows on long wooden shelves on the far wall. Sacks of meal and flour were piled against one side of the loft, but it was swept clean and had a small, round window, unglazed to let in the fresh night breezes.

"Lay her down, sir, and I'll send my boy for the leech." She put a knowledgeable hand on the fevered brow and looked grave. " 'Tis a powerful fever. Is the wound clean?"

"Red and swollen," Daniel said, bending to untie the makeshift bandage. "I know little of these matters and could do no more than wash away the blood."

The goodwife peered, sniffed the gash. "There's no reek of mortification as yet," she said doubtfully. "But 'tis early days. She'll be best out of these clothes." She began to unfasten the girl's shirt, but the figure writhed violently, swinging an arm to catch the goodwife a hefty blow on the side of the head. "Ye'd best hold her down, sir," the woman said a little grimly, rubbing her head.

Daniel fixed his thoughts on little Lizzie as he assisted the kindly body in stripping the fevered girl. It was very clear, however, that this was no little girl but a grown woman, even if a very young one, and it was with considerable relief that he saw her at last respectably wrapped in a voluminous shift belonging to their hostess.

''Now, sir, I'll send the lad for the leech, and ye'll be glad of a bite o' supper, I'll be bound.'' She bustled to the stairs again.

''I've coin aplenty, goodwife,'' Daniel said, following her down to the kitchen. ''Your kind hospitality will not go unrewarded.''

''I'd 'elp a King's man in any case,'' the woman said gruffly, before giving brisk instructions to a boy of about fifteen who was honing a scythe in the inglenook. The lad grunted and set off, narrowly missing a headlong bump with Tom coming into the kitchen.

'' 'Orses are bedded down, Sir Daniel,'' Tom announced, going to stand foursquare before the fire, warming his backside with a contented sigh. The August evening was not cold, but there was something about a fire, something ordinary and comforting, that chased battlefield horrors as kin cut down kin into the unreal world of nightmare where they belonged.

The goodwife stirred a pot on the trivet in the fire, releasing a rich aroma that set the juices running as the two ravenous men sniffed eagerly. '' 'Tis jugged hare,'' the woman declared with a complacent smile. ''No one prepares it better, my man used to say.''

''Is 'e here?'' Tom inquired, moving to sit at the long plank table.

The goodwife shook her head. ''Dead for the king at Naseby. There's nobbut myself and our Jake now.'' She ladled the succulent dark meat and gravy onto wooden trenchers, sliced thick hunks of wheaten bread, and filled tankards with good October ale. ''That'll put the heart in ye.'' Seeing Daniel glance anxiously to the foot of the stairs, she said, ''I'll go to the lass, sir, don't ye fret now.''

Relinquishing his burden of anxiety for the moment, Daniel took the advice and ate heartily, feeling strength and optimism return with each mouthful, each draught of ale. They had just finished when the door opened to admit Jake and an old man in none-too-clean smock and britches, carrying a jar of leeches and a small bag.

" 'Ere's leech," announced Jake, helping himself to jugged hare.

"Where be patient?" The old man peered myopically around the room, although his nose twitched, following the scent emanating from the pot.

"Abovestairs." Daniel rose to his feet. "The goodwife is with her." He led the way, trying to quash his unease at the prospect of this individual's employing his dubious knowledge and skill on the fragile creature raving on the cot.

The goodwife greeted the new arrival matter-of-factly, deftly removing the patient's shift, holding her still as the leeches were applied to arms and chest, lifting her so that more could be placed on her back. Daniel felt the jugged hare rebel in his belly as he saw the loathsome creatures swell, engorged with blood. With a muttered excuse, he went down to the kitchen again, leaving the physicking to those who ought to know better than he what they were about.

Loud screams came from the loft, giving way to the most heartrending sobs. He thumped his tankard back on the table and leaped up the stairs again. "Enough! Has she not lost sufficient blood already?"

" 'Tis the only way to cool the blood, sir," the leech informed him placidly, pulling his little pets off the girl's skin and dropping them again into the jar. The girl's body was covered in angry red bites and her sobs wracked the slender frame as if they would burst from it in solid form.

"Get out!" Daniel ordered savagely, striding to the bed. "She is out of her mind with pain and fever and you have done nought but add to it."

The leech looked indignant. "And what about my fee, sir?"

"You'll have it!" Daniel reached into the pocket of his doublet and pulled out a shilling.

The old man seized the coin, pocketing it and hastening down the stairs as if afraid that the gentleman would change his mind and exchange the shilling for a groat.

"Well, if ye'll not have the leech, sir, we'll have to see what we can manage for ourselves," the goodwife said. "I don't 'old with all this bloodletting, meself. Weakens 'em when they most need their strength, seems to me."

"Aye," Daniel agreed. "So why did we send for him?"

"Ye wanted a chirurgeon, sir, and 'e's the nearest we've got in these parts," the woman said a shade tartly. "O' course, there's old Dame Biddy . . . a wonder with herbs, she is, but there's those that say she 'as the evil eye. I don't 'old with it, meself, but you takes your chance."

Herbs were a deal more gentle than leeches, Daniel reflected, and he did not believe in the evil eye. "Send Jake for her."

Henrietta awoke, aware of one amazing and most glorious thing—the absence of pain. Tentatively, she twitched her toes, wriggled her fingers, moved her head. There were no ill effects, so she tried opening her eyes. It seemed to be very bright after the dark, pain-wreathed world she had been inhabiting recently, but although she was obliged to blink several times, her eyes no longer hurt and her head did not pound.

" 'Bout time too," came a mutter from across the chamber. Henrietta turned her head to see a figure who seemed vaguely familiar. A pair of green eyes, alarmingly crossed, squinted in a face wrinkled like a prune. "Nearly gave ye up." The crone shuffled across the wooden boards and Henrietta, who knew all about the evil eye, instinctively shrank back from the cross-eyed scrutiny.

The crone crackled. "I've done ye no harm as yet, little maid." She laid a hand on the girl's brow, nodding with satisfaction before turning her attention to the wadded poultice fastened to the wounded shoulder.

Henrietta relaxed, recognizing the touch and attentions as accustomed and comforting. "What day is it?"

"Monday."

But which Monday? How long had she been lying here? One week . . . two? She tried to sit up, then decided rather rapidly that perhaps she wouldn't bother. It made her feel far too peculiar.

"Y'are weak as a new-dropped lamb," said her nurse. "But y'are young. Ye'll get your strength back soon enough."

Footsteps sounded on the wooden staircase and another familiar figure from dreamland appeared at the head of the stairs. He was tall, very dark-haired, with sharp black eyes in a tanned face. Those eyes went instantly to the bed, then sparked with sudden relief. "Well, this *is* a pleasure." His voice was deep and smooth, yet seemed to carry a chuckle in its depths, as if its owner found the world and its inhabitants in general amusing.

Smiling, he came to the foot of the bed. "Is all well, dame?"

"Aye, sir, that it is. Fever broke last night and she's been sleepin' like a babe since. She'll be right as rain once she's got 'er strength back, so ye'll not be needin' me anymore."

"I'd not have you leave until y'are quite certain there'll be no relapse," Daniel said sharply.

"There'll be none," Dame Biddy declared. "I've other things to do, sir, than dance attendance on them what 'as no need of it. Five days of my time, ye've had."

"Ye'll be well paid for it."

The old dame merely nodded and began packing things into a basket. "The goodwife'll know what to do to feed 'er up and change the poultice. I'm off now." Without so much as a farewell gesture to the girl she had brought back from the edge of death, she creaked down the stairs.

"I was afeard, at first, that she had the evil eye,"

Henrietta said. Her voice sounded a little stiff, as if from disuse.

Daniel shook his head with a smile. "A fearsome countenance, I grant you, but rarely have I seen such skill. Ye've good cause to be grateful."

"Aye, I am aware." She lay looking at him, not troubling to fight the insidious weakness of her limbs but simply enjoying the sensation of her body at peace. "And to you, too, Sir Daniel, I believe."

"So you know my name."

"I seem to have heard it spoken." She frowned slightly. "I suppose I was sometimes in this world."

He nodded. "Perhaps you will return the courtesy now and tell me how you are called."

That same calculating look crossed her face and he knew what he was going to hear before she spoke. "Harry," she said firmly, closing her eyes.

Daniel considered his options. At the moment they were somewhat limited and until she was fit to travel he did not really need to know her family. "And how old are you, Harry?"

There seemed little harm in answering that truthfully, Henrietta decided, and the victory she had just gained could allow a little conciliation. "I turned fifteen on the first of August."

"And what was a fifteen-year-old maid doing at the battle of Preston?" he inquired in a tone of mild curiosity.

"I went to be with Will."

"Ah, yes." He frowned. "So you did."

There was a moment of silence, then the girl announced, "We were to be married, only . . . only . . ."

"Only you ran into a little parental opposition," he supplied helpfully. "Were you eloping when this battle intervened?"

Henrietta shook her head. "Will would not elope. He went to fight for the king, so I had to go too."

Daniel found himself unconvinced of the imperative here, but then he was not fifteen years old and in love. "Your family will be distracted with worry for you."

Her face closed again. "They will care only because if I am not there they cannot compel me to wed Sir Reginald—" She broke off abruptly.

Daniel regarded her thoughtfully. Obviously she had realized that completing the name of the intended bridegroom might give her interlocutor some clue as to her own identity, or at least to the part of the world from which she hailed.

He sat down companionably on the edge of the bed, noting absently that a week's fever had left her wan and peaky. Her hair, which he suspected to be very fair, was now lank, straggling halfway down her back in limp, dirt-darkened strands. "And why does Sir Reginald not find favor?"

Her features screwed themselves into a disgusted grimace. "He's a fat, drunken sot and his breath reeks most foully! He has no hair and his teeth are green—those that he has—and he is old as Methuselah!"

Daniel absorbed this horrifying image in comprehending silence before asking, "Why are you to be compelled to wed this less-than-paragon?"

"Oh, 'tis something to do with bonds and staple-statute. A debt my father owes Sir Reginald."

"Upon staple-statute?" When she nodded, Daniel pulled at his chin. This debt the girl's father owed would thus take precedence over all other claims on his land and property, and the man he owed could take possession of all land and property at any time he pleased until he was paid in coin of the realm. "So, this Sir Reginald will have you to wife instead. Is that it?"

"No, he will not!" she declared with more strength than a week's fever and a wounded shoulder should have permitted. "For I will not go home to be had." Her face was suddenly wiped clean of all defiance and the brown eyes shimmered with unshed tears. "If Will had not been killed, I am certain I would have persuaded him to elope. Even if it meant he *was* disinherited and I had no dowry, we would have managed somehow." She dashed the back of her hand across her eyes, sniffing dolefully.

"Love alone is an insubstantial diet, child." He stood up. "A man is like to starve with naught else to put in his belly."

"We could work. There is farm work, and I could be a dairymaid . . . But now . . ." Her voice faltered. "Will is killed, so . . . so . . ." The tears fell then, fast and furious. "It is not just," she sobbed. "He was too young and I loved him so much."

Daniel had little comfort to offer. Too many young men beloved of their maids had gone to their deaths in the last eight years of civil strife. He stroked her head, gave her his handkerchief, and waited for the storm to blow itself out.

"Now, now, what's this?" The goodwife bustled up the stairs. "Lordy, sir, she shouldn't be workin' 'erself up like this."

Thus reprimanded, however unjustly, Daniel left Harry in the charge of the goodwife and went outside into the late afternoon. The story she had told him was hardly unusual, but no less unpleasant for that. Daughters were currency and not all parents were scrupulous in the manner in which they spent that currency. It did not alter his task, however. He had no choice but to return her to her home and deliver her up to whatever fate there awaited her, for all that he was aware a runaway daughter was unlikely to draw a light sentence even from the fondest parent.

Of course, before he could do anything, she had to recover her strength and be induced to reveal her identity. Meanwhile he must kick his heels here, a mere half day's ride from Preston, where Parliament's army was still mopping up straggling Royalists. It went against all the laws of chance to imagine that the presence in this cottage of two strangers and an injured girl would go unnoticed in the surrounding countryside—and not all who heard of them would be of Royalist sympathy.

Chapter 2

It was a week later when Tom rode up to the cottage, alarm etched in every line of the leathery countenance. " 'Tis said a party of Roundhead troopers and a captain are combing the area, sir," he blurted out as he jumped from the cob. "They've already found three wounded men holed up in a barn about five miles from 'ere." He spat disgustedly on the ground. "Bastards fired the barn, although the farmer swore 'e'd no knowledge of the men hidden there. Poor sod lost 'is winter's feed."

Daniel glanced backward at the neat little cottage, the turning mill wheel, the harvested field, the round figure of the goodwife bent over a currant bush in the kitchen garden. After all the kindness shown them, they could not put the woman and her son at risk of losing their livelihood. It was time Harry was induced to tell the truth, so that at least they might flee in the right direction.

She had left her sickbed on wobbly legs the previous day, and was now sitting in the shade of a copper beech by the front door. He had been right about her hair. Freshly washed, it was the color of corn silk, feathering in soft tendrils around a heart-shaped face in which the brown eyes still appeared overlarge. She was wearing a borrowed gown that swamped her in shapeless folds, evidence of the goodwife's rather different bodily structure. However, there was nothing waiflike about the smile with which she greeted Daniel as he approached.

"Are you come to amuse me, Sir Daniel? I am sadly bored just sitting here without even a book to while away the tedium."

"Alas, child, I am come to annoy you, I fear," he said. "We must move from here without delay, and I've a need to know in what direction our way lies."

"Why, sir, how should I know in what direction your way lies?" she said, that mulish look upon her face again, replacing the previous smile. " 'Tis no business of mine."

"I think we had better continue this discussion in your chamber," he said quietly. "I intend to have the truth from you."

There was something about the quiet tone that caused Henrietta a quiver of apprehension. "I will not go home," she said as he took her elbow and drew her to her feet.

"We will see about that."

She pulled back against the hand that would lead her into the house, but even had she been restored to full health and strength her resistance could only have been token. "I *won't* go home," she reiterated on a note of desperation. "I can fend for myself if you must leave. Mayhap the goodwife will let me stay with her and earn my keep."

"You talk foolishness," he replied shortly, pushing her ahead of him up the narrow staircase. "Now, let us be done with this Harry nonsense. I want your name."

Released, she thumped down on the cot, drawing her knees up and hugging them fiercely. "I am called Harry."

"Of what family?" There was an edge now to the smooth, deep voice, and the hint of humor it normally contained was quite gone. His eyes were hard; his lips thinned.

Henrietta shook her head in mute refusal.

"If you were one of my daughters," Daniel said

softly, "I would make short work of your obstinacy. Do not try me too far."

Her eyes widened. "How many do you have?"

"How many what?" The question threw him off balance, bearing no relation as far as he could see to the matter under discussion.

"Daughters, of course." Interest laced her voice.

For a moment his expression softened. "Two, and a graceless pair they are." A shadow crossed his eyes. "They want a mother's care."

"She is dead?"

"Aye, in childbed with Ann some four years past," he replied bleakly.

"You do not seem that old," Henrietta remarked, regarding him in speculative fashion over her knees.

Daniel looked astonished. "I do not feel 'that old.' A man of nine and twenty has not exactly one foot in the grave."

"How old is your other daughter?" This was a much more appealing conversation, Henrietta decided, and might well serve to keep the other one at bay for a while longer.

"Elizabeth is eight."

"And there are no other children?" A marriage lasting upward of five years would generally produce more than two offspring four years apart.

Daniel shrugged. "Two little ones died; one at birth, the other of milk fever when he was a week old." And his Nan had never carried a child with any ease, had labored in long agony to deliver each one, until finally exhausted . . . He put away the futile train of thought and the guilt he had learned to live with.

The figure on the bed opened her mouth for another question, but Daniel, realizing how far they had drifted from the urgent matter at hand, cut her off before she could form the words. "Of what family are you?" He snapped his fingers impatiently. "This has gone on long enough."

"I cannot go home. Surely you must understand that?" The obstinacy was replaced now with a soft plea. "Do you know what they will do to me? Sir Reginald probably will not wish to marry me any longer—"

"In which case you will be spared a rank and drunken bedmate," he interrupted harshly. "I had thought 'twas that fate you had fled."

She bit her lip. "So it was. And if I had managed to wed Will, then everything would have been all right. But I am afeard to go back unwed. 'Twill be a thousand times worse if Sir Reginald says I have spoiled my maidenhead—which I have not, because Will was too honorable," she added. Daniel inhaled sharply at the slightly aggrieved note investing the addendum and he began to feel some sympathy for the girl's parents. "But he could say it was so and refuse to marry me," she finished with a helpless gesture that reminded him of how young and defenseless she was.

Daniel was defeated. There was no severity he could visit to extract the information from her that would not be surpassed by what she knew awaited her at home. He paced the tiny chamber while she sat on the bed, watching him anxiously over her drawn-up knees.

The sound of raised voices outside jarred the tense silence. Daniel strode to the window, his face paling beneath the tan as he recognized Tom's angrily protesting tones mingling with those of a stranger. Was it Roundheads? But below he saw just one man, no more than a youth, engaged in exclamatory conversation with Tom.

Henrietta stumbled off the bed, the strangest expression on her face. Her legs were still weak and the weakness was not aided by her painfully pounding heart. She clung to the windowsill at Daniel's side. " 'Tis Will!" She looked up into her companion's astounded face. " 'Tis Will! He is not killed!"

Daniel was conscious of an overpowering relief mingling with utter bewilderment as to how this salvation could so mysteriously have appeared.

"Will!" Henrietta's shriek set his ears ringing. "You are not killed!"

The young man looked up at the window, shading his eyes against the sun. "Do I look it, Harry? How the devil did you . . . ? Oh, never mind." He turned back to Tom, now stunned into silence. "D'ye see, man? I am no foe. I have been turning the countryside outside in looking for her, and those damned Roundheads are everywhere!"

Tom nodded. "Ye'd best go up, young sir."

A bare half a minute later, Will Osbert entered the attic chamber. He was a big, untidy-looking young man with a shock of red hair and bright green eyes. "Y'are the most ramshackle girl, Harry," he declared with feeling. "Where did you go? I thought ye safe in the inn." He noticed her companion for the first time and his face flushed darkly. His hand went to his sword. "What business have you with Mistress Ashby, sir?"

"Oh, Will!" wailed Henrietta, dropping onto the bed again as her legs began to wobble anew. "You have betrayed me!"

"Betrayed you!" Completely at a loss, Will stared blankly. "What do you do here with this man?"

"Daniel Drummond," Daniel said, extending his hand. "I am delighted to make your acquaintance, Master Will. I have heard much about you. But do pray enlighten me further. I cannot believe that Mistress Ashby truly goes by the name of Harry."

"Oh, no, sir, 'tis but a nickname, short for Henrietta," Will said cheerfully, quite reassured, although he was unsure why, by the manner of one who was so clearly a gentleman and seemed quite in charge of matters. "She is Henrietta Ashby of the Oxfordshire Ashbys. And I am Will Osbert, son of John Osbert, Esquire, of Wheatley in the same county."

"Oh, you are so *stupid,*" Henrietta said in disgust.

Daniel's lips twitched. It seemed he was about to hear an exchange rather resembling a schoolroom squabble than a lovers' tiff. He was not disappointed.

"I am not at all stupid," Will said hotly. "I told ye to stay in the inn, but when I reached there after the battle—and a deal of trouble I had getting there, I might add—they said you had been gone since early morning and had left no message. If *that* is not stupid, I do not know what is."

"But I saw you fall on the field," she said.

"What!" The young man gazed in disbelief. "What field?"

"At Preston. I followed you. I was in disguise anyway, so no one thought me out of place. I looked just like a trooper." She became inordinately interested in her fingers, plaiting them intricately in her lap. "I thought if you were going to die, then I would rather die with ye than be forced to return home."

"You were at the battle?" Will, in his struggle to grasp this, was aware that he sounded like a child repeating his lesson.

"I was wounded," she announced with some pride, looking up at him. "Sore wounded, was I not, Sir Daniel?"

"A pike thrust," he agreed solemnly. "I'd advise you to keep a closer eye on your affianced bride in the future, Master Osbert."

"Oh, Harry, what have you been saying? You *know* we cannot be wed." Will punched a clenched fist into the open palm of his other hand. "I have told you so more times than I care to remember. Your father will not consent and so neither will mine. You will have no dowry and I shall be disinherited. What are we to live upon?"

Daniel felt his relief evaporate. The serendipitous arrival of Master Osbert did not appear to be the salvation he had believed.

"But d'ye not love me, Will?" Henrietta spoke with painful intensity, her hands gripped tightly in her lap. "We plighted our troth. I would not have followed you else."

Will shuffled his feet uncomfortably. "Of course I love you, Harry, but we cannot be wed without money. You had no business running away as you did. *You* must understand, sir." He turned in appeal to the silent older man. "She dressed in men's clothes and ran away from home without telling me she was going to. She came up with me in London and would not go home.'' He ran his hands distractedly through the unruly thatch of red hair. ''She never tells me what she is going to do . . . just like following me to the battle when I had thought her snug in the inn.''

''But I could not tell you what I intended,'' Henrietta protested. ''You would have become exceeding perverse and said I should not.''

Daniel Drummond closed his eyes briefly. Mistress Ashby might well fancy herself in love, but from the tone of this exchange it seemed likely that love of the reluctant Will Osbert had merely offered excuse to flee the parental hearth and the prospect of wedding and bedding the ancient and unwholesome Sir Reginald. It looked as if he was not going to shed this burden for some time.

He interrupted their wrangling. ''How did you escape the field, Will? Henrietta says she saw ye fall.''

''I did not fall,'' Will said. ''If I did not recognize Harry, it is possible she mistook someone for me.''

Daniel nodded. In that hell's kitchen, clouded with gunsmoke, deafened by the clash of steel and the roar of cannon and the crack of musket shot, anything could have happened. ''How did you light upon this place?''

Will scratched his freckled nose. ''I have been scouring the countryside for days; dodging Roundhead patrols all the while. I could not see how she could just disappear, sir, so I thought if I made inquiries at every inn and in every village someone would have some news.''

''And lo and behold . . .'' Daniel said dourly with an encompassing swing of his arm at the assembled trio. ''If you heard we were here, the patrols won't be long behind.'' He walked to the window. ''Without passes, we shall have the devil's own time journeying south, and Henrietta is still far from strong.''

''I am not going,'' Henrietta declared. ''So you need not concern yourself with me. The Roundheads will not trouble me here—''

Daniel swung around from the window. ''Mistress Ashby, my patience is *not* inexhaustible!''

''But I am nothing to do with you,'' she protested with perfect truth.

'' 'Tis so, Sir Daniel,'' Will put in. ''We will shift for ourselves now that I have found her. You must look to your own safety.''

Daniel looked at the young man's flushed earnestness and smiled reluctantly. ''I appreciate your concern, Master Osbert, but I have a feeling that I can more effectively ensure Henrietta's return to Oxfordshire than you.''

Will glanced worriedly at Henrietta, who had slumped despairingly on the bed. ''She cannot return, sir. You do not know Sir Gerald, or Lady Mary, Harry's stepmother.''

Daniel frowned. ''Some punishment for such an escapade is surely merited? You would not deny that. Is it the rod ye fear?''

''There's worse things than the rod,'' Henrietta said, looking at Will, who returned her look in gloomy comprehension.

Daniel sighed. ''Very well, we will leave the question of your ultimate destination to be decided later. But we will essay the journey south together. D'ye have a horse, Will?''

Before Will could answer, footsteps sounded on the staircase and the goodwife, white-faced, stumbled into the room. ''Soldiers, sir,'' she gasped, dabbing her lips with her apron. ''Roundheads, some fifty yards down the road, Jake says. They're comin' 'ere, sir. What's to be done?'' Her voice trembled on the edge of hysteria. ''They'll burn the 'ouse over our heads, drive off the cow, they'll—''

''No, they will not, never fear, goodwife.'' It was Henrietta who spoke with sudden energy. She was pulling back the cover on the cot. ''Will, get under the bed.'' She picked up her nightcap, cramming it on her head, tucking up her hair beneath it. ''Quickly, Will . . . Oh, do not argue with me . . . Sir Daniel, you must hide in the linen chest. 'Twill be a bit cramped." She lifted the lid, and the strong aroma of camphor filled the little chamber.

"I'll not hide to be smoked out like a rat in a hole," Sir Daniel protested. "Do not be absurd, child."

"They'll not come into a plague chamber," she told him. "No farther than the top of the stairs, if that. The goodwife must tell them there is plague in the house. I will do the rest. Have you some amber pastilles, goodwife, to burn so that it seems as if you try to ward off infection?"

"Aye, that I have." The woman seemed to have steadied herself now. "And vinegar. There was plague in the next village only last month; 'twill not seem strange that we are afflicted."

It just might work; might at least give them sufficient breathing space to make their escape. Swallowing his pride and the honor of the Drummonds, Daniel clambered into the linen chest to be near suffocated by camphor as the heavy lid closed under Henrietta's impatient hand.

Henrietta struggled to remove the oversize gown before leaping into bed and pulling the covers up to her chin. The air filled with the acrid scent of vinegar as the goodwife sprinkled it over the floor and the covers. Then she lit the wick embedded in a cone of aromatic paste.

The sound of jingling spurs and the clatter of hoofs sounded from below, and Henrietta opened her mouth on a blood-curdling scream of agony.

The goodwife, who had no need to pretend to a distraught mien, hastened down the stairs as another scream rent the air. "Oh, mercy, sir, what d'ye do here at such a time?" she gasped, stumbling outside to where a troop of horsemen stood, pike and halberd gleaming in the sun sparking off the close round helmets that denoted their allegiance to Parliament.

"What the devil is it?" The captain gazed up at the window where the screams were continuing.

" 'Tis my daughter, sir. She 'as the swellings. I've tried to cut 'em, but they'll not burst."

The captain paled, instinctively bringing his hand up to cover his mouth and nose as if he could thus prevent taking in the pestilential vapors. "Ye have the plague in the house, woman?"

"Aye, sir, God have mercy upon us," she wailed, burying her head in her apron. "Out of 'er mind with the agony she is, sir."

As the captain continued to stare up at the open window from whence emanated those dreadful sounds, a figure clad only in a white shift appeared. She climbed onto the sill to sway perilously, tearing at her body with distracted hands, her eyes wild and unseeing.

"Oh, Lord have mercy, sir, she's for killing 'erself," gasped the goodwife. "The pain 'tis that bad. Will ye help me tie 'er to the bed, sir? I cannot manage 'er myself, so strong as she is when the madness takes 'er."

"Goddammit, woman! Ye'd have me infected!" The captain backed his horse away rapidly, a look of horror on his face. "Get inside, ye should all be shut up." With that, he wheeled his horse and galloped away from the pest house, his troop following, pursued by the frenzied screams that lifted the scalp and sent graveyard shivers down the spine.

"They have gone," Henrietta said matter-of-factly, stepping off the broad sill. "I have quite hurt my throat." She rubbed her throat as Daniel, choking, emerged from the chest and Will rolled out from beneath the bed. They both looked at her in some awe.

"Never have I heard such an appalling racket," declared Sir Daniel. " 'Tis no wonder you have a sore throat."

"But the ruse was successful." She beamed on them. "The goodwife was most convincing."

"For pity's sake, sir, ye'd best be away from here without delay." The goodwife appeared at the head of the stairs. "The young lady sounded just like my Martha did when the plague took her. 'Tis a sound to strike to the marrow."

"Aye," Daniel agreed. It was a somber play Henrietta had enacted, but it could not detract from his relief at her success, or from the urgency to make good that success. "Henrietta, you'd best don your britches again and travel in that guise. Ye may ride pillion with me. D'ye have a horse, Will?"

"Indeed, sir, and I have Harry's nag also," Will said. "She left it at the inn. I tied 'em up beyond the mill."

"That is all to the good, but she is not strong enough to ride alone yet. Ye may lead the nag for the time being. Make haste and get dressed now, child. Goodwife, we must come to a reckoning." The two went down to the kitchen in deep discussion, leaving Henrietta and Will.

"I do not care for this," Henrietta declared. "We are in no wise obliged to travel with Sir Daniel. While I am most sensible of his kindness to me, he holds no authority over us, Will. We will make our own way to London, and if you will not wed me, then I will find employment in some household—"

"In what capacity?" demanded Will. "Had you not better get dressed?"

"Why, as governess," she replied stoutly. "I am book-learned." A note of derision entered her voice. "There'll be many a Parliamentarian family anxious to educate their daughters in the ways of the gentry, I dare swear."

Will regarded her doubtfully. " 'Tis possible, mayhap. But y'are such a ramshackle creature, Harry, and any respectable family will want to know whose name you bear."

"I can lie." She shook out her britches, examining them critically. "These will still serve, but my shirt was torn with the pike and the jerkin is sadly stained . . . and I must procure suitable garments if I am to go as governess—"

"Governess!" The exclamation came from Sir Daniel, appearing at the head of the stairs. "I cannot imagine any man who has not escaped from Bedlam entrusting the care of his daughters to such a one as you!"

"You do not know me."

It was a simple statement, curiously dignified, and for some reason gave him pause. He smiled. "No, perhaps I do not." He turned to Will. "Why do you not fetch your mounts? Tom is packing knapsacks and could do with some assistance." Will accepted his dismissal without demur and with some relief.

"I have brought you a shirt," Daniel said. "The goodwife said it belonged to Jake when he was rather smaller than he is now, and it should do you."

"My thanks." She took the garment, unsmiling, and launched into her prepared speech. "While I am most sensible of your kindness, Sir Daniel, I must decline the offer of your escort. Will and I would not burden you with our company. We will make our own way to London."

"But if our ways lie together, it seems only practical to combine forces," he remarked casually. "We may each be of service to the other. Without safe conduct, 'tis a long and dangerous journey we undertake."

Henrietta busied herself putting on the shirt. Her shoulder was still stiff, although the gash had healed well, and the operation was a little awkward, but it gave her time to contemplate her response.

"Let me do the buttons for you." The hint of humor was in the deep voice again. She looked up and saw both amusement and understanding in the shrewd black eyes bent upon her.

"I can manage, thank you."

"I do not doubt it, Mistress Ashby, but it will be quicker if I do it. We are in somewhat of a hurry." He gently put aside her hands and fastened the buttons. "There now." A long finger beneath her chin tilted her face to meet his amused regard. "Trust me," he said softly. "I will not allow any harm to come to you." Now whatever had made him say such a thing . . . undertake such a charge? Henrietta Ashby was not his responsibility. But the words had said themselves and he could not have withheld the promise had he tried.

Surprise glowed in the big brown eyes and that fierce, prickly resolution faded from the set features. "You will not make me go home?"

"I will not allow any harm to come to you," he repeated.

A puzzled frown drew the arched eyebrows together. "I do not see how you can prevent it if I must go home. I am my father's daughter when all's said and done. He may do as he pleases with me."

"Do not be too sure of that," he said with a confidence that alarmed him. The girl had spoken only the truth after all. Who was he to interfere in a man's jurisdiction over his family? But he'd made the promise. Hopefully the means for fulfilling it would come to him when necessary. Her eyes were still fixed upon him, expressing mingled trust, hope, and doubt. Smiling, he kissed the corner of her mouth, telling himself that it was a salute of the kind he would have given Lizzie or baby Nan when they were in need of reassurance. It did not seem quite the same, though.

"Put on your britches," he said, suddenly brisk, drawing away from her. "I'm not minded to sit here waiting for Parliament's troop to return."

Henrietta turned away from him, stepping into the garment, tucking her shift into the waistband, fumbling with the hooks. Her face was unaccountably hot and for once she found herself at a loss for words. Will had kissed her often, but it hadn't made her feel like this—hot and quivery. Perhaps the fever was returning.

"Horses are saddled, Sir Daniel," Will called from the bottom of the stairs.

"I am coming," Daniel called back. "Sit on the bed, Henrietta, and I'll help ye with your stockings. You do not wish to wrench your shoulder."

She obeyed, somewhat reassured by the crisp tone that restored matters between them to their former footing. "You had better become accustomed to calling me Harry again,'' she said matter-of-factly, holding out her foot. ''Henrietta in britches is a contradiction in terms.''

He chuckled. ''Aye, y'are right.'' He smoothed the stockings over her calves and helped her into her boots. ''We must ride as far from here as possible before dark. 'Tis to be hoped your strength will hold.''

Three hours later, Henrietta knew that she had reached her limit. She sat astride the big black charger, trying not to lean against the broad back of Daniel Drummond in front of her. The charger's gait had seemed easy enough at first, but now, as fatigue softened muscle and sinew, it began to feel like balancing on a rolling wave and her shoulder started to ache unbearably.

They were traveling cross-country, keeping to the woods and the shelter of hedgerows wherever possible. There had been one heart-stopping moment when a troop of Roundheads passed on the road on the other side of the hedge while they cowered, scarcely daring to breathe, praying that one of the horses would not betray them with a whinny or a jingle of bridle.

Daniel's expression grew grimmer after this incident. The only way they would have a chance of reaching London unchallenged would be to ride by night and hide by day. Night riding was inevitably slower, and a three-week journey was going to be stretched to four weeks or more. At least Tom, in his anonymous garb, would be able to enter towns and villages to buy provisions or take a horse to the farrier if one of them threw a shoe. Not for the first time, Daniel sent a swift prayer heavenward for the loyalty and devotion that had kept Tom at his side.

So lost in thoughts and calculations was he that he only slowly became aware of the weight against his back. Henrietta had yielded the struggle to keep herself upright and now flopped against him, her head resting on his shoulder. ''Harry?''

Instantly, she drew herself upright again. ''I do beg

your pardon, Sir Daniel. I felt a little sleepy, but I am quite awake now."

"Ye do not appear to be," Will said, looking anxiously across at her. "Y'are as white as whey, Harry."

Daniel reined in sharply, twisting in the saddle to look over his shoulder. "Foolish child! Why did ye not say something?" Anxiety informed the exasperation, but Harry was too exhausted for analysis. Tears filled her eyes and fell without restraint.

"There is no need for tears." Daniel swung down and lifted her to the ground. "Is your shoulder paining you?"

"Aye." She sniffed desperately in an attempt to regain control of herself, then sat abruptly on the stubbly earth of the newly harvested field.

"We'd best rest a while, sir, 'till the maid feels stronger." Tom looked around a landscape illuminated by the mid-afternoon sunlight. "Not much shelter hereabouts."

"There's a ditch," Will suggested, gesturing with his whip toward the far side of the field. " 'Tis away from the lane and the hedge will offer some concealment."

Hiding in ditches was not a Drummond habit; then, neither was fleeing pursuit like the hare before the hound. But locked up in some Roundhead prison he'd be of little use to his children, Daniel reckoned with grim resignation. "It will have to suffice. Come." He scooped up the collapsed figure at his feet and put her back on the horse, this time mounting behind her, holding her tightly against him with an encircling arm. "Lie back, Harry. I'll not let ye fall."

"I expect you are most kind to your children," Henrietta observed, settling thankfully against the strong support of his broad chest. " 'Twould be pleasant to have such a parent."

He glanced sharply down at her, ungratified by the observation. Did she really see him as a father figure? "I am far from old enough to have sired you," he declared.

"Nay, of course not," she agreed tranquilly. "But I

still think it must be agreeable for Elizabeth and Ann to have you for a father. I do not expect you would try to compel them into a distasteful marriage, or believe everything their stepmother might say to their discredit.''

''Your stepmother does not care for you, I take it?'' They had reached the far side of the field and Daniel drew in his mount.

''She hates me with a passion,'' Henrietta said. ''She has done so from the first moment she walked into the house when I was but five years old.''

Daniel dismounted and she slipped from the charger into his waiting arms. ''Of course I was not very nice to her either, but I think she could have tried to understand that I was afeard, d'ye not agree? She was six and twenty, a widow, and she brought her three children to live with us too.'' She stood rubbing her shoulder and looking down into the ditch. ''Is it dry, d'ye think?''

''Dry enough,'' Daniel said, taking a small animal skin container from his knapsack. ''Settle down and take some rest now. I do not wish to tarry here overlong.'' He encouraged her down the little slope to the bottom of the ditch, saying over his shoulder to Tom, ''If we turn the horses loose to graze, they'll not draw attention.''

He sat on the grass, leaning against the sloping side of the ditch, stretching his legs in front of him. ''Lie down and put your head in my lap. I would look to your shoulder. The goodwife gave me some ointment to rub in if it became sore.''

Henrietta obeyed a little awkwardly, resting her head and shoulders on muscular thighs, looking up into the face bent concernedly over her. She moved to unbutton her shirt, but he brushed her hands aside with the calm injunction to be still. Her shirt came undone and he slipped the sleeve of her shift off the injured shoulder. The warm air stroked her bared skin, and for some reason Henrietta shivered.

''Are you cold?'' Daniel asked, taking the top off the

small skin container. " 'Tis warm enough, I would have said."

"Nay, I am not cold," she denied rather weakly. " 'Tis fatigue, I expect."

"As like as not," he agreed, dipping a finger into the strong-smelling ointment. "I will try not to hurt you, but I must press hard if y'are to feel the benefit."

She closed her eyes because it seemed easier and less awkward if she did not have to look up at him. Gently but firmly, he massaged the ointment into her aching shoulder. It hurt and she inhaled sharply, biting her bottom lip. The pressure did not diminish, however, as Daniel steeled himself to complete his task. But at last it stopped and her eyes opened.

"Nay, do not look so reproachful," he said softly. " 'Tis sometimes necessary to cause a little pain in order to do good."

"This pains me more than it does you? Is that what you would say?" She smiled ruefully. "That has been said to me many times, Sir Daniel, but I have never found it convincing."

Chuckling, he buttoned her shirt. "Nay, I do not subscribe to that thesis. 'Twas said to me also many a time, and I could never understand why those who wielded the rod should suffer more than those who felt it."

"Exactly so," Henrietta agreed fervently. She sat up, flexing her shoulder. " 'Tis easier," she said. "If ye wish to continue the journey, sir, I am certain I am strong enough."

"Mayhap you are," he said. "But there are those amongst us who are not." He gestured a little way down the ditch to where Tom and Will lay prone. "We'll all be the better for an hour's respite, and there's less danger of discovery if we travel under the moon." He lay back against the side of the ditch, closing his eyes. "Ye may find it more comfortable to use my legs as pillow. 'Twill provide support for your shoulder."

Henrietta looked a little doubtful, but he appeared

quite relaxed and the bare ground was certainly bumpy and unyielding. She resumed her former position; the sun bathed her eyelids, creating a warm red darkness; aching fatigue yielded to languour; the living flesh beneath her head embodied safety and reassurance. Henrietta slept.

Daniel listened to her soft, regular breathing; felt the heaviness of her unconscious body; sensed her unquestioning trust, and hoped mightily that the trust was not misplaced. He would not have chosen to flee the lost battlefield of Preston with a weakened maid and her reluctant swain in tow. A rational man would not have pledged himself to protect a runaway maid from the legitimate wrath of her parent. Yet for the life of him, he did not know how else he could have acted. Daniel Drummond slept.

Chapter 3

"Y'are a milksop, Will," declared Henrietta in disgust, picking dirt from beneath her fingernails with the sharp end of a twig. "I am certain that if you defy your father, he will admire ye for it in the end. He may be difficult at first—"

"Oh, you live in cloud cuckoo land," Will interrupted. "There is nothing feeble about facing reality. Is there, Sir Daniel?"

Daniel regarded the squabbling pair wearily. They had been at it all afternoon and he was heartily sick of it. Outside the barn where they sheltered, the rain fell in a cold, drenching sheet. Now and again a gust of wind would drive an icy wave through the unglazed window and fling the door back on its hinges. There were holes in the roof and the water dripped steadily onto the already damp straw. The horses stood, heads hanging in resigned misery; the humans huddled against the wall, cold, tired, and hungry. The odors of wet horseflesh, moldy straw, and none-too-clean people filled the dank air, adding to the desolation.

"I do not see why you should have to appeal to Sir Daniel all the time," complained Henrietta. "Why cannot ye make up your own mind for a change?"

"I have made up my mind," snapped Will. "You will just not listen to sense. My father would never forgive an elopement. He does not object to the match, but he will not permit me to marry you against your father's will. You convince Sir Gerald to permit it, and then there will be no difficulties."

"Oh, you know that is impossible!" Henrietta cried. "He would see me dead rather than happy. If we were wed, we could find work, couldn't we?"

"But I do not wish to find work," Will said, sighing heavily. "I wish to be Will Osbert, Esquire, of Osbert Court."

"Oh, I do not think you love me the least little bit!" Henrietta exclaimed. "You have no romance in your soul, and no courage."

"There are times," Will said deliberately, "when I do not even like you."

"That is the most dastardly thing to say!" Henrietta flung herself upon him, rolling in the damp straw.

With an exclamation of exasperation, Daniel grabbed the belt at the back of her britches and hauled her off her opponent. "If you do not behave yourself, Mistress Ashby, you will find yourself out in the rain!"

"Then I shall get the ague," she objected. "And I shall have the fever again, and—"

"Quiet!" But his lips twitched despite his ferocious tone. "I do not wish to hear another word out of you."

Henrietta slumped into her corner again, hugging her knees, shivering in baleful silence. The rain dripped monotonously and the wind howled; the horses shuffled on the straw; a rat scurried across the barn floor. This dismal state of affairs continued until the door was flung open to admit a dripping Tom.

"There's bread and cheese and ale," he announced, dumping his packets onto the floor. "There's more Roundheads in town than fleas on a dog. A man can't move without a pass."

"Why do we not try to acquire passes?" Henrietta asked, her usual sunny humor restored as she fell upon the bread and cheese. "We have been a week upon the road and this hiding grows monstrous tedious."

"Was it an adventure ye were expecting?" Daniel inquired dryly, taking a deep draught of ale.

"I did not think it would be quite so uncomfortably

tedious," she said through a mouthful. "But if we had passes, we could travel openly and stay in inns, could we not?"

"Of course we could," said Will, who had still not recovered his equanimity. "But we are hardly traveling in this fashion through choice. Are you suggesting we present ourselves at the nearest military post and ask politely for passes?"

Daniel raised his eyes heavenward as he waited for the explosive response to this heavy sarcasm. It did not come, however.

"I am not suggesting *you* should," she said thoughtfully, wiping her mouth with the back of her hand. "But if Tom could procure me some women's clothes, those of a servant girl would be best, I might be able to spin a tale to the officers that would suffice." She looked at Will. "I am quite accomplished at spinning tales, am I not?"

He nodded and a reluctant grin spread across the freckled face. "Aye, that y'are. 'Tis an accomplishment that has saved ye from many a scrape."

"And you," she said. "What think ye, sir? I will say that I wish to visit my sick father—a good Parliamentarian—in London. And that I would be accompanied by . . . by . . ." She frowned, one hand gesturing vaguely as if she would pluck the words from the air. "By my grandfather and my brother," she finished triumphantly. "And Tom has kindly offered to provide escort since my grandfather is rather feeble, and just one man cannot offer sufficient protection against marauding Cavaliers and highwaymen."

Daniel struggled to grasp the role of enfeebled ancient that had clearly been allotted him. "I am to grow a white beard, I assume, and adopt a shambling gait and toothless mumble."

Henrietta laughed. "Nay, I do not see why that should be necessary."

"What a fortunate man I am," he declared.

"If I spin the tale aright," Henrietta explained, ignoring the pointed irony, "there is no reason why any of you, except perhaps Tom, should have to show yourselves. They will issue the passes in the names I give, and once we have 'em no one will question them. If I say that you are nine and seventy and they put that upon the pass, then we may easily fashion a two out of the seven."

"Sweet Jesus," groaned Daniel. "Nine and seventy!"

"I do not think you are taking this seriously, sir," Henrietta said indignantly. "I am quite in earnest, I assure ye."

" 'Tis a nonsensical plan." Daniel broke off a hunk of barley bread from the loaf. "I understand you would have done with our present discomfort, but nursery games of make-believe are not the way."

Henrietta flushed at this dismissal. " 'Tis not a nursery game. I know I can make it work if I but have the clothes. Tom may accompany me. There is nothing to say that he is for King not Parliament, and I am sure he will agree to say that he is for Parliament. Would you not, Tom?" She looked in appeal at the trooper, stolidly eating bread and cheese while the debate raged around him.

"If'n it'd serve a purpose," he agreed. "But Sir Daniel has the right of it. 'Tis a crazy plan . . . moon-mad."

Henrietta said nothing, but her mouth lost its soft curve and her jaw took on a rather determined set that Will at least recognized with a stab of foreboding.

They remained in the barn throughout the sodden afternoon. Daniel attempted to soften his dictatorial rejection of Henrietta's plan, but she seemed impervious to all conversational tacks and all suggestions as to lighthearted ways in which to pass the time. In the end he gave up and lapsed into gloomy reflection. He could not accuse her of sulking, he decided, watching her through half-closed eyes. It was more as if she were deeply distracted by something.

Indeed she was deep in thought, making and discarding plans with a cool calculation. Without help, she would be obliged to carry out the scheme alone and in her present guise, but perhaps she could turn that to advantage. Suddenly aware of Sir Daniel's covert scrutiny, she closed her eyes, yawning mightily as she leaned back against the barn wall, praying that he would not notice the betraying color she could feel creeping into her cheeks.

Daniel closed his own eyes. Sleep seemed the only way to pass the interminable hours until the rain should cease and they could start out again. Both Will and Tom had followed Harry's example and there was little point in staying awake by himself. Within ten minutes, his deep, rhythmic breathing mingled with that of the others.

Henrietta's eyes shot open. Stealthily, she got to her feet. Sir Daniel's purse lay beside his saddlebags. Her furtive fingers extracted two crowns. She had no idea how much the passes would cost, but she could not appear to have great sums to spend. For a maid in her position a crown would amount to some considerable sacrifice—one that should convince the officers of her authenticity and genuine plight.

Tucking her hair into her knitted cap, fastening her leather jerkin and turning up the collar, she crept out of the barn into the gathering dusk where the rain had turned to a dismal drizzle. She ran across the barnyard, her booted feet squelching on the mud-puddled cobbles. The abandoned farmhouse, its blackened walls and roofless condition evidence of the fire that had driven away its inhabitants, loomed squat and slightly menacing in the misty gloom. She veered away across the fields toward the city of Nottingham lying some three miles distant.

Daniel was at first not alarmed by Harry's absence when he awoke a half hour later. Reasoning that she was either visiting the still-intact privy at the rear of the farmhouse or stretching her legs now that the rain had slackened somewhat, he strolled outside himself. The sky was black with cloud, not a glimmer of moon or starshine, and an autumnal chill struck hard in the dank air.

A pitch-dark night was ill for traveling, he reflected, particularly when they were obliged to keep to the fields and woods. It was all too easy for a horse to miss his footing in a fox hole or blunder into the gorse and tear the skin of a hock. Mayhap they would be better advised to spend the night in this cheerless hole and risk a daytime journey on the morrow.

Frowning as he tried to make up his mind, he returned to the barn and was surprised to find that Harry had not returned. "Wherever could she have gone?" he demanded of the air and his two companions.

Tom shrugged, but Will chewed his lip and looked uneasy. "D'ye have some idea, Will?" Daniel asked, examining the young man carefully.

A pink flush stained Will's cheeks, conflicting dramatically with the shock of red hair. "I beg your pardon, sir, for saying this, but ye shouldn't have spoken as ye did to her. Harry doesn't take kindly to having her ideas dismissed in such fashion, not when she's set her heart on something and believes it will work."

"Now, just a minute," said Daniel in a slow, horrified realization of what Will was implying. "Are you trying to tell me that she has gone off in a passion?"

"Nay, sir." Will scratched his head uncomfortably. "Not exactly. I think she has probably gone into Nottingham to try to acquire passes."

"God's good grace!" Daniel stared, horrendous images jostling in his head: Henrietta in her britches providing merry sport for a troop of lewd Roundhead soldiers in Nottingham Castle; Henrietta forced into revealing her true identity and that of her fugitive companions, together with their whereabouts; the imminent arrival of a troop of Roundheads bristling with pikes.

"A wild, hoity maid," adjudged Tom, sucking on a piece of straw. "We'd best be away afore she brings the 'ole New Model down upon us."

"We cannot leave, Tom," Daniel said sharply. "We cannot risk her returning and finding us gone."

"I will stay for her," Will spoke up. " 'Tis my responsibility, when all's said and done. If it hadn't been for me, she'd not have been here in the first place."

Daniel gave a mirthless laugh. "I am not convinced of that fact, young Will. Mistress Ashby had no intention of accepting the destiny planned for her. Following you provided romantic excuse to flee."

Will looked startled, as if such an idea had never occurred to him. "D'ye think she is not in love with me, then, sir?"

"I think she believes she is," Daniel said. "I do not mean to prick your vanity—"

"Oh, no, sir, you have not," Will hastened to reassure him. "I confess 'twould be something of a relief if it were the case."

In spite of his present dismay, Daniel could not help smiling at this frank statement. Master Osbert was no stricken swain but the hapless victim of a considerably stronger will. He strode to the door, peering out into the blackness. An owl screeched and a small animal screamed in pain and fear. They were not reassuring sounds for hunted men. "Tom, you and Will ride from here some five or six miles to the south. Find some concealment and wait for me. If I do not come up with you by mid-morning, then ye must make shift for yourselves. I will remove from the barn and find some place where I may watch for her return. There is no reason why we should be caught like rats in a trap."

They went their separate ways, Tom and Will trotting into the darkness, leading Harry's nag. Daniel turned his charger loose in a field behind the farm and found himself a broad oak tree. It was an uncomfortable resting place; although the rain had ceased, the leaves dripped dolefully down his neck, his leg muscles cramped rapidly, and his mind turned to the savage contemplation of reprisals when and if Mistress Henrietta Ashby deigned to reappear.

Henrietta reached Nottingham Castle just as the great portcullis was being dropped for the night. "I pray ye, sir, let me through," she said, genuinely out of breath.

"I would have speech with the officer who issues passes for safe conduct."

The soldiers in the gatehouse stared in astonishment. The voice was that of a country girl, the garb of a lad. "What be ye?" one of them demanded roughly. "Art wench?"

"Aye," she agreed, pulling off her cap to free the corn silk–colored mass that tumbled in profusion down her back. " 'Deed I am, good sir, but I've need of this habit. 'Tis not safe for a maid along the roads in these times." She shuddered. "There's Royalists and all sorts about, armed to the teeth and ready to make sport with a simple wench."

The soldiers laughed uproariously. "Aye, I'll be bound. Y'are a sweet morsel, wench. Come ye in, then, if'n y'are coming."

They opened the postern gate, and Henrietta slipped by them, stifling a squeak as a hand came down in an intimate pat on the curve of her backside. "I beg ye, good sir, take me to the captain in charge of passes."

"All in good time." The soldier chuckled. "Ye'll be glad of a cup of ale on a night like this. 'Tis lonely in the guardroom, is it not, Jack? We'd be glad of a little company."

Henrietta realized that she had not thought of this complication. She tugged her jerkin tighter over her breasts and showed her companions an anxious face. "If ye please, sirs, I'm in the most fearful haste. My father lies sick in London and I've to take me grandfer to 'im. 'E's fallen on terrible hard times, my father has, although 'e's powerful strong for Parliament. But if 'e passes on 'afore we reaches 'im, 'tis a pauper's grave will receive 'im."

Babbling frantically, she managed to dodge the hands that would stroke and pat, scampering up the narrow flight of stone stairs to the round chamber that housed the guards.

It was warm and cozy in there, a fire sizzling in the grate, a flagon of wine upon the stained plank table. Two soldiers, tunics unbuttoned, sat at their ease beside the fire. "Well, well, what 'ave we 'ere?" one of them said jovially. "What've ye found, Dick?"

"Why, 'tis a wench in lad's garb," chuckled Dick. "Wants passes for 'erself and 'er grandpa."

"And my brother and 'is friend to provide escort," Henrietta put in, the words tumbling over themselves. "Me grandfer is all of nine and seventy and can barely move 'isself."

"Then ye'd best leave 'im be'ind," declared Dick. "Can ye not take what's needed without the old man?"

Henrietta swallowed and improvised wildly. " 'Tis me father's last wish to see 'is father afore he passes on. They've been on terrible bad terms these last years. And Grandfer says 'e'll not rest easy 'imself without makin' peace."

Jack nodded sagely, tipping the flagon to his lips. "Aye, family troubles is bad. Was the same, as I remember, with my Uncle Job and 'is youngest. Didn't speak two words for twenty year, though they lived but a spit apart." He wiped his mouth with the back of his hand and passed the flagon to Henrietta. "Take a drink, lass. 'Tis a raw night."

"Nay, I thank ye," Henrietta said hastily. "Pray take me to the captain."

" 'Tis not the captain as issues passes, wench," one of the men by the fireside told her with a salacious chuckle. " 'Tis the sergeant, and ye'll 'ave to sweet talk 'im. Mebbe for a kiss, 'e'll be willin' to oblige."

"I thought Cromwell's men were not the kind to take advantage of a maid," Henrietta said with a doleful sniff. " 'Tis unkind when I'm in such distress." She knuckled her eyes, trying to make them water convincingly. "I've never kissed anyone, not even my Ned, 'n we're to be wed when I've got me bottom drawer together."

Peeping at them through her fingers, she saw that she had struck the right note. These rough country men had their own rules, and a girl of their own kind, affianced and virtuous, would not meet with lewd treatment.

"Cease yer weepin', wench," Dick said gruffly. "No one means ye any 'arm. 'Tis just a bit 'o fun. But ye should not be paradin' in them britches. 'Tain't decent."

"Nay, I am aware," she said with another sniff. " 'N Ned would 'ave summat to say if 'e knew. But what's a maid to do with no man to protect 'er? 'Tis terrible times we live in."

"Aye, that it is." One of the fireside sitters stood up, fastening his tunic. "Come with me, lass. I'll take ye to the sergeant. I've a maid not much bigger 'n ye at 'ome."

Thankfully, Henrietta followed the soldier out of the round chamber along a stone-walled corridor to a heavy, ironbound wooden door. The trooper knocked. A growl bade them enter and Henrietta's escort pushed her ahead of him into another fire-warmed chamber.

A bullet-headed man in an immaculate tunic sat at a big table. "Well," he demanded. "What's this then, Trooper Bates?"

Trooper Bates, standing rigidly to attention, explained the situation.

The sergeant listened impassively, his eyes fixed on the girl, who had little difficulty in looking petrified, since that was exactly how she felt. Henrietta knew only too well what happened to those suspected of treason who might have information to impart. Torture was used indiscriminately, and her sex would not protect her from the hideous fate of those who were broken in the dungeons of Nottingham Castle—broken only to meet the hangman. She shivered despite the sweat that misted her palms and gathered on her upper lip.

"Where does your father dwell, girl?" the sergeant asked when the trooper fell silent.

Henrietta had her answer prepared. "In Spittal Fields, sir, if you please."

"His name?"

"Bolt, if you please, sir."

"I'm not sure that I do," the sergeant said irascibly.

"Stop shaking, girl, no one's going to harm ye. Cromwell's New Model army doesn't wage war on women and children."

"No, sir," Henrietta murmured, shaking now with relief. "But 'tis just that I'm desperate, sir. I don't want me father to rest in a pauper's grave. They say they don't even wrap 'em afore they throws 'em in—" Great sobs burst from her lips, preventing further speech, and she buried her face in her hands.

"Odd's bones," muttered the sergeant, reaching for paper and quill. "Can't abide weeping women. It'll cost ye a crown, girl."

" 'Tis a great sum for me, sir." Henrietta sniveled, reaching into the pocket of her jerkin for one of the coins. "But 'tis worth it to see me father buried decent."

"A Malignant would give me five pound for such a pass," the sergeant informed her irritably, pocketing the crown. "What are the names to go on here?"

"Bolt, sir," Henrietta said. "I'm Meg Bolt, 'n me grandfer's Daniel Bolt, 'n me brother's Will Bolt, 'n 'is friend who's comin' fer protection is Tom . . . Tom Grant, sir."

"And y'are going to Spittal Fields?"

"Aye, sir, if you please, sir."

There was silence, disturbed only by the scratching of quill on parchment and Henrietta's noisy sniffs. At last the sergeant shook the sandcaster over the parchment, dropped wax from the candle upon it, and pressed Parliament's seal into the wax. "There." He handed the parchment to her. "Ye may travel freely from here to Spittal Fields in the city of London, but nowhere else. If ye stray from the route and are challenged, this pass will not guarantee ye safe passage. 'Tis understood?"

"Aye, sir, yer honor, sir. I can't thank ye enough, sir." Backing to the door, clutching the precious parchment, Henrietta gabbled inanely, interspersed with frequent sniffs.

The sergeant impatiently waved the trooper after her.

"See the wench beyond the gate, Bates. And I'll thank ye to bring me no more of that kind this night."

"Come along a'me, lass." Trooper Bates smiled kindly. " 'E's not a bad sort, the sergeant, but 'e don't like 'is evenings disturbed."

In five minutes, Henrietta was outside the castle, safe conduct to London for three men and a woman in her jerkin pocket, and a three-mile walk through the dark night ahead of her. But exhilaration winged her feet—exhilaration and triumph. Sir Daniel and Tom had scorned her plan and even Will had been less than encouraging. Now, without a scrap of help from any of them, she had secured the passes that would enable them to travel swiftly and in some comfort. So jubilant was she that not even the thought of what journey's end in London might bring could dampen her self-congratulation.

It was close to midnight when she reached the ruined farm. Only then did it occur to her to wonder what the others had made of her disappearance. She stood for a moment in the yard, her heart hammering, her eyes peering into the darkness, now lightened by the fleeting glimmer of a shy moon. Perhaps they believed her lost or taken by soldiers. If so, they would surely have left. They were intending to continue the journey by night as usual. Could they have done so? Abandoned her? No, Will would have known what she intended. He would have known that she could not have endured such a snub as Sir Daniel had administered without proving him wrong. Will would have made them stay for her return. He would have, wouldn't he?

With a surge of panic, she ran to the barn and stood panting in the doorway, gazing into the deserted, pitchy shed. She did not need light to tell her it was empty of all but rats. There were no horsey stirrings and whifflings and no sense at all of a human presence.

"By God, Henrietta, how dare you do such a thing! How dare you disappear in such reckless, thoughtless fashion."

She spun around with a cry, half of relief and half of alarm, at the enraged whisper behind her. "Oh, Sir Daniel, I thought you had left me."

" 'Twould be the least you deserve," he said savagely. "I have spent the last four hours in the crotch of an oak tree, and heaven alone knows how Will and Tom are faring."

"But I have a pass for all of us," she said, the words tumbling over themselves as she felt for the parchment in her jerkin. "See." She held it out to him. "I said I would do it, and I did."

Daniel stared at the document. It was too dark to make out the script, but there was no mistaking the seal. "How the devil did you achieve this?"

"I said I would." She could not conceal the smug note or the unspoken challenge, despite the feeling that Sir Daniel Drummond was not in a mood to respond to either with equanimity. "You did not believe it possible."

"I do not entirely believe that *you* are possible," he declared, pushing her into the barn. "Do not move one inch. I must fetch flint and tinder."

Henrietta remained where she had been put until Daniel reappeared. Flint scraped against tinder and a golden glow of candlelight illuminated the space where they stood. He held the candle high and examined her carefully before turning his attention to the parchment. A low whistle escaped him.

" 'Twould seem I underestimated you, Mistress Ashby. I will not do so again. And you—" He caught her chin, tilting her face. "You will never again disappear in such fashion. It is understood?"

"If you do not oblige me to do so, I will not," she said simply. "I do not think you should be vexed, Sir Daniel. I am not taken prisoner. We have lost nothing and gained much." Her big brown eyes regarded him earnestly, and her lower lip was caught between her teeth as she offered a questioning, hesitant smile.

It took a minute, but at last he laughed. It was a tiny sound to begin with, then, as relief and admiration at her outrageous audacity burgeoned to chase away the anger born of fear, gusts of mirth rose to the rafters. "You had best tell me the whole," he gasped eventually. "We must stay here until dawn, when we can go in search of Will and Tom."

"I am very hungry," Henrietta said as reality reasserted itself, quashing exhilaration under an anticlimactic wash of fatigue. "But I suppose we do not have any supper. The guards offered me wine, but I was too afeard to take any."

"With cause," he observed. "We shared the bread and cheese and ale before Tom and Will went off. There is a little left in my saddlebag. I will fetch it for you, although going supperless to bed seems an apt penalty." The amusement still lurked in his voice, however, and Henrietta heard no sting in the statement.

She ate hungrily, drank thirstily, and told her tale to an attentive audience. By story's end, she could barely keep her eyes open and her words were lost in a series of yawns. "I beg your pardon, but I seem to be falling asleep." She blinked like a dopey kitten, and he smiled, thinking not for the first time that Henrietta Ashby did have the most appealing countenance.

"Lie down then," he suggested, picking up the horse blanket. She curled onto the straw and was asleep almost before he had tucked the blanket around her.

He lingered on his knees beside the slight figure, his hand resting on her shoulder where he had been adjusting the blanket. A puzzled frown drew his dark brows together over the aquiline nose and one finger moved almost without volition to trace the curve of her cheek, flushed delicately in sleep. What was it about this indomitable young hoyden that so disturbed him? It was long before Daniel Drummond joined her in sleep.

Chapter 4

It was the end of September when they arrived in London. The safe conduct had served them well and Henrietta's dress was once more appropriate to her sex. Over her gown she wore a safeguard, the overskirt that would protect her clothes from the hazards of riding through the rain and mud. Her hair was confined beneath a round black cap suited to a member of the bourgeoisie, and a serviceable cloak of russet frieze kept out the wind. It was hardly attire of the first style of elegance, but Sir Daniel had pointed out that the less conspicuous they appeared the better, so Henrietta, with no more than minor grumbles about wearing a porringer upon her head, resigned herself to mediocrity. Will and Daniel had abandoned the lace and sash of the Cavalier and were dressed as merchants, the epitome of peace-loving men whose only interest in these troubled times was the making of money. Tom was himself, a solid yeoman riding as escort.

Henrietta had been to London but once before, at the very beginning of this adventure when she had left home in the carrier's wagon and joined Will at his lodgings close by Gray's Inn. She had found the city frenzy exciting then, and not even the foul stench of horse dung, rotting offal and vegetables, and all the rest of the filth steaming in the kennels, could detract from her pleasure. She gazed around at the jostling crowds, her ears deafened by the shouts, the ringing bells of street vendors as they cried their wares, screams and yells emanating from dark alleys. It was evening, and the night flashed with torches and lanterns carried through the press. The horses were obliged to keep to a slow walk because of the crowds; small children dodged between hoofs and under bellies, scrabbling in the cobbles in search of scraps and the abandoned treasures of the gutter.

Sir Daniel seemed to know where he was going, a fact that impressed Henrietta mightily since she could not imagine ever being familiar with this bewildering maze and hubbub. They rode through one of London's seven gates with its two square towers on either side, entering the borough of Aldersgate. Daniel turned his horse down a narrow cobbled alley and reigned in outside a pretty thatched inn with whitewashed walls.

The sign of the Red Lion creaked in the evening breeze. An ostler ran out to take their horses. "Come, Meg Bolt," Daniel said with a smile, helping her to dismount, "if y'are as sharp set as I am, ye'll be glad of your supper."

"How long are we to stay here?" Henrietta asked, looking up at the inn. There was a tremor in her voice as she asked the question that implicitly carried another. What was to happen to her now?

If Daniel heard the tremor, he gave no sign. "Until we have decided what to do next," he responded matter-of-factly. "There's none who'll question us while we stay here.'Tis only on the road that danger lies, so we may reassume our accustomed identities, I think."

"But must you not go home to see how your children are faring?" Henrietta asked, unaware that her hands were curled into tight fists and only her gloves prevented her nails from digging into her palms.

There was a strange look in the eyes he bent upon her, as if he found it necessary to weigh his response. "Aye," he said slowly. "I must, as I must discover what penalties Parliament will decide to impose upon me as a Malignant."

"If 'tis not known ye fought at Preston, then perchance they will not sequester your lands," Will broke in.

Daniel seemed to shake himself free of a reverie at this interruption. Slowly, his gaze left Henrietta's upturned face. "I live in hope, Will. Let us go in. Tom will see that the horses are cared for."

Mine host, with much bowing and scraping, was pleased to provide two bedchambers for his guests, the men sharing one as they had been accustomed to do throughout their journey. Sir Daniel's niece, Mistress Ashby, was shown a small chamber across the hall with the assurance that, unless the inn filled unexpectedly with guests, she would have no bedfellow.

"If ye'd wish for a privy parlor, sir, I've a nice, airy room along the passage," the landlord said, beaming. "My good woman will be pleased to provide a tasty supper for ye, and I've a fine burgundy."

"Aye, that will do nicely," Daniel said. "We will sup in half an hour."

"Shall I send a wench to help the young lady with 'er tiring, sir?"

Daniel glanced at Henrietta, who was unusually silent, her face set. "Yes, do so by all means," he said. "I would have a privy word with Mistress Ashby first." Taking her elbow, he eased her into the chamber allotted her. The door clicked shut behind them.

"Harry," he said quietly, "I would have your promise that you will not leave this place without telling me first."

She studied a knot of wood in the broad oak boards at her feet. "But I believe we have come to the parting of our ways, Sir Daniel."

"Aye, I rather thought your mind was running upon those lines," he said a little grimly. "Well, it will not do, my child. Ye cannot coerce poor Will into taking responsibility for you. He is barely able to take responsibility for himself. You have no monies of your own—"

"But I am strong. I can work," she declared, raising her eyes to meet his directly. "If Will refuses to wed me and I cannot find employment as a governess, then I will be a servant."

"Sleeping on straw in some kitchen, I suppose. Do not be foolish."

"I will not go home," she said fiercely. "There is nothing ye can say or do to make me."

Daniel tapped his chin thoughtfully with a long forefinger, wondering whether now was the time to tell her that when they passed through Reading the previous day he had dispatched a letter to Sir Gerald Ashby of Thame, telling him that he would find his daughter, safe and unmolested, at the sign of the Red Lion in the borough of Aldersgate. He had agonized long and hard over the decision, eventually deciding that an honorable man, the father of daughters himself, had no choice. He still intended to keep his promise that he would permit no hurt to come to her, but her future must be decided in proper fashion in consultation with her father. He had a suggestion for her future, but how he presented it would depend upon his assessment of Sir Gerald. He had no reason to believe that the man was more than a very severe parent, but he could not know until he met him. Perhaps now was not the moment to enter such a discussion with Henrietta.

"Trust me," he said instead. "Give me your word that there will be no further flights."

Henrietta walked to the small mullioned window, which looked out onto a garden of hollyhocks and delphiniums, a mulberry tree in the middle. What choice did she have but to trust him for the moment? What reason did she have to mistrust him? If the truth were told, finding herself without resources was quite terrifying. She felt as if she had an empty space inside her, a hollow void, where before she had been filled with energy and plans, never at a loss, smoothly adapting to circumstances. But matters had taken a turn that she had not envisaged when she set off so blithely in the back of the carrier's wagon all those weeks ago. She had been so certain that Will would require only a little forceful persuasion to elope, but he was proving most amazingly intransigent. Mayhap, now that they were back in London and the war was over, she could work upon him a little more.

"I cannot remain a charge upon your purse for much longer, Sir Daniel," she said gruffly. "You have been kindness itself, but—"

"Oh, Harry, such nonsense!" he exclaimed. "If it had not been for you, I would probably have been languishing in a Roundhead prison by now. On that score we are even."

Color crept into her cheeks and she smiled at him. " 'Tis kind in ye to say so, sir."

" 'Tis but the truth." He took a step toward her, touching her cheek with his finger. "Come now, give me your word."

His caressing finger, the warmth in his black eyes, the gentle amusement in the depths of his voice, had the strangest effect. She felt as if she had nothing in the world to fear. "I promise," she said.

"That's my elf." He brushed her forehead with his lips—the lightest touch, yet it seemed to sear her skin like the flame of a candle. "Wash the dust of the road from your face and hands and come for your supper."

The door closed on his departure and Henrietta remained standing at the window. He had spoken to her in the manner of guardian to ward, but he had touched her in another manner altogether, and his eyes said something quite unfathomable. It was a great puzzle, almost as great as the curious stirrings, the restless confusion that assailed her when she tried to work out the puzzle.

A knock at the door heralded the arrival of a red-cheeked wench with a copper jug of water and cheerful chatter that sent mysteries and fancies scuttling. It was a washed, brushed, and composed Mistress Ashby who presented herself in the parlor, where awaited a dish of salmon with fresh boiled peas in butter, a salad of artichoke hearts, and a plate of cheese tartlets.

"Ah, there y'are," Will said thankfully. "We have been waiting this age for ye. We're all like to starve."

Daniel gestured to a stool at the oak table. "Take your place, child. Will does not exaggerate." He poured burgundy into a pewter cup for her before sitting at the head of the table.

"Where's Tom?" She sipped the wine gratefully, then helped herself to salmon.

"He said he would feel easier in the taproom," Daniel told her. "Private parlors are for gentle folk."

"If Harry is to become a servant to earn her bread, she'll have need to accustom herself to the taproom. Why d'ye not ask mine host if he has need of a serving wench, Harry?" Will chuckled as if he had made some witticism.

Henrietta flushed angrily. Will was behaving as if her situation was in some sort a jest. "Y'are no gentleman, Will Osbert," she accused. "To promise marriage and then renege is the act of a scoundrel!"

"I never made such a promise!" A scarlet tide mounted to the roots of his bright red hair. " 'Tis you who decided these matters and—"

"Peace!" Daniel thundered. "I am not prepared to have my supper curdle in my belly with the acid wranglings of a pair of hot-tempered children. I have endured enough of it these last weeks."

"I beg your pardon, Sir Daniel," Will said, stiff with wounded pride. "I will be leaving you in the morning. I realize I have trespassed on your hospitality long enough, but I will apply to my father for the funds to repay you."

Henrietta giggled with lamentable lack of tact. "You do sound ridiculous, Will. All starchy and stiff-necked like a turkey cock."

Will began to gobble like the bird in question and Daniel fixed Henrietta with a stern eye, inquiring gently, "Do you prefer to eat your supper in your chamber?"

Henrietta shook her head vigorously, although her eyes were still dancing. She returned her attention to her platter, but after a few minutes her gaze skimmed across the table toward Will. He looked up and his lip quivered responsively.

"Y'are not in the least like a turkey cock," Henrietta said. "But y'are not really leaving in the morning, are you?"

Will shuffled uncomfortably on his stool. "I must go home, Harry. My family will not know whether I lived through the battle. You know how my mother is. She will be beside herself."

"Aye." The laughter had left her now. " 'Tis not right that she should be allowed to worry. Could ye not send a message, though?"

There was an awkward silence. Daniel continued with his supper, withdrawing from a conversation that he suspected was about to make explicit a fact that Henrietta and her reluctant swain had tried to avoid.

"But there's nothing to keep me here." Will managed to get the words of truth out eventually. "If ye will return with me, Harry, I will enlist my parents to speak for you. My mother does not hold with the way Lady Mary has treated you, and she is not in favor of your marriage to Sir Reginald. She will be your advocate."

Henrietta said nothing. Tears blinded her for a minute and she kept her eyes on her platter until she was sure she had overcome them. "Your mother has always been kind to me, Will, but I fear I have need of a more powerful advocate in this instance." She raised her eyes and smiled. It was a brave effort that deceived neither of her companions. "I did not mean to plague ye, Will. If ye truly do not wish to wed with me, then there's no more to be said. I had thought 'twas just our parents that stood in the way. But I will shift for myself now."

Instinctively, Will looked at Sir Daniel, who moved one finger in a near-imperceptible movement that nevertheless made clear to the young man that he need take no more upon his shoulders.

"More wine, Henrietta?" Daniel refilled her glass.

"If you care to, we will visit the lions at the Exchange tomorrow."

"I think I should like that." She sipped her wine. "But I should like of all things to lie abed in the morning. 'Twill be such slothful luxury. No journeying to make, no duties to perform."

"I had not thought ye a slugabed," said Daniel, laughing. "But if you wish it, then it shall be so. I've some commissions to execute in the city in the forenoon. I will return for dinner, and then we shall go out upon the town."

"A pleasing plan, sir. When will you leave, Will?" Her voice was quite steady, her expression composed. They could guess, but only Henrietta could know the wasteland as she faced the loss of the last tenuous strand of hope. Will was to have been her salvation. It was not to be, so she must rely upon herself. With the knowledge came a renewal of strength. False hopes drained one of strength, she decided, helping herself to a cheese tartlet. They diverted the attention. From now on, she would deal with reality.

"Mayhap I will visit the Exchange with ye," Will said, boyishly eager once more. "I've not seen the lions and 'tis said they're a marvel to behold. Brought all the way from the Africas. I could leave for Oxfordshire the following day."

"Then you may bear Henrietta company in the morning," Daniel said easily. "Once she has decided to smile upon the day."

"I shall frown until at least ten of the clock," declared Henrietta, entering the spirit of the discussion.

"To ensure that it is no later, I suggest you stand not upon the order of your retiring." Daniel rose and lit a small candle waiting on the oak sideboard. "Y'are weary, child. Sleep well."

She took the candle, waited for a second for a salute that seemed appropriate, but when it did not come and she received only a smile, she bade them both good night and left the parlor.

* * *

The damned animal wasn't up to his weight, Sir Gerald Ashby reflected for the tenth time in the last hour. He should never have bought from Wetherby. The man was no judge of horseflesh. Sir Gerald's spurs dug cruelly into his mount's lathered, heaving flanks and saliva frothed around the curb bit as the horse struggled to respond.

Sir Gerald cast his choleric eye around the London streets. He couldn't abide the city. Oxford was bad enough, but the capital was a foul-smelling den of thieves. And who the devil was this Daniel Drummond, Baronet, who had the disgraced Henrietta in charge? The letter had been civil enough, well penned, but uninformative as to the circumstances. If Sir Gerald had had his way, he would have consigned his whore of a daughter to outer darkness. But Lady Mary would have it that the girl could be corrected, and if she did not breed a bastard in nine months' time, mayhap Sir Reginald could be persuaded of her innocence. A tale could be told of a visit to relatives, and if the little harlot could be brought to a dutiful manner, all need not be lost. A spoiled maidenhead could be disguised on the wedding night . . . as long as there was no bastard. The Osberts would have it that Will had no part in Henrietta's disappearance, but Sir Gerald and Lady Mary knew better. Henrietta had been set on wedding with the lad these last two years and neither words nor whipping had had the least effect on her resolve. But if they'd been fools enough to elope, that could be easily dealt with. No court in the land would uphold a marriage between two minors against the wishes of the parents. Nay, 'twas only a bastard they need worry about.

A small boy ran into the lane in front of him and his horse shied, abruptly shattering these reflections. Sir Gerald cursed vilely and lashed the animal's underbelly with his whip. The horse screamed, reared, and one hoof caught the lad on the arm. The child went down to the cobbles amidst a great sound and fury as passersby surrounded him, yelling abuse at the rider who was too busy trying to control his now frantic mount to take any notice.

Laying about him with his heavy whip, Sir Gerald Ashby managed to extricate himself from the tumult and set his horse to the gallop over the uneven cobbles. The wretched animal stumbled but by some miracle managed to keep his footing as they passed through Alder's Gate.

"Hey, you . . . you!" Sir Gerald bellowed at a woman standing in a doorway, a child in her arms, two others clinging to her skirts. "Where lies the Red Lion in these parts?"

"My lad'll show ye, sir," the woman said, pushing one of the children, a mite no more than four years old. "Sam 'ere'll show ye, yer honor."

The child ventured forth into the lane, then scampered ahead of the horse, turning down a narrow alley, coming to a halt outside the thatched inn. He pointed but said not a word. As Sir Gerald dismounted, the lad mutely held out his hand, his eyes dull in the dirty face. Sir Gerald cursed him, but tossed a farthing to the mired cobbles before striding into the inn, leaving his horse to the attentions of an ostler, who muttered in disgust at the animal's condition and the bloody weal on its belly.

Henrietta was in the privy parlor with Will, playing backgammon while they waited for Sir Daniel's return. They both heard the unmistakable tones bellowing from the hall. The board fell to the floor, the draughtsmen scattered, as Henrietta leaped to her feet. Her face was gray as she turned to face the door, one hand to her mouth. How could he have discovered her? Only one person could have betrayed her, and it was the knowledge of that betrayal as much as fear of her father that brought black spots dancing before her eyes and set her heart to pounding so violently she thought she would swoon.

The door crashed back against the wall. Sir Gerald Ashby filled the doorway, every corpulent inch of him expressive of a venomous rage that the two within both knew he would make no attempt to control. "Whore!" The one word blistered in the sun-filled chamber. The door shivered on its hinges as he kicked it shut. "And your whoreson lover! Ye pair of fornicators."

"Nay, 'tis not so," Will stammered. "There has been no dishonor—"

"Don't ye lie to me, you young blackguard! I'll give you a drubbing ye'll never forget!"

"Sir, you cannot fault Will." Henrietta found her voice, taking an agitated step toward her father.

"Ye'll have your share, make no mistake," he said viciously. "But I'll deal with this whoreson first."

"Sir, I'll not be called so." Will, white-faced with outrage at the insult, drew himself upright. The next minute he fell to the floor beneath a hammer blow from Sir Gerald's fist. Will's chin cracked against the corner of the fender and he lay still before the cheerful crackling of the fire on the hearth.

"You have killed him!" Henrietta dropped to her knees beside the fallen figure.

"I've not begun yet. A taste of this will soon bring him to his senses!" Sir Gerald raised his heavy whip. "Move aside, girl."

"Nay." She looked up at him, appalled at the brutality that would horsewhip an unconscious man. "Ye'll not touch him. He's done you no injury."

"You'd prefer to be driven away, would ye?" The long thong of the whip cracked. Henrietta's breath whistled through her teeth as the pain bit deep into her shoulders, but she remained where she was, shielding Will with her body. At the next blow she cried out, but the innate obstinacy her father knew only too well kept her still, gritting her teeth, her will to resist only strengthened by the means used to break it.

Daniel Drummond heard the whip crack and the cry from abovestairs as he strolled into the inn. The innkeeper stood at the foot of the stairs, his expression both indignant and fearful. "This is a respectable 'ouse, sir," he blustered as Daniel strode past him. " 'Tis the young lady's father 'as come fer 'er. I don't want no goings-on, sir. Either the wench is yer niece or she ain't. I would never 'ave given ye room if'n I'd known."

"Known what?" Daniel snapped over his shoulder, cursing himself for not having expected this so soon. He had thought to have time to prepare Henrietta and explain his actions. "There's nothing to know!" He mounted the stairs two at a time and burst into the parlor.

"God's grace, man! Leave her be!" He covered the distance between the door and the tableau by the fire in two strides.

"And just who d'ye think you are?" demanded Sir Gerald, although he stayed his arm. " 'Tis no business of yours to come between a man and his child."

"Daniel Drummond," Daniel said shortly. "And in this instance, Sir Gerald, I claim that right. Get up, Henrietta." He held out his hand to her, but she recoiled as if he offered something noxious.

"You betrayed me," she said without expression. "You broke your promise and you betrayed me."

He shook his head. "It may look like that, but 'tis not so. Is Will hurt?"

"Now just a minute," broke in Sir Gerald. "I'll accept that I owe ye some gratitude, sir, but I've a mind to know how ye became involved with this pair of fornicators, much as it grieves me to use such a word of my own daughter."

"Then it is fortunate such a word is misapplied," Daniel said dryly. "I can assure you, Sir Gerald, that to my certain knowledge, there has been no dishonor and your daughter is still in possession of her maidenhead."

Will groaned and stirred. Henrietta bent over him again, her own pain forgotten in her anxiety. "Will, are ye all right?"

His eyes opened. "My head! What happened?" Then the face of Sir Gerald Ashby swam into focus and memory returned. "Sir, I'll not stand for your insults." He struggled to sit up, his face contorted with effort to form the words of dignified outrage.

"Y'are not in a state to stand for anything at present." It was Daniel who spoke. "Come, let me help you up. Sit yourself down and take a mouthful of brandy. Henrietta, fetch the decanter from the sideboard."

"I do not think we require your assistance, Sir Daniel," Henrietta said bitterly, getting to her feet, wincing at the smarting in her shoulders. "Or your instructions. 'Tis your interference that has led to this."

"You mind your tongue, girl!" Sir Gerald decided that he had been off center stage for long enough. "Y'are coming with me. Lady Mary will know how best to bring you to a sense of duty." He seized her arm, pushing her toward the door.

"One minute, Sir Gerald." Daniel moved swiftly to stand before the door. He had no choice and had known it since he walked into the room. A man who would take a horsewhip to his daughter while she was attending to an unconscious lad was not a man to listen with a sympathetic ear to the idea that Henrietta should be established in the childless household of Sir Daniel Drummond's sister. Frances would have welcomed her companionship, and Daniel had assumed that Sir Gerald and his lady would be only too glad to be rid of their troublesome daughter in respectable and economical fashion once such a solution was presented to them. It was commonly done, after all. When disagreement or disgrace made family harmony impossible, the cuckoo would be sent to another nest.

Now there was but one way out of this tangle. It was a tangle he had woven for himself when all was said and done, and the solution, while it had elements to alarm, for some reason did not throw him into despondency. With a calm resignation that a few weeks ago would have amazed him, he heard his voice above the gentle hiss and crackle of the fire. "There are some matters I would discuss with you before you leave."

"If 'tis a matter of what I owe ye for taking charge of this—"

"Nay, 'tis not that," Daniel interrupted. "I would ask your daughter's hand in marriage, Sir Gerald."

The silence in the room was profound. Will gawped, his jaw dropping slackly. Henrietta stared. Sir Gerald's bloodshot eyes popped in his suffused countenance.

"Why ever would you wish to wed me?" Henrietta said finally, just when it seemed as if the silence would continue forever, the figures remain forever graven in the attitudes they held.

"Why should I not?" He looked at her with quiet eyes.

Henrietta shook her head slowly. "I think perhaps this is the way you would make amends."

"You do not think that perhaps I could not in honor wed you without your father's permission?"

"And that is why you told him I was here?" Her eyes became even larger in the heart-shaped face. "Why would you not say something of this to me first?"

"Make amends?" broke in Sir Gerald, recovering from his astonishment and thus sparing Daniel the need to reply. "If ye'd make amends for a maidenhead ye've spoiled, sir, I'll tell ye now—"

"I am not Master Osbert, Sir Gerald. Ye'll cast no aspersions on my honor as if I were some young puppy!" For the first time anger flashed in Daniel's eyes. "I have said that your daughter is as chaste as my own child. Do not doubt my word."

"My daughter is promised," Sir Gerald said, a sullen note in his voice—the note of a bully obliged to back down.

"I'll not marry Sir Reginald!" cried Henrietta.

"Ye'll marry where I bid ye!" He still held her by the arm, and now he raised his other hand in threat.

She turned her head aside in a quick ducking movement that told Daniel more than anything could have done how accustomed she was to both threats and their fulfillment.

''Ye've a debt due on staple-statute as I understand it,'' Daniel said. ''Let us see if we can come to some arrangement.''

Sir Gerald looked uncertain. ''What mean ye?''

''I think 'twould be best to discuss this alone,'' Daniel said evenly. ''Henrietta, take Will to his chamber and see what you can do for him. 'Tis a monstrous bruise appearing on his chin.''

''I do not understand,'' she said. ''And I wish to.''

'' 'Tis not your place to take part in marriage discussions,'' he reminded her. ''This is between your father and myself.''

''But am I not to say whether I am willing or no?'' She would not dispute his statement, and she would not ask *this* question of her father—his answer she knew all too well. But she would ask it of the man who seemed to be assuming control of all their lives.

''When I have talked with your father, you and I will talk,'' he promised. ''You may say what you will then.''

''Come, Harry.'' Will stood up groggily. ''My head aches as if the drums of an entire regiment were beating a tattoo upon it.''

Henrietta still stood looking uncertainly at Daniel. Her father's hand dropped from her arm. ''Do as y'are bid,'' he said harshly. ''If 'tis possible to salvage something from this escapade, then ye can be grateful.''

It was clear to Henrietta that Sir Gerald had rapidly calculated that the possibility of the bird in hand was worth exploring. Sir Reginald was presumably very much in the bush at the moment. She thought of returning home, of her vindictive stepmother, of what awaited her with or without Sir Reginald at the end of it. She turned and opened the door. ''I'll see if the landlord can produce some witch hazel, Will. Ye should lie upon your bed for a while.''

The door closed behind them and Sir Daniel walked over to the sideboard. ''Wine, Sir Gerald, or do you prefer brandy?''

''Wine.'' The older man seemed to have lost much

of his former assurance under these new circumstances, but he attempted a further bluster. "I've a good marriage arranged for my daughter, sir. Ye'll have to do much to meet the terms. If y'are a Malignant, then ye'll have little to play with, seems to me."

"And what position have you taken in this war, sir?" Daniel asked smoothly, handing his guest a pewter goblet. "Kept safely out of it, I daresay."

"I'm for the king," Sir Gerald said, flushing. "But there's little sense in endangering land and family. I compounded for three hundred pounds in forty-six and I'll not risk more."

Daniel nodded. "We shall all now be obliged to compound and take the National Covenant. But tell me of this debt. If I assume it for you, then ye'll be as surely rid of it as if Henrietta married your creditor."

His future father-in-law regarded him slyly. "She's a pretty enough wench, I daresay. Good breeding stock. But she comes with no portion."

"Why is that?" Daniel sipped his own wine, asking the question almost neutrally. It was unheard of that a maid in Henrietta's social position should have not a penny to her name in the form of dowry.

"I've three other daughters to provide for. This one has been nothing but trouble from the moment of her birth." Sir Gerald shook his head disgustedly and drained his cup. "If ye want her, then 'tis good riddance. But she'll have nothing from me."

Daniel smiled wryly. "And I am to take up your bond in payment for your daughter. Is that the manner in which you will have this conducted?"

"Aye, sir, it is," Sir Gerald affirmed with that same sly look. " 'Twas ye who hit upon this, I'll remind ye. 'Tis nothing to me, for I'll have her wed to Sir Reginald once she's been brought to a proper sense of her duty."

Daniel nodded, keeping hidden his revulsion at this unnatural parent. "Then let us have done with this." He placed his goblet on the sideboard. "I would speak alone with Henrietta first, then we will draw up the documents before a justice who may perform the marriage at the same time." His eyes skimmed derisively over Sir Gerald's expression. "I assume ye'll not be interested in celebrating your daughter's marriage with any ceremony?"

"Ye assume right, sir." Sir Gerald refilled his cup, unmoved by the derision in both face and voice. " 'Tis a case of good riddance, as I told ye."

Daniel left the parlor, closing the door behind him with exaggerated quiet. He was seething with a fury greater than he had ever experienced. He was to buy a portionless bride from a brutish lout, who was now presumably smugly congratulating himself on having brought off a veritable master stroke.

The maddening reflection did not encourage a softness as he entered the chamber he shared with Will. Will was lying upon the bed, Henrietta sitting beside him holding a damp cloth to the swelling on his chin. It was clear that they had been in deep discussion by the abrupt silence that fell as he came in. Henrietta looked at him anxiously.

"Let us go into your chamber. We have things to discuss," Daniel said curtly, holding the door for her.

"Sir, I think you must be regretting an offer you made on impulse." She began to speak with difficulty, but Will interrupted her.

"Dammit, Harry, do not be so stiff-rumped. I have been telling her these last ten minutes, sir, to accept her good fortune." He struggled onto one elbow. "The devil of it is, sir, she thinks ye offered for her out of pity and not because you would really wish to."

"And why would he wish to?" Henrietta demanded, dashing angry tears from her eyes. "*You* do not wish to, and we plighted our troth two years past."

" 'Tis not that I do not wish to," Will protested, "but I do not think I am ready to wed just yet. If ye would wait until I gain my majority, then maybe . . ."

"By which time I would be wedded and bedded with some rank dotard!"

Daniel felt his anger run from him. It had not been directed at Harry anyway, and it was certainly unjust at this point that she should bear the brunt of it. He smiled reassuringly. "Come, child, *I* am ready to wed, and I trust I am neither rank nor a dotard. Surely, 'tis a better fate than any other that offers itself at present."

Henrietta frowned. " 'Tis not that I am ungrateful, but I do not understand why, if 'tis not pity, you would make such an offer."

Daniel perched on the broad windowsill, deciding that he might as well have this discussion in Will's presence as not. "I have been a widower for four years," he said. " 'Tis lonely and I would have a wife again. My daughters want the care and companionship of a mother. Y'are young, Henrietta, but not too young." He smiled suddenly. "Did ye not say that you would seek employment as governess?"

"Aye, but you said a man would have had to have escaped Bedlam to employ such a one as I," she objected.

"And you said I did not know you," he reminded her quietly. "I know you better now, and would further that knowledge." His eyes held hers for long minutes and he could read the thoughts reflected in the candid brown depths. "I would not be less than honest with you," he said finally. "And I would have your honesty in return. Is the thought of marriage with me distasteful to you?"

Henrietta dropped her eyes. A tinge of pink colored her cheekbones as she thought of the puzzling confusion she felt so often in his company, the way her body stirred so strangely when he touched her or smiled at her in a particular fashion. No, the thought of marriage with him was not in the least distasteful to her, and she could learn to be a wife and a mother to his children. It would be up to her to ensure that he did not regret his bargain.

She looked up to meet his steady regard. " 'Tis not distasteful to me, sir. I will try to be what you would have me be."

"Nay," he said softly, "I would have you be yourself."

She smiled hesitantly. "But I am a ramshackle hoity creature, sir. Ask Will."

Will was looking immensely relieved. " 'Tis true enough y'are, but my mother says ye need only the right husband and ye'll grow into a proper woman."

"Your mother said that?" Henrietta's jaw dropped.

"She did," Will affirmed. "Just as she said I was not the right husband for you."

Daniel burst out laughing. Henrietta's expression was a picture of indignation, Will's of complete confidence as if he had just quoted the oracle. "Y'are the most absurd pair of children," Daniel declared. "Will, we shall need ye as witness. Are you well enough to rise?"

" 'Tis to be done now?" Henrietta asked, startled.

"There seems little point in procrastination," Daniel said gently.

"No, I suppose not." A wistful look fleetingly crossed her face, then she shook her head in brisk dismissal. "My father will wish to return home without delay."

Daniel had not missed the wistfulness and could guess at its cause. A maid was entitled to dream of a grand and glorious wedding, with fife and drum, feasting and congratulation. Although Parliament accepted as legal no marriage that was not performed by a justice of the peace and had outlawed church ceremonies and all celebration, such ceremonies and celebrations were still clandestinely conducted. But this one would be a hasty, hole-in-the-corner affair—a father ridding himself of an undutiful daughter with the minimum of expense and fuss.

"Make yourself ready then," was all Daniel said, however. "I will find the direction of the nearest justice."

The landlord furnished the information that Justice Hazlemere was to be found at the sign of the quill on Boulder Lane, but two steps away. They dined first, an awkward party since no one seemed to know what conversational topics were appropriate in the circumstances. Henrietta played with her food, although Will's appetite seemed not impaired by his bruised chin. Sir Gerald consumed enormous quantities of a meal that would not be charged to his account, and Daniel gloomily contemplated the prospect of being saddled with a considerable debt at a time when he was bound to face crippling fines imposed by Parliament for his support of the lost Royalist cause.

At the sign of the quill, he assumed the debt of five hundred pounds owed by Sir Gerald Ashby of Thame in the county of Oxfordshire to Sir Reginald Trant of Steeple Aston in the same county.

Justice Hazlemere was a dour man with a pinched face and watery eyes. He performed his duties with expressionless efficiency. Clasping the Directory, the set of rules for public worship compiled and ratified by Parliament, he inquired of Sir Daniel Drummond if he intended to marry Henrietta Ashby. On being told that Sir Daniel did indeed intend such a thing, the justice turned to Henrietta.

"Do ye, Mistress Ashby, intend marrying Daniel Drummond, Baronet?"

Henrietta swallowed, cleared her throat, moistened her lips. "Yes," she said.

"Then," said the justice, "I pronounce you man and wife. You may pay my clerk five shillings and he will draw up the parchment witnessed and attested by me that y'are properly married in the eyes of the church and the law."

And thus it was that on the twenty-seventh day of September, 1648, Henrietta Ashby became Henrietta, Lady Drummond, wife of Sir Daniel Drummond, Baronet, of Glebe Park in the village of Cranston in the county of Kent.

Chapter 5

"I think perhaps I will seek my bed." Will yawned deeply and stretched.

"But 'tis early yet," protested Henrietta, replacing the draughtsmen on the backgammon board. "Let us play another game."

Will looked awkward. He glanced across the parlor to where Sir Daniel sat beside the fire, a book upon his knees. For a man on his wedding night, he seemed very relaxed to Will. And Henrietta was behaving as if nothing momentous had occurred in her life. It seemed to Will that the burden of recognizing this marriage as fact had fallen to him, and he did not know quite how to deal with it. Playing backgammon with the bride as the night grew late did not strike him as appropriate.

"Nay," he said, getting to his feet. " 'Tis late, and I'm awearied. You should be too." A pointed stare accompanied the latter declaration.

Henrietta frowned. "I do not feel particularly weary. I expect 'tis because I lay long abed this morning."

"Well, I am going to bed," Will said firmly. "So I'll bid ye good-night. Good night, sir."

"But you will see him in a minute—" began Henrietta, then stopped, a fiery blush mounting to the roots of her hair. She lowered her eyes to the board and became very busy with the pieces.

"Good night, Will," Daniel said calmly. The door closed on Will and he shut his book with some deliberation, watching Henrietta, who still sat absorbed with the draughtsmen. Her head was bent, exposing the delicate, vulnerable column of her neck above the deep lawn collar and white neckerchief of her dark blue gown.

"Henrietta?"

"Yes." She turned her head to look at him, her eyes very large.

"I think you should perhaps follow Will's example. We will have a long ride tomorrow and must make an early start." He smiled gently.

Her tongue moistened suddenly dry lips, but she rose obediently.

"I will come to you in a little while," he said. A jerky nod was the only sign she gave of having heard him as she hastened from the room.

Daniel stared into the fire for long moments. It was his duty to consummate this marriage, but he was not ready to father children on that slight body, not after what successive pregnancies had done to Nan. She had been sixteen when he married her and was dead at twenty-one, worn out with the carrying and delivering of children. He would not permit that to happen to Henrietta. In a year perhaps she would conceive an heir, but until then he would have to take certain precautionary measures—measures that had not occurred to the lustily eager young man he had been.

How much did she know about her conjugal duties? Nan had been completely ignorant, and he had been not much better. But they had learned together, after the first few fumbling awkwardnesses. He smiled in reminiscence. At least he could bring Henrietta the benefits of his experience and hopefully ensure that the loss of her virginity would not be unnecessarily painful.

Henrietta was trembling as if in the grip of an ague as she undressed and released her hair from its braided coronet. It fell down her back in a shining, corn silk-colored cascade, rippling beneath the strokes of her brush as she tried to achieve equilibrium with the accustomed rituals of bedtime. But questions roiled in her anxious brain. This was not, after all, an ordinary bedtime and the accustomed rituals were perhaps not appropriate. Should she take off her smock and get into bed naked? Should she put on her nightcap? Should she blow out the candle? When would he come? Would he still be dressed, or would he come to her in his shirt?

Deciding on compromise, she kept her smock on but left her nightcap off, then climbed onto the high feather mattress, pulled the sheet up to her chin, and sat gazing at the door with apprehensive eyes.

Daniel came in carrying a candle that he set on the mantel before turning to the bed. "Oh, you poor little elf," he said impulsively as she offered a tremulous smile that did nothing to disguise her apprehension. "There is nothing to fear." He came and sat on the bed, reaching up to brush her hair away from her face, allowing the silken tresses to slip slowly through his fingers. "Why are you afeard?"

"I am not," she denied, but her eyes belied the denial.

"What do you know of this business?" he asked, still playing with her hair. "Has your stepmother spoken to you?"

She blushed, shaking her head. "She has never said anything to me, and Will was always so uncomfortable if I tried to ask him . . . and there wasn't anyone else to ask."

Daniel smiled to himself at the thought of poor Will trying to deal with Henrietta's eager questions. He was fairly certain she would have shown none of her present hesitancy when it came to discussing such matters with her hapless young friend.

Catching her chin, he tilted her face, saying teasingly, "It is not like you to be out of countenance, Harry. Why do you not ask me your questions?"

Her lower lip disappeared between her teeth in the manner she had of denoting perplexity. "I don't know how to say it. Perhaps you could just show me what happens."

Daniel scratched his head in frowning silence for a minute while she continued to regard him anxiously. Then he nodded. "Very well, perhaps that is the best way." Taking the sheet, he drew it slowly away from her. The big brown eyes remained riveted to his face as he began to unlace her smock before pushing it gently off her shoulders.

He inhaled sharply at the two angry red weals across her shoulders where Sir Gerald's whip had cut. "Why did you not move when he struck you?"

"Because he was going to beat Will," Henrietta replied, adding reassuringly in case he should feel the need to stop this initiation, "it is only a little sore now."

Daniel's lips twitched, but he nodded gravely before sliding the smock to her waist. She was still looking into his face as he cupped the small, perfect breasts in the palms of his hands.

"Are . . . are they pleasing?" she whispered in a voice that did not sound like her own.

"Oh, yes." Smiling, he bent his head to graze her nipples with his lips. Henrietta gasped at the strange sensation as the crowns of her breasts hardened, tingled, setting up a chain of reaction elsewhere in her body that was as disturbing as it was delicious. He moved his hands to span the narrow, girlish waist, his lips trailing upward to press into the hollow of her throat, to stroke the line of her jaw before finding her mouth.

Her head fell back, her lips parted as his tongue pushed gently within, and at last her eyes closed. She was too busy trying to separate and define the myriad sensations engulfing her to respond to the kiss, and Daniel drew back to look down at her rapt face, eyes tightly closed, mouth still opened slightly as if she simply waited for his return. He touched the tip of her nose with his finger and she opened her eyes.

"That was not at all like kissing Will."

"Am I to take that as a compliment, elf?" The black eyes sparkled with enjoyment rather than passion, but then passion had not been on his agenda. He had had passion with Nan and did not expect to find it again, particularly not with this odd, indomitable creature, who was sometimes an exasperating little girl, sometimes a reckless and courageous hoyden, sometimes a thoughtful young woman, but always refreshingly honest in her reactions, straightforward in her attitudes to life and events around her.

''Was that not a good thing to say?'' She looked discomfited. ''I liked kissing Will, but of course I will not be doing so again. And I liked kissing you very much.''

''Well, I am glad you will not be doing so again, and I am complimented,'' he said solemnly. ''But it is not customary to talk of one man to another when it comes to lovemaking.''

''Then I will not do so again. But I did not know. It never arose with Will because I had never kissed anyone else.''

Matters seemed to be drifting off course a trifle, reflected Daniel. Conversation played havoc with sensuality. ''Lie down,'' he instructed, running his fingertips lightly over her arms, feeling her skin quiver beneath the delicate caress.

The air was cool on her bared skin as he slipped the smock out from under her, lifting her with an intimate palm that shocked her so that for a second her body went rigid. A flush seemed to creep over her entire body as his eyes roamed slowly over her, lying so still and so naked on the bed.

''There is no need to be uncomfortable,'' he said quietly, his hands following his eyes. He had seen her naked before, but on that occasion had not permitted himself the luxury of acknowledging the woman's body. Now he could do so, and it was an entrancing, lean little body, narrow hipped and long legged, her skin soft and creamy, the silken triangle at the apex of her thighs as fair as the tresses massed upon the pillow.

He kissed her belly, nuzzled her navel, feeling her skin mist, bedewed with a faint sheen of perspiration, as she half protested these attentions yet yielded to the wild turmoil of sensation. "You are very beautiful, Henrietta," he said, looking into her eyes as he parted her thighs.

She resisted the pressure of his hands spreading her wide, her head shaking in vigorous negative although she could find no words. But the inexorable trespass continued and with a shuddering sigh she gave in, allowing herself to be tossed hither and thither by weird and wonderful feelings that in her soul she thought should be shameful, yet they were not and she could not have cared if they were.

When at last he removed his own clothes and came down onto the bed with her, the feel of his skin against hers, the strange roughness of it so unlike anything she had before experienced, brought her to vibrant awareness of his physical presence. She inhaled deeply of the scent of him, felt his hair tickle her cheek, the hair of his chest slightly abrasive against her breasts, the hard throb of him against her thigh. He took the bolster and slipped it beneath her bottom, angling her body to facilitate his entrance into the tight virgin portal. She bit her lip hard, her whole body seeming to tighten against him as she looked up into his face, feeling him now as an alien presence, a stranger who would invade and possess her. His eyes were open, as if he was seeing into some other world, and he pressed ever deeper within, refusing to acknowledge her resistance. Then he looked down at her, at her fearful face, saw her confused anger at this invasion, and he lowered his head to kiss her eyelids, gentling her with nonsense murmurs, concentrating now on her so that the anger and fear left her.

For a moment he had forgotten her youth and inexperience as he reveled once more in the glory of being within a woman. For four years he had been chaste, as if by such denial he could atone for the responsibility he bore for Nan's death, and only now did he realize what a sacrifice that denial had been. It required every effort of control to delay his own satisfaction and bring all the skill he possessed to the fore, so that the girl lying so still beneath him began to relax, began to make little sounds of perplexed pleasure as she entered the realm of womanhood.

He withdrew from her body the instant before his own pleasure peaked, and Henrietta, whose education in these matters was but barely begun, thought nothing of it. She lay, feeling strangely limp, accepting the heaviness of the body upon hers, now accepting the body itself, the physical presence in all its sensory reality, that had so frightened her with its unfamiliar and invincible power.

Daniel rolled away from her, propped himself on an elbow, and dropped a kiss on her brow. A smile trembled on her lips, but she said nothing because she could think of nothing that seemed appropriate. A shyness now filled her, as if, despite the intimacy they had just shared, again she was in the company of a stranger. But Daniel Drummond had not been a stranger from the first moment she had become aware of him as a person after the battlefield at Preston. It was a paradox beyond unraveling.

Daniel read something of this confusion in her face and with quiet wisdom decided that sleep was her best medicine. He lay down, sliding an arm beneath her. Henrietta rolled into his embrace and was instantly asleep. Once he was sure he would not disturb her, he gently disengaged himself and slid out of bed, snuffing the candles and building up the fire before returning to bed in the flickering firelight.

Henrietta woke once in the night. She lay disoriented in the darkness and the befuddlement of new waking. Her nakedness surprised her for a minute, as did the presence of a bedfellow when she knew she had been granted the luxury of a bed to herself since they arrived in London. Her body in its private places didn't feel as usual either, sticky and a little sore. She touched herself and remembered. Looking up into the shadowy darkness, she twisted the heavy gold ring on her finger. It was Daniel's signet ring, all that could be produced in the haste and imperative of her wedding. Her father had ridden off immediately, without even reentering the Red Lion to drink to the health of the bride and groom. In the morning Will would leave, and she would go naked into her new life—as naked as she now was.

Kent . . . she had never been to Kent. The garden of England they called it. Orchards and pleasant rolling countryside . . . and two little girls . . . motherless little girls who were about to be faced with a stepmother. Etched into her soul was every memory of the day when Lady Mary Ashby had arrived at Sir Gerald's side to be introduced to the terrified, grieving child who Henrietta knew still existed within herself. Her own mother had been dead but six months when her father brought home his bride and her three children. And Henrietta had loathed them all upon sight in instinctive reaction to a bone-deep recognition that she herself was despised and distrusted. She had put frogs in her stepbrothers' bed and laughed merrily at their screams of repulsion. Boys were not supposed to be frightened of frogs. She expected Marie, her stepsister, to be timid and would not have teased her, except that Marie delighted in telling tales. It had become clear to Henrietta that she might as well be punished for offenses she had committed as for those she had not. So it had continued for ten years and more.

What about Daniel's little daughters? Would they view a stepmother with fearful, hostile eyes? Was he a stern father? A loving one, she believed absolutely. But how could *she* be a mother to motherless children when she had had no mother of her own, only a travesty on which to mold herself?

And how was she to be a wife? Tentatively, she put a hand against the warm back beside her. It seemed almost like spying to touch someone in this way when he was sleeping, yet she found the feel of him comforting, a solid reality to inform her unquiet conjecturing. She let her body roll against him, the warmth of his skin lapped hers, the rhythm of his breathing soothed her, seeming to insinuate itself into her own bodily rhythms, and she slept again.

Daniel woke at dawn to a deep sense of gloom. The war was over and lost, and the future looked bleak for a Malignant, particularly for one who had just acquired a five-hundred-pound debt. The land was in the grip of a vengeful Puritanism. He had been away from his home for six months and there was no knowing what had occurred in his absence. He had seen too many times the orchards cut down, the fields scorched, the gardens destroyed, the houses wrecked by Parliament's vengeance.

He turned his head to look at the sleeping face on the pillow beside him. What *had* he done? Not only had he at great expense bought a penniless bride, but she was such an odd and unpredictable little thing with a deal of maturing yet to do. Did he have the patience to let her grow at her own pace?

Henrietta opened her eyes, as if aware of his scrutiny, and saw the cloud on his face the instant before he banished it. "You look unhappy. What is it?" She touched his cheek with her fingertips and the initiative she showed with her tentative caress surprised him.

"Not unhappy," he said. "But anxious to be home. I've been too long away."

She nodded, sitting up. "Then we should rise and begone." Energetically, she sprang from the bed, then shivered in the cold dawn. "I forgot I have no clothes on." She gave him a glinting smile that could only be described as mischievously inviting, and again he was surprised, wondering if she were aware of the blatant sensuality of her expression. Remembering the shy and fearful maid of the previous evening, he decided it must be unconscious; anyway, now was not the moment to find out.

"Aye, we must get up," he said. "We've sixty miles to ride today."

Henrietta made a face. "I shall not be able to sit down for a week if I ride that distance in one day!"

He laughed, shrugging into his shirt. "Riding is apt

to work such mischief, I grant you, but you have been in the saddle every day for the best part of a month, so you should be hardened."

"Callused," she said with a mock groan, sitting naked on the edge of the bed to pull on her stockings.

He smiled. "Oh, I wouldn't say that." Swooping on her, he lifted her to her feet, turning her around to run his hands over the soft curve of her buttocks and down the backs of her thighs. "Not a callus in sight."

Blushing slightly, she gave him that same mischievous look over her shoulder. "I thought we were in a hurry."

For a moment he wished they were not. "We are." He gave her bottom a brisk pat and tossed her smock toward her. "Make haste. I will go and see mine host about breakfast." Tucking his shirt into his britches, he strode to the door.

Henrietta stood frowning at the closed door. Why did she feel so funnily disappointed? It must be hunger, she decided, and dressed rapidly in her plain riding habit of dark green cloth, braided her hair neatly, looked with distaste at the porringer, then crammed it on her head before hastening to the parlor.

Will and Daniel were already at their breakfast. Will, his mouth full of sirloin, mumbled a greeting but for some reason would not meet her eye. Henrietta wondered if he was embarrassed, knowing as he must what had transpired in her bedchamber.

"Good morrow, Will," she replied with a cheerful smile, taking her accustomed stool at the table. "I am famished."

"What may I serve you, elf?" Daniel reached for the carving knife. "Sirloin, or do you prefer bacon?"

"Bacon," she responded promptly, thinking she rather liked his name for her. She certainly preferred it to "child." "Are those coddled eggs?"

Will passed her the dish and this time looked at her directly. It was a questioning, appraising look, which she returned in her usual candid fashion.

"Ale, Henrietta? Or do you prefer chocolate?" Daniel's voice broke into the moment of silent communion.

"Chocolate, if you please." She passed her platter for the bacon he had been slicing and took the chocolate pot, pouring the dark, fragrant stream into her beaker. "Do you ride back to Wheatley today, Will?"

"Aye," he said. "But I've a mind to see the lions first. It seems a waste to be in London and not see 'em. There's no saying when I'll be here again."

Henrietta glanced wistfully at Daniel but said nothing. He was anxious to be gone from the city and her childish wish for the treat he had promised yesterday, before other things had intervened, must not hinder him.

Daniel heard the plea for all that it was not spoken. "Accompany Will if you wish. I must go to the office at Alder's Gate and see about passes, anyway."

"Will they be difficult to obtain?"

Daniel shook his head. "A man is entitled to return to his home without hindrance. I can explain a sojourn in London on business without difficulty. There is no need for anyone to suspect that we are come from Preston."

"Then I would go with Will, if y'are sure 'tis convenient."

"Lord, Harry!" Will said in tones of mock awe. "How docile y'are become."

Her eyes flashed, her mouth opened on rude protest, then she remembered that she was a married lady and closed her lips firmly.

Experience having taught him to expect an explosion in such instances, Daniel regarded her in as much surprise as did Will, but she continued with her breakfast as coolly as if Will had not spoken, although they could both guess at the effort it was costing her.

Daniel suppressed a smile. Such effort deserved a reward. "You may have until mid-morning to explore with Will. If we are obliged to spend a night on the road, it will not be a major tragedy."

"I have no desire to explore with Will," she said loftily. "We will leave for Kent as soon as you wish."

"Oh, Harry!" Daniel said with a soft laugh. "Now you have spoiled it, and you were doing so beautifully." He pushed back his stool and stood up. "I will leave you two to make peace. I must come to a reckoning with the landlord."

"If you please, Sir Daniel," Will began resolutely, his freckled face pink and earnest, "I would be glad if you would draw up an account of what I owe you. My father will repay you without delay."

Daniel nodded easily. "Furnish me with your address, and I will write to your father."

"Do you think he will do so?" asked Will, their squabble forgotten, when he and Henrietta were alone.

Henrietta frowned, playing with a crumb of wheaten bread on the table. "No," she said finally, "I do not think so, but he would not hurt your pride by telling you not to be foolish."

"But 'tis not foolish to wish to pay my way," Will protested.

Henrietta shrugged. "Ask Esquire Osbert to approach him. Daniel will perhaps feel more comfortable dealing directly with your father."

Will heard the natural use of their companion's name, unembellished with the courtesy title they had both always used. It was reasonable that a wife should call her husband by his given name, but somehow it seemed to put a distance between himself and Henrietta, as if she had entered some higher order of being, crossed some threshold that he had yet to pass over.

Her excitement at the sights and sounds of the city matched his, however, and the lions surpassed all expectation. Will found a shilling in a dark corner of his coat pocket, which bought them steaming hot gingerbread from a pastry cook and a blackcurrant cordial from a street vendor. They returned to the Red Lion, chattering like starlings, in perfect accord. But then they had to make their farewells, since the road to Oxfordshire went in the opposite direction to the road to Kent.

"Come and visit us, Will." Daniel put an arm around the young man's shoulders. "Not just to see Henrietta." He smiled. "But I shall miss you too. You have an open invitation to Glebe Park any time ye care to take it up."

He was rewarded by the miraculous drying of the tears crowding his bride's big brown eyes. "Oh, yes, that would be wonderful. You must come for a very long visit. Mustn't he, Daniel?"

"A very long visit," Daniel agreed. "But now we *must* leave if we are to be out of the city before nightfall." He waited for one last tearful embrace, then picked her up by the narrow waist and lifted her onto her horse.

Will raised a hand in farewell before trotting down the street. Henrietta sniffed, her face forlorn as she watched him go. Then she wiped her eyes, blew her nose, and straightened her shoulders. She had a new life to live now and moping over the past wasn't going to make it any easier. It would have been nice if her plan had worked and Will had married her, because he really was her best friend and she felt so comfortable with him . . . and he didn't have two daughters already. It wasn't that she didn't feel comfortable with Sir Daniel, but she had known Will forever . . . and Daniel *did* have two daughters.

"D'ye think your children will like me?" she asked, unable to keep the question in any longer.

"Of course they will," he reassured her, turning his horse in the narrow lane. "Y'are a very likable girl."

Somehow the compliment wasn't sufficient to banish her unease, and as they rode through the long day, coming into the soft green lushness of the county of Kent, she became unnaturally silent. Daniel did not notice, so preoccupied was he himself, looking about him, taking in the evidence of Parliament's devastating vengeance on some of the large manorial estates, remarking the inevitable aftermath of war—the crops unharvested because there had been no men to work the fields; the unpicked fruit, spoiled by wasps, falling from the orchard trees to rot upon the ground.

What would he find on his own estate?—an estate that had been in the Drummond family since the time of Henry Tudor. Daniel had been accustomed to considering himself a more than ordinarily rich man, but he could now be reduced to penury at the whim of Parliament. Sequestration of his estates would leave him with nothing. He would have no choice but to take his family across the Channel to shift as best they could with the other ruined noble families crowding the courts of Europe, begging and borrowing. A crippling fine would at least leave him with his house and land, and the opportunity to recover. There was land he could sell to pay the fine, depending on how heavy it was.

They were gloomy speculations and did not encourage conversation. Henrietta was left to her own reflections and the growing unease of hunger and fatigue. Tom had gone ahead the day before to alert the household to the safe and imminent return of the family's head. He had left early in the morning, so he bore no message that Sir Daniel was bringing home a wife. It would be easier, Henrietta thought, if she were expected. Or would it? If she were not, no one would have been able to build up fears or expectations.

Her stomach growled in embarrassingly loud protest. It had been a long time since the gingerbread, and an eternity since breakfast. The sun was already low in the sky. Surely they would not ride through the night? They had no escort and the roads were dangerous.

"We will stay this night at my sister's house," Daniel said. " 'Tis but another twenty minutes." He offered her a distracted smile, realizing guiltily that he had been barely conscious of her presence until her body had declared its famished condition. "Frances keeps a good table and will welcome us warmly."

"She will welcome your wife so unexpectedly?"

Henrietta asked, her heart sinking. He had never mentioned a sister.

"Of course." Daniel thought it best not to tell his bride of his original plan for her future—a plan in which Frances was to have played a larger part than her brother. "She is married to Sir James Ellicot of Ellicot Park."

"Is she older than you?"

"Aye, by some thirteen months," he replied. "And childless, to her sorrow."

"She cannot bear children?" Henrietta asked matter-of-factly. While the minute details of the process by which children were conceived had been unknown to her, the dangers of pregnancy, the process of birth, and the all-too-frequent deaths of children were part of the fabric of life, familiar to all from the moment they opened their minds to the world.

"She has never carried a child to term," he replied, equally matter-of-fact. "There . . ." He pointed with his whip toward a hill crowned by a large house of graceful proportions. "We will take the next lane and arrive in time for supper."

"For one who has had no dinner," Henrietta said, "supper will be more than welcome."

"Yes, I had gathered you were in some need." He found his preoccupation receding under the knowledge that within a short time he would hear all he needed to know from Frances and James. They would have been watching over his household and his concerns during his absence and would be able to confirm his fears or put them to rest. He touched spur to his mount, drawing away from Henrietta as they began to climb the hill.

Henrietta encouraged her more laggardly nag to keep nose to tail so that they clattered onto the driveway in front of the house looking as if they were journeying together. The door was flung open almost before Daniel had dismounted. There was a cry of joy, a flurry of skirts, and Daniel disappeared into a fervent embrace.

"Oh, Daniel, I cannot believe 'tis really you." Frances at last stood back, holding his hands, examining his face. "You escaped without hurt?"

"Aye," he said. "Is all well at home?" His voice was sharp with anxiety, but Frances nodded instantly.

"All goes well. The girls are up to their usual mischief, driving Mistress Kierston to distraction, and your house and land have so far escaped Parliament's attentions."

The tension left his face and his entire body seemed to relax. "Did Tom not pass this way yesterday? I gave instruction that he should prepare you."

"Oh, yes, he did," Frances assured him. "James is from home at the moment. He had business with the commissioners in Maidstone." Her joyful ebullience died. "He has gone to compound. You will do the same, I imagine?"

"Aye," he said heavily. "D'ye have any information . . . Oh, but there will be time and plenty later." He became aware of his sister's eyes looking over his shoulder, astonishment in their depths. With a wash of remorse, he remembered Henrietta, who was still sitting on her horse, and appeared uncertain.

"Oh, Harry, I ask your pardon." He came quickly to her, lifting her down. "Frances, may I introduce my wife . . . Henrietta, this is my sister, Frances, of whom I have spoken to you."

"I give you good even, madam," Henrietta said, curtsying to a tall, kind-eyed woman whose suit of flowered, ash-colored silk, the waistcoat trimmed with silver lace, bespoke an elegance and affluence with which Henrietta was unfamiliar, but which she knew would not find favor in Puritan eyes.

Frances recovered with admirable speed. Smiling, she embraced Henrietta, saying, "I take it most ill in my brother that he should have told you of me but have kept such a wonderful secret to himself. You are most welcome, my dear, to my house and into the Drummond family."

Daniel's sister's voice contained in its smooth depths the same note of humor as his, and Henrietta seemed to blossom under the warmth of this greeting. The anxious, preoccupied set of her face softened, her eyes glowed, her mouth curved into a broad smile. "You are most kind, madam."

"My name is Frances, my dear. Come you in and warm yourself. You must be exhausted after such a ride."

"More hungry than tired," Henrietta confided as she was hustled into a candle-bright hall of rich oak paneling and warm red flagstones. " 'Tis a very long time since breakfast."

"Really, Daniel, have you not given the child any dinner?" Frances scolded over her shoulder, before calling to a maid who appeared from the back of the house. "Janet, bring the rabbit pie to the dining room, and a jug of mulled sack . . . oh, and the cheesecakes. Make haste, now."

A bright fire sizzled in the dining room grate and Henrietta shed her cloak and the despised round hat with a sigh of relief, taking in her surroundings with an observant eye. The dull gleam of pewter and the brighter sparkle of heavy silver indicated a household of some affluence; the speed with which supper was brought and laid upon the table indicated a well-run household.

"I accept the charge of neglect, sister," Daniel said, smiling as he watched Henrietta fall upon her supper. "But I was anxious to reach here before nightfall." He sipped his mulled sack appreciatively. "I shall be glad to be done ajourneying."

"And I also," Henrietta said, her first hunger now satisfied, enabling her to concentrate on other matters " 'Tis a powerful long journey from Preston."

Frances stared. "You were at Preston?"

"Oh, yes," Henrietta said cheerfully. "Daniel found me on the battlefield." She helped herself to a cheesecake. "I was wounded by a pike."

Frances looked in disbelief at her brother, who raised his eyebrows and shrugged in rueful confirmation of his wife's statement. " 'Tis a long story, sister."

"I rather imagine it must be," Frances declared. "Are ye from the north, Henrietta?"

"No, from Oxfordshire," she replied, failing to stifle a deep yawn. "I went to Preston to be with Will. We were to be wed, but Will decided he was not ready yet."

"Harry, I think the story must be told in its entirety and begun at the beginning if Frances is not to become completely confused," Daniel expostulated, torn between amusement at Henrietta's artless explanation, which had reduced Frances to stunned astonishment, and reluctance to explain the whole absurd business to his sister, whose approval he strongly suspected would be withheld.

"I think it can wait," Frances said briskly, deciding that this story she would hear from her brother alone. "Henrietta looks in need of her bed."

"I own I am a trifle weary." Henrietta yawned again.

"Come, I will take you to your chamber." Frances stood up.

Henrietta glanced at Daniel, who showed no signs of moving. "Get you to bed, child; I will be up later," he said, refilling his goblet. "There are some matters I would discuss with Frances."

"Yes, of course." Feeling as if she had been dismissed, Henrietta followed Frances upstairs to a corner bedchamber, where a fire had been newly kindled and the bed was hung with warm velvet.

"Let me help you to bed." Frances bustled around, turning down the quilted coverlet, trimming the lamp.

"Nay, 'tis not necessary," Henrietta said swiftly. "I know you have much to discuss with your brother."

Frances looked at her uncertainly. The girl was clearly very weary, her face pale, the brown eyes large and luminous, but a constraint had entered her voice, and she was holding herself stiffly erect, as if she had been hurt and pride would have her disguise it. "Are ye sure?"

"Quite sure," Henrietta answered, slipping out of

her jacket, turning aside to place the garment over a chair, busying herself with the buttons of her shirt.

Frances wanted to offer comfort for whatever it was that had hurt her, but something about the way Henrietta was holding herself warned her that such an offer might not be welcomed. "I'll bid ye good-night then."

Henrietta turned around and produced a brittle smile. "Thank you again for your kindness."

" 'Tis no kindness to welcome a sister-in-law," Frances said gently. " 'Tis the greatest pleasure."

Henrietta nibbled her lower lip. "Will . . . will Daniel's children think the same?"

"Oh, mercy, yes!" Frances exclaimed. "They will be overjoyed, I promise you. They're a graceless pair, much in need of mothering, as Daniel will tell you, but they're very loving."

"I would love them if they will let me," Henrietta said slowly.

"They will let you." Frances took Henrietta's face between her hands and kissed her brow. "Sleep now, child. Such fears will seem less in the morning."

She left the chamber and Henrietta prepared herself for bed. That exchange had been reassuring, but she still could not banish the feeling of hurt at the manner of her exclusion from the conversation that would now take place in the dining room. She was supposed to be a married woman, and married women were not sent to bed like weary children while the adults had their adult discussions. Yet, at the same time she could acknowledge Daniel's right to be alone with his sister. Had he said this to her, in the manner of equals, she would have absented herself with instant understanding. But instead he had treated her as he was used to before last night. It was all very confusing and did nothing to relieve her unease as she hovered on the brink of this new life.

Downstairs, Frances reentered the dining room, sat down opposite her brother, and said, "Tell me the whole, Daniel."

He did so with scrupulous honesty. At story's end she sat in silence for long minutes, then she said softly, "Y'are mad, you know that, don't you? To take on such a debt when 'tis inevitable ye'll face a horrendous fine for Malignancy."

Daniel grimaced. "I could do nothing else, Frances. I could not leave her to that brute, even if I had not promised she should come to no harm."

His sister cast him a shrewd look from her own pair of bright black eyes. "Ye'd not tell me this is a love match?"

Daniel shook his head ruefully. "I cannot imagine loving another after Nan. But I've a deep fondness for her, Frances, and she's no younger than you were when you married. I've hopes that Lizzie and Nan will find if not a mother in her then an older sister who could fill the same need."

These were all good enough reasons for a widower to wed, Frances acknowledged without demur, but to wed a girl who brought only debt to the union was madness in Daniel's present circumstances unless it could be explained by love's passion. And into the bargain to wed a girl with such a penchant for falling into scrapes! It looked to Frances very much as if her brother had bought himself a mountain of trouble and aggravation in the interests of naught but a deep fondness. "You know your own business best," was all she said, however. "James will tell you what he knows of the commissioners in these parts. They seem not too unreasonable. Perhaps you can negotiate your indemnity."

"Perhaps." He shrugged. "If necessary I must sell off Barton Copse."

"Our father will turn in his grave at the thought that you would break up any part of the estate."

"What choice do I have?"

"None." Frances sighed. "But 'tis one thing to use the estate to pay your indemnity, another to pay off some debt that rightly belongs to—" She broke off as her brother's face took on an expression she knew of old. It was never wise to ignore the warning it contained.

"I think I'll seek my bed," he said, pushing back his stool. "We'll make an early start in the morning."

"Aye." Frances accompanied him up the stairs, to the door of the chamber where she had taken Henrietta. " 'Tis such a joy to have you back safe, Daniel. For all the way it has turned out, I cannot but thank God that this damnable war is at last done."

"The land is wearied of strife," he said. "We will live as best we may under Parliament's yoke."

"I have heard that there is talk of bringing the king to trial. Did you hear aught of it in London?"

Daniel's face darkened. "Aye, I heard such treason. 'Twill be a crime to stink to the heavens if they do such a thing."

"Perhaps 'tis just talk." Frances kissed him. "I will see you in the morning, brother."

Daniel went quietly into the bedchamber. The hangings were drawn around the bed, the fire low in the grate. He mended the fire, undressed, and quietly drew back the bed curtains. Henrietta was a small, curled mound on the far side of the bed, her hair tumbling loose from the lace-edged nightcap. She did not stir as he slipped into bed beside her, yet he had the feeling she was awake. But he was tired, and there was a darkness in his soul engendered by his talk with Frances, and by the memories flooding in of sharing this bed with Nan on the many occasions when they had visited Ellicot Park. He turned on his side, away from the still figure, and slept.

Henrietta let out the breath she had been holding while she had waited for him to make some movement toward her. If he had reached for her as man to wife, she would have felt less bereft, less afeard. Instead, she finally fell asleep with salt-wet cheeks and a forlorn sadness in her heart.

Chapter 6

"Stand still, Elizabeth." Mistress Kierston shook her head in exasperation as her charge wriggled impatiently, hindering the governess's attempts to straighten the lawn kerchief at the neck of the child's best gown of apple green cambric.

"But Daddy will be here soon and we must be at the gate to greet him." Lizzie tried very hard to be still, knowing full well that only thus would she be done with this irksome business.

"Tom said he was coming yesterday," put in little Nan, who had already received the attentions of Mistress Kierston and was sitting very upright on the window seat in order not to disturb perfection.

"I 'spect he stayed with Aunt Ellicot last night," Lizzie pronounced with the importance of the elder, "if he was longer upon the road than he thought to be. 'Tis a mighty long way from London, is it not, madam?"

Mistress Kierston responded to the question with a nod, pursing her lips as she examined Elizabeth for flaws. It was hardly worth the effort, of course. The child might leave the chamber as neat as a new pin, but within two minutes her hair would have escaped its ribbons, her cap would be askew, her apron smudged. And Nan, plunging headlong after her sister, would be no better.

"May we go now, madam? *Please!*" begged Lizzie, hopping on one foot. "I would be there when he comes, and the morning is half gone already. He cannot be long now."

"Very well, but try to keep yourself tidy. You have on your best gown and I would not have you present yourself to your father after such a long absence in your usual disarray. He is entitled to expect some improvement in your decorum." An expectation that would be sadly disappointed, reflected the governess with resignation as the children disappeared from the room. "Walk, do not run!" she called after them, but with little hope of being heeded.

The two slowed just until they were outside the rambling, red-brick Tudor manor house, then they scampered down the gravel driveway between lines of tall oak trees whose leaves, already turning russet, fluttered in the sharp autumnal breeze. They reached the gate set between massive stone posts and there stopped. It was strictly forbidden to venture beyond the gate without escort, and if their father should turn the corner of the lane and find them waiting outside the park, the homecoming could well turn sour.

So they hopped from one foot to the other, shivered in the wind, and peered, impatient and eager, around the corner of the gatepost.

Having made a very early start from Ellicot Park, Daniel and Henrietta were in fact but a mile away when his daughters reached the gate. Henrietta's heavy eyes and wan complexion had not escaped Frances, although Daniel seemed not to notice. His sister had waved them off with an unquiet heart, her concern of the previous evening increased rather than diminished.

Henrietta did her best to control her rising anxiety as they drew ever closer to the place that she must now call home. Daniel, despite his sister's reassurance that nothing untoward had occurred on his land, could not shake off his own sense of foreboding, which only the thought of seeing his children again could alleviate. It made them a silent pair, lost in their own preoccupations, until they turned a corner of the lane and two small figures appeared suddenly, with great shrieks of "Daddy . . . Daddy!" as they leaped into the lane the minute their vigil was rewarded.

Daniel was off his horse in the beat of a bird's wing, bending down to enfold the two little girls, who flung their arms around his neck, still shrieking their joy.

Henrietta slipped from her own horse and stood to one side, watching the reunion. It brought a lump to her throat; there was so much loving being expressed here in the middle of a Kentish lane. The thought of her own childhood, so barren of love, of even a smidgeon of affection, made her want to weep with loss.

"Merciful heaven! But what great girls you are become," Daniel said when the noise had died down sufficiently for him to be heard. Laughing, he lifted little Nan onto one hip and took Lizzie's hand in a warm clasp. "I have brought you home a surprise. There is someone very special I want you to meet." He turned with his children toward Henrietta, still standing by her horse.

"This is my wife," he said quietly. "She will be a new mother to you, and you must revere her as you would your own mother."

Henrietta swallowed, searching desperately for the right thing to say to these two children, who were regarding her solemnly with the bright black eyes of the Drummonds. Nan's thumb had disappeared into a rosebud mouth; Lizzie's button nose was wrinkled and her forehead creased as if with effortful concentration as she struggled to grasp what her father had just said.

Henrietta stepped forward. "I hope you will love me," she said, "as I will love you." Bending down, she held out her hand to Lizzie. She did not have to bend too far because Lizzie was tall for her age and Henrietta was small of stature. "You must be Elizabeth."

"Yes, madam." Lizzie remembered her manners and curtsied.

"Nay, you must call me Henrietta!" Henrietta cried, horrified at being given a title she had never thought to receive. "And you too, Ann." She straightened to smile at the child in Daniel's arms.

The little girl took her thumb from her mouth. "I am always called Nan. And Lizzie is always called Lizzie." The thumb went back in.

Henrietta nodded. "They are very pretty names. Most of my friends call me Harry, which is easier than Henrietta."

"Does Daddy call you Harry?" inquired Lizzie, who seemed to have recovered from her surprise, although she hadn't taken her eyes off Henrietta.

"On occasion," Daniel said. "But I do not think you should. It is not respectful. Let us go up to the house."

Henrietta bit her lip. She had made her first error, it seemed, but if she was to establish a friendship with Daniel's children she must do so in the way that made her comfortable.

"May we ride?" Lizzie tugged her father toward his horse.

Daniel resisted the tug. "Are ye not wearing your best gown, Lizzie?"

The child pouted, flicking disdainfully at her lace-edged apron. " 'Twas Mistress Kierston who said we should."

"I trust I shall be receiving only good reports from Mistress Kierston." Daniel smiled teasingly as he looked down on his daughter.

"Lizzie had two switchings in one week," Nan said. "For climbing the great oak tree in Barton Copse twice and tearing her petticoat when Mistress Kierston said she should not."

"Tattler!" accused her sister, a crimson tide flooding her cheeks.

"Well, I do not think we need go into that," Daniel said pacifically. "What's past is past, and 'tis to be hoped you have learned the unwisdom of tree climbing. Ye may lead my horse, Lizzie, and we will all walk up to the house."

Henrietta was rapidly coming to the conclusion that Lizzie Drummond was afflicted with a nature very similar to her own. It made her feel a great deal easier, and when she smiled at the girl as they both led the horses, Lizzie returned the smile with a reassuring promptness.

Glebe Park, Henrietta's new home, was a house that immediately welcomed one with its mullioned windows, soft weathered red brick and timbered walls, warm slate roof, and a curl of smoke from each of its three chimneys. The gardens were formal, but there were signs of neglect in the untidy box hedges, the overlong grass, the weeds in the flower beds. Men had had other things to do than gardening in these last years. Beyond the gardens stretched the park land, fields, orchards, woods, all Drummond land for as far as the eye could see. And so far, all intact. But for how long?

Daniel forced the question from his mind for the moment and allowed himself to enjoy his homecoming. He loved his house and it still stood unravished by Parliament's pikes and staves. His daughters were bright-eyed and healthy, and Glebe Park would have a mistress again. Housekeepers were efficient, but they could not lavish upon a house and household the care and attention of a mistress. Henrietta, for all her ramshackle ways, would have been well schooled in the management of kitchen, stillroom, linen-chamber, washhouse, and dairy. She would know what constituted a well-run household, and once the great bunch of keys hung at her girdle, Daniel was confident she would put childhood behind her as she assumed her new duties and responsibilities. She could teach the girls, too, as her stepmother would have taught her.

Now that this war was finished, life could assume its accustomed patterns again. There were bound to be difficulties and differences under the new order, but they would learn to adapt. It was in a much more cheerful frame of mind that he entered the great hall of the manor, one daughter in his arms, the other holding his hand, his wife at his side.

The next hour passed in a blur for Henrietta. Members of the household appeared from everywhere—steward, bailiff, housekeeper, governess, menservants and maidservants—all welcoming the master home, and all covertly examining his young bride, who tried to remember all the names and finally gave up, knowing that it would come later. As the introductions were made, she stood on the stone-flagged floor of the oak-paneled hall, dimly lit by the diamond-paned windows and the great blaze from the enormous hearth. A carved oak staircase curved to the upper stories, and heavy oak doors opened on either side of the hall.

"We will take Henrietta around the house," Lizzie announced when at last the introductions were finished and only the governess and the bailiff remained in the hall.

"Aye, that's a good thought, Lizzie. I have need to talk with Mistress Kierston and Master Herald." He smiled at Henrietta. "You look a little bewildered, elf."

"I am," she replied frankly. "But I daresay it will fall into place soon enough, and Lizzie and Nan will be able to help me."

She could see that Daniel was pleased with the way matters were progressing between herself and the children, and she began to feel much more at ease. Chattering merrily, the girls took her upstairs first, showing her their own chamber with its cushioned window seat and pretty dimity hangings to the bed. There was a spinning wheel in the corner, reminding Henrietta of her own girlhood labors, labors that in general had not been crowned with success. Nan showed her the handkerchief she was hemming. A spot of blood stained the fine cambric where the child had pricked her finger in her efforts. Henrietta had spent an afternoon locked in a pitch-black cupboard once for just such an accident.

She put the dark memories aside; they had no place here with these children who were so clearly loved, so clearly trusting. "Come, what else is there to see?" she said briskly, moving to the door.

There were some eight bedrooms on this floor, and she was shown them all. They were all well furnished;

some were guest rooms, the others occupied by the senior members of the household, Mistress Kierston and her like. At the end of the corridor, Lizzie threw open a door.

"This is Daddy's room. 'Twas our mother's also."

Henrietta stepped into the large chamber and asked the question no one had thought to ask her. "D'ye miss your mother, Lizzie?"

The child frowned, wrinkling her nose again as she considered. "I do not think so." She sat on the window seat, smoothing her apron. "I did, but 'twas a very long time ago."

"Daddy does," Nan piped up. "He told me so."

He had told Henrietta that he was lonely, she remembered. That he was lonely and he needed a mother for his children. It seemed suddenly a very great responsibility. She looked around this chamber that had witnessed the loving, the birthing, the death that lay in her husband's past. Would the life he shared with her ever overlay the memories of that past? How did one compete with memories? How could that great bed with its carved tester and rich embroidered hangings fail to remind him of all that he had lost?

Henrietta had been married for three days to a man who had treated her with the utmost gentleness and understanding. She had thought she knew the man she had married. They had spent upward of four weeks in each other's close company with no constraint. But there had been no constraint because the nature of the relationship hadn't invited it. When she had been cross and stubborn, Daniel had simply treated her as if she were one of his daughters in a cross and stubborn mood. It had never occurred to her to resent the treatment because she had not questioned the nature of the relationship. But matters were very different now, and they must deal together in very different fashion. Unfortunately, she did not know quite how to do that, just as she now realized she knew almost nothing about the man she was wedded to until death should part them.

"Shall we show you downstairs?" Lizzie interrupted Henrietta's reverie. "We cannot go into Daddy's study because he will be closeted with Mistress Kierston and Master Herald—"

"D'ye think she will tell him of the fishing?" Nan interrupted, an anxious look on her small, pointed face.

"What fishing?" Henrietta said, instantly diverted.

"With the village boys," Lizzie explained. "They were tickling trout and taught us how to do it too."

"Oh, yes, that is great play," agreed her new stepmother with unstepmotherly enthusiasm. "Did you catch any?"

"Not trout," Lizzie said with a rueful grin, "but a deal of trouble."

"Well, tickling trout is not very sportsmanlike," Henrietta said thoughtfully.

Both children regarded her with some amazement. That was the only objection their father's new wife would have to their tickling trout? They conducted the rest of the tour in great amiability and were the best of friends by the time they were summoned to the dinner table.

Henrietta had had only the briefest glimpse into the kitchen regions and retained only the sketchiest images of the housekeeper and the cook. But such matters had always been of little interest to her, so she entered the dining room without fully realizing that the next meal to appear on the long mahogany table would require some involvement on her part.

Daniel moved to the foot of the table and drew out the carved chair for her. When she stood uncertainly, he raised a signaling eyebrow. A spot of color appeared on each high cheekbone as she took the unaccustomed place, smiling up at him as he pushed the chair in for her. He assumed his place at the head of the table; the children, the governess, the bailiff, took theirs along the sides.

He must not expect too much too quickly, Daniel told himself. Being a wife was an unfamiliar role for her and she could not assume it immediately, so he directed the serving, the carving, the presentation of courses as he had done since Nan died. But he hoped, as he did so, that Henrietta was watching and preparing to assume those tasks that rightly fell to her hand.

He had listened to his bailiff's report of the condition of the estate; he had listened to Mistress Kierston's report on his daughters' progress. He could fault neither the bailiff nor the governess, but it was clearly time the proper hand took the reins in both instances. The children were animated, plying him with questions as to his experiences of the last six months, but so far no one had asked Henrietta about hers. It only just occurred to him that the tale Harry would have to tell would instantly fire Lizzie's imagination. Baby Nan might not grasp all its implications, but Lizzie would miss nothing, and it was not an edifying story.

At the close of the meal he sent the girls off to their lessons, Lizzie's ardent suggestion that today should be a holiday receiving short shrift. "Henrietta, we should discuss some details of household management, and then I will leave you to work matters out to your satisfaction with Susan Yates. She is a sound housekeeper and will be able to tell you all you need to know of the way domestic affairs have been conducted up to now." Coming around the table, he drew out her chair as he was talking. "Of course, any changes you may wish to make in the conduct of the household are for you to decide."

Henrietta stood up, smiling bravely at words that were supposed to put her at her ease but instead filled her with dread. They went into Daniel's study at the back of the house. He sat down behind a black oak desk, inviting Henrietta to seat herself in an elbow chair beside the fire. She did so, busily smoothing her skirts in an effort to disguise her unease.

"Harry, I do not wish you to misunderstand me," Daniel began slowly, "but I would prefer that you not relate to the children the story of your adventures."

"Why not?" Surprised, she raised her eyes from her lap.

''Surely you do not need me to tell you that,'' he said with a hint of impatience. ''Such an example is like to send Lizzie hot foot in search of similar adventures.''

''Oh, yes, I see.'' She smiled ruefully. ''I beg your pardon for being so stupid. Of course, I will say nothing. But had we better not construct a story to explain how we came to be wed?''

Daniel frowned, tapping his fingers on the gleaming desk top. ''I think 'twill suffice to say that I met you when I was sojourning in London and you were in your father's company. No one will question beyond that.''

''But will they not think the marriage took place somewhat precipitately?'' Harry objected.

Daniel shrugged. ''They may think what they please. But difficult times can explain much that at other times would be considered strange.''

''Aye, I suppose so.'' Henrietta stood up. ''If that is all, I will leave ye to—''

''Nay, sit down again.'' Daniel waved a restraining hand at her. ''That was but the first matter I wished to discuss.''

Henrietta resumed her seat, feeling much like a sailor trapped in a sinking ship. She fixed an attentive and hopefully intelligent expression upon her face and tried to look as if she welcomed this discussion.

''I think it will be best if you cast your household accounts yourself, and we will look at them each month,'' Daniel said briskly, tapping out the points on his fingers. ''You will have the same sum I have been accustomed to allotting Susan Yates, but if ye feel 'tis insufficient then we can examine it after the first month.'' Receiving a mute nod from his wife, he continued to the next point. ''I expect you will wish to spend two or three days accustoming yourself to the household, which you may do in Susan Yates's company. But when y'are ready to take over yourself, then ye may start to instruct the girls. Lizzie is quite old enough to begin learning the arts of the stillroom and the kitchen, and may be assigned some tasks in the dairy, I think. Nan is still too young to do more than observe, but I would have her grow accustomed early.''

Henrietta nibbled her bottom lip. Should she tell him of her own complete ignorance of these matters? It was an ignorance she had brought upon herself, of course, and one that would be hard for Daniel to believe. Any girl from her background would be assumed to know of what he spoke, would be expected to enter her husband's house and take over the domestic management without delay. On the whole, she thought she would keep it to herself. Surely she could learn by watching Susan Yates and asking discreet questions that hopefully would not reveal her abysmal ignorance? She offered another mute nod.

Daniel was frowning thoughtfully and seemed not to find anything amiss in these silent responses. ''I think 'twill be best for the moment if Mistress Kierston retains supervision of their lessons and deportment and reports to me. I would not put too much upon your shoulders at once.''

''No,'' said Henrietta faintly.

''But it would please me greatly if you would spend as much time as you can with them.'' He smiled across the desk. ''Riding together, mayhap, doing things that will give you all pleasure so that you may grow in friendship. They have need of such companionship.''

Henrietta's agreement to this was strong, since here she felt on sure ground. Becoming friends with Lizzie and Nan was a task she knew she could perform with ease.

''Lastly,'' Daniel returned to his finger counting. ''You have need of clothes, d'ye not?'' He smiled again. '' 'Tis a poor business when a bride has no time to prepare her wardrobe.''

''I have need of little,'' Henrietta said. ''I have never been accustomed to possessing a lavish wardrobe.''

''Or even an adequate one, I would guess.'' He raised a comprehending eyebrow, receiving another assenting nod. ''Well, there is no reason why you should not go into Pembury. There is a good mercer where you may purchase materials, and if you do not wish to make them up yourself, our own sempstress will do so to your designs. She is more than competent, Mistress Kierston assures me."

He pulled out an iron-banded strongbox from the bottom drawer of the desk, unlocked it, and lifted the lid. "We may as well spend this while we have it. What I do not have, Parliament cannot take."

"You expect a heavy fine?"

He shrugged, drawing out a leather pouch. "Aye, 'twould be fool's paradise to expect less. I must compound, and take the National Covenant."

To take the National Covenant meant a public oath forswearing loyalty to the king and declaring acceptance of Parliament's rule. After the act of concession, the government would set a fine based on the degree of Malignancy and the size of the covenanter's estate. In order to live within the law of the land, all previous supporters of the king would be required to compound. Exile was the only alternative. Looking at his face, set now in grim lines, Henrietta realized that the act of concession itself, rather than the fine, would cause Daniel the greatest heartache.

"This should suffice." He handed the heavy pouch to her. "I suggest you take Mistress Kierston for company and advice. She is familiar with the towns and villages around here, and all the merchants. Take the children, also, if you wish. They may make some small purchase in celebration of our wedding and my return."

Henrietta accepted the pouch, feeling its considerable weight. It seemed she had drawn a generous husband, but the thought of what he would require of her in return rather diminished any pleasure she might have in the fact.

"When should we make this expedition?"

"I must journey to Maidstone on the morrow and present myself to the commissioners. 'Tis better thus than having them search me out. I do not know how long I shall be gone, but you may see to these matters in my absence, and when I return we will start this life of ours afresh." He stood up, coming around the desk to where she still sat next to the fire. Dropping to one knee beside her chair, he reached a hand to turn her head toward him. The black eyes looked warmly upon her with that empathetic understanding that he had so often evinced in the past.

"We will manage, I believe, elf," he said softly, tracing the line of her mouth with a fingertip. " 'Tis confusing for you at present, but soon I trust you will feel quite at home. And 'tis not as if we do not know each other rather well."

"I am afeard," Henrietta heard herself whisper.

"Of what?" His finger continued its gentle caress.

"Of . . . of doing things awry," she confessed, her brown eyes huge in the small, heart-shaped face crowned with its braided corn silk–colored coronet. "I would please you, but . . . but mayhap I will not."

"Why would you not?"

" 'Tis a strange bargain we made," she said carefully. "A bargain made in haste. I would not have you regret it."

He shook his head. "Nay, Harry, I'll not regret it." He kissed the corner of her mouth. "And I trust you will not either."

She shook her head vigorously, as if the idea were unthinkable, then left the room in some haste, making her way to the kitchen, where she hoped in secret to make amends for her misspent youth. If Daniel was to be away for a few days, she would be granted some respite in which to cram the skills and knowledge she should have learned in the last ten years.

Daniel stood looking into the fire. What an odd little thing she was. A curious mixture of pride, determination, and a great vulnerability that she did her utmost to conceal. Fierce in her defense of those she cared for, she had her own special brand of courage, yet she was frequently reckless of her own safety, following her instincts without thought for the consequences. Never could he have imagined taking such a one to wife, but then he had never expected to find a wounded maid upon the lost battlefield of Preston, one who would embroil him in her own tangled webs of hurt and love.

That night, in the bed he had shared with Nan and for the last four years had occupied in aching loneliness, he found Henrietta soft and responsive. Remembering her youth and inexperience, he possessed her gently, tenderly, enjoying again the once-lost pleasures of lovemaking. He thought the body beneath him had taken its own pleasure, but the explosive glory he had shared with Nan was absent and he did not know how to re-create it. He imagined he could live quite satisfactorily without it, and what Henrietta had never known she would not miss.

Henrietta lay in the darkness of the bed curtains in the bed that would be hers for the rest of her life. Beside her slept her husband, his breathing deep and even, the warmth of his body spilling over to her. Why did she feel this vague sense of dissatisfaction? Daniel had been so gentle, so considerate of her feelings, and she had felt a spreading warmth that had been most pleasurable . . . but it had not been sufficient. How could she possibly know that something was lacking from this conjugal act when she had not known until Daniel had initiated her exactly what the conjugal act consisted of? But she did know that it was not as it could be, and that Daniel knew it too.

That sense of confusion, as if she were a little girl lost in a dark forest, swamped her anew, together with these newfound fears that she would be inadequate to the part she had so blithely agreed to play in Daniel's life. She had never before been afraid that she would fail at something. She had been too busy proving to herself and others that she would plow her own furrow and needed neither approval nor assistance to do so. And she most certainly had not needed love. Which was just as well, a wry voice murmured in her head, since it had not been forthcoming—not even from Will, if she were honest, and perhaps she had only thought she loved him. At least she had affection and kindness from Daniel. It was ungrateful to ask for more, wasn't it?

Chapter 7

Henrietta tried. In the five days of Daniel's absence in Maidstone, she stuck to Susan Yates closer than the housekeeper's shadow. She hung on every word the stilling-room maid uttered. She haunted the dairy, watching the dairymaids make the slip-coat cheeses, churn the butter, skim off the whey. At first, she attempted to hide her real purpose, to pretend that she was simply observing the manner of the household, but she had to ask questions which she knew would reveal her ignorance, so finally she gave up the pretense, well aware that she had fooled no one.

Reluctantly, she was obliged to admit that the only way to acquire the skills and learning necessary to a lady of quality who would run her own Great House was through practice—years of practice. Daniel expected eight-year-old Lizzie to begin her education in these matters without delay, but Henrietta, as a child, had flatly refused to learn to perform any of the household tasks assigned to her. Finally, her stepmother had washed her hands of her, leaving Henrietta to run wild. Delighting in the freedom that kept her away from persecution in the house, the child had never questioned the usefulness of the education she had abandoned.

Now the chickens had definitely come home to roost, Henrietta reflected glumly. The entire household knew that the master had married a complete incompetent, although they were far from unkind to her and offered her the lip service due to the mistress. Only Tom knew all her secrets, but he wasn't telling—more out of his respect and affection for Daniel than for herself, Henrietta decided. The question was: how long would it take Daniel to realize the true state of affairs?

Whenever she could, she took off with Lizzie and Nan into the fields and woods, hunting, gathering flowers, looking for birds' nests, fishing, sharing with them what she *had* learned in her childhood—the pleasures of freedom and the countryside. It did not occur to her that Daniel might not consider this learning appropriate for his daughters. She was vaguely aware that Mistress Kierston was not entirely approving, but the governess would not question the actions of her charges' stepmother, particularly in the absence of their father. Lacking the advice that might have given her pause, Henrietta simply shrugged off the raised eyebrows, the rather chilly demeanor, and blithely continued enjoying herself with her stepdaughters, who could scarcely wait until their lessons were over and the day's entertainment could begin.

Daniel returned in the late afternoon of the fifth day. He came upon the three of them trudging, weary but merry, up the driveway, their arms filled with autumn foliage. He looked askance at the grubby untidiness of his daughters, and Henrietta was in not much better condition, but they were so clearly happy that he allowed himself to be infected by their good spirits. His own spirits were so depressed by events of the last few days that it was a welcome relief to let their simple gaiety wash over him. He dismounted, walking with them through the gathering dusk back to the house while the girls prattled artlessly, constantly referring to Henrietta for confirmation, agreement, and information. She responded always with a natural ease, a ready smile, and Daniel began to feel better. He may have acquired a penniless bride and a mountain of debt, but it appeared his children had acquired the loving companion he had hoped for. The occasional torn petticoat, crooked stocking, and muddied knee were no great matter.

"You look awearied," Henrietta said, once the children had been dispatched abovestairs with Mistress Kierston. "I will have water heated in the washhouse if you would like to bathe before supper. 'Twould make you feel a little better."

Daniel looked gratified at this evidence of wifely concern. "A kind thought, Harry. Give order by all means. I should be glad to wash away the dirt of the road . . . and the stench of Parliament," he added with sudden savagery.

"It was bad?" She touched his arm instinctively. Not a trace of that gentle humor remained in his voice and the black eyes were cold and tired.

"I cannot bring myself to talk of it," he said, not meaning to sound short and dismissive but unable to help himself.

Henrietta swallowed the hurt, telling herself that he was fatigued and hungry. "I will see to your bath," she said in what she hoped was an authoritative fashion. "And I will prepare something special for your supper."

Henrietta hurried off to the washhouse. Unfortunately, she had forgotten, or rather had not been aware, that today was the one day in the month when the great copper cauldrons were scrubbed clean of scales and residue accumulated during a month of continuous heating. The fires in the washhouse had been allowed to go out and there was no hot water for a bath.

She stood chewing her lip in the cold, deserted building normally filled with steam and the cheerful bubble of boiling water. She should have known such an elementary fact of household routine.

"D'ye wants somethin', m'lady?" The cheerful tones of one of the maids came from behind her.

"Hot water, Meg," she said with a rueful smile. "Sir Daniel is in need of a bath."

"Oh, Tom'll take a tub to 'is chamber," the girl said. "There's water on the fire in the kitchen. I'll find Tom."

"Thank ye, Meg." Henrietta returned to the house, going upstairs to explain the change of plan to Daniel. To her relief he heard her explanation of a momentary forgetfulness without surprise, saying he was content to bathe by the fire rather than trekking to the wash-house.

A knock at the door heralded Tom's arrival with tub and water. "What 'appened in Maidstone, Sir Daniel?" he demanded bluntly, depositing his burdens before the fire.

"I'll tell ye as soon as I'm in the bath," Daniel said, accepting Tom's ready assistance with his boots. "They're whoresons, Tom, every last one of 'em."

They both seemed to have forgotten Henrietta, who felt like an intruder. Clearly her husband would talk with Tom of things he would not discuss with his wife. Quietly she left them, going down to the kitchen to wrestle with the matter of a special dish for supper.

The cook looked doubtful when informed that the lady of the house was going to make a cheese pudding, one of Sir Daniel's favorite dishes. However, he provided the recipe, indicated the ingredients in the pantry-closet, and retreated to the far end of the long, scrubbed-pine table to finish his baking.

It seemed simple enough, Henrietta thought. All she had to do was follow the recipe. The only difficulty was that quantities of herbs and spices were not specified. The kitchen was full of people, but they were all busy at their allotted tasks and she was reluctant to ask what must be an obvious question. Working on the principle that one cannot have too much of a good thing, she sprinkled the pepper, nutmeg, and sweet marjoram with a generous hand. Egg breaking was a little messy, but stirring, beating, cheese grating, soaking bread in milk, were all quite straightforward, and the result when it went into the pudding basin looked just as it should—a few minute pieces of eggshell would not be noticed. She set it into a saucepan of boiling water on a trivet over the fire to steam, before going abovestairs to bid the girls good-night.

As she passed Mistress Kierston's chamber, she heard the voices of the governess and Sir Daniel coming from within. The door was open and she glanced sideways as she went by. Daniel was looking uncommon grave, frowning deeply. Mistress Kierston appeared agitated. They both saw her pass and she wondered if she had imagined the uneasiness that seemed to cross their faces.

Nan was all but asleep when Henrietta went into their room, but Lizzie was in the mood for talk and Henrietta sat on the end of the bed for near twenty minutes, regaling the child with the story of how she had put frogs into her stepbrothers' bed.

"When you have a child, 'twill be our half brother or sister, will it not?" Lizzie slipped down the bed, yawning.

"Aye," Henrietta agreed, tucking the cover under Lizzie's chin. "And you will be far too grown up to tease. I was but five years old, ye must remember."

" 'Tis past time this candle was snuffed." Daniel came in, the frown still in his eyes. He bent to kiss his daughters, brushing a fingertip over a long scratch on Nan's cheek. "How did that happen?"

"Oh, 'twas from a thorn tree when we were following fox tracks." Lizzie answered for her sister, who was far gone in sleep. "Harry can tell the difference between a fox and a badger track. She knows all sorts of things like that."

"Does she?" Daniel sounded less than admiring. "I have told ye, Lizzie, that you'll accord your stepmother her proper name."

Henrietta opened her mouth to put in her own word on this, but some streak of wisdom kept her quiet. Lizzie, however, seemed to see no injustice in the reproof since it referred to matters of obedience, and such issues were always clearly defined with no extenuating circumstances.

Henrietta left them, going downstairs to the small wainscoted parlor behind the dining room where she had been told Daniel preferred to take his supper. The table before the fire was set for the meal, a bottle of good burgundy on the side table. She could see nothing amiss, but wondered gloomily if she would notice anyway.

Daniel came in, closing the door behind him and going to stand before the fire, hands thrust deep into the pocket of his britches.

"Something has vexed you," Henrietta said hesitantly.

Daniel frowned, considering. He was loath to chide her on someone else's word. Mistress Kierston had been greatly upset by the antics of her charges, although she had been careful not to lay precise blame at their stepmother's door. He had seen for himself how grubby and disreputable they had looked that afternoon, but he had also seen how happy and at ease they were with Henrietta. No, he would wait and see for himself before interfering in the progress and conduct of this burgeoning friendship.

"Do not permit the children to call you Harry," was all he said, moving to the sideboard to pour wine. "Have you had time to examine the cellars yet? Hacket will be able to show you how the various wines are stored, so you will be able to lay hands on them when they are needed."

Wine as well! She had not thought she must find time to follow the steward around also. There seemed no end to it. Henrietta mumbled something about having been very busy, said that she would fetch the cheese pudding, and disappeared to the kitchen.

The pudding unmolded quite well. She stuck on a corner that had stayed behind in the basin, and nodded with a degree of well-deserved pride. With the same pride, she placed the dish upon the table in the parlor.

"See, I have made you a cheese pudding, Daniel. I hope 'tis good."

He smiled, putting his despondency behind him. She was looking so eager, those big brown eyes searching his face for reaction. "I am sure 'tis good." He held her chair for her, then sat opposite.

Henrietta served him generously before helping herself. She watched him covertly as he took the first mouthful. A look of astonishment crossed his face. Hastily she tasted hers, then choked, dropping her spoon onto her platter. Daniel had replaced his own spoon and was looking at her with the same astounded expression.

"What ever is in it, Harry?"

" 'Tis not very nice, is it?" she said in rueful understatement.

Daniel shook his head. "I do not think I have ever tasted anything quite like it."

"D'ye think perchance it is the sweet marjoram? Mayhap I used too much."

"I wouldn't know." Delicately, Daniel removed a piece of eggshell from the tip of his tongue and took a deep draught of wine. "But I do know that I am hungry."

"Aye, I will see what else there is." She gathered up the dishes and the pudding, tears pricking her eyes. But in the kitchen she placed the pudding before the cook "Pray taste this and tell me what I have done wrong."

He took a mouthful and much the same look of astonishment crossed his face as had crossed Daniel's. Then he said slowly, "A plentiful want of salt, unnecessary nutmeg, and a great excess of sweet marjoram. 'Tis but a pinch that's needed."

"My thanks." She emptied the pudding into the pig bin by the door and went into the pantry. "What can I serve Sir Daniel instead?"

Susan Yates bustled over, ever kindly and helpful. "There's a meat pasty, m'lady, and a wheel of cheese. Meg shall bring it to the parlor. The master will be quite satisfied."

Not as much as he would have been with a cheese pudding, Henrietta thought, wishing she did not have to return to the parlor. How could she explain such an abysmal failure?

Daniel was still sitting at the table, thoughtfully twisting his pewter goblet between his hands, when she came in. "I daresay you have never prepared cheese pudding before."

"Nay, I have not," Henrietta declared with absolute truth. "Meg is bringing a meat pasty and some cheese. Will that do?"

"Amply." He lapsed into silence. The fire spurted and Henrietta sipped her wine, trying to think of something to say. Meg's arrival with supper was a welcome diversion.

"Is your indemnity very large, Daniel?" she asked, summoning up the courage at last.

"Aye, 'tis like to cripple me, if I cannot find a friend in London to speak for me to Parliament." He cut savagely into the loaf of barley bread. If he could find no one willing to intercede for him, he would be lucky to be left with more than the house and the home farm. And he was still encumbered with the debt upon staple-statute to Sir Reginald Trant.

"D'ye have a friend who might do so?" she asked.

"My brother-in-law has kin who have been strong for Parliament. They have spoken for him. 'Tis possible they will do the same for me." He pushed back his chair abruptly. "Do you go to bed when you are ready, Henrietta. I have some letters I must write."

He left the parlor for his study, and Henrietta sat staring into the fire for long minutes. She would help him if she could. But how could one help someone who did not wish to talk about what was troubling him? Anyway, how could she help anyone? She, who could not even prepare a cheese pudding, and had not thought to ask the question that would have elicited the information that the second Tuesday in the month was the day for closing down the washhouse?

Things did not improve over the next days. Daniel remained preoccupied as he wrestled with his bailiff over ways of raising the money to pay an indemnity of four thousand pounds, if he could not get it reduced. The indemnity had been fixed at such a great sum because of the degree of his Malignancy and the value of his estate as presented to the commissioners in Maidstone when he had compounded. He would have to sell off much of his productive land to meet that sum, including Barton Copse. Barton Copse was a major source of revenue, providing as it did sufficient firewood to supply the neighboring towns, as well as wood to supply all the needs of his own farm and household. Without that revenue, he would be hard-pressed to meet other expenses without selling off yet more land, and every piece he sold reduced his ability to maintain his own self-sufficiency. If they were not self-sufficient, they would need to buy from others. And so it went on—the economic facts of life. And one of the facts of his life was the price he had paid for his bride.

Henrietta, while recognizing that her husband's preoccupation was not intended to be hurtful, felt excluded nevertheless. Even the girls were affected and the dinner table was a gloomy and silent place, no longer vibrant with their cheerful prattle. Mistress Kierston sat with pursed lips; the bailiff looked like one who recognized Doomsday; Daniel seemed not to notice what he ate and drank. Henrietta tried to start conversations, but all such attempts sank like stones to the bottom of a lake and she gave up, just as she gave up her attempts to get Daniel to confide in her. He would answer her questions briefly but would enter no discussion, whether it was at the supper table or in the privacy of their bedchamber.

This preoccupation did mean that he noticed little of what went on around him. He did not question how his wife spent her days so long as everything continued smoothly, and since a series of violent November storms kept Henrietta and the children within doors, Mistress Kierston had no complaints about unladylike activities.

Henrietta continued with her self-teaching, and the entire household seemed to enter the conspiracy. Daniel assumed that his wife had taken over the reins of domestic management and no one enlightened him as to the true state of affairs. Henrietta was to be found in the dairy, the brew house, the stillroom, the wash-house, the pantry—all perfectly reasonable places for the lady of the house to be. But she could not maintain the deception forever.

Odd little things intruded on his absorption. She did not always know the answers to basic domestic questions, such as whether the October ale brew was being tunned in the sweet-wine barrel, or when the young chickens would be fat enough for eating. Suffering from a severe headache one afternoon, he had asked her to prepare him a camomile draught. It had taken her such an inordinately long time he had gone in search, finding her closeted in the stillroom, head-to-head with the stillroom maid. He had assumed they were concocting something more elaborate than the simple draught he had requested—there could be no other reason why the two of them should be involved—and had been quite taken aback when Henrietta at last brought him only the camomile.

One chilly morning in late November he was crossing the yard behind the house when sounds of commotion arose abruptly from the dairy. Pushing open the door, he stepped into the chilly shed, which was empty of all but Henrietta kicking the butter churn and swearing vigorously. "What the devil goes on here?"

"A pox upon the slubberdegullion! Oh, I will never understand this!" she exclaimed, stamping her feet on the damp cobbled floor. Despite the cold, the hood of her cloak was thrown back, revealing her flushed face and brown eyes glittering with frustration. " 'Tis the second time the milk has turned to cheese when it is supposed to be butter! I do not seem to be able to catch it at the right moment. And it is such hard work!" She kicked the butter churn again.

"Whatever do you mean?" He came toward her, and Henrietta suddenly realized what she had revealed. She fell silent and stood waiting.

Daniel stroked his chin thoughtfully as the pieces began to fall into place. The picture they formed made no sense, yet he had the horrible conviction that for some extraordinary reason it was the true picture.

"I think perhaps a few explanations are in order," he said finally. "Let us go into the house. 'Tis cold as charity in here."

Henrietta followed him into his study, where she stood by the door still saying nothing, watching Daniel as he bent to warm his hands at the fire. The silence lengthened, then slowly he straightened up and turned to face her.

"Am I to understand that your inability to manage the butter churn is not limited to something in this morning's air?"

There was no point pretending any longer. Besides, the strain of the deception was becoming unbearable. She met his grave regard. "Aye, you are to understand that. Just as you should understand that I know nothing of brewing, of cooking, of herbs, simples and physicking. I have no idea how to cast household accounts or—"

"Enough!" he interrupted brusquely. "I have grasped the point. But how should this be, Henrietta? Why were you not taught these things?"

She nibbled her bottom lip. " 'Twas not a lack of teaching but a lack of learning."

His frown deepened. "What mean you?"

"Why, 'tis quite simple," she said bitterly. "There is little point learning when one is as like to be beaten for doing something well as for doing it awry. I was safer out of the house, so preferred to absent myself."

Daniel nodded slowly, then he crooked a finger at her. "Come here, elf." She approached somewhat cautiously, and he placed his hands on her shoulders, looking down at her seriously. "Why have ye kept this such a secret?"

The slim shoulders beneath his hands lifted in a tiny shrug. "I did not know how to tell you. You seemed so certain that I would know these things, and of course I should know them . . . and I was to teach Lizzie—'' She broke off with another helpless shrug. ''I have been trying to learn, but there is so much. 'Twill take a lifetime.''

''Now, that is a great piece of nonsense,'' Daniel said, a note of severity sounding for the first time. ''I would have you learn, and you will do so quickly enough if you apply yourself. Now that you need not pretend, it is bound to be easier, and I will help you as and when I may.''

''But you have so much on your mind at present.'' She looked up into his face, searching his expression. ''I would help you there, if you would share a little of your trouble with me.''

He sighed, releasing her shoulders, turning aside to the fire, kicking at a slipping log. ''Until I hear from my brother-in-law, who has gone to London to speak to his kin for me, I can make no proper decisions. 'Tis the uncertainty that troubles me. Once I know the worst, then mayhap 'twill be easier. I can at least come to some decisions.''

She put a hand on his arm, feeling the muscles ripple beneath the slashed sleeve of his doublet. He turned and smiled down at her, interpreting the gesture for the offer of comfort that it was.

''This time will pass, elf,'' he said, bending to kiss the corner of her mouth. '' 'Tis as true of bad times as of good.''

''Aye, I know it. Why d'ye not sit beside the fire for a while and I will bring you buttered ale.'' An imp of mischief danced in her eyes. ''That is something I have learned how to prepare. If I had my guitar, I would play for you. My skill there is tolerable, and I am said to have a pleasing voice.''

''Why would you learn that and nothing else?'' he asked, sitting by the fire, his eyes teasing her.

''Because I enjoyed it,'' she replied frankly. ''And dancing also.''

''There'll be little opportunity for such amusements

now," Daniel said, the moment of relaxation vanishing. "Parliament has voted to bring the king to trial."

Henrietta shivered. "On what charge?"

"Of raising an army against Parliament, and abusing the limited power invested in him," Daniel told her heavily. "They cannot help but find him guilty. We must wait to see if they are so securely in the clutches of evil that they will sign the death warrant." He stood up, sighing. "I must ride to Longford field and oversee the hedging. Do you get back to your lessons, Harry. I will teach you how to cast your accounts after supper."

He went out into the cold, reflecting on the revelation just made to him. It fitted with what he knew of Henrietta and he supposed he should have realized that he could expect nothing ordinary from her. But she was quick-witted and would learn readily. For some reason, he found rather moving the idea of her struggling in secret to meet his expectations, although he thought it would say more for the openness of their marriage had she felt able to confess her lack of skills at the outset. He must try to spend more time with her, he resolved, as he rode over stubble fields through the raw November air. The girls would benefit from more paternal attention too. It was high time he came out of his self-absorption. It was not achieving anything at present.

Daniel's resolutions served well and the household returned in some measure to its previous cheerfulness, until disaster struck.

The foul weather that had kept Henrietta and the children within doors for so long at last lifted, bringing bright sunshine, blue skies, and crisp cold air in its place. The three of them resumed their afternoon rides and rambles, returning to the house at dusk, rosy and weary, and in great accord. Mistress Kierston pursed her lips and looked sourly at the muddied petticoats, the missing buttons, the tumbled hair. She could not punish the children, however, since their stepmother had been their escort, and was frequently as untidy as they. Unfortunately, Sir Daniel had gone on a visit to Ellicot Park and could not be told of this resumption of undesirable activities, so she was obliged to bide her time.

Daniel returned on a Saturday afternoon. His visit to the Ellicots had brought no cheerful news. James had pled his brother-in-law's case in London, but no decision was as yet forthcoming, and when he reached home he found waiting for him a demand from Sir Reginald Trant for repayment of the debt and interest thereon accumulated over the last ten years that he had assumed on behalf of Sir Gerald Ashby. The demand was couched in no polite terms, and Daniel whitened with anger, crumpling the parchment and hurling it into the fire.

He had assumed he would be able to repay the debt in installments, although it would be a heavy drain on his resources once he had sold off the goods and land necessary to pay the indemnity. He would be obliged to reduce drastically the number of people he employed around the house, gardens, and estate, and the thought of the hardship that reduction would cause those he must dismiss brought him to a white heat as he raged at the insolence of Trant's letter and the blatant manipulation of the brutish Ashby.

It was at this inauspicious moment that Mistress Kierston chose to bring certain matters to his attention. She had hastened down the stairs as soon as she heard of his return, anxious to speak with him while his wife and daughters were away from the house. He heard her out in silence. His daughters were become saucy and unmanageable; the governess could not be held responsible when her authority was usurped; digging in fox holes, climbing trees, fishing the streams, had always been forbidden activities until . . . Here she pursed her lips and fell silent. It was not necessary to continue the sentence and she would not stand accused of openly criticizing Lady Drummond.

"They remain forbidden," Daniel said curtly, "You may leave this matter with me, Mistress Kierston."

He marched out of the house into the December afternoon. The sun was low in the sky and there was an icy bite in the wind. He pulled his cloak more tightly around him, wondering where to begin his search. The stables produced the information that they had not taken horses, which meant they would not be too far afield.

He heard Nan's excited shriek coming from the orchard. "Can ye catch him, Harry? Oh, poor little thing . . . I hope he won't fall!"

"Cats do not fall, silly," came Lizzie's scornful tones, sounding somewhat muffled. "Anyway, Harry has him."

The explanation for the muffled tones was apparent as soon as he entered the orchard. Lizzie was crouching in the crotch of an ancient conifer at the edge of the orchard, peering upward to where Daniel could make out a smudge of blue in the higher branches. It was the blue of Henrietta's skirt. Nan, too small for tree climbing and for the moment unaware of her good fortune, was jumping around the tree trunk, piping shrilly.

"Elizabeth!"

At the sound of her father's voice, Lizzie nearly fell off her perch. Nan ceased her piping and, as was usual in moments of tension, her thumb went into her mouth.

Daniel removed the thumb. "Y'are grown too big for such babyishness. Go at once to Mistress Kierston."

The child scuttled away without a word, and her sister dropped out of the tree. She stood, hands behind her back, staring at some spot beyond her father's shoulder.

She had pieces of fir in her hair, grass stains on her skirt, a smear of mud upon her cheek. Daniel thought of the child's mother, such a neat, fastidious person Nan had been. So graceful and womanly, so well-versed in the duties and responsibilities of womanhood.

"You have been forbidden to climb trees, have you not?"

"Yes, sir."

"Go to your room. I will come to you shortly."

Lizzie went with dragging step. Henrietta, who had made her own descent discreetly on the far side of the tree, moved out of the shadow. She held a tiny, ginger-striped kitten in her arms.

"I do not think it would be just for you to punish Lizzie," she said, slowly and clearly. "I expect she thought it was not forbidden since I was doing it."

"An error which it is now my disagreeable duty to correct," Daniel said harshly. All his pent-up rage and frustration rushed to the fore as he looked upon this wife and thought of the other. Here was a wife who could teach daughters none of the arts of housekeeping, none of the gentle skills of womanhood, since she knew them not herself. She knew only hoydenish tricks and the spirit of rebellion, and she had brought him nothing but the weightiest addition to a load of trouble that alone threatened to crush him.

"I will not permit my daughters to become unruly, ill-conditioned, romping tomboys."

Henrietta was in no doubt that the precise description applied to herself. Each word struck as a body blow, but she held herself straight, determined that Lizzie must not suffer for her stepmother's failings.

"Let me talk to her," she said urgently. "I will explain the way things must be so that she will understand. The kitten was crying so piteously because it was stuck up the tree, and we did not think of anything but rescuing him."

"There are men and boys aplenty to do such work," he declared, still harsh. "I am told that my children are become saucy and unmanageable under their stepmother's influence. It is not to be."

"No," Henrietta said swiftly. "If, indeed, 'twere the case, then you would be right to correct such faults. But I do not believe it to be so."

"And how should *you* be the judge?"

She winced, but said boldly, "Because I know the difference between exuberance and rebellion. Others may not." Sensing a hesitation in his manner, she pressed on vigorously. "Only let me explain matters to Lizzie, and I will promise you that such a thing will never happen again."

Daniel hated punishing his children, although he would no more risk spoiling the child than any other parent of his acquaintance. It was simply an unpleasant duty. But if an alternative offered itself, he was always responsive. Now, he stood thoughtful, his anger subsiding as he saw the situation clearly. Henrietta, for all her untidiness and the kitten clutched to her breast, seemed, at this moment, more of an adult, less of a child, than he had ever known her. Maybe both she and Lizzie would learn a valuable lesson if they had to work this out between them.

"I promise you such a thing will not happen again," Henrietta repeated, absently scratching the kitten between its ears.

"It had better not," Daniel said, turning on his heel, indicating tacit acceptance.

Henrietta looked down at the ginger kitten. " 'Tis all your fault," she said disgustedly. "I could wring your scrawny little neck." She set the creature on the grass, then stared in disbelief as it scampered across the ground and clawed its way up the fir tree, only to begin its pitiable mewing once it reached the middle branches. "Oh, no! How could you be so stupid!"

At this infuriated wail, Daniel swung around. "What the devil's amiss now?"

" 'Tis the kitten," she said, between weeping and laughing. "It has gone up the tree again."

"This must be what Bedlam is like," Daniel muttered, before telling her vigorously, "Leave it where it is. It may teach it something about survival."

"Oh, I cannot, Daniel. Only listen to it." She wrung her hands in distress. "If you would just lift me up, I could reach it easily enough. 'Twould not be the same as climbing the tree."

There was an instant of complete disbelief. He felt much as he had when she returned from Nottingham with safe conduct for them all. Laughter welled deep in his chest, inconvenient and inappropriate in light of the last minutes. Striding back to her, he spun her around so that she faced the tree and could not see his expression.

"You are utterly incorrigible!" Catching her by the waist, he lifted her, feeling her light and supple between his hands as she stretched upward into the branches.

"I have him. My thanks." He set her on her feet again, and she turned, holding the scrabbling kitten tightly. "Daniel, I believe you are laughing."

"I am not!" he denied fiercely. "I have never been less amused, as it happens."

"No, of course not," she said meekly. "I cannot imagine how I made such a mistake."

"Neither can I. Take that wretched animal back where it belongs, and before you go to Lizzie for heaven's sake tidy yourself!" On that hopefully firm note, Daniel strode back to the house.

Not displeased with the way things had turned out, Henrietta deposited the kitten in the stables with the rest of the litter, stopped at her chamber to change her dress and comb her hair, then went to Lizzie.

The little girl was sitting on the bed, but jumped to her feet, her expression apprehensive, as the door opened. She looked surprised at the unexpected visitor. "Is Daddy coming?"

"No," Henrietta said, closing the door. "But I think 'twould be as well if you were to spend the rest of the day in some diligent pursuit with Mistress Kierston." She sat on the bed, patting the space beside her. "Sit down, Lizzie, we have to talk. There are some things we must both try to understand."

Chapter 8

It was an hour before Harry left Lizzie's bedchamber. It had been a most uncomfortable task, explaining to an eight-year-old that her father's wife was not always a reliable example and was herself in frequent need of reminders about correct deportment. Feeling rather small, but a great deal wiser, she went into her own chamber in search of a composing solitude.

She was not left alone for long, however. Daniel came in after about five minutes. "Tell me about this Sir Reginald Trant," he said without preamble. "I am aware that he is ancient, has green teeth, and stinks to the heavens, but I would know of his character."

Henrietta frowned in thought as she arranged a sheaf of copper leaves in a big brass jug. "I have met him but twice. It seemed to me that he was a man of ill humor, rather like my father." She stood back, judging her arrangement with a critical eye. "Why d'ye wish to know?"

"I owe him money, or had you forgotten?" he said, unable to conceal the acid note in his voice.

Henrietta flushed awkwardly. "It slipped my mind for the minute. Has he made demand of you?"

"Aye. In the most insolent fashion, he demands immediate repayment of the entire sum with accrued interest." Daniel paced the room. "The devil of it is, I do not know where I am to lay hands on such a sum at this moment."

"But can you not use my portion?" She adjusted a

branch. "I do not know how you arranged matters since I was not permitted to remain in the room for the discussion, but surely—"

"Your father would settle nothing upon you," Daniel interrupted. He had not intended to apprise her of this humiliating fact, but in response to her direct question there seemed little point in prevarication.

Henrietta swung around to face him. "That cannot be! I was wed with his approval."

A case of good riddance, Daniel remembered sourly. He shook his head. "Nevertheless, Harry, he refused to settle a penny upon you."

She shook her head vigorously, setting the two heavy corn silk-colored braids swinging against her back. Her eyes were wide with anger. "Then he has tricked you, Daniel! My mother's jointure in the event of her death was entailed to me upon my wedding, so long as I did not marry against my father's wishes. That money is mine. I did not expect a groat from *him* . . ." Scorn and disgust laced her voice. "He would not give me the parings of his nails. But he has no right to my mother's jointure. 'Tis all of three thousand pounds, if I heard Master Filbert correctly, and—"

Daniel raised an imperative hand. "Just a minute. Who is Master Filbert?"

"A lawyer from London," she said impatiently. "I listened at the window when he was talking with Esquire Osbert and my father. There was much shouting." She pulled a face at the memory. "Esquire Osbert had come to discuss the possibility of my marriage with Will. My father said he would not consent, and if I married without his consent, then I would forfeit the jointure. And Master Filbert said it was so, but that was the only condition on which the money could pass to my father. 'Twas for that reason that Esquire Osbert would not agree to Will's wedding me."

Daniel saw again in the eye of memory the sly smile on Sir Gerald Ashby's face as he had thrown down his ultimatum. He had thought to be rid of his staple-statute debt *and* keep his daughter's inheritance in his own hands.

"Would you have known about this jointure if you had not listened at the window?" he asked slowly.

Henrietta shook her head. "I was never told anything. But afterward, Esquire Osbert explained it all to Will, and Will told me all the details." Comprehension dawned. "Of course, my father did not know that I knew. If I had wed Sir Reginald, part of my mother's money would have paid off my father's debt. As 'tis—"

"As 'tis," Daniel finished for her, "your father has rid himself of debt and presumably has his hands on your entitlement. He would assume you could not claim something of which you had no knowledge."

"He is a whoreson!" Henrietta exclaimed. "And do not tell me that is something I should not say, for I know it. But I say again: my father is a whoreson!"

Daniel chuckled, despite his own anger. "Y'are an undutiful daughter, Harry."

"How could I be otherwise?" she returned smartly.

"How indeed!" Then he became serious. "I do not suppose you know the direction of this Master Filbert?"

"Cheapside," Henrietta said promptly. "And I would know Master Filbert again if I saw him. He looks like a filbert—smooth and round and brown as a nut. Do we go in search of him?"

Daniel looked doubtful. "*I* certainly have that intention, but—"

"Oh, you cannot leave me behind!" Harry exclaimed. " 'Tis *my* money by rights. Of course," she added, chewing her lip, "if 'tis mine, then 'tis yours by rights. But I think I should be permitted to fight for my own."

She looked so intense, so determined, every muscle in that lean little body taut with indignation and resolve, that he was forcibly reminded of the Harry of the battle of Preston, the Harry of mettlesome negotiations at Nottingham Castle. Lady Drummond struggling with butter churns and household accounts and the realities of stepmothering was a rather different person.

He had not married Henrietta Ashby simply because he needed a housekeeper and a companion for his children and she needed a refuge. For the first time, he found himself looking beyond the overt reasons that had led to his impulsive offer that September morning in London. He had been drawn to certain qualities she had, and by an instinctive feeling that when she had matured somewhat in her new role as wife, she would be a rewarding and loving companion. Apart from her unfortunate tendency to lead Lizzie and Nan away from the paths of righteousness, she had given him no reason to suspect that he had been wrong in that assessment. But they had had little time for developing a companionable relationship since their marriage. Both immersed in their own troubles and preoccupations, they were less close now than they had been on the journey from Preston. Perhaps the excursion to London would provide opportunity for a renewal of that easy intimacy.

"I am coming," Henrietta said, fiercely interrupting this musing. "I will not be left behind."

At that, he caught her chin, tilting her face. "Madam wife, if I say you will not come, you will not come."

Words of protest rushed to her lips, then something lurking in the black eyes bent upon her gave her pause. Two dimples peeped responsively in her cheeks. "But you will not say that, will you?"

He pinched her nose. "Nay, we will make the journey together. But only because I had already decided that we should before you came out with that intemperate declaration."

Henrietta grinned cheerfully. "When do we leave?"

"In the morning." He sat on the bed to pull off his riding boots. "Lizzie and Nan may pay a visit to Frances and James in our absence. It will give Mistress Kierston some respite from taking sole charge of them."

"And 'twill give Lizzie and Nan some respite from

Mistress Kierston's sole charge,'' she responded, bending to take his booted foot between her hands and yanking. With wicked intent, Daniel withdrew his foot from the boot very abruptly, catching her off balance. She plopped onto the floor with an undignified thump and an indignant ''Ouch!''

''The price of impertinence,'' Daniel said, offering her his other foot before continuing thoughtfully. ''Mayhap, if I plead my case for reduced indemnity to the commissioners at Haberdasher's Hall in person, I might get some results.''

''I will accompany you and appear very pathetic,'' Henrietta said. '' 'Twould be better, of course, if I could sport a swollen belly.'' Two spots of color appeared on her cheekbones as she busied herself with his other boot. ''D'ye not think I should be with child by now?''

Daniel's jaw dropped. It had never occurred to him she did not recognize that he had been taking what precautions he could to prevent such a happenstance.

''Oh, dear,'' he said softly. ''It seems there is something we have to discuss.''

Henrietta remained sitting on her heels as she listened to his explanation. '' 'Tis so mortifying!'' she said when he had finished. ''Why do I not know these things?''

''You cannot know what you have not been told,'' he said. ''The error was mine.''

Henrietta was frowning, her fair eyebrows scrunched in fierce contortion. '' 'Tis not that I feel any great need to have a child at present, but I would have had some part in the decision.''

''When you have the desire, you have merely to tell me,'' he said quietly, bending to take her hands, drawing her up so she knelt at his knee. He cupped her face and kissed her mouth. ''I thought only of you.''

She moved her mouth back to his, her lips lingering against his as she savored their yielding pliancy, and inhaled of the wind-freshness of his skin. Raising her hands, she ran them through his hair, so dark as to be almost black in the lowering afternoon light. "I would give you a son, Daniel."

He nodded. "And so you will, God willing. But there's no hurry, and I've more than enough to do with two daughters." Catching her hands, he turned them palm up and pressed his lips into each one. "Two daughters and a tomboy wife."

"Am I not pardoned?" Henrietta was quite unaware that the look she gave him was pure coquette.

Daniel had seen that look only once or twice before, but he found that it stirred him most powerfully. "Aye, minx, y'are pardoned," he said huskily. "As well you know." Catching her under the arms, he pulled her onto his knee. "And if you look at me in that fashion, I cannot imagine failing to grant pardon for any offense."

Look at him in what fashion? Henrietta wondered, as he brought her face down to his. It would be useful to know the formula for instant forgiveness. Kissing in the middle of the afternoon seemed to have a deliciously illicit feel, and she discovered that with her head above his she had more freedom of movement; indeed, in essence she was in control of what happened. Experimentally, she moved her mouth from his, trailing her lips across his cheek, tasting his skin with the tip of her tongue, flicking upward to brush his closed eyelids. Daniel's hand slid beneath her skirt and petticoat, smoothing over her stockinged leg. She shivered as his fingers brushed lightly over the bare satin softness of her thighs, above her stocking tops. When they reached farther, probing delicately within the moistening furrow, she shifted on his knee with an incoherent murmur, her legs parting involuntarily to facilitate his play.

Amusing himself in this fashion had been far from Daniel's mind when he entered the bedroom. Both the present and the future had acquired a gray patina that filled him with despondency. His fury at Trant's insolence and Ashby's blatant manipulation was mixed with anger at himself for having been made a fool of—

or so it appeared to him. And despite the resolution of the business with the children in the orchard, he was still annoyed with Henrietta, uncertain whether permitting her to deal with the matter with Lizzie had not been simply a way of avoiding an unpleasant duty.

Now, however, life had assumed a different complexion. Three thousand pounds would mean that even if he could not get his indemnity decreased, he would not be reduced to penury, and would be able to recover financially in a relatively short time. Defeating Sir Gerald's ploy would give him great personal satisfaction, and he would be rid of the staple-statute debt . . . and his wife could be quite enchanting at times, when she was concentrating on being a wife. He would take time to encourage that concentration, he decided, smiling with satisfaction as her wriggles and moans told him she was nearing the peak of arousal.

"Daniel!" His name broke from her lips in an urgent whisper as she shuddered in ecstasy, her body rigid against his until the wave receded and she collapsed against him, her breath swift and shallow.

He kept his hand where it was for a long minute, feeling the pulsing of her core against his fingers, while his other hand stroked the tumbled hair from her brow and he murmured soft nonsense words against her cheek as her head drooped on his shoulder.

"Why did you do that?" she asked at last in bewildered wonderment at sensations more intense than any she had ever experienced.

"Because it gave me pleasure," he answered, smoothing down her skirt. "Did it not pleasure you also?" His eyebrows lifted teasingly.

"Most powerfully," she answered in the same wonderment. "Unlike anything I have felt before. But it is the middle of the afternoon and we still have our clothes on and are not in bed."

He laughed at her candid surprise, so expressive of her lack of experience in these matters. "Loving does not always require darkness, sheets, and nakedness, my elf. Neither must it always take the same form."

Still chuckling, he tipped her off his knee. "We must make preparations for leaving tomorrow. Do you go and inform Mistress Kierston of our plans. I must confer with Master Herald about estate matters, since I do not know how long this business in London will take."

Harry stood up, a look of uncertainty in her big brown eyes. "D'ye not think Mistress Kierston might resent my telling her? Would it not be better if you talked with her?"

Daniel shook his head. " 'Tis your task, Henrietta. Y'are the mistress of the house, and now the mother of my daughters. If you begin to accept that, then mayhap you will find it easier to behave accordingly."

There was no hint of reproof in his tone, which was simply matter-of-fact, stating a truth as he saw it. Henrietta nibbled her lip, frowning, then with an accepting shrug, she went to the door. It was the truth, and she had already shouldered the burden once today when she took upon herself the responsibility of setting Lizzie to rights. It had most definitely *been* her responsibility, though a few weeks ago she would not have seen that.

The Ellicots welcomed them warmly. Sir James was rotund and rubicund, with a personality to match. He embraced his new sister-in-law heartily, pronounced her a dear little thing, and bore his brother-in-law off to his parlor, declaring that the women and children were best left to their own business. The prospect of spending time with their aunt, clearly a great favorite with Daniel's daughters, did much to compensate Lizzie and Nan for Henrietta's imminent departure. Frances took due note of the affection her nieces bore their stepmother, an affection obviously reciprocated, and began to feel a little more sanguine about her brother's whimsical marriage. Daniel appeared more cheerful, also, and his wife more at ease than when she had last been at Ellicot Park.

They spent one night with Frances and James. It was the week before Christmas, but since public celebration of that festival was now forbidden except by solemn attendance at church, there seemed little point in delaying their departure in order to be together. There would be no twelve days of festivities, no mummers, no dancing, no Lord of Misrule, no Twelfth Day cake, no mistletoe and ribaldry. Even an unhappy childhood offered good memories of Christmas, Henrietta thought, as she rode at Daniel's side through the bitter cold morning. Would today's children ever have the opportunity to garner such memories?

London bore a strange atmosphere, very different from that Henrietta remembered. An aura almost of menace hung in the freezing air, and the entire city seemed to be holding its breath, waiting, not for some pleasant happening but for the unthinkable. People scurried, huddled into cloaks, along the filth-encrusted cobbled lanes under the biting wind. Somehow it seemed to Henrietta that everyone avoided meeting another's eyes, all keeping their heads down as if watching their feet. Was it shame or fear they felt, inhabiting the city where the King of England was on trial for his life?

''Where will we stay?'' she asked as they rode through unfamiliar streets.

''In lodgings near St. Paul's,'' Daniel replied. ''We may as well be as close to Master Filbert on Cheapside as we can, since I imagine we shall be spending much time in his company.'' He glanced sideways at her. ''One thing, Harry. Y'are not to leave the lodging without my permission and an escort. It's understood?''

She frowned. Never before had he placed any restriction on her movements, and it was the one thing of old that had unfailingly driven her to rebellion. ''Why may I not?''

''There is violence in the air,'' he said somberly. ''Do not tell me you cannot feel it. The people are uncertain, and they are angry because of their confusion. I'll not have you risking the streets alone.''

Harry was silent, unable to argue with his impressions yet reluctant to accept a proscription that might prove inconvenient on some as yet unforeseeable occasion. Fortunately, Daniel appeared to read her silence as acceptance and made no demand for a verbal promise. They turned off Cheapside onto Paternoster Row, then down a narrow lane where the gabled roofs on either side touched to form an archway over the cobbles and neighbors across the street could shake hands from the top-floor casements.

"Here we are." Daniel drew rein about halfway down the alley before an ironbound door set in a lath-and-plaster wall. The stoop was well honed, the glazed windows gleamed, and even the cobbles in front of the stoop were swept and washed clean of mire. "My old nurse," Daniel said with a smile. "She wed an ostler and they set up house in London. If ever I plan an extended stay in the capital, there is always room and a welcome for me here." He swung down from his horse and hammered upon the great brass knocker, gleaming evidence of housewifely pride.

The gray gloom of early evening was banished as the door was opened. A tiny woman, small-boned as a sparrow, bobbed into the opening, saw her visitor, and burst into a great twittering of pleasure. Daniel, laughing, lifted her easily, enclosing her in a bear hug so that she seemed to Henrietta's eyes to disappear altogether, except that her excited trilling continued unabated.

"Dorcas, my dear Dorcas!" Daniel exclaimed when he could be heard. "You never grow any bigger. See whom I have brought to you."

Henrietta had slipped from her horse during the exuberant welcome and now stepped forward as Daniel held out his hand.

"This is my wife. Henrietta, this is Dorcas, who knows more to my discredit than anyone has the right to."

" 'Deed, Sir Daniel, that's not so. An angel child you were," exclaimed the tiny figure, bobbing a curtsy to Henrietta even as she scrutinized her with a pair of sharp, bright blue eyes that to the girl seemed uncomfortably circumspect. "I bid ye welcome, Lady Drummond. Pray come within. Our Joe'll look to your horses."

Our Joe, a lad as burly as his mother was minute, appeared promptly, responding to Daniel's greeting with a bashful smile and a tug of his forelock. He led away the horses and Henrietta accepted the invitation to precede her hostess into a minuscule hall.

"I'll put ye in the chamber above the parlor, Sir Daniel," Dorcas said, ascending a narrow flight of stairs. " 'Tis quite the largest, and ye'll be needin' space now y'are married again."

"I'd not cause you trouble, Dorcas," Daniel demurred.

"Lord-a-mercy!" Dorcas flung up her hands in horror at the very idea. "Don't you be a-talking such nonsense!"

Harry couldn't stifle a grin at the idea of this little woman taking the large and authoritative Daniel to task in such brisk, matter-of-fact fashion. Daniel appeared to find nothing unusual about it and simply shrugged in accepting fashion.

They were shown into a clean and pretty chamber, not luxuriously appointed but comfortable enough with heavy winter hangings to the bed and a big fire in the grate. A small mullioned window looked down onto the street.

Dorcas bustled around, placing a screen between the window and the fire, twitching the coverlet straight, fiercely polishing a gleaming gateleg table with her apron. "There now," she pronounced, satisfied, looking around her with proprietorial eyes. "Ye'll not find neater than this in all of London town, though I says so myself. How long'll ye be stayin', Sir Daniel?"

He frowned, unclasping his heavy riding cloak. "That depends. I have business with a lawyer, a Master Filbert of Cheapside. Think ye, Dorcas, that Joe would go and find his direction for me? It should not be too difficult."

"Aye, I'll send him straightway. Ye'll be sharp set,

I dare swear, after a day's riding, so come on down to the parlor when ye've settled in and I'll have supper waitin' on ye.''

The door closed on her energetic departure, sending flames shooting in the grate. Harry bent to the blaze, holding her chilled hands to the warmth. She had the unmistakable impression that Daniel's old nurse was reserving judgment where his new wife was concerned. Apart from the initial words of greeting and that close scrutiny, she had directed no further words or observations in Henrietta's direction.

''I expect Dorcas was very fond of your first wife,'' she said, still gazing into the fire.

''Aye, she was,'' Daniel agreed readily. ''She delivered Lizzie and I think believes that if she had been there for the others Nan would still live.''

''I expect she will find the idea of your remarrying rather hard to become accustomed to,'' Harry said.

''Not at all. She has never lost an opportunity in the last few years to tell me to take another wife.'' He regarded her averted back, sensing the tension in the hunched figure. ''Harry? What troubles you?''

''Why, nothing.'' She managed a dismissive half laugh. ''I am most dreadfully hungry.''

''That can be easily remedied if ye will but make haste,'' he pointed out dryly. ''Crouching over the fire will not get your cloak off, your hair tidied, and your face washed.'' Coming over to her, he took her shoulder, turning her to face him. ''More than hunger troubles you.''

''Oh, 'tis just that sometimes I feel uncomfortable.'' She shrugged. '' 'Twill pass when I have supper.''

Daniel frowned, unwilling to accept this half explanation. ''That will not do, Harry. What makes you uncomfortable?''

Being married to you. Not an answer one could easily give. And it wasn't as if it was a constant source of discomfort. It was just that sometimes she could see herself through the eyes of others looking upon Sir Daniel Drummond's wife, and the impoverished, ramshackle creature she saw made her feel awkward. Perhaps if she felt a little more confident in the role herself she would not feel the implicit judgments. She shook her head. " 'Tis just silliness, Daniel. I am awearied and famished and so inclined to be fanciful."

"I think y'are inclined to fibbing," he responded, still frowning.

Harry flushed. "I am not lying."

Daniel contented himself with a raised eyebrow, releasing her shoulders and going over to the dresser to pour water from the ewer into the basin. "As soon as we have supped, I will pay a call upon Master Filbert, if Joe has managed to discover his direction."

"I will come too," Henrietta declared, shrugging out of her cloak.

"No, not tonight. Y'are awearied, as you have said, and I would prefer to make the initial approach alone."

Harry bit her lip. "I am not so tired that I cannot accompany you. And I will remember Master Filbert and can remind him of the conversation I overheard, so that if he attempts to dissemble I can face him with the truth. He is my father's lawyer when all's said and done, and there's no knowing whose side he will be on. Maybe my father has bought his silence."

Daniel splashed water on his face. He could well imagine the effect Harry's outrage at her parent's chicanery would have on a conventionally minded lawyer, particularly if he felt himself implicated by this importunate and indignant young woman. He would need Master Filbert as ally and certainly did not wish to put his back up this early in the game.

"Not tonight," he repeated, drying his face. "When I have discovered the truth, then mayhap you will make Master Filbert's acquaintance. Come and wash away the dust of the road." He stepped away from the dresser, indicating the bowl and ewer.

"But 'tis *my* money," Harry protested, fire in her brown eyes. " 'Tis only meet I should be involved in exposing my father's theft."

"That is not the way I wish to present the matter,"

Daniel said shortly. "There's to be no talk of theft." He, too, was weary and still had a long evening ahead of him. "I don't wish to argue further. The subject is closed."

"But that is so arbitrary!" she exclaimed.

"Husbands on occasion are inclined to be arbitrary." He went to the door. "Come down to the parlor when you are ready."

On that unsatisfactory but undeniable pronouncement, he left her alone to her ablutions. She thumped on the bed with a colorful oath. If he was going to exclude her from the business that had brought them to London, why had he allowed her to accompany him in the first place? Forbidden to go outdoors without her husband's permission, she was presumably expected to sit twiddling her thumbs in this house where she was regarded with only dubious acceptance. 'Twas as bad being a wife as a daughter!

Only hunger drove her belowstairs when the mouth-watering aromas of roasting mutton wafted beneath her door. Daniel, his spirits somewhat restored by the second glass of burgundy, smiled in conciliatory fashion as she entered the parlor.

"I do not see," Henrietta said, "why you would permit me to accompany you here if I am not to be allowed to take part in the business. 'Tis as much my business as yours."

"Later," Daniel responded, "you may do so. But not tonight. Sit down." He pulled out a chair for her. "May I carve you some mutton?"

Henrietta glowered and contemplated a martyred return to the chamber abovestairs. Only the reflection that such a gesture would probably not cause Daniel the least remorse and would certainly cause her considerable regret made her take the proffered seat.

"I suppose you expect me to sit by the fire and do fine sewing," she said, before addressing a heaped platter of roasted mutton and floury boiled potatoes.

Daniel regarded her quizzically. "Somehow I had the

impression that you were not too handy with a needle."

Harry, recognizing her error, skewered a large piece of mutton and wisely devoted her attention to the consumption of her meal. "Well, what *am* I to do?" she demanded at last, wiping her mouth with her napkin. "Perhaps I should return to Kent. At least there I can go out and about without hindrance."

Daniel refilled his goblet, choosing his words carefully. He was forcibly reminded of the way she had responded on a previous occasion to a perceived snub, and of Will's statement that one must tread cautiously where Harry's pride was involved. He had no wish to be obliged to grapple with his wife's open defiance of his orders. Matters could become exceedingly unpleasant between them. However, he did not find this persistence bordering on impertinence in the least appealing and was sorely tempted to deal it the short shrift he would have accorded his daughters in such an instance.

But Henrietta was his wife, and if she was to learn to behave as a wife then she must be treated as one and not as a recalcitrant child. "Mayhap you did not hear me correctly," he said quietly. "I said only that I wished to meet alone with Master Filbert *this* time. On subsequent occasions, I shall welcome your company, your assistance, and your opinions."

Put like that, the matter assumed quite a different complexion, Henrietta found. She cast him a suspicious glance across the table, but he was eating his supper quite naturally, his expression as calm as ever, except that the glint of humor she was accustomed to seeing in the bright black eyes was absent. That in itself was warning enough. It was clearly time to offer her own conciliation.

"Mayhap I did not quite understand," she said a little stiffly. "Would you be so good as to hand me the carrots, please?"

The remainder of supper passed, if not exuberantly, at least with amicable politeness. Joe appeared with the information that Master Filbert was to be found beside the sign of the Golden Cock on Cheapside, and Daniel left soon after.

Henrietta piled up the dishes from the table and ventured toward the kitchen with them. It seemed somehow wrong in this house, where they were neither family guests nor formal lodgers, to take herself abovestairs, leaving the table uncleared.

''Goodness me, Lady Drummond!'' exclaimed Dorcas as she came timidly into the kitchen. ''There's no call for ye to be a-doing such work.''

''I wished only to help,'' Harry said, yielding the pile of plates to her hostess. The kitchen was cheerful and warm, Joe and Dorcas's goodman sitting at their ease in the inglenook, the smell of baking coming from the bread oven set into the wall beside the range. ''I did not mean to intrude.''

Dorcas looked at the girl and did not miss the wistful shadow in her large eyes. For all her married status, she rather resembled a lost child, and Dorcas's soft heart banished whatever reservations she might have had. It was lonely in the chamber abovestairs, and still early for bed. ''Sit ye down,'' she said. ''I'll be bringing some apple tarts out of the oven in a minute or two. They're at their best when they're fresh baked. And a mug of hypocras will not come amiss, I'll be bound.''

The sweet spiced wine was one of Harry's favorite drinks. The goodwife's tone was brisk, yet welcoming; for all her smallness of stature, she carried an air of authority—the authority of one on her own ground. The prospect of apple tart, despite her ample supper, Harry found irrefusable. ''If y'are sure I'll not be intruding.''

''Such nonsense, child. Sit ye down.'' Dorcas gestured to the long bench beside the kitchen table. ''I didn't reckon as how Sir Daniel would wed such a young'un again, I have to say,'' she observed, setting a mug of hypocras before Henrietta.

''I don't think he intended to,'' Harry confided, quite

at her ease now that the issue was in the open. "But he is kind, and my circumstances were such that . . ." She stopped, and shrugged a mite self-consciously. "But ye don't wish to hear that. I do want to be a good wife, but I fear that I am not succeeding."

Dorcas pursed her lips, her head nodding busily so that she resembled a small bird pecking in the dust. "Sir Daniel never did summat he hadn't thought about, not even when he was still in short coats, so don't you fret about that, child." She opened the bread oven, releasing a cloud of fragrant steam into the room.

"What sort of child was he?" Harry found she could not resist the question. "Lizzie and Nan are always into mischief. I cannot believe he was not also."

Dorcas chuckled richly, drawing out the flat griddle with its burden of toasty brown, gently steaming apple tarts. "Aye, that he was, but always with such a smile and a twinkle you couldn't be vexed with him for long."

"I can imagine." Henrietta settled down with a sigh of pleasure, deciding that she would much prefer to be in this warm room facing apple tarts and hypocras than treading the freezing streets of London on a dark winter's night in search of a lawyer and a matter of conflict.

Dorcas did not skimp with her homespun wisdom lacing the stories of Daniel Drummond as child and man. As she began to talk of his first marriage, she saw Henrietta grow more serious, chin resting upon her elbow-propped hand, eyes gazing into the middle distance. Her mouth was soft, yet there was a hint of determination, of resolution, in the fine line of her jaw.

Henrietta was hearing about a young couple deeply in love. She imagined Daniel as a young man, eagerness and passion augmenting the natural humor and gentle consideration he showed her. She knew instinctively that their own lovemaking lacked something. And she knew without a shadow of doubt that Daniel's loving with his Nan had not lacked anything. Had he decided that one lifetime could only supply such glory once? Or did the fault lie with her? Or was it simply that if one did not truly love, one could not reach whatever heights were to be reached?

If the latter was the case, then the future looked, if not dark, then not rosy with promise either—more a featureless, grayish landscape. Fifteen seemed very young to Henrietta to accept such a commonplace existence. If Nan had had more, why should *she* settle for less? Could love and passion be kindled? If they were intertwined, then creating the one should inevitably produce the other.

That was an intriguing thought, and a novel one. Henrietta was not inclined to wait passively for things to happen, and the idea that one could invariably do something positive to change matters for the better had always been her credo. Maybe it was time she took a hand in this. She knew enough about it now, after all, to be able to exercise her imagination. Why could a wife not seduce her husband? Daniel had taught her some of the things that gave him particular pleasure, but he had never expected her to take the initiative in matters of loving. It happened when he decided it was to happen, and in the form he decided it should take. Until now, she had never questioned this, had simply assumed it was the natural order. But why should it be?

On that thought, she took herself to bed, to a sleep enriched with formless yet stirring dreams. When Daniel finally returned, to crawl wearily into bed beside her, she curled in her sleep against his back with a whimper of satisfaction that would have startled him had he been alert enough to notice.

Chapter 9

Henrietta awoke before Daniel. Still infused with resolutions, she slipped carefully from bed, anxious not to disturb him. The fire was a mere ashy glow and she shivered in the frigid dawn, pulling on her clothes over her smock with more haste than care. The water in the ewer had a crust of ice and she decided rapidly to blink the sleep from her eyes. A quick comb through the corn silk massed on her shoulders and she twisted it into a knot at the nape of her neck, securing it with wooden pins. Then she crept from the chamber, running down to the kitchen from whence came sounds of life.

"I give you good morrow, Dorcas," she greeted cheerfully, entering the warm room with relief. " 'Tis cold as the grave abovestairs."

"Aye," Dorcas agreed, turning from the range where she was frying eggs for Joe and the goodman, sitting ready at the table. "I thought not to disturb ye for a bit with fresh coals, but seein' as how y'are awake—"

"Oh, but Sir Daniel is not," Harry interrupted. "I thought to prepare him his favorite breakfast."

Dorcas smiled. "Veal collops and eggs."

"Aye," Harry agreed with a responding smile. "If ye will direct me a little."

"Sit ye down and break your own fast first," Dorcas said comfortably. "Ye'll work better on a full stomach."

That was not a fact with which Henrietta would argue, so she smiled at her companions and took her place at the kitchen table. The goodman sliced sirloin for her and Dorcas slid two eggs swirled in butter upon the platter beside the beef.

"Well, this is a fine case of neglect!"

At the tone, only half humorous, Henrietta spun around on the bench at the table. "Oh, Daniel, I thought ye still abed."

" 'Tis past seven," he said, "I am not such a slug-abed, as well you know. Good morrow, all." He came into the room, rubbing a hand over his chin. "If ye've hot water on the range, Dorcas, I'll take it abovestairs and shave."

"I would have brought it for you," Henrietta said in apologetic tone, "but I thought to let you have your sleep. I was going to make your breakfast, also."

Daniel looked sharply at her, and a glint of amusement returned to his black eyes. She looked thoroughly discomfited, as if accused of dereliction of wifely duty. He had not intended to sound sharp, but if truth were told, he had been rather put out at waking to an empty bed in a freezing bedchamber, and the sight of her cheerfully addressing an enormous platter of eggs and sirloin had not lessened his sense of grievance.

"I trust 'twas not to be cheese pudding," he teased, turning to take the jug of hot water from Dorcas and thus missing the flash of hurt crossing the heart-shaped face.

"Joe'll bring a scuttle of coals up and mend the fire for ye, Sir Daniel," Dorcas said. "And there'll be veal collops and eggs waitin' on ye in the parlor."

Harry turned back to her breakfast, her own offer having been spurned. She did not believe he'd meant the unkindness. Daniel did not know, after all, of the plan that had sent her so sweetly to sleep and that had brought her so energetically awake. A plan that was to start with evidence of her new-learned skills in the realm of domesticity, and was to proceed to a demonstration of skills and ingenuity in that other branch of wifehood. But she could hardly blame Daniel for assuming that, as usual, she had forgotten the tasks that fell to her hand—forgotten them or ignored them; either way, the result was the same.

Daniel and Joe went abovestairs, bearing coals and hot water. "Shall I prepare the collops?" Henrietta put down knife and spoon on her clean-scraped trencher.

"Nay, child, I'll do it," Dorcas said. "You run along abovestairs. Sir Daniel may have need of ye."

"I don't imagine so," she replied dolefully; then, with customary resolution, she put the setback behind her. She would simply start the day anew. Gathering up her skirts, she hurried upstairs, entering the bedchamber with eager step.

"Did you find Master Filbert last even?"

Daniel was in the process of drawing a swath through his lather-smothered face and jumped at this precipitate arrival, nicking his chin. Irritated, he peered at his wavering image in the beaten steel mirror. "Was it necessary to startle me while I'm shaving, Harry?" he demanded crossly.

Harry bit her lip. Picking up one of his tall boots, she began busily to shine the leather with her handkerchief. "Your pardon, I did not realize."

Daniel wiped his face with a warm, damp towel and turned to look at her, his expression pained. "God's grace, child! Go down and ask Dorcas for a rag for those boots. 'Tis no work for a lace-edged handkerchief!"

She dropped the boot abruptly, her mouth taut. "I will not polish them if you do not wish it."

"But I do wish it," he replied calmly, oblivious of her vexation. "Only not with your handkerchief. 'Tis all black now, and you are bound to forget and use it at some point, transferring all that dirt to your face."

Tight-lipped, Henrietta went down to the kitchen, fetched a rag, and returned to the bedchamber. In silence, she resumed her task.

Daniel finished buttoning his shirt, then stood examining her as she sat on the edge of the bed, head bent over his boots. "Y'are most dreadfully untidy this morning, Henrietta."

It was the last straw. "There was ice on the water in the ewer and the chamber was freezing!" she exclaimed in indignant defense. "I am sorry if my appearance causes offense."

Daniel just laughed. "Nay, elf! That it could never do. Y'are far too pretty."

She blushed rosily at this unexpected compliment, coming as it did so hard upon the heels of his criticisms so relentlessly heaped upon her this morning. She set to polishing the buttons on his doublet with unwonted fierceness and changed the subject. "But will you tell me about Master Filbert?"

"Ah." Daniel frowned, straightening the falling band of lace-trimmed lawn at the collar of his shirt. "Master Filbert is a most cautious lawyer. However, your father's signature as witness to the marriage document convinced him that y'are wed truly with his permission. He has undertaken to go into Oxfordshire and visit your father on your behalf."

"When will he do so?"

"I trust within the week," Daniel told her, taking his doublet, nodding at the shine on the silver buttons. "I will visit him again this morning so that we may draw up documents of formal request for the release of your jointure. How your father responds to the request will dictate what we do next."

"But does Master Filbert believe that I may recover the monies?"

"Aye," Daniel said, hooking the waistband of his britches onto the underside of his doublet before stepping into his boots. "But how long it will take for your father to concede is another matter. He could drag the issue out for months, if he so chooses, and while he does so we must kick our heels in London."

"Which is an additional expense," Harry said slowly. "And you must pay Master Filbert for his services, also."

"Aye," Daniel agreed. He arranged the falling band

of lawn over the small collar of the doublet. "But 'tis an outlay I must bear if there's to be three thousand pounds at the end of it."

"I will accompany you this morning." There was the faintest hint of challenge in the statement.

Daniel regarded her with mock gravity as he turned the lace edging of his boot hose over the tops of the freshly shined leather boots. "In your present state of untidiness, my child, unwashed and unbrushed, with the sleep still in your eyes, you will not."

"Now there is hot water, I may tidy myself," she said, tossing her head, abandoning her attempts to respond with mature dignity. "If you have left me any, that is. Do you go for your breakfast before it spoils."

"Yes, madam," he said solemnly, bowing with teasing formality before taking himself off, leaving Henrietta to wonder what devils were about this morning to render stillborn her every effort to show herself in a new light.

She washed and dressed anew in a fresh gown of russet velvet with a crisp but plain lawn collar. The material was rich, although the flowing, high-waisted style was simple enough not to offend Puritan sensibilities, and the color deepened her eyes and set off her hair most satisfactorily. She braided her hair and secured it in the coronet that framed her face in pleasing fashion, put on her sturdy leather shoes with the silver buckles, took up her hooded cloak and gloves, and ran down to the parlor.

"Some considerable improvement," Daniel observed, setting his empty ale mug upon the table. "That gown suits you. I would have you pay more attention to your wardrobe when we return home."

"There seems little point dressing up in the country," Henrietta pointed out, standing on tiptoe to check her reflection in the glass above the mantel.

"When y'are about your household duties in the daytime, then obviously you should dress accordingly. But in the evening, I would have you dress to please me."

Henrietta looked at him in surprise. "You have never said such a thing before."

"No." Daniel gave a puzzled shake of his head. "I never concerned myself about it before." Then he smiled. "I daresay it is because you look so fetching at the moment, I have just realized what I have been missing."

Matters were improving, Henrietta decided, contentedly giving her hair a pat. "Shall we visit Master Filbert now?"

"Aye." Daniel stood up, frowning. "But if y'are to accompany me, Harry, you must understand that there are to be no intemperate accusations against your father. They will embarrass Master Filbert and are not his business."

"But he must realize that my father has deliberately withheld my portion," exclaimed Harry. "Why else would we be consulting a lawyer?"

"What he realizes for himself and what he is told are separate issues," Daniel said firmly. "I have simply presented the situation as one of misunderstanding. You will sit quiet, if you please, offer smiles and soft words, and answer any questions in moderate language and accents. The affair is unpleasant enough as 'tis."

Henrietta made a face. "I do not see why we should pretend that my father is simply absentminded or—"

"If you do not see why, then you must remain here," Daniel interrupted brusquely. "That look of a thwarted child ill becomes you, and most certainly does not go with your attire."

Henrietta rearranged her expression, showing him a bright smile and wide, innocent eyes. "I will speak only when spoken to and will refer to my father only in the most dutiful terms."

Daniel's lips twitched, but he said gravely, "I trust so. Let us go."

A few flakes of snow broke loose from the leaden sky as they hurried along the streets. The faces they passed seemed as sullen as the sky, but Harry was looking around her eagerly, absorbing the sights, sounds, and smells of the city. She was also in search of a vendor of specific merchandise and found what she sought some quarter of a mile from their lodgings. She took due note, reflecting that the opportunity to slip out without Daniel's being aware was bound to present itself.

Master Filbert was to be found in a dim little room above a tailor's shop. "My congratulations, Lady Drummond," he offered, ponderous and punctilious. "Pray be seated. May I offer you a morning draught of sack?"

Henrietta realized with a shock that this was the first time anyone who had known her in the past had treated her with the deference accorded a married lady. If the lawyer remembered the straggle-haired, untidy, rebellious girl of last spring, he gave no indication. She accepted both seat and refreshment with a gracious smile and an inquiry about Master Filbert's health.

Daniel had little difficulty understanding what was happening and was both amused and relieved. It would seem that if his wife was treated as a grown woman of some status, she could be trusted to respond accordingly.

Her temperance was sorely tried, however, as the discussion continued. Master Filbert had had in his possession documents relating to the disposition of Mistress Ashby's inheritance, entrusted to him by the late Lady Ashby, but Sir Gerald had since claimed them. Master Filbert coughed awkwardly. Sir Gerald *was* the young lady's father, and there was no reason for the lawyer to refuse to hand over the charge to such a one.

"But surely you know my—" Harry's impassioned beginning died a sudden death under an icy glare from Daniel. She subsided, gazing intently at an intricate series of cracks in the plaster wall.

"Of course," Daniel said smoothly. "You acted quite correctly, Master Filbert. As I have said, I am sure this is simply a misunderstanding. But am I to understand that without those documents, my wife cannot lay legal claim to her inheritance?''

''That is so,'' the lawyer said, as ponderous as ever. ''I will journey to Thame and present your claim to your father-in-law. I have drawn up a letter stating the facts of your marriage, Sir Gerald's approval of such, and the terms of the jointure. I am certain there will be no difficulty.''

''Of course there will be,'' Henrietta stated impatiently. ''Surely you should be preparing to begin legal action. It could drag on for years, and the sooner 'tis begun the better.''

''Come now, Lady Drummond. I am sure, as your husband says, there has simply been a misunderstanding, something overlooked,'' said the lawyer in soothing accents.

Henrietta glanced at Daniel, who was looking most annoyed. She spoke up resolutely. ''I did not mean to embarrass you, Master Filbert, but I see little point in prevarication. There are only the three of us here, and we all know what is the true situation. What virtue can there be in beating about the bush?'' She was speaking to the lawyer, but looking at her husband.

Daniel sighed. He should have known, of course. Henrietta did not have the patience or the personality for these social dissemblings.

''There is every virtue,'' said Daniel. ''You cannot accuse someone of a crime without evidence. Your father has not yet openly withheld your inheritance. He has not yet been asked for it.'' He spoke sharply.

''Indeed,'' agreed Master Filbert hastily. '' 'Tis hardly a seemly matter and one must be careful whom one accuses in these times, and of what. Let us call it a misunderstanding and treat it as such. I am sure 'twill be remedied without delay.''

Henrietta shrugged. ''You may believe that if you choose. I know better, I fear.''

Daniel stood up. ''I think enough has been said. If you will let me look over the letter you have drawn up,

Master Filbert, we will be on our way, and wish you godspeed and success."

The lawyer shuffled papers on his desk, drawing out a neat black-penned parchment, handing it to Sir Daniel. Henrietta, deciding that she was already in so deep a further indiscretion could make little difference, stood up and went to peer in most brazen fashion over Daniel's shoulder, reading the crisp, lawyerly script that turned such an emotional issue into a dusty matter of legal terms.

"Have you finished?" Daniel said, dryly pointed, when he reached the end.

"Yes, thank you."

"I trust it meets with your approval."

"If it meets with yours," she said meekly.

Daniel was far from mollified, but he said nothing. Master Filbert's sensibilities had been scraped sufficiently for one morning. He handed the document back to the lawyer, and they went out again into the cold street.

"Y'are vexed?" Harry said without preamble.

"Very," Daniel agreed. "But as much with myself as with you. I should have known you would not be able to behave correctly."

"I do not consider I behaved incorrectly," Harry said stoutly. "Why should I not read the letter? It concerns me as much if not more than you."

"You are my wife," Daniel said quietly. "As such, anything that concerns you concerns me directly. Wives behave with a degree of decorum; you did not. While it may be well enough for you to go on in your customary ramshackle, hoity fashion when we are private, in public I would have you abide by the rules. I do not care to be put to shame by my wife's conduct."

Henrietta looked for a defense but could not find one. She knew that a wife was required to be gentle, obedient, and bow to her husband's greater sense and knowledge in all matters. Wives did not set themselves up in opposition to their husbands, or argue with their husbands' judgment and manner of conducting their affairs. Wives did not intrude upon those affairs. Such a wife would indeed bring shame upon her husband. She knew all these things, but it did not mean she could accept them.

Daniel glanced down at her as she walked, head bent and in silence, at his side. She was so far from the conventional mold, it seemed futile to try to refashion her. Somehow or other, he was going to have to come to terms with that, but Henrietta was going to have to come to terms with public realities.

In the interests of encouraging this coming to terms, he offered no softening during a silent dinner of Dorcas's preparing, and at the end of the meal told his wife that he had business to attend to and would be back later in the afternoon. She should occupy herself about the house as best she could.

If he had but known it, such a plan suited Henrietta to perfection. When Daniel returned to the house, he would find a very different wife waiting for him, one who would hopefully cause him to forget utterly any unwifelike indiscretions in lawyers' offices.

She had two crowns left over from the money Daniel had given her for household necessities before they left Kent, and armed with these she left the house, her cloak drawn tight around her. Dorcas did not seem surprised or doubtful when informed of the impending excursion, so presumably was unaware of Daniel's proscription on unescorted journeyings. She offered no cautionary advice either, which led Harry to the conclusion that Daniel had been unnecessarily anxious. Anyway, she was not going far, just to the shop they had passed earlier where she had seen scents, soaps, and dried herbs for sale.

As she passed the entrance to a narrow alley, a small boy, begrimed, his clothing ragged, shot out in front of her. He was clutching half a loaf of bread. From behind him came the familiar sounds of a hue and cry, the bellow of "Stop, thief!" He tripped over a stone at Harry's feet, and a white face, haunted by a pair of terrified eyes, gazed up at her as he waited for her to lay hold of him.

Swiftly, she bent and pulled him to his feet. "Make haste!" She accompanied the urgent whisper with a shove in the direction of another alley across the street. Without so much as a backward glance, he was off, streaking between the wheels of carriages and the massive hooves of dray horses, to be lost in the throng.

" 'E came out 'ere, I swear it!" A constable, scarlet with exertion, appeared in the entrance of the alley, flourishing his staff of office; behind him came a mountainous man whose flour-dusted apron bespoke his trade.

"Thievin' brat!" the baker declared, wiping his moist brow and looking around him. His eye fell upon Henrietta, who still stood with apparent nonchalance, gazing about her. "Eh, miss, you seen a brat around 'ere in the last minute?"

Harry raised a haughty eyebrow as if to indicate she was unaccustomed to being addressed by such as he. "I have not," she declared. "Brats do not interest me."

"Hoity-toity!" murmured the baker, but the constable, who knew gentry when he met it, touched his forelock, muttered a word of apology, and dragged his companion in the opposite direction.

With a satisfied chuckle, Henrietta continued on her way, ducking under the low lintel of the little shop where heady scents of dried lavender, musk, and beeswax filled the air. In the country one prepared such things oneself and it would be unheard of to purchase them, but she swallowed the prickle of guilt at spending coin in this profligate fashion and gave her order to the dame sitting on a low stool beside the smoking fireplace. Dried lavender, a small jar of distilled rose water, and, most precious and important of all, a cake of soap, not of the kind they made at home from lye and animal fats, but soft, delicately scented with verbena, and most dreadfully costly. But Daniel would consider the cost as naught, she determined, squashing her conscience at the pathetic sixpence that was all the change she received for her two crowns.

With her purchases buried deep in the pocket of her cloak, she hurried back down crowded Cheapside and onto Paternoster Row. A yelling mob had formed a circle outside a butcher's shop and, curious as always, she moved to see what was causing the ruction. She pushed her way to the front of the crowd, disregarding the curses and shoves of protest, and then promptly wished she had not. Two youths had tied a burning brand to the tail of a scrawny, one-eyed cat. The crowd was roaring with laughter, tossing clods of mud, stones, and anything else they could lay hands on as the poor tormented creature screamed in pain and rage, trying desperately to escape the fire.

Henrietta was not unaccustomed to country brutalities, but there was a different quality to this vicious crowd-pleasing torture. It was aimless, pointless, just something to pass the time. She plunged into the circle and tried to grab the cat, but it evaded her grasp and the crowd laughed louder, enjoying this new spectacle. Weeping with anger and frustration, she flung every stable oath she knew at the mob, and then quite suddenly a bucket of slops was emptied from an overhanging window all over the cat, effectively dousing the fire and splashing Henrietta's skirt and boots. The casement closed with a decisive snap and the crowd grumbled.

"Eh, Lady Drummond, what be ye about? Ye shouldn't be 'anging around 'ere." Dorcas's goodman appeared from nowhere it seemed, his face anxious, his customary taciturnity vanished. He took her arm and hustled her through the crowd as the murmurs swelled and took on an ugly note. "They'd be accusing ye as a spoilsport next," he muttered, "then there's no knowin' what would 'appen."

Henrietta shuddered, feeling queasy. Perhaps Daniel had not been overcautious. The mood of the crowd had been such that little consideration would be paid to her age, sex, and social position. The goodman escorted her to the door and saw her within before going off about his business again, and Dorcas came hurrying from the kitchen, exclaiming at Harry's white face.

" 'Twas some louts torturing a cat," Harry explained. "It made me feel as if I would puke."

"There's worse than that goin' on in this city," Dorcas said darkly. "They'll be killing the king next, you mark my words."

Henrietta unclasped her cloak, beginning to recover her equilibrium as she remembered the purpose of her errand. "I'd like to bathe, Dorcas. D'ye have a tub I could fill in the bedchamber?"

Dorcas looked a little surprised but agreed readily enough to supply tub and hot water, and Harry hastened upstairs, hoping Daniel would remain absent long enough. She laid her purchases upon the tiring table, the afternoon's unpleasantness forgotten as she contemplated her plan. Was she being naive to think it could work? Nay! She dismissed such feebleness with a brisk wave of her hand. Daniel was going to come home to a pleasant, and hopefully exciting, surprise.

Ten minutes later, she stood naked before a steaming wooden tub. She shook the contents of the rosewater jar into the water and stirred it vigorously. The delicate scent filled the room, enhanced by the fire's warmth. The lavender she sprinkled on the surface of the water, then she stepped in, sinking down into the hot, soothing fragrance. The precious sliver of soap was unlike any she had ever used, smooth as velvet, and when she rubbed it between her hands it lathered instantly with verbena-scented froth.

She poured a jug of hot water over her hair and soaped it thoroughly, then rinsed it with a second jug. Then she simply lay back, her knees drawn up, head resting on the edge of the bath, and closed her eyes to lose herself in a luxurious, sensuous, wickedly extravagant dream of desire.

"Sweet Jesus! 'Tis as if all the perfumes of Araby have come here to roost!" Daniel stepped through the door, chilled by his walk through the snow-threatening evening, and stood blinking. The room was fogged with scented steam, wreathing and curling in the warm air.

Lazily, Henrietta turned her head to the door and smiled. ''Y'are earlier than I expected.''

''What the devil goes on here?'' He stepped over to the tub, drawn by that smile although not quite realizing it. He stood looking down at her. Her face was flushed with the warm water . . . and with something else. That something else lurked behind the dreaminess in her big brown eyes, danced over the curve of her smiling mouth. He allowed his eyes to drift down her body, pink and pearly beneath the lavender-strewn water, her breasts peeping rose-tipped above the surface, and he was suddenly breathless. It was as if he were seeing her for the first time, as if the lean little body with which he was familiar had taken on some other quality, as if there were secrets here that were his to discover. And in the eyes fixed upon his face there lingered the invitation to discover.

He shook his head, as if to dispel the strange sensation, but it remained, and he began to wonder if he were bewitched, if perhaps Harry, his child-wife, had disappeared, a changeling in her place. Slowly, she stood up, the water flowing from her body. Stretching her arms behind her head, she caught the soaked mass of hair and wrung it out between her hands, her eyes never leaving his face. Where the devil had she learned such a seductive movement, such a wickedly inviting smile? She reached out her hands to him and he took them without volition. She stepped from the water, coming close to him, enveloping him in her mingled lavender, rosewater, and verbena aura.

''If you wish to bathe also, I will wash your back,'' she whispered, standing on tiptoe and lightly brushing his mouth with her lips, before moving to unclasp his cloak.

''You'll catch cold if you do not dry yourself,'' he managed to say through a husky throat. Turning aside with some considerable effort, he picked up the towel. "Let me do it for you."

She stood still for him as he gently blotted the water from her skin, his bare hand occasionally brushing her as if to satisfy himself that she was truly dry. He could feel her skin, soft as rose petals, flutter at each touch, and her nipples stood out, hard and wanting. Her legs parted as the towel moved down and intimately within, then he turned her sideways, placing one arm across her waist, bending her over it as he dried down her back and between her buttocks and thighs, missing not a nook or cranny.

When he could find no further damp spots for excuse, he rubbed her hair vigorously, then stood back.

"Now 'tis your turn," Henrietta said softly, reaching for the buttons of his shirt. "I will maid you, sir." And quite naked, she proceeded to do just that.

It seemed to Daniel that he had slid into some trance-like universe where everything accustomed had been turned topsy-turvy, and one whom he had thought he knew in all her facets had become some other person. Her touch was sure, as if undressing a man was something with which she was quite familiar. She seemed to weave and wreathe around him, all soft and pliant nakedness offered to his eyes and hands, as her lips brushed, her fingers tiptoed, over each fraction of his body she unclothed.

Scented steam, the occasional crackle of a hot coal, the soft yellow glow of candlelight enhanced the dreamy lethargy created by her attentions, yet beneath the lethargy lust's dragon stirred for the first time since Nan's death, twitched a fierce tail, played a waiting game.

Henrietta had discovered the power of fantasy. With every move she made, every whispering touch of her skin with his, the erotic dream grew stronger. Excitement flowed through her veins, set her skin to gleaming rosy and translucent, moistened the deep recesses of her body so she moved with more abandon, and demand began to infuse the way she touched him.

Leaning over him where he lay in the bath, she brought her mouth to his, her tongue pressing deeply insistent within, the hard crowns of her breasts tingling against his damp chest. He groaned with pleasure, running his hands down her back, nipping the firm flesh of her buttocks between finger and thumb. Her teeth closed over his lower lip in urgent, bold response and her hand slid between their bodies to grasp the rising shaft nudging her belly.

"You are going to taste the water again, my elf," Daniel murmured, his eyes now burning as lust's dragon abandoned the waiting game. His hands spanned her back, holding her against him as he twisted. Water slopped over the rim onto the waxed floor; there was a brief, ungainly tangle of limbs, then Harry found herself back in the tub looking up at him as he knelt astride her.

Her body, moist and slippery in welcome, took him deep within; her eyes, huge pools of hungry wonder, were fastened upon his face; her tongue, damp and eager, ran over her lips; her hands gripped the corded muscles of his upper arms as he braced himself against the rim of the tub.

Slowly, wickedly, he withdrew to the very edge of her body and held himself there at the nerve-stretched tender opening. Her hips shifted in the now-cooling water and her body quivered around the tantalizing tip of the pleasure bringer. A warm languour spread through her lower body. It filled and then engulfed her so that she heard her own voice from a great distance making strange, incoherent sounds. Then, as he drove deep within, the bottom fell out of the universe and she felt herself sinking, without shape, without identity, into delight's embrace.

Daniel shuddered in glory on his own mountain, looking down at the heart-shaped face rapt with joyous wonder beneath him. There was a moment when her eyelids fluttered, opened, and the wide eyes gazed into his, their expression one of tenderness and an amazed gratitude, as if she had been given a priceless gift. And he knew that his own expression would mirror hers. She had indeed gifted him this day and laid to rest the ghosts of past glories he had thought never to re-create.

He felt her shiver suddenly and the world reasserted itself. They were once more a man and a woman with limbs entangled in a bathtub of tepid water, and the fire was getting low, and the wind fingered its way through cracks in the casement. "Come," he said softly, brushing a wet tendril of hair from her brow. "I think you have bathed sufficiently for one day." He drew himself upright, stepping from the water.

Henrietta lay, still too languid to make the effort to move, feeling the water lap her skin where, despite the chill, a faint sheen of perspiration glowed. Daniel bent and splashed water between her breasts, ran a cleansing hand delicately between her thighs, then lifted her from the tub. She smiled dreamily at him, making no attempt to reach for the towel. He pushed her close to the fire, grabbed the towel, still damp from her previous bath, and rubbed her down vigorously, with none of the lingering caresses of before. It served to bring her back to herself and the world again, and she shivered anew.

"Put on your nightgown, love." Daniel threw a scuttle of coals upon the fire, poked it fiercely, and the flames spurted high, throwing out renewed heat. "Quickly," he said, as she huddled toward the warmth, reluctant to cross the room to fetch her fur-trimmed nightgown of dark blue wool.

She paused for a moment, savoring the endearment he had never before used, warmed to her core by the softness of his tone, the ease and naturalness with which he had spoken it.

Daniel fetched the gown himself, tossing it around her shoulders. "Y'are bewitched!" he said with a laugh, setting to dry himself. "And I can hardly blame you. I think I am myself."

"I had thought to create such a wonderland," she said, finding her voice at last and sounding just a little smug.

"Mmmm." He put on his shirt, stepped into his britches, then stood regarding her quizzically. "Such a sweet-scented wonderland, it was. May I ask how you acquired such luxuries?"

A tinge of pink colored her cheekbones. "I spent a little of the money you gave me for household expenses last month. I thought 'twould not be a bad use."

"No," he said thoughtfully, "I will not quarrel with that. Did you ask Dorcas to make the purchases for you?"

She turned aside, busying herself with the girdle of her nightgown. "Not . . . not exactly." She bent to pick up the discarded towel, shaking it out, hanging it over the firescreen to dry.

"Harry?" He spoke softly and she turned to face him.

" 'Twas not so very far, Daniel, but a quarter of a mile along Cheapside. I told Dorcas I was going and she made no objection; she did not even tell me to have a care, so she must have thought 'twas quite safe."

Daniel stroked his chin pensively. Then he crooked a finger at her. "You face me with a dilemma, Henrietta." He pinched her nose as she came up to him. "I must excuse you on this occasion, because to do otherwise would be the act of an ingrate and I'll not bear such a charge. But you must understand that I forbade you to go out alone purely in the interests of your safety and my peace of mind. Y'are not city bred, elf, and the temper of the city at present is ugly and uncertain."

She thought of what she had seen that afternoon and kept silent. Daniel pursed his lips, his eyes grave. "Obedience is a quality much prized in a wife," he observed solemnly.

She looked up and thought she could detect just the flicker of a smile behind the gravity. She murmured a demure assent and waited for the smile to blossom as she somehow knew it was going to.

Daniel shook his head in mock exasperation. "I suppose, if we are to live in peace, I must learn to command only where you can easily comply. Only in this instance, I *will* insist. You will not again leave the house without escort. Is it understood?''

She put her arms around his neck, standing on tiptoe to nuzzle his throat where it rose strong and clean from the open neck of his shirt. ''I do not think I shall wish to again. But 'twas to be a surprise, and I could not surprise you if I had to have your company.''

Daniel groaned in defeat, catching her wet hair and pulling her head back. ''Will I ever make a proper wife of you?''

Her eyes sparked mischief. ''But I thought you had, sir . . . a most proper wife. Must I demonstrate your achievements again?''

He laughed, even as his loins stirred anew and the fresh blood of eager youth seemed to course in his veins. ''Later you shall do so, but for now I have need of my supper and 'twould be as well to tidy up the chamber. I would have you demonstrate the more pedestrian talents of domesticity.''

''I should have a care, sir, before you reject my offers in such cavalier fashion.'' She danced away from his swinging hand, put her tongue out at him over her shoulder, and left the chamber with a light step and a singing heart.

Daniel made to follow her, his step no heavier and his heart no less musical than hers.

Chapter 10

It was a week later when Daniel, shaking snow off his cloak, entered the house to be met by sounds of a violent altercation coming from the parlor. His wife's voice, shrill with fury, was ringing to the rafters yet was almost drowned out by a raucous bellowing that he immediately recognized.

"Oh, my heavens, Sir Daniel!" Dorcas, her habitual calm destroyed, scurried from the kitchen. "Thank goodness y'are back. There'll be murder done in a minute."

"Not if I have anything to do with it," he said grimly, placing the shapeless parcel he was carrying carefully against the wall before flinging open the parlor door. The small room seemed full of people, but for the moment the only thing that interested him was the sight of his wife standing upon the oak table in the middle of the chamber, stamping her feet and yelling her head off.

"What the devil do you think you're doing?" Two long paces brought him to the table. "Get off there this instant!" Seizing her by the waist, he swung her down. "Just what were you doing?" he repeated, still holding her.

"I was trying to make myself heard," Henrietta said somewhat breathlessly into the sudden silence. The hands at her waist were warm and steadying, imparting reassurance.

"Well, stamping your feet on the table is a novel,

not to say thoroughly indecorous, way of achieving such an object,'' Daniel declared without heat, critically examining her flushed face and damp forehead. ''Y'are thoroughly hot and bothered.'' He glanced quickly around the room. ''You also seem to have forgotten your duties as hostess, Henrietta. You do not appear to have offered your guests any refreshment.''

Under the circumstances, the reproving reminder, one suited to ordinary social congress, struck Henrietta as quite extraordinary and her jaw dropped. But some of the tension slipped from her body.

''Bravo, Sir Daniel. Will said you were a sensible man, and I can see he was quite right,'' a voice said approvingly. The owner of the voice stepped away from the fire and Daniel turned to face a tall lady of ample girth and commanding stature. Green eyes twinkled in a worn countenance that nevertheless carried the marks of its previous beauty.

Daniel smiled, glancing at Will, standing beside his mother. ''The resemblance is unmistakable, madam.'' He bowed, raising her hand to his lips. ''I am delighted to make the acquaintance of Will's mother.''

''When we heard from Master Filbert that you were in London,'' Mistress Osbert said, gesturing toward the lawyer, who looked as if he wished he were anywhere but there, ''we determined to pay you both a wedding visit. And I know that my husband wishes to settle certain affairs with you. We cannot thank you enough for your kindness and your care of Will.''

Daniel shook his head, laying an arm across the young man's shoulders in careless affection. ''Will proved an invaluable companion and I can assure you there is nothing to settle.''

''Ah, I beg to differ, sir.'' Esquire Osbert hurried forward. ''I have heard the whole from Will and—''

''Oh, this is not the point!'' Henrietta exclaimed in an agony of frustration. ''They came with my father, Daniel, and he—''

''Where are your manners?'' Daniel broke in as her voice began to rise alarmingly again. ''What can you be thinking of to interrupt in that discourteous fashion?''

The hectic flush died on her cheeks and she took a deep breath, turning toward Will's father. ''I beg your pardon, sir. It was most ill-mannerly. I forgot myself for the moment.''

''That's better,'' Daniel said gently, caressing her cheek with a fingertip. ''There is no need to be so agitated. I am here now. Why do you not go abovestairs and tidy yourself while I find some refreshment for our guests?''

Henrietta shook her head. ''Nay, I wish to stay. If you had not sent me away the last time you had dealings with my father, we would not be in this tangle now.''

''Why, you . . .'' Sir Gerald sprang forward, and Daniel swiftly interposed himself between the man and his daughter.

''How delightful to see you again, Sir Gerald,'' he said with a bland smile.

Sir Gerald came to an abrupt stop, head lowered rather in the manner of a charging bull meeting an immovable object. '' 'Tis no damn pleasure for me,'' he blustered. ''This damned lawyer comes to me with some insolent demand—''

''Insolent!'' exclaimed Harry. ''How can you possibly stand there and—''

''That will do!'' Daniel swung around on her, real annoyance now in his face and voice. ''If you wish to remain in the room, then be silent. I can make sense of nothing when you constantly interrupt in this intemperate fashion.''

''A very sensible man,'' Mistress Osbert reaffirmed with a nod. ''Ye need have no fear, Henrietta. We are here to see fair play, and I can assure you it will be done.''

Sir Gerald turned an alarming shade of puce and began struggling for words. Master Filbert coughed. ''That's right, Lady Drummond,'' he said. ''There's nothing for you to worry about. This misunderstanding is in a fair way to being settled."

"*Misunderstanding!*"

"Henrietta, I said that will do!" thundered Daniel.

"I don't know what damned business this is of yours, Osbert," Sir Gerald exploded into the moment of quiet. "Or of some damned whey-faced lawyer." He glared at Master Filbert. "There's no documents to be found and I'll not stand here listening to you tell me otherwise, just because some damned jackanapes has greased your palm!"

Daniel rightly assumed he was the "damned jackanapes" in question but decided to ignore the insult. His father-in-law seemed to suffer from a paucity of adjectives, he reflected. "May I offer you wine, gentlemen? Since Henrietta has omitted to do so."

"Thank'ee," Esquire Osbert said with heartfelt relief. "But ye shouldn't blame Henrietta. 'Twas a shock for her when we all turned up. But as Amelia says, we'll not stand by and see her done out of her due. As soon as we heard what was in the wind, Amelia said we must do our bit this time; we've turned a blind eye too often in the past." He scratched his nose, as freckled as Will's. "It's hard to know what to do, though, Sir Daniel. Can't interfere between a man and his child even if you don't hold with what's going on, and I don't say Henrietta was an easy child . . . never biddable. But this is different, as Amelia says . . . a matter of right and wrong and what I know. I saw those papers myself when there was talk of a match between Henrietta and Will, and I'll stand up in a court of law and say so. As will Master Filbert." He drank deeply of the goblet handed him and sat down at the table with the air of a man who has said his say, shooting a glance of ineffable distaste at Sir Gerald, who was becoming more apoplectic by the minute.

"I cannot believe that will be necessary," Daniel said, thanking his stars for Amelia Osbert, who clearly saw where her duty lay and had no hesitation in taking the path and marching others along with her. He raised an eyebrow at the fulminating Ashby. "Come, Sir Gerald, let us discuss this in a reasonable fashion."

"Reasonable?" A sly look appeared in Ashby's bloodshot eyes. "Reasonable, ye say? Where are these documents, then? The ones everyone says they've seen? You show 'em to me, then mayhap we'll have a 'reasonable' discussion." He drained his goblet and slammed it down on the table with unsuppressed violence.

"Oh, I'll show them to you." Henrietta spoke quietly. She was very pale but seemed perfectly in control of herself as she stepped forward. "I know exactly where they are." She offered her father a glinting, mocking smile. "Shall I tell you? Or should we all journey into Oxfordshire and I will lay hands upon them myself? Which would you prefer . . . Father?"

The last word was invested with a wealth of bitter irony that chilled Daniel to the marrow. He stared at her in the stunned silence that wrapped them all. She was holding herself rigidly straight and still, and seemed to be concentrating every ounce of energy, every fiber of strength, every strand of willpower, upon the volcanic bulk of the man she called Father. It was as if she would defeat him with the power of herself, as if she believed he would crumble into inoffensive, harmless dust before the force of her will.

What Daniel did not know, what no one in that room except Henrietta herself knew, was that she was playing a hunch. Her father was an obsessive magpie. He kept everything, whether it had any apparent use or not, on the grounds that one never knew what the future would hold. If he had not destroyed the documents, she knew where they were. And as she impaled her father with the probe of the knowledge she thought she had, she saw that she had been right. The lines of his face seemed to blur, uncertainty to swim in his eyes.

"They are to be found beneath the false bottom of Lady Mary's jewel casket behind the panel beside the fireplace in your bedchamber," she pronounced with a thrill of triumph that she could not disguise. It was a triumph that led her to recklessness and her voice took on a taunting ring. "And with them will be found the deed of covenant for the tenants in the Longshire cottages. The deed giving to the families the cottages in perpetuity for a peppercorn rent in recognition of their services to your grandfather. The deed you denied ever existed when you evicted those families and sold the cottages to pay your gambling debt to Charles Parker."

So heady was the sensation of victory as she read the truth and incredulity in Sir Gerald's face that her habitual instincts of caution went by the board. She had come very close to him as she made her statements, and when his hand flashed, powered by the full force of his arm, she ducked an instant too late. The next second a chair crashed to the floor under the dead weight of Ashby's bulk staggering beneath the impact of Daniel's fist.

"Oh dear, oh dear," Master Filbert whimpered, wringing his hands as he looked at the devastation around him. "This is most unseemly."

Daniel ignored him. He bent to scoop up Henrietta, who was on her knees against the wall. "That was foolish," he said almost roughly. "You had already made your point without talking of cottages."

"Maybe so, but it served to prove the point," she managed to retort, triumph still in her voice.

Catching her chin, he turned her face sideways. "Y'are going to have a very black eye."

"Not for the first time. Anyway, it was worth it." She glanced at her father, who was struggling to his feet, shaking his head like a bewildered bull, and said rather wistfully, "I wish you'd knock him down again."

"Bloodthirsty little wretch!" Daniel exclaimed. Will snorted with laughter, then coughed, reddening under a hard glare from his mother, who marched across the room to Henrietta.

"This has become disgracefully out of hand. Come with me, Henrietta. We will see if the goodwife has some red meat to put upon your eye. It will draw out the swelling."

"Oh, please, no." Harry made a face. "I do hate it, all bloody and wet and cold. 'Twill be all right if we leave it be." She shot a pleading glance at Daniel with the eye that was open. "Will it not, Daniel?"

"Go with Mistress Osbert," he said, impervious to the plea. "Your part is well played and I would play mine now without hindrance."

"I would not hinder you," she said softly. "I wish to hear what is decided. Am I not entitled?"

"I can see that marriage has not made you any the more biddable, Henrietta," declared Mistress Osbert. " 'Tis not a woman's place to take part in these discussions."

Henrietta squinted fiercely. "I do not think you believe that, madam. And if 'tis not true where you are concerned, why should it hold for me?"

Will gave vent to another ill-concealed chortle and Esquire Osbert regarded his wife with some interest, waiting for her response. "Y'are impertinent, Henrietta," she said at last, but there was a twinkle in the green eyes.

"I know, madam," Harry agreed cheerfully.

"Well, I cannot help but feel compassion for your husband." Mistress Osbert glided to the door. "You had best sit quietly and I will fetch something for that eye."

Victory achieved, Harry sat on the settle beside the fire without demur. Although she would cut her tongue out rather than admit it, she was feeling distinctly quivery all of a sudden and her eye was beginning to throb painfully. She rested her head against the tall wooden back of the settle, content to let the voices swell around her, knowing she had nothing further to contribute but still fiercely clinging to her right to be there.

Daniel looked at her for a minute, a deep frown in his eyes as he wrestled with the urge to carry her off to bed willy-nilly. She looked so fragile with that great purple swelling marring the small, heart-shaped face. But she was entitled to remain if she wished, old enough to make her own choices and decide for herself if she felt well enough to implement those choices. He turned to his father-in-law, who had managed to drag himself into a chair, where he sat in the stunned and sullen silence of a bully who has met his match.

"Now perhaps we may have that reasonable discussion, Sir Gerald," Daniel said pleasantly. "Pray take a seat, Master Filbert. There will be some papers to draw up and we might as well waste no further time. I am sure Esquire Osbert will lend his services as witness."

Sir Gerald put up no further resistance and Harry offered only token protest to the large slab of raw flesh firmly placed on her eye by a resolute Mistress Osbert, who then sat down at the table with the air of an adjudicator.

"How did you know, Harry?" Will whispered, sitting beside her on the settle. "Not that anything you could do would ever surprise me anymore, but how could you be so sure where the papers were?"

"I wasn't," she confided with an attempted smile. "But it seemed worth trying. I know that's where he hides precious things because I found the hiding place one day when I was poking around their bedchamber. No one knew I had discovered it."

Will looked a mixture of shock and admiration. "What were ye doing poking around your parents' bedchamber?"

She shrugged. "Just looking for things. I often used to do it. That and listen at doors and windows. That's how I heard about my mother's jointure in the first place."

" 'Tis dreadful behavior, Harry," Will said.

"I am aware," she replied, quite unrepentant, "but think how useful it has turned out to be. Besides, I had to look out for myself. There was no one else to do it."

Will nodded, silenced by the truth of this. "You do

look sick, you know," he said after a minute. "D'ye not think you should lie down?"

"Aye, perhaps I will." She took the slab of meat off her eye and put it on the platter with a grimace of distaste. Then, despite the weakness still affecting her knees, chuckled wickedly. "D'ye think I should offer it to my father, Will? 'Tis a powerful bruise he has on his chin."

Will choked with laughter as he helped her to her feet, maintaining his hold on her elbow as she swayed slightly. "I'm going to help Harry to her chamber," he said to the room at large.

"Aye, I think I'll rest for a little while," Henrietta said with careful dignity.

Daniel glanced quickly in their direction, then nodded calmly. " 'Tis wise of you, I think. You'll feel more like your dinner after a rest."

"A most sensible man," murmured Mistress Osbert, fully appreciating the effort it was costing him to keep his seat and leave his wife with the conviction that she was making her own decisions. A spark of humor glowed responsively in the black eyes as he met her smiling gaze.

"I am learning, madam."

Much later that afternoon, Henrietta awoke in the darkened bedchamber, aware first that she was starving and then that one side of her face was twice its usual size. Memory rushed back and she forgot her ills immediately. They had won, and without a lengthy and expensive legal battle. She was free, once and for all, from her father's long-armed malevolence. But where was everyone? Had they forgotten all about her? Such neglect seemed unjust after the part she had played in the morning's drama. She sat up gingerly. Her face throbbed, but she felt perfectly strong.

The sound of voices reached Henrietta from the parlor—cheerful voices and the clink of knife on pewter. As she came down the stairs, the rich aromas of Dorcas's cooking filled the narrow hall, wafting from both kitchen and parlor, and her mouth watered. She pushed open the parlor door and stood in her nightgown in the doorway, taking in the scene around the table where sat Daniel, all three Osberts, and Master Filbert. They were all flushed with good food, wine, fire-warmth, and good company.

"I see my father did not join you for dinner," she said. "And I take it mighty ill in you, Daniel, that ye'd not wake me."

Daniel pushed back his chair and came toward her. "Now, do not be vexed, Harry," he said, laughing at her cross expression. "We have saved your dinner, but thought you'd enjoy it more when you'd had your sleep." He caught her chin, holding it as he studied her blackening eye. "Does it pain you?"

She shrugged. "Some, but not as much as my belly, which is cleaving to my backbone."

"Come and sit down. There are grilled pigeons and a hash of rabbit and lamb. Which d'ye care for first?" He drew her to the table, and she found it impossible to maintain her aggrieved pout under this determined refusal to acknowledge either the pout or the reasons for it. The Osberts were all smiling solicitously, and Master Filbert bowed most punctiliously, as if she were not in her nightgown with a swollen face and her hair in a pigtail.

"The hash, if you please."

There was a holiday atmosphere around the table, as if an enormous weight had been lifted. Henrietta for once said little, but she found herself taking an inordinate pleasure in Daniel's relaxation. She knew what this injection of capital meant to him, and the fact that she had been instrumental in acquiring it made her feel warm and glowing inside, as if she need no longer see herself as the impoverished suppliant rescued on a whim, as if she now had a place of her own in Daniel's life, one that she was in a fair way to earning.

"I bought you a present this morning," Daniel said suddenly, his eyes soft on her face. "I left it in the hall when I found you dancing a hornpipe on the table."

"A present!" Harry choked on her wine in surprise. "Why would you buy me a present?"

"Some mad and foolish whim," he said with a teasing grin, wiping wine from her chin with his handkerchief. " 'Twas a risky purchase, too. Such things are not looked upon kindly by those in authority these days."

"Whatever could it be?" Her one open eye widened, giving her such a lopsided look that he burst into laughter.

"It's in the hall," he told her. "By the door."

Harry leaped to her feet, running into the hall to retrieve the shapeless parcel Daniel had come in with that morning. "I know what it is," she cried excitedly. "I can feel the shape of it under all this wrapping."

"Well, what is it?" demanded Will impatiently.

" 'Tis a guitar," she said in wonder.

"I trust y'are as accomplished a player as you said you were." Daniel smiled delightedly at her pleasure as she pulled aside the wrapping and held up the instrument.

"Oh, indeed she is," Mistress Osbert said. "And a most pretty voice."

Henrietta flushed at the compliment, stroking the smooth curved wood with a delicate hand before plucking a string, tilting her head to listen to the note. " 'Tis a true note," she said, plucking another string. "Why, 'tis a fine guitar, Daniel. I will teach Lizzie and Nan to play."

He nodded, still smiling. "But now will you play for us?"

"If you wish it." She brushed a stray lock of hair off her forehead and gave him her own smile, a little shy, as if she would say more but could not for the moment. With a tiny frown of concentration, she plucked the strings almost at random. Then she began to sing, her voice rising sweetly in the quiet room as she sang a haunting ballad of love and loss to the gentle resonance of the guitar. When it was finished, without pause, she launched into a lusty folk song dealing with country matters, her voice mischievously inviting, the strings dancing beneath her busy fingers.

"Don't introduce that song to Lizzie for a year or two, if you please," Daniel said, laughing with the others as she ended on a singing chord.

" 'Tis time we made our farewells." Amelia Osbert stood up reluctantly. "There'll always be a welcome for ye both at Osbert Court . . . and your family," she added. "Don't you let Henrietta go running around, Sir Daniel, until the swelling's gone down. It'll only make it worse."

"I won't," he said solemnly. "And I do not know how to thank you enough."

"Nonsense!" Amelia declared in dismissal. "If there's to be any thanking, it'll be on our part." And with thanks and protestations on both sides, the Osberts and Master Filbert went out into the cold January night to make their way to their respective lodgings.

"Will we go home now?" Harry hugged her breasts convulsively in the shaft of freezing air lingering in the hall as the front door closed.

"Not immediately." Daniel hustled her back into the parlor. "I have still to see the commissioners at Haberdasher's Hall, and . . ." A shadow crossed his face, wiping away the previous warmth and elation. He bent to poke the fire.

"And . . ." Harry prompted.

"And I would wait for the outcome of the king's trial," he said, straightening. "I saw him this morning as they were taking him again to Westminster. He was on foot, going to take the barge at Gardenstairs, surrounded by those treasonous louts with their pikes." His mouth twisted in contempt. "Such a sweet smile he had and a greeting for all his people lining the streets to watch him pass."

Harry drew closer to the fire. "What was the mood of the people?"

Daniel shook his head. "Angry, confused. They were mostly silent. A few muttered 'God save the King,' but they were quickly hushed by those around them. Such prayers are considered treason, after all, under Parliament's tyranny.'' He almost spat the words. ''God help me, Henrietta, but if they murder His Majesty, then I'll not stand by.''

Such deadly purpose infused the quiet statement that she shivered involuntarily. What choice would he have? He had compounded, pledged allegiance to Parliament, in order to protect his family and his lands. Would he renege on that pledge? And if he did, what would happen to them all? Somehow, she could not bring herself to speak the questions, but the day's satisfactions seemed to have lost their gilt. She picked up the guitar again. ''Shall I play some more for you?''

''If you've a mind to,'' he responded, but the music did not seem to soothe him, or banish the dark thoughts, and after a while he stood up restlessly. ''I think I'll take the air for a while, Henrietta.''

''I will accompany you.'' She laid aside the guitar and stood up. '' 'Twill take me but a minute to dress.''

He shook his head. '' 'Tis too cold, Harry. Your face will hurt most dreadfully in that wind. Ye'll be better in bed with a sack posset.''

The latter prospect was definitely more appealing than venturing forth in her present state, she had to agree, but she could not shake off the conviction that concern for her health was but excuse for his refusal of her company on this occasion. It seemed he felt he could not share the devils plaguing him with one whose political understanding was ill-formed by virtue of her age and sex. She would ask him to instruct her, except that she did not think the request would find favor in his present frame of mind.

The tension increased throughout the next week until the day came when Charles Stuart was sentenced to death by beheading, ''as a tyrant, traitor, murderer, and public enemy of the good people of this land.'' He was led out of the court at Westminster with the cries of ''Justice! Execution!'' ringing to the skies as the soldiery bellowed their demand for the blood of the man they believed was responsible for the blood of all those slain during the years of civil war.

Henrietta was there with Daniel, who stood stark and still as the previously unthinkable became a certainty. All around them rose a hum of voices, some in angry dissent, some in confused dissent, others loud in their support of the court's sentence. " 'Tis God's law," an ascetic-looking man beside Henrietta stated with cold precision. " 'Tis God's express words: 'that blood defileth the land, and the land cannot be cleansed of the blood thus shed therein, but by the blood of him that shed it.' "

Henrietta felt the current of anger strike through Daniel as a bolt of lightning will cleave a tree and she was suddenly afraid of what would happen if he loosed that anger here, in this throng. She tugged desperately on his hand. "Let us go back."

As if in a daze, he looked down at her face, upturned, anxiety swimming in the big eyes, her temple and cheekbone faintly shadowed with the residue of Sir Gerald's bruising hand.

"Please," she said insistently, tugging his hand again. "Let us go back now. My head aches most dreadfully."

Concern sparked in his eyes, banishing the unfocused glare of anguished fury. "What ails you, elf? 'Tis not like you to be sickly."

"Oh, I'm sure 'tis nothing," she said hastily. "Just the wind. But I would go back to the house. If Dorcas will prepare some physick for my head, it will be better directly."

"Very well. There is nothing to keep us here anyway." Acid edged his voice, but he turned toward a side alley, holding Henrietta's hand firmly. The crowd was breaking up around them, but the mood was somber and scuffles erupted here and there. A stone flew through the air, cracking against the cobbles at Henrietta's feet so that she jumped back in alarm. Daniel's grip tightened on her hand. "This place has an unhealthy air,'' he muttered. '' 'Tis no time for a woman to be abroad.''

''But I am not the only one,'' she protested, gesturing to the eddying throng.

''Most of the others look well able to have a care for themselves,'' he said shortly, lengthening his stride so she was obliged to skip to keep up with him. His free hand rested on the hilt of his sword and his gaze was everywhere.

It was certainly an accurate observation, Harry reflected, looking around her. The women were hard-eyed and grim-faced, their wooden pattens clacking on the cobbles, their frieze cloaks showing signs of much wear. Many of them held small children by the hand or in their arms, and the men who walked with them were marked with toil and poverty, their expressions devoid of expectation. Was this the face of a nation that would applaud the murder of its king? Or would they simply let it happen as an act that had nothing to do with them, an act decided upon by the wisdom of those in power, who must, by definition, know what they were about?

She would have liked to discuss the question with Daniel but hesitated, afraid to scrape on open sores; and when they reached their lodgings, she was given no opportunity for conversation, serious or otherwise. An attempt to maintain that her headache had somehow miraculously disappeared during the walk home met with an incredulous raised eyebrow, and she was obliged to submit to being put to bed and fed a loathsome draught of Dorcas's concoction. It must have had poppy juice in it, because she fell heavily asleep long before supper and was dead to the world when Daniel finally came to bed, to lie wakeful, his heart leaden, staring into the blackness as he struggled to come to terms with his own needs and convictions, to weigh practicality with violated belief and loyalty.

During the next few days, he seemed to retreat into himself. Henrietta tried to pierce his absorption with music and talk, with the softness of her hands and body in the big bed, and when all else failed she tried to persuade him to return to Kent. The commissioners at Haberdasher's Hall had agreed to a reduction of a thousand pounds in his indemnity, and there was now no business to keep them in the city, but he would not leave London. It was as if he had to wait with his king, for whom he had fought most of his adult life, until the ax finally brought the enterprise to an end.

Dawn broke on Tuesday, January 30. Daniel rose in silence, dressed in silence, and strode in the same silence down the stairs to the front door. Henrietta ran after him, struggling with the hooks and buttons of her riding habit.

''I am coming with you.''

''No, you are not!'' he pronounced with ferocious vehemence, more shocking coming as it did after the prolonged silence. ''You will stay here within doors until I return.'' The door opened, a lance of freezing air thrust through the damp chill of the hall, then the door slammed.

She stood for a minute, huddling into her still-unfastened jacket, numbed fingers fumbling with the hooks.

''Come you into the kitchen and feel the fire, m'dear.'' Dorcas spoke at her back, one hand rubbing her arm in gentle comfort. '' 'Tis best to leave him with his devils; and this day is one when evil runs rampant.''

''Aye.'' Henrietta turned and followed Dorcas into the kitchen, where the fire blazed in the range, the lamps burned, defying the lowering gloom of a January dawn, and Joe and the goodman sat stolidly breaking their fast, as if the king was not to die this day at the hands of his people.

Dorcas set a bowl of curds and white bread before Henrietta, and a redcurrant cordial that instantly brought warmth to the cold, empty pit of her stomach. It was soothing nourishment, which strengthened as it soothed, and Henrietta finally rose from the table with quiet determination.

"My thanks, Dorcas. 'Twas much needed. I go to Whitehall, now."

"Sir Daniel will not be pleased." Dorcas made the statement neutrally, almost as if she felt it her duty to do so, but her duty extended no further.

"I will not be excluded from this that touches him so nearly," Henrietta said quietly. "If my husband is to stand in suffering, a helpless observer, then I too will suffer that. I cannot share it else."

"You must do what you must." Dorcas cleared platters from the table. "But have a care. The streets will be uneasy."

"They have been so these past weeks."

Dorcas simply nodded. It was for each wife to decide where wifely duty lay. If this one saw it thus, then she would not argue with her. "Joe will go with you."

The youth did not look overjoyed at the prospect of the excursion, but his mother slapped his shoulder. "Great lump!" she said. "Get along with you and make sure Lady Drummond meets with no offense."

Although she would not have asked for it, Henrietta accepted the escort with relief, and once they were out in the city, her relief became heartfelt. The streets were filled with a tide of people, moving inexorably in the same direction, slow yet purposeful, like some behemoth closing in on its prey. Once they had joined the tide, turning aside was an impossibility. One became a part of the beast.

Thin, wintery sunshine broke through the clouds as they neared Whitehall, illuminating the scaffold set up outside the Banqueting House. The crowd surged forward, and Henrietta found herself part of a group flowing ahead of the rest. Without intending it she was in the front lines of the spectators, who fell dreadfully silent as they looked upon the scaffold with its grooved wooden block. The executioner stood there already, his long-handled instrument of justice in his hand. The sun caught the wicked curve of the silver blade. What did it feel like to know that your arm would strike off the head of the King of England?

Henrietta stared at the man as if she could read his thoughts, but the mask lent him an unreal air, separated him from the hard shapes and contours of the real world. She looked around her for the large, bumbling familiarity of Joe and could not see him. There were just strangers' faces, registering every emotion from lust to horror as they waited. Panic quivered in her belly. She tried to inch backward, away from her proximity to the scaffold, but the human wall at her back was impermeable. Desperately, she scanned the crowd, praying for a glimpse of Joe, or maybe Daniel. He was here, she knew. But where?

Then a low murmur grew in the throng, swelling to a sound part anticipatory, part horror-struck as a troop of soldiers emerged from Whitehall gate. Charles Stuart walked in their midst. His head was bare. To see the king bareheaded amongst his covered subjects struck Henrietta as the most dreadful aspect of this dread affair. It was absurd, she knew, to fix upon such a thing, but it seemed to symbolize the almost hallucinatory quality of the morning.

Now, she could do nothing but gaze as the scene played out before her. The king mounted the scaffold, which was immediately surrounded by ranks of soldiers so deep that when His Majesty turned to address the crowd his voice could not carry far enough. He gave his coat to an attendant, scorned the blindfold, spoke words of forgiveness to his executioner, and knelt. Now there was a silence so immense it seemed impossible it could ever be broken. Sun sparked off silver as the blade rose and fell in one clean, sweeping movement. A mighty groan broke from the crowd; a groan of despair and disbelief; a sound to wrench the vitals, rising, swelling in the air. Tears poured unheeded down her cheeks as Henrietta heard her own keening, mixing with the sound all around her.

Then someone shouted, the crowd surged, pressed forward, then ebbed as people struggled to break rank. Troops of horses were bearing down on them, their riders brandishing pike and halberd, intent on the speedy dispersal of the grieving throng. One troop marched on them from the direction of Charing Cross, another herded them toward Charing Cross, so that all was confusion as the crowd scattered hither and thither, desperate to avoid the rearing, plunging horses and the prodding pikes.

Henrietta concentrated on keeping her footing. Nothing else seemed important. She had no control over where she went, but she knew that if once she slipped and went down beneath the stampeding feet, she would never get up again. Her small stature was a grave disadvantage, and she lamented bitterly at having lost Joe's bulky support. He could have held her up as she was tossed forward, backward, sideways, according to the ebb and flow of the tide.

Salvation came in the dark, narrow opening of a doorway. Just before she was carried past, she managed to duck beneath the arm of a burly individual brandishing a heavy stave and gain the safety of the doorway. Gasping for breath, she huddled against the door frame as the tide swept past her. She had no idea where she was, but at least she could stand upright and still, and at some point this great, milling mass of bodies would have gone.

Daniel was on horseback. Anticipating the possibility of mayhem, he had stationed himself well away from the press, and had left before the troops began their maneuvers. Thus, he reached Paternoster Row with little difficulty, hearing the swelling murmur of the crowd behind him. He felt cold, drained, empty of all feeling. It was over. That was all he could think of. He was too numbed to feel outrage anymore. In fact, he had done his grieving in advance and now lapsed into torpor . . . until Dorcas informed him that Henrietta had gone to Whitehall with Joe.

He snapped back to his senses as if his head had been held under a pump. "But I forbade her to leave the house!" He stared at Dorcas as images of the rioting crowd filled his vision. "Sweet Jesus!" He turned and ran back into the street, gazing wildly around, wondering which way to go. It was madness to go toward the crowd, but he could not just stand there like a paralyzed dolt. Then he saw Joe running toward him. Joe, but no Henrietta.

"Where the hell is she?" he demanded, grabbing the youth's coat front with a violent jerk.

"I lost her, Sir Daniel," Joe blurted. "I'm sorry, sir, but I couldn't 'elp it. One minute she was there, close to the scaffold, then she wasn't. I looked everywhere, but there's so many, 'tis impossible." His breath was coming in sobs, not helped by the continued jerking as Daniel without conscious thought shook him. "I came back as fast as I could, sir. I did, really."

The words finally penetrated. Daniel released him abruptly. "I beg your pardon, Joe. I did not mean to handle you roughly," he said, trying to clear his head, to focus on what really mattered. "You lost her at Whitehall?"

"Aye, sir." Joe nodded vigorously.

"Before the . . . before they killed the king?"

"Aye, sir." Joe's face darkened. " 'Twas a dreadful sight."

"Fetch my horse. I have just taken him back to the stable." It was probably futile, but he could not keep an anguished vigil, praying for her reappearance. He mounted and set off to retrace his steps.

Henrietta stayed in her doorway until the tide became a trickle. It was a long wait, but nothing would prevail upon her to leave her haven until the mêlée had dissipated. There were still soldiers, but they took no notice of her as she slipped out of concealment and stood, bewildered, wondering where she was and in what direction lay St. Paul's. Plucking up courage, she approached one of the troopers, who gestured with his pike. "That-a-way, mistress."

She thanked him and wearily trudged off. It seemed a much greater distance returning than coming, but earlier she had not yet seen what she had seen, endured what she had just endured. Every bone in her body felt bruised, her muscles ached, her skin was sore, and the dreadful memories would not leave her, sapping her of all remaining energy.

Daniel saw her just as he was beginning to think he could not control his panic any longer. He had kept down all thought of what might have happened to her as he combed the streets, the main thoroughfares, and the alleys, seeing only the shocked faces of strangers stumbling in their bewilderment. Then, as he came down Ludgate Hill from St. Paul's for the second time, he saw the small figure dragging herself up the hill, eyes on the ground as she put one foot in front of the other with conscious deliberation. She had lost her hat and the neck ruffle of her shirt was torn.

He descended on her in a squall of pounding hooves. She looked up, shocked and fearful, at the imperative menace of the sound. Then the horse came to a heaving halt and Daniel twisted sideways in the saddle, catching her under the arms and hauling her up. For one horrified moment, she thought he was going to fling her facedown across the saddle in front of him, such wild fury she had seen on his face in the bare second before he seized her. But she landed with a thump on the saddle before him, dazed and bruised but upright. He said not a word, simply turned his horse and rode back to the house.

In the absence of invitation to speak, Henrietta also kept mute, but her insides were churning with alarm. This was not the Daniel she knew. His face was a mask of anger, the black eyes saber tips of fury, and the body at her back was rigid with the effort at restraint.

Outside the house, he flung himself from the horse, pulled Henrietta down, and stalked into the hall, bellowing for Joe to see to his mount. Joe and Dorcas both appeared in the kitchen doorway. Dorcas's hand flew to her mouth as she saw Daniel's expression and Henrietta's white-faced alarm. She started to say something, but Daniel marched to the stairs, half dragging, half carrying Henrietta with him.

"You dare to disobey me, on this day of all days!"

He spoke at last, kicking the bedchamber door shut behind them.

"I did not go alone," she stammered. "Joe was with me. Only we became separated—"

"I did not give you permission to leave this house with Joe or with anyone," he bit out, still gripping her arms. "Do you think I did not know what was going to happen in the streets?"

Henrietta swallowed, trying not to flinch from him as he held her. "I had to go," she said. "I knew you would be suffering, and I had to be a part of it so I could understand how you felt." She shivered suddenly, and tears filled her eyes. "I saw it! I saw the ax fall . . . I saw him, bareheaded, with the soldiers who kept their heads covered . . ." Tears clogged her throat and she put a hand up to massage it as if the external pressure would ease the internal.

Daniel released her suddenly. "Go and stand by the window. I am so angry I cannot trust myself near you." He swung away from her toward the fire, and she scuttled across the room to stand on the far side of the bed.

"I would not be excluded from your pain," she said with difficulty, clasping her hands tightly in front of her. "You would not take me, so I had to go alone."

Daniel rested his arms on the mantel shelf, letting his head drop onto his hands. "Do you have any idea what could have happened to you?"

"Yes, of course," she replied. "I managed to find safety in a doorway until the crowd had passed, but I saw what happened to some. I knew that I must not lose my footing or—" Her teeth began to chatter as a shock wave of cold and nausea washed across her.

Daniel turned from the fire, running his fingertips across his lips as he looked at her and allowed the meaning of her words to penetrate his fear-fueled anger. She had gone to Whitehall in order to experience his suffering, so that she could understand it and share it. It was an extraordinary thing to do, yet, if he really thought about it in the light of Henrietta herself, it was entirely reasonable. It bore all the marks of the determined courage she exhibited in the cause of others. He had thought her too young, too naive and inexperienced in the ways of the world, to be involved in his agony. He had refused to confide in her, so she had taken matters into her own hands in a predictably simple and direct fashion. And she had suffered for it. He looked at her as she stood, shivering, gray-faced, the big eyes haunted by what they had seen.

Without saying anything, he left the room and went down to the kitchen. When he returned ten minutes later with a tray on which stood two steaming tankards and a plate of gingerbread, she was still standing as he had left her, except that she was looking out of the window onto the street below.

"Come to the fire," he said quietly, setting the tray on the side table. "Y'are in need of warmth. There's mulled wine and some of Dorcas's gingerbread straight from the oven."

It would seem the tempest had passed. Hesitantly, she came toward him, rubbing her crossed upper arms with her hands. " 'Tis not cold in here."

"Nay, the cold is within yourself," he replied, taking her hands and chafing them vigorously. "We will never forget what we have seen today. No one who saw it will ever forget it. But we must go on, nevertheless. The fight must be continued because no honest man can live under the rule of regicides."

She swallowed. "What mean you, Daniel? You have compounded, taken the Covenant."

He shook his head. "I did not swear allegiance to regicides. Charles the First is dead. Charles the Second lives, and to him I owe my fealty."

"What will you do?" The question was barely a whisper.

"I go to The Hague," he said simply. "To the king in exile, and pledge myself to his cause."

Henrietta nodded slowly. "There are many families in exile. We will not feel strange amongst their number, and the children will learn much from such travels."

Daniel stared at her for a minute. Not thinking further than his own imperative, he had intended leaving Henrietta and his daughters safe in their Kentish backwater. But his wife had already once today demonstrated her views on the way in which a marriage partnership should be conducted.

He smiled and cupped her face, running his knuckles against the high cheekbones. "Think you Mistress Kierston will take to life in exile?"

Light and life returned to the previously solemn brown eyes. "Must we take her?"

He nodded. "I am afraid so, elf. You will have enough to do as my wife at court without caring single-handed for Lizzie and Nan."

"At least there'll be no butter to churn," she said with a roguish glint in her eyes.

"And no trees to climb," he replied solemnly. "You must learn to be a courtier."

Henrietta contemplated that prospect. "I do not suppose it can be any harder than anything else I've learned to do." She grinned suddenly, reaching up to put her arms around his neck, standing on tiptoe to kiss him. "But I do not suppose it will be as pleasurable as some other things."

"Probably not," he agreed, holding her lithe body against his length, feeling her warmth and eagerness, feeling his own stirring in response. Abruptly, he was engulfed by an urgent desire, a need for the body he held, as if in passion's union would be found a healing of the day's unhappiness.

Henrietta felt the change in his hold, saw passion chase all else from the black-eyed gaze bent upon her. And with her own wanting came a curious sense of triumph as she drew him to the bed.

Chapter 11

"Nan, do stop dawdling." Henrietta reached for the child's hand, her voice impatient. "We have tarried overlong as 'tis."

"I expect we shall be late for dinner again," said Lizzie cheerfully from behind an armful of fresh-cut lavender.

"And Daddy will prob'ly have invited guests," Nan chimed in with what Henrietta considered uncalled-for insouciance.

"Highly likely," she muttered, increasing her speed along one of the narrow cobbled streets that meandered through the busy city of The Hague. Cries of street vendors enticed the children, unaccustomed to city living, and she had constantly to tug one or the other of them away from the seduction of a smelly fish stall or the nimble fingers of a basket maker or the succulent aromas of a pastry cook's. It was not that she did not understand their perpetual fascination; indeed she shared it. But they had spent too long picking lavender in a field just outside the city and the household would be waiting dinner for them.

Daniel would, as usual, have spent the morning at court, where fevered plans were being concocted to raise another army against Parliament with the support of the still-loyal Scots. He had not said he would be bringing guests home, but it was a not-infrequent occurrence since they kept open house for the many impoverished exiles in the city. An absentee hostess and delayed dinner did not reflect well upon the quality of the hospitality.

Finally they reached the stone house with its steep gabled roof that was the Drummonds' home in The Hague. It was not an insubstantial house: by the standards of the majority of this court-in-exile, whose estates had been sequestered, Daniel was moderately affluent. They had managed to leave England unnoticed by the authorities and had brought with them a considerable sum. It required careful husbanding, however, since he could not risk returning to England to raise more funds from the estate. Parliament's agents were now watching the ports, on the lookout for those active in the exiled king's cause, and he had no desire to be identified as such and thus jeopardize his property.

The house stood in a quiet square of similar houses and boasted a pretty walled garden at the rear. The April wind carried the smell of the sea and the scent of wallflowers, and it was with some reluctance that Henrietta closed the front door on the spring day. Voices rose in soft cadences from the parlor to the left of the hall.

"I wonder who 'tis?" Lizzie, inveterately curious, ran to the door, putting her eye to the keyhole, straining to hear through the heavy oak.

"Lizzie!" Henrietta protested, half laughing, when the door swung open.

Lizzie tumbled off balance into the doorway at her father's feet. Daniel looked down at her with a raised eyebrow. "Have you dropped something, Elizabeth?"

"Nay . . . nay, sir. I t-tripped," the child stammered, scarlet with embarrassment as she scrambled to her feet and bobbed a hasty curtsy.

"How unfortunate," Daniel murmured solicitously. "I trust ye did not hurt yourself."

"No, sir." Lizzie curtsied again, shooting her stepmother an anguished look of appeal.

Henrietta came swiftly to her rescue. A quick glance into the room beyond Daniel told her who his visitors were and she now stepped forward, tossing back the hood of her cloak as she pushed the children in front of her. "My Lord Hendon, Mr. Connaught, I do not think you are acquainted with my stepdaughters . . . Elizabeth and Ann."

"Indeed not." The Earl of Hendon put up his glass and smiled vaguely at the two little girls. "Delighted, my dears. Charming, Drummond . . . quite charming."

"Thank you," Daniel said dryly. "However, their governess is waiting for them abovestairs, so I trust you will excuse them."

The children curtsied a little too precipitately for true decorum and beat a thankful retreat.

"It's to be assumed you had a productive morning," Daniel observed, regarding Henrietta with a smile in his eyes. She seemed to have brought the spring day in with her, sparkling in her eyes, glowing in her wind-pinkened cheeks, scenting the tumbled corn silk-colored curls and the damask of her skin.

"We have been picking lavender to dry for potpourri," she said, giving him that irresistibly coquettish look she habitually produced when she might conceivably be at fault. "I trust I haven't kept you waiting too long for your dinner, but I am afraid the time ran away with us."

"Your hospitality, Lady Drummond, is most generous." William Connaught spoke up in customary ponderous tones, his air of importance not a whit diminished by his shabby broadcloth doublet and the fake silver buckles on his down-at-heel shoes. " 'Twould be the height of gracelessness to find fault."

"Nevertheless, we are a trifle sharp-set," Daniel pointed out. "It being all of three of the clock."

"I will take my cloak abovestairs and instruct the cook to serve dinner directly."

Henrietta went up to the bedchamber, examining herself critically in the glass. On the whole, she was not displeased with what she saw. She also knew that these days Daniel was actively pleased with what he saw. Her face seemed to have changed in the last months, but it was hard to identify the changes. They were mostly in her eyes, she decided, then blushed slightly. The truth was that her eyes always looked as if she had just been making love . . . glowing and knowing and utterly satisfied. It was an accurate reflection of the way her body felt most of the time.

The thought set up a tingling sensation in the pit of her stomach and she hurried downstairs again, trying to think of dinner and the responsibilities of a hostess. The cook, who was broad and Flemish and spoke little English, had early taken charge of the kitchen with sufficient skill to enable Henrietta to take credit for the table without having to do anything significant about it. Now, he nodded in stolid comprehension when she appeared in the kitchen and gestured toward the bubbling pots on the trivet in the hearth. With a sweeping movement, he removed the lids, inviting her inspection and compliments. She peered knowledgeably, smiled and nodded at the rich mutton stew, the potato dumplings, the dish of peas with lardons of bacon. With a mixture of signs and monosyllables, she managed to establish that the children and Mistress Kierston had already been served in the schoolroom abovestairs. The cook invited her to exclaim suitably over the apple tart he had prepared especially for Lizzie, who had not the least difficulty communicating her preferences and was frequently to be found in the kitchen chattering nineteen to the dozen to the silent but attentive cook, the lad who came in daily to do the heavy household work, and the little maid who lived in the attic.

Dinner was a cheerful meal, but Henrietta immediately detected a suppressed tension in Daniel. It was excitement rather than anxiety, she sensed, and there was a question in his eyes whenever they fell upon her as she served their guests, refilled glasses, chatted pleasantly.

Somewhat to Daniel's surprise, she had taken to the role of hostess with much enthusiasm when they had set up house in The Hague last July. Her efforts had been amply rewarded by flattering attentions and plentiful compliments, and she had blossomed quite amazingly. Their present guests were frequently at the Drummonds' generous and open table. Both Hendon and Connaught had fled England after Preston, leaving sequestered estates and all their worldly goods. They lived, in company with the majority of Englishmen at present at The Hague, from hand to mouth, relying on the generosity of those better placed and whatever they could borrow. In this, they were no different from their king, who, as penniless as they, was obliged to beg and borrow from his fellow monarchs throughout Europe. The universal revulsion felt throughout the Continent over the bloody execution of his father generally ensured an openhanded response.

Daniel Drummond was about to take a decisive part in the king's cause, and his present excitement came from the knowledge that his king had made a request of him—a request embodying the trust King Charles II had in his subject, Sir Daniel Drummond. However, he did wonder how Henrietta would react to the news, and even more whether she would be able to undertake the tasks and responsibilities that would be laid upon her.

"So, Lady Drummond, how d'ye think ye'll like Madrid?" The astonishing question came from the earl, who was looking pinkly well fed and well imbibed, although as sartorially threadbare as his friend.

"I beg your pardon, my lord." The knife she was using to slice the apple tart slipped from her fingers to clatter on the pewter platter.

"I have not yet had the opportunity to speak of the journey to my wife, Hendon," Daniel said, greatly chagrined by his guest. " 'Twas only mentioned when I had audience with the king this morning."

"Oh, I crave pardon!" Hendon looked suitably confused. "Of course it was. Can't think what I was thinkin' of."

"Madrid?" Henrietta stared across the table at Daniel.

"His Majesty has asked that I go as ambassador to the king of Spain, to ask for funds to raise another army," he told her quietly. "But let us discuss it later."

"Aye, if you wish it." She lowered her eyes to her platter, pushing her tart aimlessly with a spoon while questions roiled in her head. It was this that had presumably caused Daniel's excitement. It would be a most hazardous journey; Spain was a wild and savage land, was it not? Yet with a court governed by the most rigid rules of etiquette. How could she possibly perform as an ambassador's wife? A comparatively short time ago, she had been racketing around the countryside in boy's clothes . . . It was an utterly terrifying prospect.

She stood up suddenly. "Pray excuse me, gentlemen. I will leave you to your wine as I have some household matters to attend to."

Daniel rose and went to open the door for her. "We will talk about it in full very shortly," he said softly. "But one matter you might deal with without delay . . ."

"Yes?"

"You might instruct Lizzie that if she wishes to discover what is happening on the other side of a door, it is perfectly simple to knock upon that door."

For a second, she forgot the issue of Madrid and her eyes danced mischievously. "But 'tis not nearly so amusing, Daniel."

He schooled his features sternly. "Listening at keyholes is devious and unprincipled, Harry."

"But on occasion useful," she pointed out.

"Nevertheless, if I find Lizzie engaged in such an activity again, in your company or no, she is going to have a very uncomfortable time of it. So if you wish to spare her some trouble, I suggest you make certain she understands that."

Henrietta frowned. "Why must I tell her? Surely you should do so."

He shook his head, and a smile twitched at the corners of his mouth. "I strongly suspect she believes you do not disapprove of such behavior, and I would have you disabuse her of that notion without delay."

She looked so conscience-stricken that his smile found full expression. "My elf, you have simply to explain to Lizzie that, unlike you as a child, she has no need to develop questionable habits."

She nodded ruefully. "Y'are right, of course. And I did laugh. I will talk to her."

"We will talk about this other matter as soon as our guests have departed," he promised, tipping her chin with a warm forefinger. "There is no reason to be uneasy."

"No," she said, sounding unconvinced. "I will send Hilde to clear the table."

Half an hour later, she was sitting pensively beside the open window in her bedchamber, overlooking the pretty walled garden, Lizzie and Nan playing cat's cradle on the floor at her feet, when Daniel came in.

"Have they gone?"

"Aye," he said easily, bending to examine the elaborate structure his daughters were creating. "Take that strand, Nan, then you will have it."

She beamed up at him, following the advice, and Lizzie cast him a quick, speculative glance from under her lashes. Clearly, Henrietta had had her little chat. He pinched the child's cheek, shaking his head in gentle admonition, and she smiled tentatively.

"I wish to talk to Harry," he said, having long given up his prohibition on the girls' use of the nickname. "Run along to Mistress Kierston now."

"Oh, but Daddy, if we go to the schoolroom she will make us go to church with her," protested Lizzie. "She always goes to the evening service and it is so drear."

"And we cannot understand anything that is said," Nan piped up.

"But 'tis good for the soul," he teased. "And yours are in great need of redemption. Off with you."

They went without further overt protest, although with muttered grumbles and dragging feet.

"Will we take them to Madrid?" Henrietta asked, playing with the silk fringe of her shawl.

Daniel shook his head. "Nay, I'd not expose them to the hazards of the journey, or of the climate." Dropping to one knee beside her chair, he laid a hand over her restlessly plaiting fingers. "Or you, elf, if ye'd rather not."

"Oh, how could you suggest such a thing?" she cried, springing to her feet. "You would leave me behind to attend church with Mistress Kierston while you amuse yourself with the grandees at the Spanish court!"

Laughing, he rose from his knees. "Nay, I would not. But do you truly wish to accompany me?"

"Not if you do not wish me to," she declared, tossing her head. "I had thought married people essayed most dangers together, but if you think otherwise . . . Oh!" This piece of mock-dignified mischief ended on a squawk as Daniel caught her by the waist, dumping her unceremoniously onto the poster bed.

"You are sailing in very dangerous waters," he informed her pleasantly, pinning her hands on either side of her head and kneeling astride her as she wriggled helplessly. "I should have a care, if I were you."

She became quite still, summoning an expression of the utmost docility, except that her eyes burned with a quite different message, and her tongue flickered over her lips.

"Merciful heaven," Daniel whispered, "sometimes I wonder what happened to the little innocent I married."

"Do you?" she whispered in return. "Would you have her back?"

He shook his head. "Only in play, love."

"Shall we play now?"

He moved his hands to her bodice, unlacing it carefully, his eyes never leaving her face. "If you've a mind to."

"What shall we play?" She lay very still as he slowly bared her breasts and the cool evening breeze fingered the softly mounded flesh, caressing her nipples as they hardened in growing excitement.

"I would have a Spanish gypsy in my bed," he said, moving his hands to unpin her hair, combing it with his fingers, tossing the thick silken mass over the pillow, where it lay fanned around the small face. "A bare-breasted, tangle-haired Spanish gypsy who will pluck wild enchantment from the strings of her guitar."

"And weave bewitchment as she dances." A dreamy, unfocused glow appeared in the brown eyes. Her hands moved to her breasts, stroking delicately. Daniel moved away from her, his gaze fixed upon her hands, upon the proud, sensual flesh that she was offering with every loving touch of her fingers. Slowly, she stood up, her gown opened to her waist, her hair pouring over her shoulders, seduction in her eyes and softly parted lips.

She picked up the five-stringed guitar resting on the window seat and cradled it, feeling the smooth, cold wood against her breasts as if it had life, so exquisitely tuned were her senses. Her head bent as she struck a chord, and then another. Music rippled from her fingers; it was indeed magic music, sometimes wickedly inviting, sometimes aching with the need for something unknown, the vague yearnings of the soul and the flesh. Then abruptly her mood seemed to change. Her fingers moved with amazing speed, filling the room with a tripping, trilling melody that set the toes tapping and brought an involuntary chuckle of delight from Daniel. She threw back her head and laughed joyously. Setting aside the instrument, she sprang to her feet, kicking off her shoes, twirling, her hair and skirts swirling, the creamy swell of her breasts somehow mischievously sensual. The tune she had just played bubbled from her lips as she danced for him, a wild, exotic dance of promise, moving ever faster until she was nothing but a whirl of corn silk and turquoise linen and he thought she would dissolve in motion. But she slowed finally, sinking gracefully to the floor, hands outstretched toward him, head tilted as an impish smile played over her lips and she invited his applause.

"God's grace," he murmured, taking her hands and drawing her up against his length. Cupping the curve of her cheek, he kissed her mouth, his other hand resting on her bosom against the impatient jarring of her heart. She moaned softly, moving against him as if the passion exemplified by her dance must now find another outlet. She was fumbling with her opened gown, pushing it off her body, and he drew back slowly.

"Yes," he said on a husky throb, "take your clothes off for me."

She did so as if she were still the dancing gypsy, but her movements now were slow and sinuous, infused with erotic promise so that his breath caught in his throat and the blood pounded hotly in his veins. When she was naked, he reached for her, reveling in the feel of her bare skin, the planes and contours of her body, slipping beneath his hands; but she was making urgent demand of him, in thrall to the passionate mood she had created, now slave to her own creation, clinging to him, rubbing herself against the hard shaft pressing through his buckskin britches as her teeth nipped his mouth and she sucked on his lower lip as if it were a ripe plum.

Daniel gloried in this abandonment that made her supremely responsive to his lightest touch, the merest brush of a fingertip, the dewy caress of his tongue. It was his turn now to play the instrument, and he played upon her with the delicacy she had used with the guitar, drawing the high notes of perfection from her so that she shuddered on the peak again, and yet again, and he held back from his own mountaintop all the better to enjoy hers. But there came the moment when restraint was no longer possible and he kicked free of his britches, pushing her back onto the edge of the bed, standing over her to raise her legs, fitting her to him. Her legs curled around his hips, her toes kneading his buttocks as the muscles tightened, driving him deep within her center.

Looking down upon her as she lay, the very image of a wanton, arms stretched above her head, breasts flattened against her ribs, hips lifting rhythmically with his movements, he was suffused with a wondrous tenderness. Her eyes were closed, her lips slightly parted, a faint sheen of perspiration misted her skin, then her eyelids fluttered open and she smiled radiantly up at him as the glory filled her. He was lost instantly, falling forward to gather her against him, and her hands stroked his back while the intense wave of pleasure curled, crashed, and finally receded, returning him to the world again.

"I do envy you, Harry," Julia Morris said wistfully the next morning. The girls were perfect foils for each other. Where Henrietta was small, Julia was tall and Junoesque in stature; where one was fair and white-skinned, the other was dark and olive-skinned; but they were much of an age and the best of friends.

"Why would you?" Henrietta asked, going to close the casement as a sudden squall blew in off the sea, darkening the sky and sending a shower of fat raindrops plopping to the ground. She had never had a girl friend before, had never experienced the luxury of sharing confidences with any but Will, and men were different. The instant liking that had sprung up between herself and Julia was one of the major sources of her present contentment, and was viewed with great approval by both Daniel and Lord and Lady Morris, who, like so many, had chosen exile and poverty when they had followed their sovereign.

"I would be married," Julia now said, plying her needle on her tambour frame with great diligence. "Ye have so much freedom, Harry. You can order your life as you wish and there's no one to say you nay."

Henrietta smiled slightly. " 'Tis not entirely the case. But y'are right, Julie, 'tis very pleasant being married for a lot of reasons.'' Memories of the previous evening glowed warm in her mind, but those she would not share, not even with Julia.

''And y'are going to Madrid,'' Julia continued, looking up from her embroidery. ''It is such an adventure! And I must stay here and be dutiful, and practice fine sewing.'' She grimaced in disgust. ''You do not have to sew.''

Harry laughed. ''That is because I do not know how to.''

''Yet you found a husband,'' her friend declared unarguably. ''But if I try to tell that to madam, my mother, she says she will give me a strong purge to rid me of ill humor.''

''I trust you have not told her how I met Daniel?'' Harry shuddered slightly at the thought of the stiffly correct Lady Morris hearing such a scandalous tale.

Julia went into a peal of laughter. ''Do not be absurd, Harry. She would never believe it. She thinks Sir Daniel far too respectable.''

Harry's toes curled within her leather pumps at the thought of just how unrespectable—and unrespectful—her husband was capable of being. The sound of the great brass knocker interrupted this delicious musing. ''Whoever could that be? I am not expecting anyone, and Daniel is at court.'' Then she froze, listening to very familiar tones. With a squeal of joy, she flew to the parlor door, exploding into the hall. ''Will . . . 'tis Will. Whatever do you do here?''

''Lord, Harry, give a man a chance,'' Will protested as he found his arms full of Henrietta.

'' 'Tis raining cats and dogs, love. Let us get in.''

She had not seen Daniel behind Will, and now stepped back, laughing. ''Where did you find him?''

''In the street.'' Daniel shook rain off his cloak as he came into the hall. ''He was coming in search of us.''

''So I should hope.'' Taking Will's arm, she pulled him toward the parlor. ''You must stay with us . . . must he not, Daniel?''

Will began to demur, then the words died as he saw

the occupant of the parlor. Julia smiled shyly and curtsied.

''Oh, Julie, this is my dear friend Will, who has come to The Hague,'' Harry burbled excitedly. ''Only he has come just as we are to go to Madrid.''

''Madrid!'' Will took his eyes off Julia for a minute. ''How is that?''

''All in good time,'' Daniel said, injecting some order into the proceedings. ''Allow me to perform introductions correctly, since Harry appears to have lost her wits . . . Mistress Julia Morris, Master Will Osbert.''

''How d'ye do.'' Will bowed, blushing to the roots of his fiery hair. ''I am honored, mistress.''

''Oh, do not be so formal,'' Henrietta instructed with a dismissive wave. ''Julie is quite my best friend, after you, so you must not stand on ceremony with each other.''

''A glass of canary, Will, or d'ye prefer ale?'' Daniel's calm offer gave Will the opportunity to recover himself. ''Julia, you prefer sherry, I know. Henrietta, would you fetch ale from the kitchen, please? And had you better not tell the cook we have extra guests?''

''Oh, I cannot stay for dinner,'' Julia said, flustered.

''Whyever not?'' Harry demanded, flinging her arms impulsively around Will, hugging him again. ''You always do.''

Julia was saved from response by the precipitate opening of the door. ''Harry, Mistress Kierston has the headache and says she will not come down for dinner.'' Lizzie and Nan tumbled into the room, shining-eyed at the prospect of their governess's absence upon her sickbed, and then both stopped dead at the sight of their stepmother embracing a strange man. ''Who's that?'' Nan blurted the question her sister's greater age and experience had caused her to swallow.

''I beg your pardon?'' Daniel said ominously.

''Oh, she did not mean to be impolite,'' Henrietta said. ''Did you, Nan?'' Nan shook her head vigorously, and her thumb disappeared into her mouth. Daniel automatically removed the thumb before turning with a resigned sigh to the sideboard and the wine decanter.

"This is my friend Will," Henrietta said, taking the girls by the hands and drawing them forward. "Will, this is Lizzie, and this is Nan."

Will smiled in friendly fashion at Harry's stepdaughters, who regarded him with considerable interest. "Harry told us all about you," Lizzie said, remembering her curtsy somewhat belatedly.

"Oh." Will glanced uneasily at Harry. "And what did she tell you?"

"Oh, all sorts of things . . . about all the scrapes you both used to get into." Lizzie warmed to her theme. "About the time when you accident'ly shot the squire with your catapult and—"

"Enough!" Will exclaimed, torn between laughter at this ingenuous recitation and embarrassment at the audience. "Harry, you had no right."

Henrietta shrugged and winked at Julia, who seemed to have recovered from her shyness with the arrival of the children and was laughing as heartily as the rest of them. "It made a good bedtime story. Lizzie, go to the kitchen and tell Cook that we have two extra guests for dinner, and bring a pitcher of ale back with you." Lizzie scampered off importantly, and she turned to Nan. "Would you go and ask Mistress Kierston if she would like a tray in her chamber? Perhaps she would like some broth, or a tisane."

Having disposed of both children and her own errands in satisfactory fashion, she accepted a glass of canary from Daniel and sat on the broad window seat. "I cannot believe y'are really here, Will. What has brought you?"

He shook his head, frowning at her, and did not immediately answer her question. "Y'are different, Harry. Not completely, of course, but . . . I do not know what it is." He shook his head again. "Just since the time in London, you have changed . . . Mayhap 'tis because y'are a mother." He nodded this time, as if certain he had hit upon the solution to the riddle.

Daniel hid his smile, then caught the knowing glint in his wife's eye and turned away hastily. Let Will believe what he wished.

"Shall I pour the ale, Daddy?" Lizzie came in, staggering under the weight of a brimming pitcher.

"I think it might be safer if you held the tankard for me and I poured," he suggested diplomatically. " 'Tis rather heavy for such a little scrap."

"I'm not a scrap!" the child protested, laughing. "I'm almost as tall as Harry."

"Who is most definitely not a scrap," announced the lady in question. "And don't you dare disagree, Daniel."

"I don't," he said, chuckling. "Y'are far too fierce."

"Aye, that she is, on occasion," agreed Will. "Have you not found it so, mistress . . ." He coughed, blushed anew. "I mean, Julia?"

Julia shook her head in laughing confusion. "Nay, I have not."

"Dinner is ready." Nan popped into the room. "And Mistress Kierston says she would like some broth, please, and I do not think we will be able to have any lessons this afternoon."

"What a dreadful prospect," murmured Daniel, shooing them out of the parlor and into the dining room next door. "You must be quite desolated."

They giggled delightedly at this absurdity. Nan fetched the cushion, without which her nose barely topped the table, and Daniel lifted her onto her chair. Lizzie hitched herself up and looked expectantly around the table, waiting for the entertainment of adult conversation to begin.

"So, Will, what brings you to The Hague?" Henrietta asked again. "Is all well at home?"

"Aye." He skewered a mouthful of oyster-stuffed capon. "But 'tis wretchedly dismal. There's no music allowed, not even in church, and every man goes in fear of his neighbor. It takes but one hint that a man is not truly Godfearing and the preacher has him held up to ridicule and public penitence the next Sunday."

"'Tis as bad as church here, then," Lizzie put in. "That is dreadfully drear also, and you cannot understand what is being said."

"You've a quick tongue, little maid," Will said, laughing. "But I think ye'd find the climate at home harsher than here."

"Have you come to aid the king?" Daniel asked, shushing Lizzie with a swift gesture as her mouth opened eagerly to respond to Will's statement. A degree of license could be permitted around the family dinner table, but in company children should generally be seen and not heard.

Will nodded vigorously, taking a deep draught of his wine. "The Scots will fight for him as soon as he has an army and comes to Scotland at its head. We will defeat Cromwell and his New Model yet."

"That is why we go to Madrid," Henrietta said. "Daniel goes as His Majesty's ambassador to the king of Spain to ask for funds to raise an army."

"I wish we could go too," Lizzie bewailed.

"And I also," said Julia. "Such an adventure!"

"Wouldn't it be," agreed Will, meeting her eyes across the table.

Henrietta intercepted the shared glance and her jaw dropped in surprise. She looked at Daniel, but he was cutting a recalcitrant piece of fowl for Nan and could not have noticed anything.

"Why do you not stay here while we are gone, Will?" she suggested thoughtfully. "There is plenty of room. It would be a good idea, do you not think, Daniel, to have someone to keep watch over things?"

"Why, certainly," he agreed readily. "But how does Will feel about sharing houseroom with two children and their governess?"

"He will not mind it in the least."

"Perhaps you should permit Will to answer for himself."

"Oh, do say you would not mind it," Lizzie pleaded, before the startled Will could reply. "We would be very, very good . . . not the least trouble, and we could all—''

''Elizabeth! If you insist upon interrupting, you must leave the table.''

She fell silent, but Will found himself subjected to two pairs of pleading eyes fixed upon his face. He scratched his freckled nose. ''I would not mind it in the least, but I could not impose on your hospitality in such fashion, sir.''

''Nonsense!'' Daniel said in the tone he had used to Lizzie.

''So there you are.'' Henrietta beamed around the table. ''You will live here while we are gone, and I'm sure you will make many friends.''

''I trust so,'' Will replied, looking at Julia.

Chapter 12

It seemed to Henrietta that she had been at sea all her life. Her body moved easily with the motion of the ship, the taste of salt was always upon her lips, and her hair was constantly tangled by the wind.

They had been storm tossed in the Bay of Biscay and she had been so sick she had wept for death. Daniel had wrapped her up and carried her on deck, where even the lashing wind and the drenching spray were preferable to the stuffy confines of the tiny cabin, where the floor would not keep still and her stomach slavishly followed its gyrations. For hours, she had shivered in his arms while he patiently coaxed brandy between her lips until enough had stayed down to provide a little warmth in the pit of her aching stomach. Eventually she had fallen asleep, waking six hours later, still in his arms, still on deck, to find herself starving hungry and the continued bucking and heaving of the vessel no longer in the least troublesome. Daniel, on the other hand, had been so stiff, frozen and cramped by his long vigil, that he could barely move.

Henrietta leaned her elbows on the port rail, lifting her face to the fresh breeze, finding it possible to smile at the recollection of that hideous experience.

"What is so amusing?" Daniel's light voice reached her, and she looked up at the quarterdeck, where he had been talking with the ship's master, an irascible Dutchman who required much diplomatic handling from his passengers.

"Nothing." She shook her head, still smiling, not about to shout for all to hear that she had been thinking of her husband's loving care and the smile had been not one of amusement but of warm contentment.

Daniel came down the ladder to the foredeck. "Y'are a fibber," he accused, administering an admonitory tap to her behind.

She laughed. "Maybe so, but I'll hold my own secrets."

"With a prosperous wind, we should make landfall by morning," Daniel said. "Once we have rounded the Straits of Gibralter, 'tis but a short sail to Málaga." The ship's master had refused to put in at Bilbao for them to disembark, insisting that his cargo was bound for Málaga, and if they had wished to disembark at Bilbao, they should have taken a ship with that destination. The fact that there had been no ship from Amsterdam sailing to that port at the time when they had to leave had fallen upon deaf ears, and there had been no inducement Daniel could offer to persuade him to change his mind. So they slogged along the coast of Portugal, through the Gulf of Cadiz, and were now headed for the Straits.

"And a long ride to Madrid," she said.

"Aye, but we'll take such rest as we need," he replied, gazing across the blue Mediterranean, sparkling under the May sun. They were hugging the coast of Spain as they approached the Straits and the sea was dotted with small craft, feluccas and fishing boats for the most part. "What the devil is that?" Daniel said suddenly as an unfamiliar shape rounded the Straits. His question was answered by a shout from the lookout in the mizzen top.

"Man-o'-war!" the cry rang out, and the ship came alive with scurrying figures. Daniel pounded up the ladder to the quarterdeck, where the captain, glass to his eye, was staring out to sea.

"What kind of man-of-war?" Daniel demanded.

"Turkish galley," the Dutchman said. "Under full sail. We'll never outrun her."

"Merciful heaven!" Henrietta arrived on the quarterdeck just in time to hear. "Shall we fight them off, sir?"

He ignored the question and instead bellowed for brandy. The flagon appeared immediately, and he drank deeply before handing it around the crew gathered on the quarterdeck.

"What the devil d'ye intend doing, man?" A corpulent figure, wig askew and coat unbuttoned, clambered up the ladder, a panting, red-faced lady at his heels. A bellicose merchant and his cowed wife, they were the only other passengers on the vessel. Daniel was studiously polite to them, but Henrietta had the lamentable tendency to burst into giggles when in their company.

"Oh my . . . oh my!" gasped Mistress Browning, fanning her heated face with her hand. "Oh, we are quite undone! We shall all be carried off for slaves!"

" 'Twill be a Turkish harem for you and me," Henrietta said with wicked relish, turning eyes wide with horrified innocence upon the lady, who seized the railing with a moan of terror.

"Your sense of humor is at times gravely misplaced," Daniel said in sharp rebuke, as Henrietta stuffed her fist into her mouth to keep from laughing aloud. "If it comes down to battle, we are ill equipped to beat them off."

"But our ship carries guns," moaned Mistress Browning.

"Sixty guns and two hundred crew," her husband snapped.

"But little enough ammunition," the Dutchman declared, wiping his brow with his spotted neckerchief.

"How should that be?" Henrietta lost all desire for mischief.

"We're carrying too much merchandise," Daniel informed her succinctly. "Our master in his wisdom decided there was no need to spare room for unprofitable cargo like gunpowder and shot."

"What will happen if they board us?"

"Your tasteless jest may well prove to be no jest," he said.

"We will surrender the cargo. Surely they will be satisfied with that." Master Browning was beginning to lose some of his high color and more than a little of his bluster.

"Goddammit! But I'll not lose my ship. 'Tis worth all of thirty thousand pounds!" swore the captain, taking another swig of brandy. "Give the men a tot, then clear the decks," he bellowed at the bosun. "We'll fight with what we've got. Good Dutchmen are more than a match for those heathens!"

"By its speed, it would appear to be well manned," said Daniel thoughtfully, staring across the expanse of blue water at the rapidly approaching vessel. "But we might bluff 'em."

"How so?" Henrietta asked the question a little hesitantly, unwilling to risk again the cutting edge of Daniel's tongue, for all that she was now obliged to admit its justice.

"With a show of strength." He turned to the ship's master. "Master Almaar, if the galley sees only a man-of-war, and no sign of booty, 'tis possible they will see no profit in a fight. If 'tis merchantmen they're after, they will go in search of other prey."

"Aye." The Dutchman nodded. "We'll run out the guns, muster the crew fully armed, clear the decks of all but cannon. Get the women below. There's no place for women on a man-o'-war, and if the heathens get a smell of 'em, we'll not carry the bluff through. You, too, sir." He waved dismissively at Master Browning. "Ye've the look of a merchant about ye . . . too soft by half."

The merchant huffed indignantly, but turned to the ladder, pushing his wailing wife ahead of him, muttering that he hadn't paid good money for passage just to fight for the protection of the captain's cargo, so he wouldn't lift a finger anyway.

"Fool," Daniel observed dispassionately. "Come, Henrietta, you must go to the cabin. I will fetch my sword and pistols, Master Almaar, and join you directly."

"Oh, but you cannot expect me to stay below while y'are in danger," Henrietta protested, pulling back on his hand as he took her own. "I will stay hidden behind the foc'sle."

"Sweet Jesus, Henrietta! When will you begin to take this seriously?" Daniel exclaimed, jerking her forward. "Those are Turks in an armed galley bearing down upon us, and they are not coming to pass the time of day!"

"No, I realize that. 'Tis for that reason that I would be with you," she said with what she considered perfect reasonableness.

Daniel did not trouble to reply. In the cabin, he fastened his sword belt, slung a bandolier across his shoulder, and thrust two pistols into his belt. Catching her chin as she sat disconsolately on the narrow cot that served them both as bed, he tipped up her face, saying with a teasing smile, "Sulking does not become you, elf." When her expression did not alter, he offered in placation, "It is not that I would not have you at my side, love, but if I am concerned for you, then I'll be of little help to Almaar."

"And if you are killed, then I daresay I shall be quite content to be a slave in a harem," she said, turning her head away from his capturing hand to hide her trembling lip.

"I do not think you are destined for such a fate," he said briskly, deciding he could spare no more time in attempted conciliation. "I will be back as soon as 'tis safe." He left the cabin, closing the door firmly. He took a step toward the companionway, then stopped, turning back to the cabin, frowning. He remembered Nottingham, and he remembered the king's execution. Reluctantly, he shot the outside bolt on the door.

Within, Henrietta heard the unmistakable grating sound and stared in disbelief. Tears of hurt and anger scalded her eyes. Leaping to her feet, she jumped the small space to the door and hammered on it with her fists, bellowing at the top of her voice.

On deck, Daniel found the ship stripped for action. Two hundred men, bristling with swords, knives, and pistols, lined the deck rails or stood at the ready beside the guns, rolled out, pointing their blunt muzzles at the approaching galley. Not a sign of softness showed, no hint of the bales of silk and cotton, the Venetian glass, the Dutch porcelain, the Flemish tapestries, that made up the vessel's rich cargo.

Daniel took up a place beside the master on the quarterdeck. When Almaar handed him his glass, he took it without a word, training it on the approaching galley. Under full sail it was a magnificent sight, water foaming beneath the curved prow. A hundred pairs of oars cleaved the water in rhythmic rise and fall, augmenting the power of the wind, and as the galley drew close the most foul stench wafted over the water, sullying the fresh, salt-tanged air of the open sea.

"God's death!" Daniel covered his mouth and nose, and the captain beside him spat over the rail.

" 'Tis the galley slaves. They're chained to the oars, never released, just hosed down when the reek becomes too much for the delicate noses of their masters." He called over his shoulder to the man at the wheel. "Bring her 'round into the wind, helmsman." The great ship swung slowly, head into the wind, so that the sails now flapped idly, and she came to a stop on the smooth water.

Below decks, Henrietta became aware of the change in motion as the floor beneath her rolled gently from side to side under the slap of the waves. Her fists ached from pounding the door, and her throat was hoarse with shouting, but she continued nevertheless, deaf to the voice of reason, almost beside herself with the passionate need to escape her imprisonment and see for herself what was happening on deck. Only by being there could she judge how best to help.

Then, miraculously, the bolt scraped, the door

opened, and an alarmed cabin boy stood there, staring wide-eyed at the tearful, distraught Henrietta.

"Oh, quick!" she said, her tears drying. "Ye must lend me your clothes. Here." Running to the sea chest, she drew out a leather bag, selecting a half crown, which she held out to the stunned lad. "Make haste."

He took the coin, turning it over in his hand, then shrugged. It was no business of his to question the whims of this crazy woman, and half a crown was half a crown. He took off his blue wool cap, heavy tarred jacket, and worsted britches, handing them to the impatient Henrietta, before taking himself off in his shirt and drawers.

Henrietta dressed rapidly. The lad could have been no more than twelve, but she still needed to secure the britches with string at her waist, and the bulky jacket swamped her slight figure. Her braided hair disappeared under the blue cap. She left her feet bare and crept from the cabin, up the companionway and out onto the deck, where all motion seemed suspended and a tense silence hung almost palpably over the scene. She found she was not in the least fearful as she slipped into the line of sailors at the deck rail. A quick glance upward satisfied her that Daniel was still standing, alive and healthy, at the captain's side, and for safety's sake she decided to remain on the main deck, where she could watch both him and the proceedings from a discreet distance.

The galley had come head-to-wind on the starboard side, and now swung gently in the breeze, great white sails flapping, oars still. On the high poop deck stood a group of men, bearded and swarthy, the breeze flapping the loose material of their baggy trousers, the sun sparking off the wickedly curving scimitars at their belts.

The wind shifted slightly and Henrietta choked as the dreadful stench wafted like a miasma over the deck where she stood. The men around her coughed, swore, covered their mouths and noses. For long minutes the two vessels and their crews and commanders assessed each other under the sun.

Then one of the Turks came to the rail of the poop deck and called up to Master Almaar in heavily accented English, the lingua franca of the sea. It was a demand for identification. The Dutchman returned answer that his was a Dutch man-of-war, patrolling the seas as protection for Dutch merchantmen. Silence greeted this; the men on the galley conferred.

"A gesture of goodwill on our part might serve us well at this point," Daniel remarked thoughtfully.

"Aye, 'tis a good notion." Master Almaar drew a pouch of tobacco from the pocket of his jerkin. The pouch was of intricately worked leather, the tobacco the finest Dutch. He walked to the edge of the quarterdeck, looked down on the main deck, scanning the crew until he made out the small figure of the cabin boy.

"Hey, lad. Come here!"

Henrietta did not realize it was she who was being addressed until her neighbor nudged her. "Eh, master wants ye, boy."

Her heart in her throat, she approached the ladder to the upper deck, keeping her cap low, her eyes on her feet.

"Take this and give it to the man with the gold chain," Almaar instructed, dropping the pouch at her feet. "Look lively, now."

"Come on, lad." The bosun stepped forward, swinging his rope's end. "Over the side with you."

Over the side! They were telling her to climb down the sickeningly unsteady rope ladder swinging against the ship's stern and drop onto the poop deck of the galley amongst all those savage barbarians with their dreadful knives. How could she possibly do such a thing? How could she possibly refuse without revealing her identity, and thus betraying everything?

Swallowing convulsively, she bent to pick up the pouch, stuffing it into the capacious pocket of the capacious jacket, and slunk to the ship's side, staring down at the frail ladder banging in the breeze. The rope's end stung her shoulder in rough encouragement, and she swung her leg over the rail, grabbed the coarse hemp of the ladder, and lowered herself onto it.

The deck so far below seemed to pitch and roll impossibly. It had not looked nearly this far down from the safety of the ship's deck, but swinging perilously on a frail piece of rope far above the limitless depths of the ocean was more terrifying than anything she could have imagined in her wildest flights of nightmare.

The ladder stopped a couple of feet from the deck. Closing her eyes tightly, Henrietta dropped, and the first sensation as solid wood cushioned her feet was one of the utmost relief. Until she looked up and found herself in a circle of grinning, dark-skinned, white-toothed men. She looked for the one with the gold chain and saw him standing a little apart. He was scrutinizing her with a strange expression in his eye. Dear God, surely he had not guessed? Her clothes so swamped her, there was no possible way of telling the shape beneath the ample folds. But what of her face? Her complexion? Surely she could pass for a mere boy not yet touched with the man's beard? Keeping her eyes down, she darted through the circle of men, holding out Almaar's gift.

Someone made a comment in a strange tongue, and they all laughed, but not unkindly it seemed. Emboldened, she risked a quick look up as she reached her goal. He took the pouch, examining it with interest, for the moment ignoring the messenger. The others gathered around and Henrietta looked about her more openly. She found herself gazing down into the galley from whence emanated the reek that seemed trapped in her nostrils now, like some noxious gas. All she could see were backs, gleaming, dark, sweat beaded. Most of the heads attached to the backs had fallen forward as if in exhaustion as they rested their oars in this moment of respite.

Anger and revulsion chased away fear and, for a split

second, caution. She turned away, and her eyes flashed at the man with the gold chain. The speculation on the swarthy face became pure interest. "Such a pretty boy," he said softly in her own tongue. "What a waste to make a sailor of you. 'Tis a life to coarsen such comeliness."

Laughter rose again. It had a strangely knowing quality, but Henrietta was completely bemused. She had no idea what the man could be talking about. He stepped forward, touching her cheek with a surprisingly delicate finger, tracing the curve of her jaw. "Such fine skin." He smiled, and it was a smile that made her shudder with that same revulsion, yet she did not know why. It was certainly not a threatening smile, yet she felt threatened.

"Stay with me," he said softly, his eyes lingering on her face with a look of longing. "Be my catamite and I promise you only luxury, ease, and comfort."

Henrietta shook her head violently, speechless at an invitation she did not understand. She knew only that she must get away. She turned from him and ran for the rope ladder. It held no terror to match the nameless one posed by the man behind her, and she sprang for the bottom rung with an agility that surprised her. She scrambled upward as speedily as if she had been doing such a thing from childhood, tumbling over the deck rail, panting, wild-eyed with shock and fear, to come face-to-face with an ashen Daniel.

He did not know when he realized exactly who it was down amongst the Turks. The knowledge seemed to seep into his bones as he stood watching the scene being played out below. He could hear nothing of what was said, could make little of the figure lost in that enormous jacket with the string holding up his britches. But the suspicion grew to become certainty. He stared, numb with terror as the galley's captain pawed her face, seemed to devour her with his eyes. If he had guessed her sex, they were all lost, and none more so than Daniel Drummond's wife.

How had it happened? He could not begin to piece

together the sequence of events that had led to her standing, quite unprotected, in the midst of hostile Turks who, if they realized what she was, would have no compunction in carrying her off as the spoils of war. And he dared not breathe a word to anyone of what he knew for fear an incautious gesture or exclamation would betray her; he must stand in his agony, his chest so tight with fear and tension he could not draw breath without pain.

When she broke away from the man and ran for the ladder, he could control himself no longer. An oath broke from his lips and his hand went to his pistol as he waited for them to pursue her. When they did not, Almaar turned to him with a laugh. "Wonder what they said to make him jump like that?" But Daniel was already on his way to the main deck, reaching the top of the ladder a minute before she tumbled over the rail.

Still he dared not say or do anything that would betray the presence of a woman on board. "The master wants you on the quarterdeck," he said as if in explanation of his presence. It seemed to satisfy the listening crew, who patted the cabin boy's back heartily and made jocular remarks about his coming up faster than he went down.

Henrietta kept her eyes on the ground and shook her head at them, unable to speak even had she wanted to. She followed Daniel up to the quarterdeck, but the master was exchanging a few more words with the master of the galley and did not immediately spare the lad a glance. Then guttural orders were shouted from below. Sheets and halyards creaked as the galley swung onto the port tack and the sails bellied. At another harsh command, a hundred pairs of oars lifted as one, cleaved the water as one, and the curved prow moved slowly away.

Master Almaar let his breath out on a long exhalation and turned with a smile to Daniel. "Odd's bones! I'd not willingly endure another half hour of that kind." His gaze fell on the lad at his passenger's side. "You did well,'' he said. ''But there's no need to look so whey-faced.''

Without a word, Daniel removed the blue cap from his wife's head. Almaar's mouth opened and closed in the manner of a landed fish. ''Quite so,'' Daniel said dryly, when it seemed that the master would remain bereft of speech for some considerable time. ''My reaction exactly.''

''Lady Drummond!'' Almaar breathed finally. ''How the devil . . . ?'' He fell silent again, shaking his head in disbelief. Then he looked at Daniel in horror, as if struck by a dreadful thought. ''I could not possibly have known, Sir Daniel. I . . . I thought she was the cabin boy . . . the clothes . . .''

Daniel nodded. '' 'Twas not your responsibility, Almaar. It was mine.''

Henrietta spoke up for the first time. ''Actually, I think it was mine.''

''Then the consequences are yours to bear,'' Daniel said gravely, his black eyes unreadable.

Henrietta nodded slowly. ''I only wished to see if I could be of help, but I'll not deny your right to be angry.''

''Angry!'' He passed a hand wearily over his eyes. ''I am beyond anger. Go below and give those appalling clothes back to whomever they belong.''

She went hurriedly, aware of a rustle of whispers as she crossed the deck, anxious for a few moments' solitude in which to review the extraordinary experience and prepare, if not a defense, then a position at least with which to face her husband.

Daniel became aware that Almaar was regarding him with something like compassion. He looked over the deck rail to where the rope ladder swung and considered Harry's perilous return journey. ''Jesus, Mary, and Joseph!'' he muttered.

Almaar coughed. ''Ye'd have to admit it was plucky. One false move and we'd all have been lost.''

Daniel gave a short, assenting laugh. She had certainly endured the unforeseen consequences of her impulse with customary courage, and the impulse had been born of that need she had to share in every aspect of his life, her complete inability to stand aside if she believed him threatened or in any way in need of her assistance. He had earlier thought her impulses motivated simply by a powerful sense of loyalty, but now he knew that love was the foundation. And being loved by Henrietta was a hazardous business, he decided, massaging his temples with thumb and forefinger. Hazardous, but for all that vastly rewarding.

He went down to the cabin. Henrietta was sitting on the cot, once more clad in her gown of russet linen with its demure lawn collar and full, beribboned sleeves. Her hair hung loose, massed to her shoulders, feathering around her face, in the fashion she knew he liked best. It was well nigh impossible to see in this demurely pretty girl the monkey of the rope ladder. She offered him a tentative smile, her eyes wider than ever.

He decided not to be seduced for the present and demanded curtly, "How did you get out of here?"

With a sigh, she dropped the penitent air and told him the tale. "And I paid the cabin boy half a crown for the use of his clothes," she said, as if ridding herself of the final confession.

"A gross overpayment, considering their quality and fit," he commented caustically, leaning against the door, studying her.

"It would have been perfectly all right, Daniel, if the captain hadn't sent me on that . . . that errand," she offered. "I would have just stood with the others until it was over. I had to know what was happening. You could not expect me to stay in safety while you were in danger."

"Could I not?" he asked rhetorically. "And what was *I* supposed to do while *you* were in danger?"

Her startled expression indicated that that aspect had not occurred to her. "Were you afeard?"

"Terrified."

She bit her lip unhappily. "I ask your pardon, Daniel. I would not frighten you deliberately. It was just that matters did not work out as they were supposed to."

"They frequently do not."

There didn't seem much else for her to say, Henrietta thought, plaiting her fingers in her lap while she waited for whatever unpleasantness was about to ensue. She did not deny Daniel's right to be punitive, but she did wish he would get it over with. When the silence seemed to have lasted an eternity, and he still stood against the door in frowning consideration, she took a deep breath. "What are you going to do, Daniel?"

"Do?" His eyebrows shot up in punctuation. "About what?"

"Oh, please do not be odious," she begged. "You know what I mean, but I cannot bear this dreadful anticipation. I have been frightened enough for one day."

"No more than you deserve," he responded, and her head drooped in defeat. "Ramshackle creature," he said. Her head shot up and she saw the laughter in his eyes.

"Oh, you were teasing me!" She sprang into his arms in one movement, burying her head against his chest. " 'Twas not kind to do so when I have been so afeard."

He stroked her hair and held her tightly as she clung to him with fierce need for the safety of his arms. He was able to lose the bitter taste of his own fear as he held the live, warm body.

"Daniel, what is a catamite?" The question was muffled against his chest and he did not think he could have heard aright.

"What is a what?"

She lifted her head, showing him curious brown eyes. "A catamite."

"Where on earth did you hear that word?" He stared down at her.

"The Turk," she said. "He wanted me to be one . . .

His, actually. I did not know what he meant, but I knew it was something horrid, just by the way he was looking at me."

"Good God! Was that why you suddenly ran like that?"

She nodded. "I couldn't help myself."

"Your disguise was amazingly convincing." His voice shook with suppressed laughter. He had been petrified that the Turks would guess her secret and instead . . . The laughter of relief rocked him and he fell onto the cot, tears running down his cheeks.

"Oh, what is so funny? What *is* a catamite?"

He sat up, wiping his eyes. "Sweet innocent, 'tis a young boy who serves a man in the bedchamber in the ways of a woman."

She gaped at him. "How could he do so?"

Daniel sighed and explained, and her eyes grew rounder. "My heavens," she said at the conclusion. "Is it not painful?"

"My love, I do not know," he replied. " 'Tis not a practice I have ever indulged. But those who do apparently enjoy it."

"Oh." She sucked in her lower lip thoughtfully. "It seems very strange when 'tis so pleasant between a man and a woman. But I suppose people are entitled to do what pleases them best."

"As long as it does not hurt others." A serious note found its way into his voice and she looked at him, reading his meaning correctly.

"I would not hurt you, love," she said. " 'Tis just that I cannot seem to master the need to be with you at such times. You may think I cannot be of help, but 'tis always possible I might be, so I have to be with you just in case."

It was such a simple statement, one that told the truth as he had come to accept it, and he could find no words of dispute. He would simply have to take that truth into account in the future, since he did not think he could cure her and locking doors upon her was clearly no solution. But God only knew into what trouble this unmastered need and rash impulse to be of service would plunge them both next time, if he failed to circumvent it.

Chapter 13

Madrid: a landlocked city of narrow, winding streets and wide squares; a hot, airless city of strange customs. Henrietta toiled up a steep street, a basket of figs and pomegranates on her arm. The June sun was hot and she hugged the shade of the lime-washed houses lining the street, wiping beads of perspiration from her brow with her sleeve. At the top of the hill, she stopped at a gate set into a high stone wall. Behind the gate lay a small courtyard shaded with a vine-covered trellis.

Daniel was sitting on a bench beneath an orange tree reading a sheaf of papers. He looked up as she came in and smiled. "What have you there?"

She crossed the courtyard, bending to receive his kiss. "Fruit from the market by the cathedral." She held out the basket for his inspection. " 'Twas so delicious-looking, I could not resist."

He leaned back, squinting up at her as she stood dappled by sun filtering through the trellis. "But was that what you were sent to buy?"

"How did you know?" She grinned ruefully.

"Because the señora has been complaining to me most volubly about your unreliable shopping habits," he told her. "Yesterday, she asked you to buy eggs and you came back with cheese. Today, she wishes for tomatoes for a sauce for dinner."

"But I did not have enough money for tomatoes as

well as the fruit," Henrietta pointed out logically. "We will eat figs and do without the sauce."

"You tell that to the señora."

"Oh, she will wail and wave her arms at me," Henrietta said. "And I am only trying to help her by doing the marketing."

"I think perhaps she would prefer to do without your help," Daniel said carefully. " 'Tis most frustrating when she has planned a certain dish and she can never be sure you will return with the necessary ingredients."

"I suppose so." She sighed, looking at her basket of produce. "But shopping is such pleasure here. I would never have enjoyed it so at home, or even in The Hague."

"Ah, Doña Drummond . . . Doña Drummond!" A dark-clad figure bustled from the stone house at the rear of the courtyard and hurried over to them.

With a conspiratorial grin at Daniel, Henrietta held out her basket. A stream of Spanish greeted the sight and Señora Alvara raised her hands in an appeal to the heavens. While the precise meaning of the words was beyond Henrietta's comprehension, the sense was perfectly clear. Daniel dug a coin out of his pocket and handed it to the wailing señora, who, with another heavenward gesture, ran out of the courtyard into the street in search of the necessary vegetable.

"Have a fig." Henrietta sat on the bench beside Daniel. "How was your morning?" She bit deep into the succulent flesh.

"It's hard to say . . . messy brat." He pulled his handkerchief from the pocket of his brown silk doublet and scrubbed trickling fig juice from her chin.

"I'm not messy." She wiggled away from this ignominious ministration. " 'Tis inevitable when they're so juicy. Why is it hard to say?"

Daniel frowned. "They are all so very polite and welcoming, yet I cannot get close to the king's chamberlain, without whose acceptance and patronage I will never have audience with King Philip. No one ever says anything in direct denial, but nothing happens. They smile, chat, are most hospitable, but avoid all serious subjects. I do not know whether it is because they do not know exactly how to treat the unofficial representative of a deposed king. There's nothing in the rules of protocol to cover such a position." He shook his head ruefully. " 'Tis also possible that they suspect the nature of my errand, and if King Philip is either unable or unwilling to oblige King Charles, they may feel it easier simply to prevent the request's being made."

"How frustrating," she said with true feeling. Henrietta had not been to court, since women were not welcomed at a man's court and she had not yet been received by the queen, so she could not attend at Her Majesty's side of the palace. But she had received visits from the wives of Daniel's acquaintances, visits that had to be returned punctiliously and had to follow certain rigidly prescribed rules of etiquette, so she understood well the kind of atmosphere Daniel was describing. "What are those papers?"

"Dispatches from The Hague." Daniel folded the documents he had been reading when she came into the courtyard and thrust them deep into the pocket of his doublet. "The messenger arrived this morning."

"From the king?"

"Aye."

"Well, what do they say?"

Daniel shook his head. "I cannot divulge the contents, elf. His Majesty commands that I keep them to myself."

"But I am your wife."

He tweaked her nose. "Not even my wife would persuade me to break the king's confidence. Anyway, they touch upon matters that will not interest you."

"How can you know that?" she demanded. "What interests you interests me, or d'ye think me too young and feebleminded to understand your weighty affairs?"

"Now you *are* being a foolish and importunate

child," Daniel chided unwisely. "I do not consider ye feebleminded, but y'are as yet inexperienced in matters of state and will find nothing of interest in the dispatches, even were I at liberty to divulge their contents."

Henrietta flushed indignantly and stubbornly persevered. "I know more than you think. Is it news of the Scots, or of the court at The Hague, or of England?"

Daniel regarded her gravely for a minute, then he stood up. "Did you not hear me aright, Henrietta?"

She followed him into the house and up to the shuttered bedchamber with its cool tiled floor and whitewashed walls, watching as he put the documents into the strongbox standing on the marquetry chest. "I cannot imagine what could be so secret that I cannot know of it."

Daniel simply shrugged. "We have been invited to an entertainment given by the Duke de Medina de las Torres this evening. Don Fuentes, the duke's secretary, presented me with the invitation this morning at court."

As he had hoped, the news diverted Henrietta from her grievance. " 'Tis the first social invitation we have received. Could it mean something important?"

"Perchance," he replied. "I certainly think we should go and see."

"What shall I wear?" She ran to the enormous clothes press. " 'Tis such a shame that we have only plain Puritan clothes when everyone here is so magnificent."

Daniel said nothing, simply watched her as she rummaged disconsolately through the sober-hued garments. Then her restless movements stilled.

"Whatever is this?" Wonderingly, she drew out a mass of cherry-striped silk and ivory taffeta. " 'Tis beautiful. Who does it belong to?"

"Well, it won't fit me," Daniel said solemnly. "And I do not know who else keeps their clothes in that press."

"Where did it come from?" she asked, quite unable

to respond to his teasing in the face of this amazing surprise.

"From the sempstress," he replied.

"Oh, Daniel, you know that is not what I mean." She shook out the folds. "Is it for me? Truly for me?"

"Try it on," he said. "The sempstress worked from one of your other gowns, but if there is need of alteration she can do it this afternoon."

The gown was a cherry-striped silk with a deep lace collar and matching lace frothing at the edges of the elbow-length, richly puffed sleeves adorned with cherry velvet bands and ribbon knots. The underskirt was of ivory taffeta, delicately embroidered with silver flowers. Henrietta had never owned such a magnificent garment.

Daniel nodded with satisfaction when she stood arrayed in her finery, twirling for his inspection. The fit was perfect and the color complimented her skin, hair, and eyes exactly as he had envisaged.

"It must have been monstrously expensive," she said with a worried frown. "And we do not have very much money."

"More than enough for a few new gowns," he reassured her. "You must select materials, and we will instruct the sempstress to make you some others."

"But what of you?" Still troubled, she regarded him, her head tilted to one side. " 'Tis hardly fair that I should have such wonderful new clothes and you should have to wear your old ones."

"Will I shame you?" he teased, then caught her hands as she drove a small fist into his midriff. "That is not the way I would be thanked. I would prefer a kiss."

She stood on tiptoe and planted a series of darting kisses on his mouth. "Is that enough, or would you like more?"

"More," he replied. "Many, many more."

Daniel watched her that night with pride in his eyes. The girlish prettiness was somehow enhanced by an air of confidence, exemplified in the way she held herself, in the way she moved, in the clear ease with which she was conversing, mingling in a society so vastly different from any she had known hitherto. In fact, he thought, it would not be too much of an exaggeration to call her beautiful tonight. The elegant gown set off her slight figure to perfection. Caught up high under her bosom, it fell open in soft, graceful folds to reveal the embroidered underskirt. High-heeled satin pumps displayed the turn of a dainty ankle, matched by the curve of her forearm, the fragility of her wrists emerging from the frothy lace at her sleeves. She wore her hair drawn back from her face, held in place with a circlet of creamy pearls, a matching necklace clasped at her throat. They had been his wedding gift to Nan, but he did not suffer the slightest pang at seeing them adorn Henrietta, so perfect were they for the pink and ivory of her skin, the rich glossy corn silk color of her hair. No, his child bride was become a most pleasing young woman, a wife in whom a man could justifiably take pride.

"Our gathering is much enriched by Doña Drummond's presence, Sir Daniel. She is a veritable jewel." The elaborate compliment came from one Don Alonzo Jerez, who bowed deeply, a vision himself in a scarlet satin doublet and wide petticoat britches, a profusion of diamond-studded Belgian lace at his wrists and throat.

"Forgive the conceit, Don Alonzo, but I must agree with you." Daniel returned the bow with matching depth. Don Alonzo Jerez had the ear of King Philip IV's chief chamberlain.

"Doña Teresa would like to visit your wife in the morning. I trust she will be receiving."

"She will be honored," Daniel said, and bowed again. Don Alonzo's wife was chamberlain to the queen and such a visit could only herald an invitation for Henrietta to attend upon Her Majesty. Maybe they were progressing in this elaborate dance of protocol, but he could not help a tiny stab of unease. For all her newfound beauty and confidence, Henrietta was still unsophisticated and unschooled in matters of diplomacy, and the queen's court was a hotbed of intrigue and gossip. He could not follow her there, so she would have to find her own path through the maze without his guidance. Daniel was not entirely sure she was ready to do so.

Henrietta, unaware as yet of the plans being made for her, was enjoying herself. She seemed to be receiving the most flattering attentions from men and women alike, the music was entrancing, and she seized eagerly upon the long-denied opportunity for dancing, her pleasure so clearly evident in her smile, the sparkle in her eyes, the lightness of her feet, that those in her vicinity basked in her enjoyment and found their own heightened.

"How much do you think she is in her husband's confidence, Doña Teresa?" The question came from a tall woman, gray hair hidden beneath a most delicate, jewel-encrusted mantilla, black eyes sharp in her painted face.

" 'Tis hard to say, but I understand he is a sensible man," replied the other, a plump lady whose eyes were no less sharp and face no less painted than her companion's.

"One who would not share state confidences with his young wife?" The marchioness of Aitona raised an eyebrow as she looked across the crowded room with its rich Persian carpets and cloth of gold hangings to where Sir Daniel Drummond stood in conversation. "He keeps a close eye on her, I think . . . and a fond one."

"She is young, and 'tis to be assumed still naive," said the other thoughtfully. "If there's affection between them, we may be able to work upon it . . . she will wish to be of service to her husband."

"Indeed," murmured the marchioness. "I understand dispatches arrived from The Hague this forenoon."

"And an envoy extraordinary is expected from the

English Parliament,'' mused Doña Teresa. ''I understand from the queen that His Majesty is most anxious to discover whether the court at The Hague has a reliable spy network in England. 'Twould be revealing to discover if the dispatches for The Hague contained information about the imminent arrival in Madrid of Parliament's envoy extraordinary.''

The marchioness simply nodded, her eyes on the slight figure under discussion. ''She's a taking little thing. The queen will find her pleasing, I think.''

''And useful.''

''And most useful, if we play it aright.''

It was well past midnight when Daniel moved across the still-thronged ballroom toward the doors standing open onto a balustraded terrace hanging over lush gardens, where fountains played and majestic elms lined the winding walks, the whole lit with flambeaux glowing under the star-filled velvet blackness of a southern sky.

Henrietta was standing at the edge of the terrace, a glass of Venetian crystal in her hand, her face upturned to her interlocuter, a young and most handsome grandee with shining brown eyes and a neat little beard. Daniel became suddenly aware of the shabbiness of his own clothes beside the silken, laced, and brocaded richness of Harry's admirer—and it was very clear he was an admirer. It was also very clear that Lady Drummond was greatly relishing the admiration as a delighted trill of laughter broke from her lips and she tapped her courtier's hand with her fan in flirtatious mock-rebuke.

Daniel stroked his chin pensively, deciding that he didn't care for his wife to play the coquette with anyone but himself. However, he was not about to act the jealous husband; it was far too demeaning a role. He made his way across the terrace toward her.

''It grows late, my dear wife,'' he said, bowing before her, taking her hand and raising it to his lips.

Henrietta looked thoroughly startled at such an unusual salute from her husband. ''I had not thought it so. Are you acquainted with Don Pedro Escobal? He has been amusing me most wonderfully with some very wicked stories." Her lips curved in an entrancing smile at Don Pedro. "May I introduce my husband, sir."

"Sir Daniel." The Spaniard bowed deeply. "I have heard much of you and am delighted to make your acquaintance at last. I must thank you for permitting me to enjoy your wife's company this evening."

"Did he permit it?" asked Henrietta, forgetting for an instant the punctiliousness of this society. "I had thought 'twas I who permitted it."

Daniel's lips twitched as he watched the young man search for an appropriate response to this unconventional declaration.

"You are too kind, Doña Drummond," Don Pedro said, bowing over her hand. "But 'tis even kinder of your husband to deprive himself of your company in order that others may enjoy it."

"Oh, bravo, sir!" Henrietta clapped her hands admiringly. "That was most neatly said."

"But I fear I must now take my wife away," Daniel said easily. " 'Tis time we made our farewells."

"Is he not the most handsome man?" Henrietta breathed as she walked off on her husband's arm.

"Tolerable," Daniel replied in an offhand fashion. "If you care for little beards and pointed chins."

"Daniel!" She stopped dead at the entrance to the reception room. "Y'are not jealous!"

"Of course not," he said loftily. "What an absurd idea."

She peeped up at him through her eyelashes. "Y'are!"

"Am not!" The black eyes danced at her. "You have too great a conceit of yourself, my child."

She touched her lips with her tongue. "I do not think so, sir. I have received a great many compliments this night."

" 'Tis the Spanish way," he said in airy dismissal. " 'Tis not to be taken seriously."

"Nay, I suppose not," she said in a small voice, looking down at her feet.

Instantly remorseful, Daniel patted her hand. "It was but in jest, love. Y'are looking radiant tonight; 'tis no wonder you have received compliments." When she made no response, but continued to walk with her eyes on her feet, he pulled her toward a secluded window embrasure, shielded by a richly hued tapestry where silver and azure thread mingled in an elaborate design. "I did not mean to hurt your feelings, elf. Surely you know that." Catching her chin in customary fashion, he tilted her face toward him. Her eyes were brimming with mischievous laughter.

"Wretch!" he scolded vigorously. "For a minute, I really believed I had upset you."

"You have but yourself to blame," she informed him, tossing her head.

He probably had, Daniel thought. There was a quality to this Henrietta he had not seen before. Then she put a hand on his arm and whispered, "He is not nearly so handsome as you."

"Oh, you do not have to spare my feelings," he said, tracing her mouth with his fingertip. "I am aware I cannot hold a candle to such youth and elegance."

Henrietta looked stricken. "How could you believe such a thing? Y'are a thousand times more elegant and handsome; and I do not care for callowness."

"I think you are going to have to prove to me that you prefer the graybeard to the youth," he said softly, holding her gaze until the deep velvety pools of her eyes seemed to engulf him.

"Let us go home at once." On this imperative statement, she turned and marched out of the embrasure, her skirt flowing gracefully around her, her heels clicking on the black-and-white marble floor, a purposeful tilt to her small head. "Come quickly," she commanded over her shoulder. "I do not wish to tarry with this demonstration and it cannot take place here."

"Indeed it cannot," he murmured, following her impetuous progress across the reception room. "But we must make our farewells in decent fashion."

"Oh, pah!" Nevertheless, she slowed, allowing him to take her arm and direct her toward their hosts.

He could feel the vibrating impatience in the hand resting on his arm, could hear it in her voice as she struggled to master her eagerness to be off, and responded with suitably leisured courtesy to the Duke and Duchess of Medina. At last, however, they were free to make the last curtsy, the last bow, and hasten into the warm night.

"I thought we would never get away." Henrietta breathed a sigh of relief and skipped on the cobbles. "Kiss me."

"Here? In the middle of the street?"

"Yes." She nodded vigorously. "'Twas you who created a powerful excitement with your talk of demonstrations."

"So I did." He lowered his mouth to hers, tasting the wine-sweetness of her lips, inhaling the delicate fragrance of her skin.

Abruptly, she took over what had been intended as a gentle salute, a mere preliminary to what would ensue in the bedchamber. Her tongue pushed insistently between his lips, her arms went around his neck, her hands riffling through his hair to palm his scalp, gripping his head tightly as her body moved passionately against his.

"What the devil are you doing?" He pulled back, his breathing ragged. "'Tis not the place for this."

There was a wildness in her eyes and she laughed, a gay and heedless laugh. "You would have me prove something to you. I will prove that passion for my graybeard husband transcends all caution. I would make love under the stars, husband. Now."

"Dear God," Daniel exclaimed under his breath. "'Tis the full moon!"

She laughed again, looking up to where the great golden round hung benevolently in the star-filled sky. "Maybe so. Let us go in here." She darted through a small gate leading into a darkened garden, quiet and still, heavy with the scents of honeysuckle, sweet basil, and roses. She came into his arms again, her hands moving intimately over his body, busy with the fastening of his britches, sliding within to caress him with deft strokes and assured touches. And all the while she kissed him, his throat, his chin, the corner of his mouth, his eyelids, fire-tipped kisses that heated his blood and drove all thoughts of caution from his head.

An arbor of rosebushes beckoned and they moved almost blindly to within its deep, scented darkness. Daniel drew her toward a carved wooden bench as she nibbled his ear, whispering to him, softly erotic. He was drowning in the warm, whispering, fragrant wonder of her. He sat down and she understood without words what he wanted of her, drawing up her skirts and petticoats as she stood in front of him, baring herself under the night's soft touch, so that he could run his hands down the creamy, gleaming length of thigh, over the soft roundness of her knees, up to play in the moon-washed, corn silk-colored tangle at the apex of her thighs, slipping between to feel the heated readiness of her. When he drew her down astride his lap, she took him within her self, tightening around him, willing him to become a part of her, part of her essence. Her knees held fast to his thighs and her body moved with a rhythmic vigor that carried them both, until she slowed, eased into a gentle, languorous motion that lapped them in a sensuous sea of delight. Daniel was content to leave the play to her direction. When he would have lifted her from him at the moment of climax, she placed her hands on his shoulders and held him tightly within, glorying in the throbbing pulsing of his release, until a cry broke from her and she fell forward to rest her lips against his forehead as the waves of joy broke over her.

"Mayhap we have made a son," she whispered, when she could draw breath again.

Daniel stroked her narrow back, feeling the fragility of her shoulder blades through the rich silk of her gown, feeling the warm flesh of her thighs pressed to his own. "I never seem to anticipate your impulses," he said ruefully. "And ye have more than a fair share, my elf."

She raised her head to look down at his face in the shadows. "Would ye not have had that happen?"

A finger of moonlight pierced the shadowy darkness, touching the planes of his face, sparking in the black depths of his eyes. "I'd prefer you to be safe at home when y'are with child," he said.

"Well, we cannot be nine months in this land," she said practically, "so I will be brought to bed at home."

He smiled, shaking his head slightly. "We can but wait and see. Lift up, now." He slipped his hands beneath her, raising her from his lap. "Naughty one. I wonder whose garden we have just made such shameless use of."

She laughed, smoothing down her skirts. "Not shameless use, but the best and most wonderful. I trust I have now set your mind at rest on the subject of graybeards."

"You have," he agreed, fastening his britches. "And I do not feel in the least like a graybeard. I do not think elders make reckless love to importunate young women in strangers' gardens."

"No, I am sure they do not." She slipped her hand in his. "Let us go home and do it again, just to prove to me that my husband lacks none of the energy of youth."

"You will need your sleep," he said. "I forgot to tell you that you may expect a visit from Doña Teresa Jerez this forenoon and you must be at your best."

"She is chamberlain to the queen, is she not?"

"Aye, and it can only help my mission if y'are accepted at that court," he replied. "If you have audience with Her Majesty, then I cannot be refused the same privilege with King Philip."

"I will do whatever is necessary to be accepted," she assured him as they reached their own house. "I will become a veritable Spanish lady."

* * *

She was rather too true to her word for Daniel's taste. He came into the bedchamber at mid-morning and stopped in horror. "What the devil are you doing, Henrietta? Take it off immediately."

"But why? All Spanish ladies paint, from the queen to the fisherman's wife. 'Tis surely only polite to adopt the same customs," she protested with seeming innocence, rubbing a little more vermilion on her cheekbones and patting chalk-white powder on her forehead.

"Take it off!" he ordered, revolted. "You look like a whore."

Henrietta pouted with her rouged lips. "Why do I look like a whore if the Spanish ladies do not?"

"Who said they do not? You, however, are my wife and I will not tolerate such a thing. Now, wash it off!"

"But you said I should do everything I can to be accepted at the queen's court . . . Ow, Daniel!" She squealed in shrill protest as he took her ear between finger and thumb and forced her inexorably to her feet. It occurred to her somewhat belatedly that her teasing had not fallen upon receptive ground as she found herself hauled thus unceremoniously across to where the ewer and basin stood on the marble-topped tiring table.

"If you will not wash if off yourself, then I will do it for you," he said grimly, still holding her by the ear while he scrubbed her face with his free hand and she spluttered and squirmed.

"I would have done it!" she cried when he finally ceased. "I was only jesting."

"I do not find it in the lest amusing," he snapped, dabbing at a patch of red he had missed. "Whatever possessed you to do such a thing? Seldom have I been more revolted."

"I only wished to see what it would look like," she said, aggrieved, rubbing her ear reproachfully. "I thought it funny, like a clown . . . There was no call to be so rough and vexed."

"For some reason you failed to convince me of the

humor of the situation,'' he commented tartly. ''The Lord knows, I'm no Puritan, but paint on women has always disgusted me. And on you . . .'' He shook his head, unable to describe what he had felt at the sight of her fresh, soft prettiness sullied by the red-and-white mask. ''I did not hurt you,'' he said as she continued to regard him reproachfully.

''You pulled my ear as if I were some scrubby urchin instead of a wife.''

Daniel laughed at this disconsolate yet undeniable statement. ''Come, I will kiss it better.''

She stood still as he brushed the offended feature with his lips, then squirmed away as his tongue darted within. ''Oh, you know I cannot bear it!'' She struggled in his hold as his tongue explored thoroughly, every contour and whorl, wickedly aware of every exquisitely sensitive spot.

''Oh, how could you be so unkind?'' she gasped when at last he released her.

''Unkind?'' he protested. ''I thought only to give you pleasure . . . and you know it does.''

She tried not to smile, but her lips curved despite her efforts. ''I cannot deny it, but 'tis a strange kind of pleasure.''

''Cry peace,'' he said softly, opening his arms to her.

She stepped into his embrace. ''I could not imagine not being at peace with you.''

''There is no reason why that should ever be,'' he said. ''We understand each other far too well, my elf.''

It was a statement they were both to remember in the weeks that followed.

Chapter 14

"A wise woman, my dear Doña Drummond, always ensures she knows and understands her husband's business." Her Catholic Majesty, the Queen of Spain, smiled with apparent benignity at the young woman. Her eyes, however, were hooded, the drooping eyelids touched with kohl, and the smile from rouged lips seemed to crack the red-and-white mask of her complexion.

Her Majesty was seated upon a pile of rich satin pillows on a dais under a lavishly embroidered canopy of state. The ladies of her court were also seated upon cushions, their proximity to the queen determined by rank. Henrietta had been bidden to take a cushion at the queen's feet. Sensible though she was of the honor done her, she was at a loss to understand why she should have been singled out for such gracious attention on only her second visit to the queen's court at the palace of Buen Retiro.

Doña Teresa Jerez fanned herself lazily and copied her queen's smile. "Indeed, Doña Drummond, it is one of those little secrets that women keep from their husbands. We permit men to think of us as empty-headed and unknowing of the truly important things in life—those matters that men like to consider purely the masculine province—but little do they know how many of their decisions are influenced by the quiet words, the gentle encouragements, the tactful maneuverings of their helpmeets.'' A delicate rustle of assenting laughter ran among the listeners grouped around the queen.

Henrietta found this doctrine rather appealing, yet she felt a little uncomfortable, almost as if, by listening and laughing with the rest, she was in some way being disloyal to Daniel. But that was absurd. '' 'Tis surely hard to know such business if one is not in one's husband's confidence,'' she ventured.

''Such innocence!'' exclaimed the marchioness of Aitona, popping a sugared almond between scarlet lips. ''Dear child, husbands do not share confidences in these affairs. It is for us to discover things for ourselves, and having done so to use that knowledge in our husbands' best interests.''

'' 'Tis a well-known fact, Doña Drummond, that men do not always know what is in their best interests,'' gently put in the queen. ''They do not always see the undercurrents. Your own husband, for instance . . .'' She paused to take a sip from a small silver cup of steaming, fragrant chocolate proffered by one of her ladies.

Henrietta stiffened involuntarily, waiting for the queen to continue, but strangely she did not, turning instead with a murmured comment to Doña Teresa.

The latter rose from her cushion, announcing, ''Her Majesty will retire.''

Henrietta rose to her feet with the rest, curtsying low as Her Catholic Majesty swept from the room accompanied by her chamberlain and several of her maids of honor.

''What did Her Majesty mean?'' Henrietta inquired of the marchioness of Aitona, who seemed to have been allotted the role of Lady Drummond's guide and mentor at these court functions. ''She was about to say something concerning my husband.''

The marchioness smiled and patted Henrietta's hand. ''Her Majesty has taken quite a fancy to you, my dear Doña Drummond. If she deigns to give you a little advice, you would do well to heed it.''

Henrietta nodded slowly. ''I would do so, madam,

if I could but be certain what the advice was. It seems Her Majesty talks in riddles."

"Not so. Let us walk a little in the gardens." The marchioness glided through the presence chamber where ladies remained chattering like so many bright-plumaged birds. Henrietta followed her down the wide sweep of stairs, through lines of bowing footmen, and out into the peaceful gardens that gave the palace its name. Fountains plashed softly into marble basins, ornamental lakes glistened like jewels set into the lush verdant grass, and great oaks offered shady and secluded walks.

The sun was hot and Henrietta's companion showed no hurry as they progressed far too slowly for the impatient and eager Lady Drummond in the direction of an orange grove. "I pray you, madam, unravel this mystery for me," Henrietta begged once they had attained this privy spot.

The marchioness sat upon a stone bench at the edge of a lily pond, carefully arranging her emerald taffeta skirts before patting the seat beside her in invitation. "Her Majesty simply meant, my dear, that affairs of state should be as much the domain of women as of men. Indeed, a woman who understands these things will be much beloved of her husband." She glanced shrewdly at Henrietta to see if the bait had been taken. The look of eager speculation in the girl's eyes boded well. "Of course," she continued casually, " 'tis often as well to keep the extent of our knowledge to ourselves, but simply to use it as it would best benefit our husbands."

"Forgive my stupidity, madam, but I do not see how one can use knowledge without revealing that one has it," Henrietta pointed out with her usual logic. "How could I be of assistance to my husband and thus earn his gratitude if I must keep close the means by which I do so?"

The child was not the simpleton they had thought her, reflected the marchioness, dabbing her upper lip with a lace-edged handkerchief whilst plying her fan vigorously. She picked her words carefully.

"In some cases," she said with a conspiratorial smile, "virtue must be its own reward, augmented, of course, by your husband's satisfaction in achieving his goals, even though he may be unaware that he owes his success to your intervention." She paused to allow the import of this to sink in before continuing almost casually, "At court, 'tis sometimes necessary to employ devious means to achieve one's object. One must know always who is the best person to approach, what approach will succeed with different people, and one must always have at hand certain bargaining counters." Again she paused to allow her listener time to absorb this, before continuing in the same level tones. "Sometimes people do not always realize that they must have these bargaining counters, and then they do not achieve their object."

Henrietta thought of Daniel and his continually frustrated efforts to gain audience with King Philip. Always he was faced with a warm, friendly, hospitable, utterly courteous wall of implicit denial. Was there something he should be doing, some card he should be playing, to unlock the deadlock? "Pray, be more explicit, madam," she requested. "I take it you refer to my husband's mission and his present inability to progress in that cause."

The marchioness sighed. "You are very direct, Doña Drummond. 'Tis not always wise to be so. One must move by side roads, speak with caution. Those who are meant to understand will do so." She rose from the bench. "The afternoon grows too warm for taking the air, my dear. You must be anxious to return to your house for the siesta."

Henrietta acquiesced in correct manner with this discreet closing of the subject. She had learned enough in the past weeks to realize that nothing would be gained by transgressing the rules of etiquette governing Spanish society. They returned to the palace and the marchioness, with punctilious courtesy, gave order that Doña Drummond's litter be summoned, then waited with her in the anteroom, making polite conversation.

When the footman appeared to announce her ladyship's conveyance, the marchioness took her hand. "I have enjoyed our little talk, Doña Drummond. You must miss your home in The Hague."

"A little," Henrietta admitted. "I miss my stepdaughters rather more. I wish they could have accompanied us."

"Yes, to be sure. It is always hard to leave one's family behind." The marchioness smiled brilliantly, but the experienced eyes were hard and calculating. "I am certain your husband must receive regular dispatches from The Hague. I trust they bring good news of his household."

"I do not think such domestic matters are referred to," Henrietta replied frankly. "My husband would have told me if there were such news." In the silence that greeted this artless statement, certain knowledge burst upon her. Dispatches from The Hague lay at the core of this strange part interrogation, part lesson that had been delivered this afternoon.

"Don Drummond does not share these dispatches with you?" gently questioned the marchioness. "Perhaps he considers their contents no concern of yours?"

"Perhaps," Henrietta agreed neutrally. " 'Tis not a subject we have discussed." The lie came easily and she kept her eyes down lest her interlocuter read the truth and the speculation they contained.

"Remember, my dear, that affairs of state are as much a wife's concern as they are a husband's," said the marchioness. "Your husband will certainly benefit from any interest you may take on his behalf."

Henrietta smiled vaguely, murmured a polite farewell, and seated herself in the litter, heaving a sigh of relief as the curtain fell shut, enclosing her in solitude as she was carried through the streets of Madrid by the four stalwart bearers.

Coach and horses were expensive to maintain and Daniel had early decided they were unnecessary. Mostly, he himself went about his business on foot, and Henrietta also whenever her errand was of an unofficial kind. But she could not pay social visits in such manner, so the litter and bearers were now always at her disposal and she was rapidly becoming accustomed to traveling in this style. It certainly granted her the privacy to think, and the thoughts now raced through her head, tumbled in confusion, before falling into a readable picture. Somebody was inordinately interested in the dispatches Daniel had received from The Hague . . . and Daniel was clearly not being forthcoming about the contents. If he would not tell her, it stood to reason that he would not tell anyone else.

But what did they contain that was of such interest? Whatever it was would unlock the door to the king's presence chamber. That much had been made crystal clear to Henrietta this day. Just as she had been told where, in the eyes of the queen's court, her own wifely duty lay.

In essence, she had been told to spy upon her husband. This unpleasant truth was in no wise mitigated by the benefits she had been told would accrue to Daniel from such an act. Yet some aspect of the doctrine imparted to her did appeal. She did resent being excluded from this area of her husband's life. He still thought her too young and inexperienced to understand the diplomatic complexities with which he daily wrestled, and the temptation to prove him wrong was more than great. She did feel that she could and should be of more service to him than that of simply playing her social role. Maybe it was time to demonstrate that she had both the understanding and the ability to take a larger part in this business. And, as always, when the opportunity presented itself to help him when she thought him in need, Henrietta could not master the urge to seize that opportunity.

Thoughtfully, she stepped out of the litter when the bearers set it down outside the high-walled courtyard of their lodging. Somehow she must use the knowledge she'd been given this afternoon to smooth Daniel's path, yet she must do so without betraying him. It was out of the question to deliver the contents of the dispatches to the queen without Daniel's permission, and he would definitely not give it. But once she had discovered what the dispatches contained, why could she not play her own devious game at court? If she could discover exactly what it was they wanted to know, then maybe she could feed them misinformation that would still act as the bargaining counter for Daniel. But she had to know the true contents before she could do that convincingly. And how was she to find out?

In the relative cool of the shuttered bedchamber, she thankfully removed her gown of turquoise satin and the stiff taffeta underskirt. While she enjoyed this new wardrobe, the rich elegance of court dress had its disadvantages in the heat of a Madrid summer, and the extraordinary fastidiousness of the Spanish nobility was easily explained. Their love of cleanliness had at first surprised Henrietta, who was so accustomed to the odors of unwashed bodies, occasionally overlaid with heavy perfumes, that she barely noticed. She had been used to bathing infrequently, but she had discovered the pleasures of following the example of her host country and now relished the sensation of clean skin and sweet-smelling hair. It was an example Daniel also followed and one she was determined they would carry with them when they returned home.

She hung her garments carefully in the clothes press and released her hair from its pins. The Spanish habit of sleeping through the hottest part of the day was also a custom she had adopted with enthusiasm. Going to the casement, she pushed open the shutters, resting her elbows on the broad stone sill as she looked down onto the somnolent, sun-drenched courtyard. The heat laved her breasts through the thin linen of her smock and struck upward from the hot stone of the sill. She closed her eyes, feeling the sun's warmth probing her lids, creating a red darkness that lulled her into an almost hypnotic trance. When arms banded her waist from behind, her heart jumped in shock.

''Sun worshiper,'' Daniel said with a chuckle, pushing aside her hair to nuzzle the soft, fragrant nape of her neck. "Come to bed."

"I'd like to make love under the sun," she said dreamily, turning into his arms. "To feel it on my bare skin."

He smiled. "Your wish is my command, madam. Let us first ensure the bare skin." Deftly, he unfastened the ribbon tie of her smock before catching the hem and lifting it up her body. "Raise your arms."

Henrietta giggled at the brisk, matter-of-fact instruction and complied, wriggling her head free of the folds of linen. "Now what?" She planted her hands on her hips and regarded him mischievously, her head on one side. "Am I to go outside like this?"

Daniel looked her up and down in a teasing appraisal before placing his hand on the top of her head and twirling her around so he could view her back in the same fashion.

"Do you like what you see, sir?" she inquired sweetly.

"Beggars can't be choosers," he observed solemnly.

"Why you . . . you . . ." Speechless, she spun on him, pummeling him with her small fists while he doubled over with laughter, making no attempt to defend himself until at last he caught her against him, pinning her arms at her sides, his hands flattening warmly against her bottom.

"What a humorless termagant I have taken to wife! Be still, now."

" 'Twas not in the least amusing," she declared with an attempt at lofty dignity. Unfortunately, lofty dignity and nakedness were not natural partners, she discovered, particularly when that nakedness was clasped so firmly to a powerful and fully clothed body. Her skin rippled where it touched the softness of silk, the cold silver hardness of a button. Her nipples peaked; her buttock muscles clenched involuntarily against the hands holding them. She felt amazingly vulnerable, but it was a heady sensation and not in the least alarming. She looked up into his face and saw in his eyes the recognition of what she was feeling. A dark eyebrow lifted quizzically, and a tremulous smile hovered on her lips in response.

'Well, now,'' he drawled softly, ''I seem to have discovered the way to tame a virago.'' Her tongue ran over her lips, but she said nothing. ''Fetch the pillows from the bed and put them on the floor by the window in the sun,'' he instructed, slowly taking his hands from her.

She obeyed in silence, her blood coursing swift with anticipation, the sweet juices of arousal beginning to flow. Then she stood by the makeshift bed, watching him undress.

He sat on the chair to pull off his boots. ''Lie down and close your eyes. Imagine y'are in the garden, lying naked and alone under the sun.''

She did as he said, closing her eyes, yielding herself to the warm air, the play of the sun fingering her skin as she shifted to catch it, the sensuous depths of the cushions beneath her. Her hands roamed slowly over her body, feeling the living heat of her skin, the shape of herself, the languid power of rising desire, and when those other hands joined her own in delicious exploration, she slipped into a dreamland of delight, where the mind held no sway and only the sensations of the flesh were of importance . . .

When she awoke, the sun was low in the sky and shadows lurked in the corners of the chamber. She stretched, lazy and languorous on the pillows, and her mouth curved in a smug smile of memory as she opened her eyes.

''You look like the cat with the cream,'' Daniel said with a chuckle from the chair, where he had been sitting watching her as the sun went down.

'' 'Tis how I feel.'' Still smiling, she rolled onto her side and propped herself on one elbow, examining him. He was once more in shirt and britches. ''Did you not sleep?''

He shook his head. ''Nay, the play that sent you to sleep merely served to refresh me, and I would not miss for a minute the enjoyment of such an entrancing sight.''

Her eye fell on the strongbox resting on the marquetry chest, and other memories pushed to the forefront of her mind. Perchance, in the soft glow of after-love, Daniel would be more responsive. She sat up on her cushions and regarded him speculatively. ''D'ye love me?''

A tiny frown appeared in his previously tender eyes. ''Why would you ask such a silly question, Harry?''

It was not encouraging, but having fixed upon this course she decided to pursue it regardless. ''Well, I do not see why, if you truly love me, you would not share with me what is in those dispatches.''

The love light died completely from the black eyes. ''We have had this discussion once. I do not care to repeat it.''

Henrietta uncurled herself from the cushions and came over to him. ''Please,'' she coaxed, bending to kiss his forehead. ''I *am* your wife and a part of you. 'Twould not be betraying the king's confidence to tell me.''

Daniel sighed and stood up, putting her from him. ''I do not wish to grow angry with you, Henrietta, but if you persist in this fashion I shall become so. I have said no, and I meant it. 'Tis past time you learned that I mean what I say, and I do not tolerate pestering.''

Henrietta flushed with annoyance. ''There is no need to talk to me as if I were Lizzie.''

''If you were Lizzie,'' Daniel said deliberately, ''there would be no need for me to say this. She is far too well schooled. Mayhap you should take a leaf from her book.'' He stalked to the door, then stopped and turned back to her, shaking his head ruefully. ''Oh, come now, sweetheart, let us not quarrel. 'Tis the last thing I wish to do.''

''I do not wish to either,'' she said with perfect truth, cuddling into his arms. '' 'Twas only that I thought . . . Oh, well, never mind. We will not talk of it further.''

Daniel accepted this apparent compliance without question. He kissed her and told her to hurry with her dressing as they were expected at the Prada for a reception. "I've a powerful thirst for that Rioja I acquired from the wine merchant last week. I'll go down to the cellar and fetch up a bottle." So saying, he left the chamber, closing the door after him.

Henrietta reached absently for her discarded smock, slipping it over her head, tying the ribbon, flicking her hair free of the collar, a preoccupied frown drawing her fair eyebrows together. She looked again at the strongbox and her feet seemed to take her across the room without order from her brain. Slowly, she lifted the lid. It was not locked. Daniel only locked it when they were traveling, and, besides, there were only themselves and the señora, who knew no English, in this house. The crisp white parchment lay at the bottom of the box, the royal seal imprinted in wax. It would take but a second to apprise herself of the contents, then she could play her own little game and outwit the Spaniards who were so intent on outwitting her. And then, when Daniel had achieved his object, she would tell him the whole and he would count this little trespass as naught. And he would surely realize that she could be taken into his confidence in all matters, and could be trusted to behave with skill and care in the trickiest of situations.

Slowly, slowly, her hand went into the box, hovered over the parchment, closed suddenly over it, and lifted it clear. Feverishly, she opened the sheet, which crackled under her fingers, and gazed upon the hard, clear penmanship flowing over the paper.

The door opened behind her. She whirled, guilt and confusion flooding her cheeks with scarlet. Daniel stood in the doorway, a bottle and glasses in his hands, utter incredulity on his face. Then the incredulity vanished, to be replaced with a look of cold disgust that started a deep, trembling chill in the pit of her stomach. She tried to say something . . . anything . . . but her throat seemed to have closed and she could do nothing but stand there with the incriminating parchment between her hands.

He put the bottle and glasses on a side table and crossed the room, his boots clicking on the tiled floor. Without a word, he held out his hand, snapped finger and thumb imperatively. She held out the document. He took it, replaced it in the strongbox, and locked the box, pocketing the key. Throughout, his expression remained the same and the chill in her stomach threatened to overwhelm her. But he turned from her, poured wine, and began to dress in the formal garb suitable for an evening at the Prada. In silence, Henrietta did the same.

She was to remember that evening for the rest of her life. It was a memory that came to her whenever the hour was dark and the spirit low, inevitable conditions on occasion. She remembered it mostly for the quality of the silence. Even in the thronged palace, where the lilting strains of musicians and the constant rise and fall of voices provided a background of continual sound, she heard only her husband's absolute silence. Not a word had he spoken to her and whenever she felt his eyes upon her they held that same cold disgust. It was a look she had never encountered before, from anyone, and to have it directed at her by that loving, tender, humorous man, who in conflict had never shown her anything less than understanding and anything more than the occasional flash of annoyance, cut her with a hurt and shame so deep she felt as if she were bleeding from her soul.

Somehow, she managed to talk, to smile, to move as if she were not impaled by dread and shame. The magnitude of her error increased the more she thought of it, and she began to see herself through Daniel's eyes: poking, prying, refusing to acknowledge his right to privacy, refusing to accept that for him that privacy was a matter of honor, wanting only to satisfy her own gratuitous curiosity in whatever fashion conveniently presented itself. It was an appalling picture, yet she had not intended deception of that despicable kind.

She had intended nothing but good, had transgressed, she thought, only temporarily and with good cause—a cause that Daniel would acknowledge willingly once all that was supposed to happen had happened. But now there was to be no good conclusion to justify the offense, and she stood condemned by her own hand and judged in her husband's silence.

It was barely midnight when she felt him come up behind her as she stood listening to an enthusiastic discussion about an upcoming feast of the bulls.

"Have you attended a feast, Doña Drummond?"

"Not yet, Don Alva," she replied, hearing her voice as quite level although her stomach seemed to be sinking into the toes of her dainty satin pumps as Daniel appeared at her shoulder. "But I understand 'tis a most magnificent sight." She looked up at Daniel, her smile brittle, and said, "I do trust we will still be in Madrid on the next occasion."

"Possibly," he replied, barely looking at her before directing some casual comment to one of the members of the circle. Wretchedly, Henrietta started to move away, but his voice, cold and level, arrested her. " 'Tis time we made our farewells."

After a seeming eternity of smiling, curtsying, and murmuring the polite but necessary inanities, Henrietta was enclosed in the litter, Daniel, as was his custom, walking beside as she was carried home. Surely he must say something when they reached the house. Say something . . . do something. In her innocence, she thought it didn't matter what he said or did, so long as this dreadful, condemnatory silence was broken.

The litter halted and she stepped out. Daniel held open the gate of the courtyard and she brushed past him, wondering sickly if she imagined his recoil as her arm touched his sleeve and her skirt swished against his knee. Inside the small, candlelit hall, he lit a carrying candle for her from the bigger one on the marble-topped table. She took it and went ahead of him up the stairs to the bedchamber. It was only as she reached the head of the stairs that she realized Daniel had not followed her.

The casements stood open to the warm night breezes carrying the fragrance of hibiscus and lavender from surrounding gardens. The pillows that had formed the love couch of the afternoon had been replaced on the bed, presumably by the señora when she tidied up after they left for the Prada. The memory of the sensual glories of the afternoon brought an agonizing wrench. It seemed to her in this dread wasteland to have happened in another time, another place, to another person.

She undressed, listening fearfully for the sound of Daniel's footstep on the stair. The door opened at last as she stood in her smock, brushing her hair with ritual, repetitive strokes that faltered as the door closed gently. She remained with her back to the room, yet hearing his every move in the continued silence as he took off his cloak, his sword belt, his wine-red satin doublet with the sleeves slashed to reveal the fine lawn of his shirt.

Daniel sat down in the armless chair beside the bed, looking at the slight figure, who remained with averted back, again rhythmically brushing the gleaming corn silk-colored cascade as if the normality of the act would restore the world to its accustomed course.

"Henrietta, come here."

The quiet command crashed into the silence she had begun to imagine would never be broken. Her heart jolted against her ribcage, and she turned slowly to face him. He presented such a picture of grim purpose, sitting in his shirtsleeves, arms folded across his chest, that the painful pounding of her heart increased and her stomach churned.

"Why?" she heard herself ask tremulously.

"Come here."

Hesitantly, she went to stand in front of him. He leaned back in the chair and closed his eyes for a minute as if in utter weariness. "I do not know what to do," he said in a near-expressionless tone. "I have been racking my brains all evening to decide upon the appropriate course of action for a man whose wife creeps behind his back to pry into his most private affairs, who sees nothing repugnant in ransacking his possessions, possessions he has expressly forbidden her to touch, who will not accept reasons of honor—"

"Please," she interrupted despairingly. " 'Twas not like that."

"Do you deny, then, that I walked in here and found you holding my private papers?" he demanded, cold and harsh, before she could continue. "Do you deny, then, that I took those same papers from you?"

Henrietta shook her head. What was the point of explanation when the act itself was for this man so clearly inexcusable and unpardonable?

"For some reason, I had believed it impossible that you would resort in my household to the duplicitous, dishonorable tricks of your childhood, but I should have realized, of course, that such ingrained habits of dishonesty die hard."

Henrietta began to weep helplessly, unable to stop the tears of pain and shame welling from deep within her, but Daniel, unmoved, continued to flay her from his own depths of hurt and disappointment until her bitter sobs filled the chamber and he felt himself drained and empty of all emotion. Then he got up and left her.

She crawled into bed, shivering, aching as if she had been savagely beaten, but the bruises were to the spirit, not the flesh, and she curled tightly over her hurt, enclosing it within her, praying in futile despair for this day not to have dawned.

Chapter 15

When she awoke, she was still alone, and she knew that she had been alone all night. Her body told her so as clearly as the cool, unruffled space beside her in the bed. She lay in the dawn-washed chamber, leaden with misery, her eyes still so hot and swollen with weeping that she knew the tears must have flowed even during her exhausted sleep. How had it happened? How had something so catastrophic occurred from only the happiest of motives? She had only wanted to help him. How could they continue to live together after such a horrendous happening? After those dreadful things he had said to her? She felt as she had as a young child, facing yet another day in the wilderness of rejection and unlove, before she had built up the carapace behind which the hurt soul could shelter. She had torn down that carapace since meeting Daniel, but now it seemed she must rebuild it.

He came into the bedchamber just as she had reached that melancholy conclusion. "Good morning." The greeting was curt, and he barely glanced in the direction of the curled figure in the big bed, who mumbled a response, peeping over the bedcovers to see what he was doing. If he had slept, he had done so in his clothes, it seemed, judging by their rumpled condition as he changed shirt and britches with brisk, impatient movements.

She had to do something; in a voice hoarse with

weeping, she managed to form some words. "Daniel, 'twas because the queen wanted—"

"What?" He whirled round, staring with that same stunned incredulity. "You were spying for—"

A knock heralded the arrival of the señora with his shaving water. Her greeting was cheerfully voluble as usual, and if she noticed any lack of enthusiasm in the responses she gave no indication.

"Just do not say anything further." The instruction came hard and clipped, once they were again alone. "I am sickened by the whole sordid, disgraceful affair."

Henrietta gasped with the sharp pain of his words and despairingly watched him sharpen the knife blade on the leather strop, watched him go through all the routine morning actions that she knew so well. But it was if she were watching a stranger, and when he was finished and was once again his daytime, immaculate self, he left the room without a further word.

Slowly, she rose, washed, dressed, brushed and braided her hair, examined her image in the glass: a wan, swollen-eyed picture of misery. She could not possibly go out looking like this and she was supposed to attend a morning party at the house of one of the English merchants resident in Madrid. Perhaps she could send a message excusing herself. But no, she could not do that. She had somehow to lead her life as if it had not collapsed in dust around her. If she retreated into herself, she would shrivel away with self-pity.

Resolutely, she reached for the pot of rouge and applied the lightest touch to her cheekbones and lips, wishing in a perverse fashion that Daniel would walk in and object as vociferously as he had once done. Such a trivial show of annoyance could only be a relief. But he did not come in, and when she went belowstairs, she found that he had breakfasted already and had left the house.

She went to Mistress Troughton's party, sat sipping lemonade and nibbling grapes and sliced pears as if nothing had occurred to disturb the even tenor of an existence she shared with the other young and not-so-young matrons making the best of their residence abroad. But Betsy Troughton, some six years older than Henrietta, the mother of two small children and the bearer of a third, saw something in the young woman's face that she thought she recognized.

''My dear Henrietta, you look a little peaky,'' she observed, sitting down on the wooden settle beside her guest, fanning herself languidly. ''Perchance y'are feeling a trifle queasy? I suffered most dreadfully myself with the first and the second, but it has been much easier this time, although the heat is at times insupportable.'' She smiled confidingly and patted Henrietta's hand.

Sweet heaven, Betsy thought she was with child! Henrietta floundered, searching for the discreet words of disclaimer, and then drew breath sharply, remembering that glorious joining in the garden two weeks past. Her impulse had not been repeated since then, at Daniel's behest, and she had almost forgotten the whispered possibility that they had made a son under the Spanish moon. What if they had? Such an event would have to heal the deepest breach.

She returned Betsy's smile, letting the statement go by default, but her mind seized upon the possibility and held on with the grip of a drowning man. If she carried Daniel's child, then all would have to be well.

Once she was home again, the possibility began to take on the shape of probability. She sat in the courtyard under the orange tree and dreamed of a child, her clasped hands resting protectively on her stomach. Daniel would forgive her and they would put this dreadful time from them.

But there were no signs of forgiveness over the next few days. Daniel tried to look at the event dispassionately, to see it simply as an act of childish defiance perpetrated out of pique, an act he could have dealt with in disagreeable but straightforward fashion. But this was an act that flouted every tenet of their marriage—of any marriage. Wives did not spy upon their husbands and take the fruits of their spying to the enemy. He had known her to be inexperienced and unsophisticated, but he had believed her honest, one who would recoil in horror from such a contemptible suggestion. Instead, his wife had violated his trust and his privacy in the most despicable fashion, demonstrating her utter rejection of his values of decency, honesty, and respect. He tried to find excuse in her childhood, but she had been perfectly aware of her wrongdoing. He could not get out of his mind's eye the image of her, standing there holding his papers, the crimson tide of guilt and confusion flooding her cheeks. Shaken to the core, his implicit faith in her honor destroyed, he could not imagine how he could ever trust her again. And without trust of the most fundamental kind, how could they possibly live together in any degree of harmony?

He behaved toward her with a distant courtesy and slept in a small room adjoining the bedchamber. Rarely looking at her, he failed to see the effects of this treatment as she struggled with despair and loneliness, becoming drawn and pale. Despite her earlier resolution, she retreated from the social round and hugged tightly to herself the hope, rapidly becoming conviction, that soon she would be able to give him news that would bring instant pardon.

Absorbed by unhappiness, Henrietta ceased to plan, to attempt to alter anything in the drear life that had descended upon her, even to pay attention to what was going on around her, until one morning, when the marchioness of Aitona paid her a visit.

''My dear Doña Drummond, we have missed you at court,'' she said, examining her hostess with sharp eyes. ''I trust you are not ailing. Her Majesty is most concerned to know that all is well with you.''

''Her Majesty does me too much honor,'' Henrietta replied, and surprised herself with a slight caustic note in her voice as she remembered that Her Catholic Majesty had been largely responsible for the present wretched state of affairs. ''I am perfectly well, madam.

May I offer you some refreshment?'' She pulled the bellrope for the señora. ''A cup of chocolate, perhaps?''

''Thank you.'' Her guest smiled with only her lips and arranged skirts and petticoats around her as she took a seat. ''It has been very hot. I can well understand why you would prefer to remain at home in the cool. But I do trust you will attend the concert at the palace on the morrow. I bring Her Majesty's most ardent invitation.''

Refusal was impossible if she was not upon her deathbed, and Henrietta acquiesced as graciously as she could, pouring chocolate for her guest and offering a bowl of the sweetmeats so beloved of the ladies of the Spanish court. Then the idea hit her with the speed and illumination of a shooting star. Her happy plan to aid Daniel's mission had gone devastatingly awry, but that did not mean she could not still pursue the original goal. In the second or two before Daniel caught her red-handed, she had read some portion of the king's dispatch. The damage was already done, so what did she have to lose, and mayhap she could still do Daniel some good even if he would never lay the credit at her door.

''I have been thinking about our little talk, marchioness,'' she said carefully, and was rewarded by a swift flash of interest in the other woman's eyes, a slight stiffening of her shoulders.

''Indeed, Doña Drummond?''

Now what had she read exactly? Something about the expected arrival of an envoy to the Spanish court from Parliament . . . would that be of interest? Why would it? Presumably it was news the king of Spain already possessed, so why would he need to hear it from Daniel? ''It is a matter of some amazement to me how King Charles's messengers manage to deliver His Majesty's dispatches to such far-flung places,'' she said cautiously, sipping her chocolate, finding that some life seemed to have returned to her body to energize her numbed brain.

"It is certainly amazing," concurred her visitor. "It's to be assumed that His Majesty King Charles must have a most efficient information network. I am sure he would know, for instance, about the diplomatic activities of his father's murderers . . . of where they might be sending envoys, perhaps."

So there it was. The Spanish court wanted to know how much King Charles knew. Daniel would be as completely impervious to the question direct as to gentle hints, and for as long as he withheld this information, so the king's audience would be withheld from him. King Charles had enjoined Daniel's silence, so presumably His Majesty preferred to keep the nature and extent of his own spying activities a secret from all but those of whose loyalty and support he was assured. King Philip IV had not yet made overt and unconditional offer of either.

"It's to be assumed Parliament would wish to gain acceptance in the courts of Europe," Henrietta said noncommittally.

"Yes," murmured the marchioness. "One would assume so. How is your husband's mission progressing, Doña Drummond?"

Henrietta smiled blandly. "Unfortunately, not as speedily as he had hoped, madam. His Catholic Majesty appears monstrous busy these days and has little time to receive visitors."

"Her Majesty, like all clever wives, has her husband's ear, my dear," spoke the marchioness deliberately. "And like all such wives, uses her influence with great care. I am certain she could be persuaded to advance Don Drummond's cause."

"That would be most kind in Her Majesty," responded Henrietta. "I understand from my husband that King Charles is greatly concerned about Parliament's diplomatic activities. He would be less so, I think, if he had some idea of how extensive they were." She picked at a loose thread in the lace of her sleeve. "In the isolation of The Hague, 'tis proving difficult to hear who has been approached by Parliament's envoys extraordinary . . . or so my husband says." She looked up and smiled innocently, before adding the sauce to the dainty dish of her mixing. "I understand our king has charged my husband with the additional task of discovering whether His Catholic Majesty has been approached, or can expect such an approach. I do not suppose you would know, would you, madam? If I could pass such information on to my husband, it would certainly impress him with my acumen, and I daresay he would confide in me to an even greater extent in the future."

And that should be thoroughly convincing, Henrietta thought with the first flash of contentment in days. If King Charles did not wish the Spaniards to know what he knew, then she had done her bit to ensure that they were completely at sea. Her visitor was murmuring that it was not the sort of information she was privy to, but Doña Drummond should keep her wits about her and her eyes and ears open. Thus would she surely learn much that would assist her husband.

"I trust I have already done so in some small measure," Henrietta said directly, rising as her guest began to take her leave.

The marchioness merely smiled and nodded. "You have much wisdom, my dear, for one so young."

"I have been most fortunate in my teachers," Henrietta replied pointedly.

But Harry's elation did not last long once her guest had left and the hot, stifling silence of the house settled around her again. She heard Daniel come in, and her heart sank with the now-familiar unhappiness at the way she knew he would greet her.

He came into the small parlor. "You have had a visitor?"

"The marchioness of Aitona," she agreed dully. "I am bidden to a concert at the palace on the morrow."

He stood looking at her for a minute and her heart yearned toward him, begged for a smile, just the hint of affection in the black eyes, just a touch of the old humor. But there was no change in his expression as he went over to the side table and took up the sherry decanter, filling a goblet to the brim with the rich golden wine. "I understand that the Troughtons are leaving Madrid. They are journeying overland to San Sebastián and taking ship for France."

"Oh," she said."Do you know when?"

He shrugged. "At the end of the week, so I heard. 'Tis a little sudden, but they were brought news of the ship sailing from San Sebastián and decided to take it, not knowing when there would be another. You should visit Mistress Troughton and bid her farewell."

" 'Tis too hot for visiting," she said listlessly.

"Nevertheless, you cannot remain immured in the house indefinitely," he returned. Strangely, Henrietta had not realized he had been aware of her retreat from the outside world. "Besides," he continued with an edge of sharpness, "you cannot be backward in the courtesies. Mistress Troughton befriended you when you arrived. You owe her a farewell visit."

"Aye," she agreed in the same flat tone. "I will wait upon her in a day or so." She thought she would choke in this deadly atmosphere with this complete stranger in her husband's body and hastily rose to her feet and made for the door, her fingertips pressed to her lips as she concentrated on keeping back the tears.

Daniel sighed as the door closed behind her, and he massaged his temples wearily. Would he ever be able to put this behind him? He could not punish her in this fashion indefinitely, yet neither could he help himself. His anger and hurt seemed not to have diminished in the least. Perhaps, when they could leave this city that seemed to have become an airless prison, he would feel differently. But the futility and mortification of his present anomalous position at the Spanish court merely exacerbated his deep sense of disappointment in one whom he had believed to be utterly straight and honest, for all the rashness of her impulses.

Two days later, however, he was informed by the king's chancellor that His Catholic Majesty would grant

King Charles II's unofficial ambassador an audience on the following forenoon. Wondering what could have brought about this unheralded change of heart, Daniel returned home in a more cheerful frame of mind, only to be informed by the señora that Doña Drummond had not left her bed that day. Frowning, he strode up the stairs and into the bedchamber, where the shutters were pulled tight, allowing only thin bars of sunlight to filter dimly through the cracks. It was close in the room, yet Henrietta lay behind the drawn bedcurtains, in airless darkness, smothered by the quilt.

"What ails you, Henrietta?" He pulled back the bedcurtains and peered down at the small, curled mound. " 'Tis as hot and stuffy as Hades in here!"

"I have the headache," she mumbled. "The light makes it worse."

His frown deepened. "Can I fetch ye something to ease it?"

A sniff was the only response, and he placed his hand on her brow. Her skin was warm and damp, but that was hardly surprising in the overheated room. "Y'are not feverish, I think."

" 'Tis just the flowers," she said in a tiny voice, curling up more tightly.

"Then 'twill not last long," he said matter-of-factly, straightening up. Her monthly terms rarely caused her significant indisposition. "I'll leave you to rest."

Tears squeezed under her closed lids as the bedcurtains fell back, enclosing her once again in darkness, and she heard the chamber door close softly. He had not even remembered that this month she might have conceived. It meant nothing to him that she had not, and he had not considered for one instant whether it might have mattered to her. He had known that she hoped for it and he had forgotten. He did not know, of course, how very important the possibility had become, how it was to heal this gaping wound in their marriage. But now, as her body shed the hope, she was filled with a great emptiness . . . a void that grew from utter helplessness. There was nothing she could do. Her husband despised her; she had no useful part to play in his life, no possible claims upon the love that she had destroyed. The years of her growing had been spent in the thin, dry soil of dutiful caretaking. No love had informed the duty and she had fled the barren ground as soon as she could, searching for warmth, for affection, for someone who would want her. She had chosen Will, and had been chosen by Daniel. But he no longer wanted her. And she would not again stay where she was unloved and unwelcomed.

It was a decision born from utter misery, but at least it was a decision and alleviated the paralysis of helplessness. With the decision came the planning. Betsy Troughton was leaving Madrid for France. She could not refuse to provide escort and companionship for Henrietta, who would tell her she needed to return to The Hague in advance of Daniel because of some ill news they had received of family matters. It was not in the least an unusual occurrence. She could pay for her passage on the ship, and for her hospitality on the road, but she could not travel alone. The Troughtons would understand that. The major difficulty would be the timing. She must present her request with great urgency and at the last possible moment, so that there would be no time for the gossipy piece of news to spread, as it inevitably would, before she was well away. Daniel would not permit her to leave, regardless of how little he wanted her. He was far too honorable a man to cast off even a dishonorable wife. So she must go in stealth.

An hour later, she was on her way to wait upon Betsy, ostensibly to pay her a farewell visit and wish her godspeed and good health and fortune upon her journey. She found the merchant's house in an uproar and Betsy distracted as she tried to direct the packing, soothe a fretful baby, and control a rambunctious toddler.

"Oh, Henrietta, how good of you to call," she said breathlessly, dabbing her forehead with her handkerchief. "Is it not insufferably hot? No, John, you may not have that!'' She lunged sideways to snatch a crystal jar from her son, who instantly began to bawl. ''Oh, I do not know what to do, Henrietta. The nursemaid has the toothache, baby must have the colic, and John will not be good! And how we are to be away from here by the morning, I do not know.''

''Y'are leaving so soon?'' Henrietta wiped the toddler's running nose. ''I had not realized.''

''My husband is anxious that we do not miss the ship's sailing from San Sebastián. And, indeed, I'll not be sorry to be away from this heat. 'Tis greatly tedious in my condition.'' She patted her rounded belly and Henrietta winced under a sharp pang of envy. ''Oh, no, Maria, those platters must be wrapped in cloths. They cannot go into the cases like that.''

''Give me the baby,'' Henrietta said, taking the keening infant from her friend's arms. ''Come, John, let us go into the garden and see what we can find. I will entertain these two for you so you may deal with the packing, Betsy.''

''Oh, y'are too kind, Henrietta.'' Betsy yielded up her children with a sigh of relief, and Henrietta took them out into the garden, where the afternoon heat lay like a heavy quilt. The baby stopped wailing as if it were too great an effort suddenly, and little John began to scrabble in a flower bed, a pursuit that his present guardian decided was both quiet and relatively innocuous.

Walking slowly along the paths, she worked out her plan, her mind amazingly clear. She would come here in haste and apparent distress at dawn tomorrow, just as they were about to set off on their journey. She would beg a seat in the carriage, saying that her husband had received bad news from The Hague, and as he could not yet leave Spain himself, he had sent her on ahead of him. No one would question her story. It was a far too common one in these unsettled times. Betsy would welcome her company and her help on the journey, and once they reached France, she would leave the Troughtons and fend for herself. Daniel was as generous with money as he could afford to be, and she had a fair sum left over from this quarter's allowance. If it should prove insufficient, she must sell the pearls. They had been a gift, not a loan, and were hers to dispose of as she pleased.

Of course, if Daniel still slept in the conjugal bed she would be unable to steal away in the dawn; but if he still shared her bed she would not have the need to do so. The doleful truth simply strengthened her purpose.

She left Betsy in her chaos and went home to the seclusion of her bedchamber, where she selected what she would take with her. The smaller her bundle, the better . . . a portmanteau would be far too cumbersome and she must be able to carry it herself. She chose a light wicker hamper with strong handles and carefully packed clean linen, her brushes and combs, sturdy boots, a cloak for climes less mellow than the Spanish heartland, and two of her simplest gowns. The elegant court wardrobe with which Daniel had furnished her would have no place in the life she must construct for herself.

She hid the packed hamper beneath the bed, then undressed and got underneath the covers. She was not in the least sleepy, but bed seemed the safest place at the moment. Daniel would assume she was still feeling indisposed and would not disturb her during the evening. In fact, she might not even see him before the morning . . . and in the morning, she would not see him.

Henrietta turned her head into the pillow and wept, grieving for the loss of a love that had become indispensible for happiness. Without that love, it ceased to matter what became of her.

Daniel spent a quiet evening in the parlor, preparing for his audience with King Philip on the morrow. He knew he would have only the one chance to present his king's request, and he must somehow convince the Spanish monarch that financial assistance in raising an army would not be wasted. He had to paint an optimistic picture of the support King Charles already had, of the Scots so eagerly awaiting his arrival at the head of an army, of the dispersal of Cromwell's disciplined New Model in the chaotic aftermath of the war and Charles Stuart's execution. Unfortunately, Daniel was not entirely certain how correct such an optimistic picture was. It was hard to be convincing if one was not totally convinced oneself.

As a result, he was preoccupied and, apart from sending the señora abovestairs to see if Henrietta wished for any supper, he did not trouble himself unduly about her retreat. Once his mission here was accomplished, successfully or no, then he would tackle this great morass of misery that enwrapped them both.

Henrietta slept little and was up and dressed long before the first gray showed in the east. She picked up her hamper and crept from the room and down the stairs, slipping the heavy bolt on the front door with exaggerated care.

Señora Alvara, in her little chamber off the kitchen, heard the soft footfalls in the courtyard and sat up abruptly, her thoughts full of robbers. But when she tiptoed to the casement, she saw only Doña Drummond, carrying a wicker hamper, slipping through the gate. Frowning and curious, the señora pulled on a wrapper and ran out into the dawn in her nightcap. Peering down the steep street, she saw Doña Drummond turn the corner at the bottom, heading in the direction of the cathedral square. Whatever could she be doing? Not out for an ordinary stroll, that was for certain.

Señora Alvara stood nodding to herself, her lips moving, as if she were debating with some invisible person. She knew matters were not right between Don Drummond and his lady. There was no laughter in the house anymore, and the lady no longer smiled mischievously and teased both her husband and the señora. But of most consequence: Don Drummond now slept in the little chamber adjoining his wife's. And Señora Alvara was grown accustomed to these lodgers for whom the pleasures of the bedchamber were manifestly important.

Still nodding and muttering, she returned to the house and went upstairs with a firm, purposeful tread.

Chapter 16

"Oh, my heavens, Henrietta, you poor dear! But of course you must accompany us. There is ample room in the coach, is there not, John, particularly now you intend to ride." Betsy appealed to the saturnine figure of her husband, who had listened in silence to Lady Drummond's breathless explanation and request.

"But of course," he said politely, bowing to Henrietta. "We are happy to be of service, Lady Drummond. Does your husband not come to see you safe away?"

"He . . . he could not," Henrietta said. "I did not wish to tarry in case I missed you, and he had letters of instruction he wished to write without delay in order that they may go back immediately with the messenger who brought the bad news. The messenger will be able to make better speed than we, you understand."

"Indeed." He bowed again, but Henrietta could not help the uneasy feeling that his eyes carried a glint of skepticism at this explanation for her unceremonious departure. However, he turned to a postilion. "Have Lady Drummond's basket put on the roof."

"Oh, I cannot tell you how wonderful it will be to have your company," chattered Betsy, clambering cumbersomely into the coach, where the wan nursemaid, her aching jaw wrapped in cloths, already sat, holding the baby. Master John, still half asleep, was whining ominously in a corner of the coach.

It was going to be a *long* journey, Henrietta reflected miserably, squeezing onto the leather-squabbed seat beside the nursemaid. However, she had no other options, and once they were away from this city that had brought so much unhappiness, she would perchance feel easier. It was hollow comfort.

The six horses pawed the cobbles of the square outside the Troughtons' lodging. The postilions mounted the near side horses; the outriders took up their positions alongside the vehicle. John Troughton cast a final searching glance around the deserted square and up at the coach roof to check that the luggage was securely fastened. Henrietta plaited her fingers, twisted the slender gold band that had replaced Daniel's signet ring, and resolutely swallowed the lump in her throat—when she saw her husband stride into the quiet square, nestling under the bulk of the cathedral.

It was clear that he had dressed in haste. He was bareheaded, wore no doublet beneath his cloak, his sash was twisted, the collar of his shirt opened. But the set of his jaw, the line of his mouth, a grim anxiety in his eyes, indicated a purpose that transcended the obligations of sartorial neatness.

"Ah, Drummond, y'are come to bid your wife godspeed, after all." John Troughton, in the act of mounting his horse, greeted the new arrival matter-of-factly.

"On the contrary," said Daniel. "Where is she?"

"In the coach with Betsy and the children." Troughton took his foot from the stirrup. "Is something amiss?"

Daniel ignored the question. Walking to the coach, he pulled open the door.

"Oh, Sir Daniel, what a lovely surprise," exclaimed Betsy. "Y'are come to bid farewell to Henrietta. I cannot tell you how overjoyed I am at the prospect of her company. You could not have hit upon a happier plan." Then she reddened slightly. "I do beg your pardon, I did not mean to make light of your grave news from The Hague."

Daniel appeared not to have heard a word of Betsy's

bubbly burble. His eyes were on his wife. "This is not necessary," he stated evenly.

"Oh, d'ye mean there's better news of your family?" exclaimed Betsy.

Daniel had no idea of what she spoke, but decided that an affirmative seemed safest. "Aye, thank you, madam. And we shall be leaving ourselves for The Hague within the month." He held out his hand to Henrietta. "Come."

"I shall want your company," Betsy said to Henrietta a little disconsolately. "But I can be thankful for ye." She brightened bravely and patted her friend's hand.

Henrietta, momentarily in the grip of unreality, made no move and could find no words.

Daniel saw the small, heart-shaped face white with despair, her eyes great dark puddles of unhappiness, and his heart turned over with remorse. Absorbed in his own angry hurt, he had not seen how deep were her wounds—deep enough to cause her to take this drastic action. It was time for the balm of forgiveness, and someday he would forget. "Come," he repeated. "This is not necessary, Henrietta."

She swallowed and seemed to come out of her trance. "I think 'twould be best if I continue with Betsy, even if you have had better news from home."

"Indeed, perhaps it would be so," Betsy said eagerly.

He shook his head. "Nay, I do not give leave for that."

Betsy sat back, resigned. When husbands spoke such words in such a tone, wives could only accede.

She could not continue this argument here in the coach, Henrietta realized. The proprieties had to be observed and not even Betsy would openly aid a runaway wife. Meanwhile, Daniel was standing in the open door, his hand outstretched in an invitation that embodied command. For the sake of appearances, she let her fingers brush his as she bent to climb down, but his hand closed hard over hers, his free hand cupping her elbow, and she felt his breath on her cheek, the muscular tension in his frame as he assisted her to alight.

She stepped away from the coach, out of earshot, and spoke with soft, fierce intensity. "I think it is right that I leave now."

"I do not," he replied quietly. "Running away is never the answer."

"I am not running away," she denied, soft and fierce still. "I am simply leaving because I cannot live where I am not wanted. I have spent enough years in such a situation and I will not endure it again. You cannot wish me to remain either, if you are truthful, so let us have done with this—"

"This is no subject for the open street," he interrupted, brusque because he could not bear to hear her talk in this fashion, comparing the neglect and unkindness of her childhood with her life with him, could not bear to see the pain etched upon her face. "We will continue in the privacy of home."

"No." She stood her ground. "I will not cause you embarrassment, if you will only let me do what I must." She turned back to the coach. Exasperation came to his assistance.

"Must I carry you, Harry?"

The question struck her as too absurd to require response and she stepped toward the still-open door of the coach.

Daniel glanced at Betsy's puzzled face peering through the opening. He cast an eye up at John Troughton, now mounted and looking a trifle askance at this strange, whispered parley. Daniel shrugged. Let them make of it what they would. Gossip was the least of his worries at the moment. Without further words, he scooped his diminutive wife off the ground and settled her in his arms.

"Oh, my Lord," squeaked Betsy, as Sir Daniel began to stride down the hill with his momentarily stunned burden. "Had we better have Henrietta's hamper taken back to their house, John?"

"It would seem so, my dear," replied John, apparently unperturbed. "I gather there has been a change of plan."

"Put me down!" Henrietta demanded, recovering breath and wits together.

"If you wriggle in this fashion, I shall be obliged to put you over my shoulder," said her husband calmly. " 'Twill be even less dignified, I fear."

Henrietta instantly offered a creditable imitation of a corpse. "I will walk."

"I do not think so," Daniel said in the same calm tone. "I feel more confident we will attain our destination by this means. Y'are not in the least heavy," he added reassuringly, as if such a consideration might be preying upon her mind.

Confusion swelled, fogged her brain. This was the old Daniel talking to her, holding her. Yet it could not be. He could not suddenly return, wiping out that cold, harsh stranger, eliminating that disastrous happening as if it had never been. But her every nerve and fiber yearned to believe that it could be so.

"Ah, Don Drummond, you have brought her back!" The señora greeted their return in customary voluble and enthusiastic fashion, flinging up her hands and exclaiming with pleasure, apparently not a whit surprised at the captive position of the retrieved wife, who was herself shrinking with embarrassment.

"Yes, thanks to you, señora," he replied in her own language, looking down at his speechless, red-faced burden and switching to English. "Fortunately, Señora Alvara heard you creeping out and woke me up. When she told me she had seen you going toward the cathedral square, I was able to draw the correct conclusion and thus spare us both a most tedious amount of trouble." So saying, he marched up the stairs and into the bedchamber, kicking the door shut behind him.

He set her on her feet, but kept a hand on her waist while his other gently cupped the curve of her cheek. His eyes were now grave, not a trace of amusement in his voice as he said, ''It is over now, elf. We will not speak of it again.''

Henrietta wanted to believe him with all her heart, wanted to accept the simple words of forgiveness and forget the whole dreadful business, but she could not. She moved away from him, shaking her head. ''No, it can never be over if you will not understand. You will always remember and you will always despise me. You will never trust me again.'' Her voice was low and she was biting her lip fiercely.

''What is there to understand?'' he asked quietly, unable to dispute her statement for all that he was determined to put the wretched business behind them.

''I did not think I was violating your trust,'' she answered in the same low voice. ''I only wanted to help you—''

''Help me!'' Daniel broke in. ''God's grace!'' He ran his hands distractedly through his hair. ''I suppose I should have guessed. 'Tis always when y'are feeling at your most helpful that the worst trouble occurs.''

Henrietta made no attempt to contest this melancholy truth, saying only, ''I do not know why that should be. It seems unjust.''

''I rather suspect 'tis because y'are incurably impulsive.'' Daniel sighed. ''I think it's time you told me the whole, don't you?''

''I do not suppose it will make any difference to the way you feel,'' she said. ''I had thought it an excusable trespass, but I must have been mistaken.''

''Let me hear the excuse.'' He listened attentively as she told him of her conversations with the queen and her ladies, of her deductions, and of her plan.

''It seemed so clever,'' she said at the close. '' 'Twas such a good idea. But when you would not share the dispatches with me, I thought . . .'' She paused as the dreadful memory of those moments of discovery returned in full force. ''I was going to tell you all about it once I had put the plan in action, so I was not intending to deceive you at all. But when I tried to explain that to you, you would not listen. You were only interested in what you thought I was doing."

Which was perfectly true, Daniel reflected. He had not been in the least interested in her motives for her underhandedness, and he had been far too shocked and angry to listen anyway. "So, you were intending to confess the whole, were you?" When she nodded, a tiny smile born of relief glimmered in his eye. "I see. But it was still an abominably unprincipled act, Harry, even if you intended no deception."

"I know," she acknowledged simply.

"I do not imagine you will ever do such a thing again," he prompted carefully. The look of horror that crossed her face was answer enough. "Just one more question; although I am certain the answer is perfectly clear, I don't seem to be able to hit upon it. Why on earth did you not come to me immediately you had realized what the queen wanted of you, instead of attempting to deal with it alone?"

Her eyes widened in surprise at such an obvious question. "But that would have been so ordinary!"

"Ordinary," Daniel murmured. "Yes, of course. I knew the answer had to be staring me in the face. How stupid of me." He shook his head and tutted as if annoyed with himself.

Henrietta regarded him suspiciously. "I wanted to show you that I could be skilled at intrigue. I want to be a part of what you do, but I do not think you always accept that I can. I am not such a baby, Daniel, as you believe me."

"I do not think you a baby," he said, smiling. "But y'are still only sixteen, love. There are things about the world you have not learned yet."

"Well, I will not learn them if you do not give me the opportunity," she pointed out reasonably.

"I suppose that is true." He glanced at the watch hanging at his side. "Hell and the devil! 'Tis past eight of the clock and I'm bidden to the king's presence at ten."

"Oh, it worked!" Henrietta clapped her hands involuntarily, a radiant smile chasing away the drawn look she had worn for so many days.

"What worked?" He went to the clothes press, drawing out his best suit of richly brocaded silk edged with silver lace.

"Why, my plan, of course . . . Oh, I forgot to tell you about what I did when the marchioness came to visit."

"Tell me." He listened incredulously to the details of her conversation with the lady. "What an astute little thing you are," he said finally.

"Did I say the right things?"

He nodded. "Exactly what I would have said myself, had I the wit to conceive of such a clever plot."

"Y'are pleased?"

He nodded again. "I'd have to be a monster of ingratitude not to be."

She plaited her fingers, staring down at them with an air of great concentration. "Then perchance you think that 'twould be wise of you to take me into your confidence in the future?"

"I beg leave to tell you, madam wife, that y'are an artful wretch," Daniel declared roundly. "Yes, indeed I have learned the unwisdom of excluding you from my affairs, just as I trust you have learned the unwisdom of unprincipled behavior, regardless of the purity of the motive."

"I could not endure such a time again," she said quietly, holding out her hand to him. "To have you say such things to me again."

He took her hand and gently pressed his lips into the palm. "I was unwontedly harsh, elf, and I ask your pardon. But I was cut to the quick. Let us put it behind us, now."

"I do not care for this place any longer," she declared. " 'Tis hot and devious, and nothing goes aright. I would go back to The Hague and the girls, and bear you a child."

Daniel laughed softly. "Such wishes are not beyond the granting. But do not be in too much of a hurry for the latter.'' He touched her lips with a long finger. ''Were you greatly disappointed when the flowers came?''

''I thought you had forgotten.''

He shook his head. ''Nay, love, I had not forgotten your impulsiveness in the garden. But let us wait now until we return home.'' A shadow crossed his face. ''Home? God knows, but I would have you brought to bed at Glebe Park, as is right and proper. Will this damned war never be done so that Englishmen may go home and tend their lands and look to their families again? 'Tis been all of ten years since England was truly at peace.''

''You will fight again?'' A chill arrowed through her, as she suddenly confronted what that would mean. Somehow, she had not thought of the inevitable conclusion of Daniel's open support of Charles II . . . Had not permitted herself to think of it, she realized. He would face the battlefield again.

In confirmation, he said gently, ''You know that I must. I am committed to my king's cause. There must be one last attempt.''

''And if King Philip will not lend his aid?''

''Then we must do without it.''

I do not think I could bear your death, she thought bleakly, but she kept the thought to herself, turning toward the door. ''D'ye wish to break your fast before going to the palace?''

''Just bread and meat and ale,'' he replied, following her change of subject because he knew he could offer no comfort on the other that would not be a lie.

''I will fetch it for you.'' She went down to the kitchen, wondering what had happened to the maid who had herself plunged headlong into the Battle of Preston not that long ago, quite fearless, all unthinking of what the realities of battle were, seeing only adventure and excitement. Now, such a prospect filled her with the greatest dread, not for herself, since such battlegrounds were no longer in her destiny, but for those she loved. There would be Will, also, fighting for his king. And what of Julia? Had that spark between them ignited? Would Julia also begin to live in fear for the man she loved?

With grim determination, Harry dismissed the gloom that had abruptly arisen. She had too many blessings to count to sully her newly returned peace with the anticipation of pain.

That night, the big bed was no longer the chill, lonely wasteland of the past nights. The warmth and security of Daniel's body enveloped her as she cuddled against him in the tight circle of his arms. Curiously, after such an absence, it was not the rough-and-tumble of lust she craved, the glorious wanderings in passion's garden, but just the feel of him once more holding her, the familiarity of his body and the sound of his breathing. Apprehension, speculation, and wretched memory drifted from her as she drew strength and renewed vigor from the haven of his presence, reacquainting herself with the touch and scent of his skin, the hairiness of the legs curled with hers and of the chest beneath her cheek, the ridged muscles of thigh and abdomen beneath her hand. She smiled contentedly to herself in the warm darkness as he slept and she could enjoy him in secret, reveling in her private pleasure.

A week later they left Madrid, taking an evasive answer from the Spanish king back to The Hague.

Chapter 17

"'Tis time Elizabeth was abed, Master Osbert." Mistress Kierston appeared, starched and purposeful, in the doorway of the parlor. "Nan has been in her bed these twenty minutes."

Lizzie opened her mouth to protest, then closed it again. Her governess had the look of one who might respond unpleasantly to protest. The child gazed in appeal at Will, whose intercession might have better success, but he did not seem to notice. In fact, she reflected in some annoyance, he was monstrous distracted this evening, and somehow had not even appeared amused by her valiant efforts to entertain him during the last hour. She was quite unaccustomed to such failures and now, with a pout of pique, slid off the window seat.

"I give ye good night, Master Osbert." A punctilious curtsy accompanied the valediction.

Will blinked in surprise at this extraordinary formality from one who was more likely to hand out kisses than curtsies. "What's amiss, Lizzie?"

"I have to go to bed," she said.

"That is hardly unusual." He could not help smiling at the disconsolate face. "But why do I think I have offended ye in some way?"

Mistress Kierston sniffed audibly and smoothed down her apron with brisk pats, indicating her impatience at this further delay.

The sound of carriage wheels rattling on the cobbles outside drifted in through the parlor window, standing open to the mild September evening. Lizzie, inquisitive as ever, turned at the sound, then ran to the window. "Oh, 'tis Daddy and Harry, they are come back," she squealed, jumping excitedly onto the window seat. "Daddy . . . Daddy!"

Daniel had just stepped from the coach. He turned, beaming with delight. "Lizzie . . . Lizzie!" he imitated, striding to the open window. Catching her around the waist, he lifted her through, hugging her tightly before kissing her and setting her on her feet. She ran immediately to Harry, who felt the most amazing joy sweep her at this loving welcome, at the child's trusting expectation that that love would be returned.

"Where's Nan?" Laughing, her father interrupted Lizzie's hugging, kissing, and unchecked prattle.

"She's abed, already—"

"No, I am not!" The excited shriek came from an upstairs casement from which Nan was leaning perilously, her hair tumbling loose from her nightcap, her hands waving frantically.

Daniel looked up. "Careful! I am coming inside." He ran to the open front door, where Will stood, waiting to greet them. Henrietta followed, holding Lizzie's hand. Nan scrambled down the stairs, tripping over her smock in her haste, to jump from halfway down into Daniel's waiting arms.

"I was nearly asleep," she burbled. "If ye'd come in five minutes I would have been, 'n then you'd have had to waken me!"

"Oh, I wouldn't do that," Daniel teased, smoothing back the thick brown hair, burying his lips against the smooth, warm, roundness of her cheek. "I'd have waited 'till morning."

"You would not!" Then she saw Henrietta and wriggled impatiently. "There's Harry!"

Daniel put her down, watching the ecstatic reunion with an inner smile of contentment. He turned, hand outstretched, to Will, who was discreetly standing aside. "Will, how are ye?"

"Well enough, Sir Daniel. 'Tis good to see you back

and safe." Will moved out of the shadows to take the hand. "The children have missed you both."

"Aye, as we have missed them," Daniel replied. "Five months is a long time."

"Oh, Will, there you are." Henrietta freed herself from the girls and came swiftly toward him. " 'Tis so good to see you again." The embrace they shared was the most natural expression of loving friendship, and Daniel found to his dismay that it caused him a slight pang, which was manifestly absurd since they were like brother and sister. Except that they were not. He remembered them with their squabbles and teasing on the journey from Preston. They had been little more than children then, and confused children at that. But they were both very different now. Will carried himself with the confidence of manhood, and Henrietta . . . you only had to look at her to see the beauty and poise of awakened womanhood.

Mistress Kierston was standing in the parlor door, patiently awaiting acknowledgment. Daniel dragged his eyes away from his wife embracing her dearest friend and returned to duty.

The children were finally put to bed, and Will and the returned travelers sat down to supper. "How wonderful it is to be back." Henrietta looked around the dark paneled dining room with a sigh of satisfaction. "You cannot imagine how hot it is in Spain, Will. 'Tis like Hades." She helped herself to eel pie and passed the dish across the table.

"But was it exciting?" Will asked, taking a small spoonful.

Henrietta did not immediately answer. "Why d'ye take such a tiny portion, Will? You love eels."

He shook his head. "I do not seem very hungry. But was it exciting?"

Henrietta glanced ruefully at Daniel. "Sometimes, but mostly it was very tedious and uncomfortable, and matters were always going awry. Were they not, Daniel?"

"Often enough," he agreed with a chuckle, refilling

Will's wineglass. "But what's past is past. Tell us, Will, of what has been happening here."

Will shrugged. "Ye've heard of the defeat of the Scots army at Dunbar, I imagine."

"Nay, we have not." Daniel's fork clattered onto his plate. "When was this?"

"At the beginning of the month," Will replied in distracted tones. " 'Twas a rout, the Scots army decimated, and all for about thirty English lives."

It was far too momentous a piece of news to warrant such a listless tone. Harry stared at him, noticing for the first time the tension in his eyes, the drawn line of his mouth, his general air of dejection. Somehow, she was convinced such obvious despondency was not due to the political situation. "Whatever is troubling you, Will?"

He started, flushed. "Nothing at all. Why should you imagine there should be?"

A few months ago, Henrietta would have badgered him for the truth without pause for thought. Now, it occurred to her that he might find Daniel's presence inhibiting if he was going to unburden himself to his closest friend. He did not know Daniel as well as she did, after all, and still treated him with the deference he had shown when they were journeying under his protection. No, she would wait and have it out of him once they were alone.

"What of the king?" Daniel asked. "D'ye know how this news has affected his plans?" He took a pear from the fruit bowl and began to peel it carefully.

Will frowned. " 'Tis said he makes plans to journey to Scotland himself. He goes to encourage the Scots with his presence to reform and rise again against Cromwell. If he succeeds, then a Royalist force will land in England."

"And if he does not . . ." Daniel mused, quartering the pear and laying it on Henrietta's platter. "If they will not, then the Royalist force must try its strength, anyway."

"But surely that would be foolish," Henrietta said,

nibbling with suddenly diminished appetite on the fruit. "If the Scots army failed to defeat Cromwell, then a Royalist force, much smaller and ill-equipped, will have even less chance alone."

Daniel shook his head wearily. "Perchance that is so, but we must attempt it one more time."

Henrietta shivered, demanding with sudden passion, "Why must we? Why must ye all risk your lives again, when you know the cause is lost?"

The two men looked at her in silence for a minute, then Daniel said evenly, "You know why, Harry. 'Tis a matter of honor and principle, and we must fight for both."

"And you will lose, and probably be killed, or sore wounded, and 'twill all be for nothing," she said fiercely. "And the land will be filled with the widows and orphans of honor and principle."

"Lord, Harry, you talk like a woman," Will said in amazement. "I never thought to hear you say such things."

"I *am* a woman," she declared. "Not a silly child with my head full of adventure."

Daniel smiled. "Aye," he said. "So you are, my elf . . . so you are . . . sometimes."

Will looked between them and decided abruptly that he was de trop. "If ye'll excuse me, I've a card game planned with some friends." He stood up, then said awkwardly, "I'll find myself alternative lodgings on the morrow, if that will be all right."

"Oh, nonsense," Harry exclaimed. "You'll do no such thing. Will he, Daniel?"

"I think that's a matter for Will to decide," Daniel said quietly. "He is welcome to stay, but he may prefer to set up his own establishment."

"Oh." Henrietta chewed her lip. "You mean he might have friends he would wish to invite." Her eyes suddenly danced mischievously, chasing away the intensity of the last few minutes. "Or loose women, mayhap. Is that it, Will?"

To her surprise, Will flushed crimson. "That is not

amusing, Henrietta. 'Tis in bad taste. I would have thought ye'd have learned better by now. I'll bid ye both good-night.''

The door closed on him and Henrietta swallowed uncomfortably, her own cheeks pink. ''Why did that upset him?''

''Well, it was not a very proper thing to say.''

''Oh, pah! I am never proper with Will.''

''Perhaps 'tis time you became so,'' Daniel said. ''Y'are no longer children together, Harry, and Will has his dignity.''

She lay in bed later, considering that. Somehow, she did not think it was a question of offended dignity. Will was not himself, and it clearly behooved her to find the cause.

With this worthy aim in mind, she descended to the dining room the following morning and greeted Will cheerfully, as if the previous evening's unpleasantness had not occurred. He returned the greeting a little sheepishly, then said, ''I ask your pardon, Harry, for being so sharp last night.''

''Oh, 'twas nothing.'' She bent over him as he sat at the breakfast table and kissed his nose. ''Daniel said I offended your dignity, and I am very sorry if I did.''

Will laughed, circling her waist with one arm and giving her a quick squeeze. ''Nay, you could never do that. I do not have any where y'are concerned, anyway.''

''There,'' she said triumphantly to Daniel. ''I told ye so . . . Oh, is something amiss? You look very stern.''

Daniel, who had been watching the little play over his platter of sirloin, realized he was frowning. He shook his head briskly. ''No, nothing amiss, but do not talk of loose women around the girls, will you? Lizzie will inevitably demand a complete explanation of the term.''

''Of course I will not. Anyway, where are they?''

''Gone to church with Mistress Kierston,'' Will told her. ''Under protest, I might add. The lady has become so devout these past months she attends evening service every day, and often enough morning as well, and perforce they must accompany her."

"Oh, how drear," Henrietta exclaimed, buttering a slice of wheaten bread. "Could they not go every other day, Daniel? They may spend the time studying the guitar with me, or some such."

"If you think it will be better for them," Daniel said amicably, draining his mug of ale and pushing back his chair.

"Perhaps not better," said Henrietta with scrupulous honesty, "but certainly more amusing."

Daniel laughed. "I have complete faith in your judgments in such matters, Harry. Decide what you will, and tell Mistress Kierston."

Harry wrinkled her nose at this latter prospect, but made no demur, accepting the task as her own. "Where do you go?"

"To court. I must seek audience with the king and make my report. I would also discover what plans are being made."

"Aye." She raised her face for his kiss. "But you will return for dinner?"

"I trust so."

"I may as well be hung for a sheep as a lamb," Henrietta declared as the door closed on her husband. "If I must face Mistress Kierston's frozen-faced disapproval, then I shall tell her that the girls need only attend church on Sundays, when we all go."

"For which you will earn their undying gratitude," Will observed, but his grin lacked its customary sparkle.

She propped her elbows on the table, resting her chin on her clasped hands, and regarded him gravely. "What troubles ye, Will?"

A deep sigh was his initial response, but she kept silent, waiting. "I am in love," he got out finally, flushing crimson with embarrassment at such a confession.

"With Julie? I knew it would be so!" She jumped up and ran around the table to hug him.

''How could you know?'' He struggled free from her embrace, still blushing.

''Oh, 'twas obvious from the first moment . . . the spark between you,'' she replied. ''That was why I suggested you stay in the house while we were away. I knew Julie would come to see the children sometimes, and you would have excuse . . .'' She shrugged. ''Anyway, it worked.''

Will shook his head. ''Nay, it did not, Harry.''

She looked astonished. ''Is Julie not in love with you, then?''

Will dropped his head in his hands. ''She loves me as I love her, but her parents have forbidden it.''

''Why ever should they do so?'' Indignation laced her voice.

''They do not think a mere esquire's son good enough,'' Will said wretchedly.

''And just who do they think *they* are?'' Harry demanded, outraged at this arrogance. ''Impoverished, exiled petty nobility! Oh, 'tis ridiculous!'' She paced the dining room. ''Have ye talked with them?''

''Of course. I did everything in the correct manner, asked Lord Morris for Julie's hand, told him of my estate, my expectations, my lineage . . . My family is as old as theirs,'' he added with a sudden resurgence of vigor. ''But not only did he refuse me, he has forbidden us ever to meet. Julie is not permitted to write to me, or to go out without her mother, and then only to certain very specific places.''

Henrietta looked horrified. ''But that is such tyranny. 'Tis as bad as my parents!''

''But what am I to do, Harry?'' Will looked utterly wretched. ''I cannot bear to be without her. Just to catch a glimpse of her would be balm, to hear her voice, anything . . . but this absolute desert is killing me.''

''Well, I do not think it is doing that,'' Henrietta said practically, ''but 'tis certainly making ye most dreadfully miserable, and I will not permit that.''

Will managed a glimmer of a smile at this energetic statement. ''There is nothing to be done, Harry. Lord and Lady Morris are adamant and Julie cannot defy them."

"Not openly, I agree," she said pensively. "But in secret, she could. I will go and visit her this morning. I was intending to anyway, and her parents have always looked with favor upon our friendship so they will give her leave to receive me."

"What are you thinking, exactly?" Will was well accustomed to his friend's methods and the speed of her decision making. It could make him uneasy, but it also created a flicker of hope. Henrietta rarely failed when she set her heart on something.

" 'Tis perfectly simple," she told him with a happy smile. "You must remove from here without delay, for if ye continue to live here then it stands to reason Lady Morris will not permit Julie to visit me as she was used to do. But she will not forbid my friendship with Julie because she and Lord Morris hold Daniel in such esteem; and when Julie visits me, or we walk together, then you will 'accidentally,' or do I mean 'coincidentally,' happen to come along. No one need ever know." She frowned suddenly, biting her lip. "I think we had better not tell Daniel that y'are forbidden to meet with Julie. He might not like your meeting together here in defiance of her parents. But if he does not know 'tis forbidden, he will think nothing of it. Y'are both my friends and are often in my company."

Will looked doubtful. " 'Tis not honorable, Harry."

"Why is it not? 'Tis just disobedience and has nothing to do with honor," she said stoutly. "But if you do not care for it, then you must think of something else, for I cannot. You could wait until you come of age, of course, but that is eighteen months away, and Julie must wait forever. She is the same age as I am. Can you wait that long without ever seeing her or talking to her? And in the meantime, her parents might marry her off to some ancient but suitably noble suitor."

"Oh, I could not bear it," Will said, anguished at such a prospect. "Besides, who is to know what is going to happen in this damnable war? I would be with her, Harry, for whatever time is allotted us.'' His voice had lowered, heavy with an unhappiness bordering on despair.

Harry looked at him, her head on one side as she waited for him to reach the right decision.

''If you think 'tis all right—'' he began again, hesitantly.

''Of course it is,'' she interrupted with vigor. ''I will go and visit Julie straightway, and you must find yourself lodgings. I will tell her parents that you have removed from the house now that we are back. 'Twill sound quite reasonable.''

Julie received her friend with an enthusiasm that could not mask her low spirits. Henrietta paid punctilious and dutiful respects to Lady Morris, talked of Spain and the strangeness of the Spanish court, sipped an elderberry cordial, mentioned casually that Master Osbert was leaving Sir Daniel's roof for his own, and pretended that she had not noticed Julie's sudden pallor at the mention of his name, or the tightening of Lady Morris's already thin lips.

''Well, I daresay you girls have much to talk about,'' Lady Morris said after about half an hour. ''I have certain matters to attend to, but I give leave for you to remain with Lady Drummond, Julia, if she is not anxious to be gone.''

''Not at all, madam,'' Henrietta said demurely. ''I am most grateful for the permission.''

Julie murmured her own gratitude, but she kept her eyes lowered until her mother had left the room.

''God's grace,'' said Henrietta in imitation of her husband. ''Are ye really kept so close that you must have leave to be alone with a visitor in your parents' house?''

''Oh, 'tis awful, Harry! You do not know what has happened—''

''Oh, yes I do,'' she broke in. ''Will has told me the whole, and we have come up with a plan.''

Julie listened to Henrietta's forceful presentation of

this plan. "If 'twere ever discovered . . ." She gasped. "I cannot imagine what would happen."

"I can," Harry said a trifle grimly. "But there is risk in all things worthwhile. If you wish me to help you both, I will do so with all my heart. But if ye've not the stomach for it—" She let the sentence hang.

Julie was silent for a minute, her face pale. "I know 'tis wrong to defy one's parents," she began hesitantly, "but I cannot see why it should be wrong to love someone."

"It is not. 'Tis your parents who are in error, and in such an instance 'tis not wrong to defy them." Since this was the maxim by which Henrietta had conducted her life up to now, she pronounced it with utter conviction, and Julie nodded, much comforted.

"But what of Sir Daniel?" she ventured. "What will he say?"

Henrietta shifted uncomfortably on her chair. "Well, I think 'twould be best if he did not know of it. It should be between the three of us. He is a parent, you understand, and a parent of daughters, so I think he might view the matter a little differently."

"Oh, dear," Julie whispered. "I do not think I have your courage, Harry." She sat silent for a minute, then suddenly spoke with resolution. "Yes, I do have. I will do it."

"Oh, bravo! Now all that remains is for us to receive your mother's permission for you to visit me alone."

Either Lady Morris felt she could begin to ease the strictness of her daughter's confinement, or she simply felt that Sir Daniel Drummond's wife could only be an unexceptionable companion for Julia, but she gave leave for the visiting and the plan went into action.

Daniel first became aware of something a little odd when he returned home one afternoon and surprised his wife and Will in deep conclave in the parlor. That would not ordinarily have caused him a second's questioning, except that Harry jumped away from Will as her husband entered the room, and two bright flags of color flew in her cheeks.

"Oh, Daniel, you startled me," she offered in explanation of this peculiar reaction. "D'ye wish for ale, or wine, perhaps? Shall I tell Hilde to bring some?"

"There's both upon the sideboard," he reminded her on a dry note. "Good day to ye, Will."

"Good day, sir." Will stood up a little awkwardly. "I was just leaving."

"Don't go on my account," Daniel said. "Take wine with me."

Will could not refuse the invitation without discourtesy, and a stilted conversation then ensued that puzzled Daniel mightily. Why on earth should these two, with whom he had shared so much intimacy, be behaving as if in the presence of a stranger? The opportune arrival of his children, newly released from the schoolroom, brought some ease as their cheerful prattle took over the conversation, and Will and Henrietta encouraged their chatter until Will could decently take his leave.

"Will you be walking tomorrow, Harry?" Will made the apparently casual inquiry as he went to the door.

"In the afternoon," she replied as casual as he. "By the sea wall, I believe."

"Can we come?" Nan piped up.

"Yes, indeed." Her sister added her own urging. "We have not walked there this age."

"Not tomorrow," Henrietta said. "We will go there the next day, if you wish it."

"But why can we not?" they chorused, unused to being excluded from such excursions.

"Because Henrietta says not, and that should be sufficient," Daniel put in, inadvertently rescuing Henrietta, who had been desperately searching for a convincing reason. The truth was that she would not permit them to participate in any way in the clandestine meetings of Will and Julia. In many ways, their company would have provided the perfect foil, the perfect image of innocence, to those walks and 'accidental' meetings, but the idea offended her deeply.

"But that's silly," Lizzie unwisely muttered. "There has to be a proper reason."

"Your pardon, Lizzie, I did not catch that," Daniel said pleasantly. "Could you repeat it, please?"

"I do not think she is going to do anything so foolish," Henrietta said, seizing the child's hand. "Come and say farewell to Will." She hauled the far from reluctant Lizzie outside. "That was a stupidly impertinent thing to say, wasn't it?"

"But there does have to be a reason," Lizzie persisted, knowing it was safe to do so with this audience.

"Yes, there does, but 'tis not one I am prepared to vouchsafe," Henrietta said. "And you will have to accept that, I fear."

"All right," Lizzie said after a considering silence. "But I knew there was a reason." Deciding that it would perhaps be imprudent to return to the parlor immediately, she went upstairs.

Will exchanged a rueful grin with Henrietta as they walked out into the street. "She's very like you, Harry."

"I know," she said, strolling with him to the corner. "Unfortunately, the characteristics she shares with me are those that her father does not look upon with a tolerant eye . . . at least, not with his children," she amended. "He does not seem to mind them in me."

"That is fortunate," Will said, chuckling. "But I daresay he feels 'tis a lost cause."

"I daresay."

They both laughed, and Will hugged her. "I will meet you and Julie at the sea wall tomorrow."

"Aye." She touched his face lightly. " 'Tis good to see you happy again, love."

Daniel stood in the open front door, watching them, wondering if he were jealous of that spontaneous, easy affection. They were both so young and vital, so sure of each other, had such a shared history. Perhaps it was not unreasonable to experience a lover's pang at the special quality of their relationship. Then Henrietta turned, saw him standing in the doorway, and gathered up her skirts to run smiling to join him.

''Did ye come looking for me?'' She stood on tiptoe to kiss him.

''You did seem to be taking a powerful long time to bid Will farewell,'' he replied, putting an arm around her shoulders, enjoying the pliant warmth of her as she eagerly leaned into his embrace. He banished the lover's pang as a piece of arrant foolishness.

''I just thought to walk a few steps with him. 'Tis a beautiful afternoon. Shall we walk a little?''

''If you wish it,'' he acquiesced, turning with her into the square. ''What did you do with my impertinent daughter?''

''She went abovestairs. It probably seemed to her the most prudent thing to do in the circumstances.''

Daniel laughed slightly. ''Probably it was. But why may they not accompany you on your walk tomorrow?''

She hadn't been expecting the question and could not help the sudden stiffening of her shoulders beneath the embracing arm. ''Oh, Julie and I wish to talk secrets,'' she said, recovering.

''Ahh.'' Daniel found nothing strange in the explanation, but he did wonder what had caused that uncomfortable reaction to his question. ''Are they secrets that cannot be shared with your husband?'' he ventured.

Color flooded her cheeks. ''Why . . . why should you think . . . well, perhaps . . . perhaps they are . . . but . . .''

Daniel stopped in the street and turned her to face him. His eyebrows lifted quizzically. ''Harry, just what mischief do you brew?''

She put her hands to her burning cheeks and cursed this inability to lie to him convincingly. She had never suffered this difficulty with anyone else. ''No mischief.'' She gulped. ''But they are Julia's secrets.'' That at least was the truth and she felt her flush die down.

''I see.'' He let the subject drop and they continued

their walk, Henrietta recovering to chat in her customary fashion, to listen to his account of the latest doings at the court, and to question him with sharp intelligence on his own views as to what was going to happen now that the king had made definite plans to sail for Scotland.

"I am not to sail with the king," Daniel told her. "He would have me remain here for the present. I and others are charged with the organizing of a Royalist army here, ready to sail for England as soon as it is needed."

"In what way needed?"

"To join with the Scots reformed army in an invasion of England," he said levelly.

Henrietta shivered but said nothing.

Daniel's arm tightened around her shoulders. "It means our time in Flanders will soon be at an end. We shall breathe English air again." He looked down at her seriously. "Will you be glad to be home in Kent, elf?"

"I will be glad to have the time to make it my home," she responded with thoughtful candor. "We were not there many weeks before we went to London, and then we came here almost immediately. And while we were there, I felt it to be your home, not mine."

"And will that still be so?"

"Nay, 'twill be quite different," she averred. "Because it is different between us now."

"Mmmm," he murmured, "that it is."

"I think it might be wise for us to retrace our steps," Henrietta declared. "Just so that we may demonstrate the difference in a degree of privacy."

And in the seclusion of the bedchamber she offered him such overwhelming evidence of the difference that he forgot the afternoon's oddities. Unfortunately, the amnesia did not last for long.

Chapter 18

"Oh, I do beg your pardon, Sir Daniel!" Breathlessly, Will excused himself.

"Think nothing of it," Daniel replied, recovering from the effects of having been nearly knocked off his feet at his own front door. "Y'are in somewhat of a hurry, I gather." He regarded the scarlet-faced, red-headed young man with a questioning quirk of an eyebrow. "Were you going in or out?"

"Out, sir. I have been visiting Harry."

"I rather thought that must be the case," Daniel said gently. "It generally is. Well, do not let me detain you, my friend, since y'are in such haste."

Will, much flustered, tried to admit that he was in a hurry whilst disclaiming that Daniel could in any way be detaining him. He managed to tie himself into such knots that his companion stared at him in astonishment. When the young man had finally taken his leave, Daniel went in search of his wife, who might conceivably be able to shed some light on this extraordinary behavior.

He found her in the January-bare garden at the rear of the house, cutting holly. "Just what is the matter with Will, Henrietta?"

She started at the question, dropping the armful of berry-laden foliage to scatter richly at her feet. "I don't know what you could mean, Daniel. Why should anything be the matter with Will?"

"He appears to find the sight of me a trifle unsettling

these days,'' he said carefully, bending to pick up the prickly branches. ''Which seems strange, considering how often he is in the house. Indeed, I begin to wonder why he bothered to move out.''

Henrietta pinkened. ''D'ye object to his presence?''

''No.'' Daniel shook his head, carefully filling her arms with the retrieved foliage. ''Not in the least. Should I?''

The pink deepened and the brown eyes slipped away from his steady gaze. ''Of course not.''

''Henrietta, if something is going on, I think 'twould be politic in you to apprise me of it sooner rather than later,'' he said. ''Somehow, I have the impression these last weeks that y'are hip deep in mischief again, and it is making me very uneasy.''

''Y'are not suggesting I might be behaving improperly with Will?'' she exclaimed, seizing on this absurdity as a convenient way of altering the direction of the conversation.

''You are always in his company,'' Daniel replied.

''But he is my friend.''

''That is what is making me uneasy. You wouldn't be trying to help him in some way, by any chance?''

She began to polish a deep green leaf with a gloved finger. ''Why should Will need my help?''

''If he has a grain of common sense, he will ensure that he does not,'' Daniel replied, looking down on the bent head, resisting the urge to kiss the soft exposed nape, to run his finger along the groove in the slender column of her neck, where curled feathery corn silk–colored tendrils.

''That is not very kind,'' she mumbled.

''The truth often isn't.''

''I do not know what you are talking about. I must arrange these before dinner . . . Julia is here . . . There is a shoulder of mutton with redcurrant sauce, which I know you like so I hope you have an appetite.'' Rattling on in this fashion, she hurried across the garden and back into the house, leaving Daniel even more mystified than ever, and even more uneasy.

He did not really believe that Will and Henrietta were conducting themselves as anything but friends, despite his occasional pang of envy at the special nature of that friendship—a dimension he could never have himself with Harry, based as it was upon such a shared past. But whenever he came upon them together these days, instant constraint sprang up. It had been so since their return from Madrid in September, and the only explanation he could think of was that they shared a secret from which he was excluded. Daniel Drummond did not like that explanation in the least.

Frowning, he followed Henrietta into the house. Nan and Lizzie were engaged in some competition on the stairs. It seemed to involve constant jumping, considerable excitement, and not a little altercation. Irritably, he administered a sharp rebuke that sent them upstairs shooting hurt looks at him over their shoulders.

He turned toward the parlor and paused, his hand on the latch. There was no mistaking the urgent quality to the low voices coming through the oak. He rattled the latch loudly before he lifted it and pushed open the door, saying, "Henrietta, those children are not to be permitted to play in the hall. Where is Mistress Kierston? Ah, I give you good day, Julia." He bowed to the young woman, who had jumped up from her chair at his entrance and curtsied, blushing. For some reason, the very sight of him these days seemed to put everyone to the blush, Daniel thought humorlessly.

"She's at church. I did not think they were doing any harm," Henrietta said.

"They were making an unseemly amount of noise." He walked to the sideboard. "If you do not wish to take charge of them, then they must accompany Mistress Kierston to her devotions. May I pour you a glass of wine, Julia?"

"No . . . no, I thank you, sir," Julia murmured uncomfortably. "I was just leaving."

"But you were to stay for dinner," Henrietta protested.

"No . . . no, I cannot, really. But I thank you." Julia

headed for the door. "Perhaps you could visit me tomorrow, Harry."

Henrietta accompanied her friend to the front door without demur and offered no excuse for her husband's ill temper. She knew the reason for it, and sharing that knowledge would do nothing for Julia's already fragile equilibrium.

"I am sorry the children were noisy," she said in an effort to placate Daniel on her return to the parlor. "I did not realize it would annoy you so. But 'twas quite my fault."

Daniel looked at her over the rim of his wineglass. What on earth had she been whispering about with Julia in such intense fashion? At the moment she looked as if butter wouldn't melt in her mouth, so demure with her hands clasped in front of her, her head a little to one side, her voice softly anxious.

"What *are* you up to?" he demanded.

Henrietta decided rapidly upon the combination of attack and half truth. "I am not up to anything, but I have told you that Julia has certain . . . well, certain private matters to talk over with me, and now you have frighted her with your bad temper. 'Twas not at all courteous. And it was not just to be vexed with the girls simply because you were in ill humor."

Daniel gave up. It was perfectly reasonable for Julia to confide in Henrietta, and they would hardly be confidences that would interest him. The girl was probably in love, or in some parental trouble. And whatever was going on between Master Osbert and Henrietta would presumably be revealed all in good time. Whatever it was could not possibly be too important.

"Just how often does Mistress Kierston go to church these days?" he asked, as if there had been no acrimony in the last minutes.

"Once, sometimes twice, a day," Henrietta replied, barely missing a beat as the mood inexplicably changed. "Today, there is a preacher come from London and she wished to hear him. I understood him to be a proponent of hellfire and brimstone, a doctrine that appeals to Mistress Kierston."

" 'Tis not a doctrine she has been successful in imparting to her charges," Daniel observed with a wry smile. "I will fetch them for dinner." He went abovestairs and Henrietta, relieved but with the uncomfortable feeling that the relief was only temporary, went into the kitchen to give order to the cook and Hilde.

Daniel came into the dining room, hand in hand with his now-merry daughters, whose sense of grievance had vanished with their father's smiling summons to table. Dinner was a cheerful meal, much enlivened by the absence of the governess, although everyone forbore to comment on this fact. Afterward Henrietta went riding with the girls, allowing their chatter to wash over her as she wrestled with the new problem now facing Will and Julia—the problem that had led to Will's precipitate departure and air of disarray, thus prompting Daniel's uncomfortable questioning.

Lord Morris had been bidden by the king to set sail for Scotland without delay. He was intending to do so within three weeks, and his wife and daughter were to sail with him.

Will was in despair at the news, and Julia had seemed paralyzed. Neither of them thought there was anything they could do to prevent the separation, which left plotting to circumvent it to the considerably more energetic Henrietta. At this point, she could see only two alternatives. Julia could run away and Will return to England with her on the next ship, and they could throw themselves upon the mercy of his parents. Mistress Osbert was a thoroughly pragmatic soul, and would accept the situation after the initial scolding, which would no doubt be fierce. Or Henrietta could persuade Lady Morris to leave Julia with the Drummonds, on the grounds that it would be safer for her, more convenient for the Morrises until the fate of the Royalist cause was settled one way or the other, and Henrietta would love her company.

On the whole, Henrietta favored the first course as

being the most decisive, but suspected that the protagonists would prefer the second for its general lack of decision. It would simply prolong the entrancement of courtship without requiring them to face any hard choices. However, it was their affair, she reminded herself, and her role simply that of facilitator. She would need Daniel's permission to issue the invitation, of course; indeed, the invitation should properly come from him. Lady Morris would certainly consider it so.

"Harry, is that a kestrel? Is it, Harry?" Nan's repetitive piping at last intruded on her reverie, and she looked up into the gray winter sky to where a hawk hovered seemingly immobile over a stubble field.

"Nay, I think 'tis a goshawk," she said. " 'Tis too big for a kestrel, and it has short wings. D'ye mark them?"

Nan squinted earnestly upward, and Henrietta hid her smile. She was such a little figure sitting on her small, barrel-bellied pony, her dark green riding habit a miniature of Henrietta's own; and the bright black eyes of the Drummonds were so like her father's. Would her own child have those eyes, also? Henrietta wondered. Daniel had at last agreed to take no more precautions against conception, and she waited with ever-increasing impatience for the moment when she could tell him she was bearing his child.

"Come, I think we should go home," she said, suddenly realizing the time. The January evenings closed in abruptly.

At supper, she brought up the subject of Julia's visit. "I should miss her most terribly if she goes, and she does not wish to leave in the least. I am certain, if you issued the invitation, her parents would let her stay with me for a little while. She could travel to England with us, if . . . when you must go and fight again." She licked the tip of her finger and picked up breadcrumbs littering the table top, saying in a low voice, "I would draw much comfort from her presence at such a time."

Daniel was silent for a moment, unsure whether he

wanted to share his wife with Julia. It was bad enough having Will around so much of the time. But that was selfish of him, he decided. She had made no secret of her fears over the prospect of another battle, and they were not fears he would make light of. If Julia's company would give her comfort and strength, then he would not deny it.

"Very well," he said. "You may take my invitation to Lady Morris in the morning. I will write it tonight."

But the invitation did not get written that night. An imperative knocking abruptly sounded at the front door, bringing Daniel to his feet with an exclamation of annoyance. "I trust that is not Will again."

"Of course it is not," Henrietta said with a touch of indignation as she defended her friend. "He would not come without invitation at this time of night. You know he would not."

"I suppose I do," Daniel agreed, going to the dining room door as he heard Hilde struggling with the bolts in the hall. "Why, Connaught, what the devil's amiss to bring you out at this time? Come in and take wine."

"Thank'ee, Drummond." William Connaught came into the dining room, his usually ponderous mien enlivened by an air of excitement. "Lady Drummond, I do beg your pardon for disturbing you at supper."

"Not at all," Henrietta said politely. "Pray join us. D'ye care for some venison pasty?"

"Nay, I have supped, thank'ee. But I'll be glad of wine." He sat down and looked around the table with that same portentous air. "Drummond, news has just arrived that the Scots have crowned His Majesty at Scone. 'Tis a direct challenge to Parliament—one they cannot ignore."

Daniel whistled softly, and Henrietta, feeling suddenly queasy, took a deep gulp of her wine. So, it had come at last—the inevitable that she had prayed would somehow be averted. Her husband would take sword, with so many other husbands and fathers, in a battle that both sides believed they fought for honor and principle, and in the name of God. And she would watch and wait, not caring who won or lost just so long as this husband and father came away from the field sound of wind and limb.

Daniel glanced across the table at her, reading her thoughts in her pallor and the liquid depths of those big brown eyes. " 'Twill be some time, love, before Cromwell can respond to the challenge. We must wait for order from His Majesty."

She managed a wan smile. "Then I will delay my fears 'till then."

"I will call upon Lady Morris myself in the morning," he said, hoping to comfort her.

Henrietta just nodded, feeling as if some natural justice was at work. She had used her fear as an added inducement to persuade Daniel to do what she wished; now it seemed she had received her just deserts, had somehow provoked the ill news. Did Daniel consider it to be ill news? Of course he did not.

Wordlessly, she clung to him when they were at last able to retire; but he had no need of words to tell him what she was feeling. He held her for a long time, imparting the reassurance of his strength until he could feel the peace of acceptance enter her, then he made love to her with slow gentleness, leading her down a long, winding road to oblivion. And then, when he knew her to be truly at peace, he possessed her again with a fierce passion that exorcized the demons of fear . . . for them both, he realized with a flash of self-knowledge the instant before all possibility of coherent thought was lost to him and the maelstrom engulfed them both.

"I love you," she whispered against the salt-sweet slickness of his chest, where his heart still pounded beneath her cheek as she curled into his embrace.

"And I you, my elf." He reached down to stroke the soft curve of her bottom with a lethargic hand.

" 'Twould be a criminal act to keep apart two people who love each other in this way," she murmured. "Do you not agree?"

"Utterly criminal, elf." He yawned mightily. "But

not as criminal as keeping me from my sleep after exhausting me so thoroughly.'' He kissed the top of her head and fell instantly asleep.

His wife followed suit, but not before she had decided that he had given his implicit approval of her efforts to ensure just such a happy conclusion for Will and Julie.

When she awoke in a cloud-dark dawn, this was also her first thought. It made her feel immensely more cheerful, for some reason. Propping herself on one elbow, she leaned over Daniel's sleeping figure, drinking in the strong lines of his face that even unconsciousness could not weaken; the sharply delineated eyebrows; the long, curling black lashes that many a maiden would envy; the firm mouth, now relaxed. Without the habitual humorous quirk of his waking countenance, and the gentle amusement in the sharp black eyes, there was something a little intimidating about him, she found. Her hand roamed over his body, slipping beneath the covers to slide over his belly and between his thighs. With a contented smile, she felt the softness stir and harden beneath her gently squeezing fingers. She reached further, her fingers twining in the crisp, curly hair to caress the twin globes filling and hardening in their turn.

''What are you doing?'' Daniel's sleepy voice, that note of amusement lurking richly in its depths, drifted down.

''Do you not know?'' she exclaimed in mock amazement. ''And I thought I was doing rather well. Clearly, I should redouble my efforts.'' With an agile twist, she dived beneath the covers, seeking him with her mouth in the warm darkness where the loamy scents of arousal, the languid melding of limbs and skin, mingled to create a hothouse and the flower of passion sprang into bloom at the first dampening stroke of her tongue.

Daniel yielded to the glory of the moment, his hands running over her pliant back, pressing into her spine, kneading her buttocks, drawing her backward until he could match her dewy caresses with his own, and the morning exploded with shared pleasure.

Daniel was in shirt and britches, humming smugly to himself as he shaved, and Henrietta was still lying naked and languidly abed, enjoying the moment of lassitude before she must rise and put on the day, when an urgent tapping came at the door.

"Daddy!" It was Lizzie's voice and Daniel went instantly to open the door.

"What is it, love?"

" 'Tis Nan." Lizzie was still in her smock and nightcap and carried an air of importance mixed with alarm. "I think she has the fever, and Mistress Kierston has gone to church."

"I think 'tis time the church put the bread in Mistress Kierston's belly," Daniel muttered for Harry's ears, before striding into the passage.

Henrietta struggled into her smock and tumbled out of bed, following him into the children's bedchamber. Nan was tossing and turning, kicking off the bedcovers.

"My head aches," she moaned fretfully, as Daniel leaned over her, placing his hand on her forehead.

"She's burning," he said, unable to conceal his anxiety. "Pray God 'tis not the smallpox."

"I doubt it is," Henrietta said, feeling the child's brow for herself. "There's been no cases in The Hague for several months. Do you go about your business, for I know you have much to do today. I will look after her."

Daniel's uncertainty was for a moment writ clear upon his face. There were many things Henrietta could do better than anyone with his children, but she was not skilled at nursing, knew almost nothing of the art if the truth be told. Yet there was something about her present demeanor that inspired confidence, and she returned his look with a tiny smile that contained the hint of challenge.

"Very well," he said quietly. "Mistress Kierston should be back soon."

"I do not need Mistress Kierston," she said, turning to Lizzie, who stood by the door, wide-eyed and big-eared. "Hurry and get dressed, Lizzie; then you may fetch some lavender water and bathe Nan's forehead while I prepare a soothing draught."

Daniel hesitated for one more second, then turned and went back to the bedchamber to complete his own dressing. When he returned to the children's room, Henrietta asked him calmly to lift Nan while she removed the child's soaked smock so that she could bathe her with the cool lavender water. He did so, holding the hot little body gently as Nan moaned and complained that her skin was sore.

"There's no sign of a rash," Henrietta reassured him, seeing the alarm in his eye. " 'Tis only because of the fever. It's always so. D'ye not remember from when you were ill yourself?"

He did and nodded ruefully. "I seem to forget everything sensible when they are unwell."

Henrietta only smiled and slipped a clean smock over Nan's head. "There, she will be more comfortable now. You may put her back on the bed and go off and do what you have to. You must have many people to see after last night's news."

"Are you trying to be rid of me?" he asked, raising a questioning eyebrow.

"Aye," she confirmed affably. "I am. You will worry too much if you stay here, and there is nothing you can do that I cannot do as well." She shooed him toward the door. "You can go downstairs and make sure Lizzie has eaten her eggs. You know what she's like about breakfast if no one is watching her, and then she gets so cross and hungry long before dinner."

He kissed the tip of her nose and did as she said, reaching the dining room just in time to forestall his elder daughter's attempt to dispose of the detested eggs out of the window.

"Let's pretend I did not see you," he suggested amiably. "Sit down and eat them all up."

Lizzie complied without demur, far too relieved by his suggestion to do more than wrinkle her nose at the laden platter in front of her. "Is Harry going to look after Nan?"

"It would seem so," her father replied, helping himself to bacon. "You will have the great pleasure of Mistress Kierston's undivided attention."

"But d'ye not think I should help Harry?" Lizzie regarded him hopefully across the table.

"And leave poor Mistress Kierston with nothing to do?" he exclaimed in mock horror. "How could you be so unkind, Lizzie?"

Lizzie did not look as if she appreciated this little joke. She finished her breakfast with a moue of distaste. "May I go, Daddy?"

He glanced at her empty platter and nodded. "Ask Harry to come down and have her own breakfast. You may sit with Nan until Mistress Kierston returns."

Lizzie scampered off, and Henrietta came down within five minutes, just as Daniel was preparing to leave the house. "How is she?"

"Sleeping," Henrietta replied. " 'Tis the best medicine."

"Aye." He stood frowning, his hand on the door latch. "Should I summon the physician, d'ye think?"

"We will see how she is at dinnertime. Did Lizzie eat her breakfast?"

"With a degree of encouragement. I arrived just in time to rescue the eggs." He still hesitated at the door. "You had best have your own, Harry."

"I am not in the least hungry. Now do go, Daniel." She gave him a little push. "D'ye not trust me to look after things?"

Daniel didn't know whether he did or not. She still struck him as such a little person, but she did seem to be radiating a fair degree of confidence at the moment. "I will be back as soon as I can," he said, and left her smiling in the hall.

When he returned at dinnertime, he found all peaceful, Henrietta calmly in charge in the sickroom, Mistress Kierston and an obedient if resentful Lizzie at their lessons in the schoolroom, the cook in the kitchen, from whence emanated toothsome aromas, and Hilde polishing the furniture with beeswax.

"I cannot imagine why I expected to find chaos," he said, bending over Nan, who offered him something resembling a smile. "How's my little one?" He kissed the hot forehead.

"I'm very sick," Nan informed him in a croaky voice. "But not as sick as this morning."

Daniel glanced at Henrietta, who nodded in confirmation. "Well, that's good to hear," he said cheerfully, sitting on the bed. "Does your head not pain you anymore?"

"Not much," Nan croaked. "Harry's been playing her guitar and it makes me go to sleep."

"I'm not sure whether to take that as a compliment or not," Harry said with a chuckle. "I'm going to fetch you some broth, and Daddy will help you eat it."

Lizzie catapulted into the room at this point. "You do not know how lucky y'are to be sick, Nan," she announced disgustedly. "I have been learning dreary psalms all morning, and I think it's quite stupid."

"I do not think y'are qualified to be the judge of that, my child," Daniel said. "And 'tis certainly not an opinion I care to hear you express."

Lizzie, crestfallen, looked at her stepmother for support. Harry winked at her. "Run down to the kitchen and ask Cook to give you a bowl of broth for Nan."

Lizzie disappeared, grinning, and Daniel, who had not missed the wink, said sternly, "If I take issue with Lizzie, I do not expect you to undermine me, Henrietta."

"But they *are* dreary," she said. "And it is stupid to waste a whole morning learning them. There must be more useful things she can learn."

"Like self-discipline and restraint," he declared. "Learning psalms will teach her both."

Henrietta's eyebrows lifted in skeptical response and Daniel could not help laughing. "Oh, mayhap y'are right. 'Tis probably past time I reviewed matters with Mistress Kierston."

"Will ye tell her we're not to learn psalms?" Nan's question reminded them that they had an audience, and Daniel shook his head ruefully at Henrietta.

"That is no concern of yours, Nan," he said firmly. "Here's Lizzie with your soup."

"Daddy's goin' to tell Mistress Kierston that we're not to learn psalms anymore," Nan, shamelessly taking advantage of the license permitted an invalid, informed her sister as Daniel lifted her against his shoulder.

"I did not say that," her father insisted. "I said any conversations I have with your governess are no concern of yours."

"But that's what you meant." Nan opened her mouth for the spoonful of soup he held.

Lizzie clapped her hands gleefully. "Will ye tell her this afternoon, Daddy?"

Henrietta doubled over with laughter in the doorway as Daniel floundered. "Get out of here," he ordered. "Y'are nothing but trouble!"

Still laughing, she went downstairs.

Daniel joined her in a short while. "You are the most appalling influence," he declared. "I am beginning to regret the errand I ran for you this morning. You do not deserve the consideration."

"Oh, did you visit Lady Morris?" In all the morning's concerns, she had completely forgotten that complication in her life.

"I did. Canary?"

"If you please." She took the goblet and waited patiently for him to continue. When, wickedly, he remained silent, apparently savoring his wine, she came over, stood on tiptoe, and kissed the corner of his mouth. "I crave pardon for being nothing but trouble. I had thought I was rather useful this morning."

He dipped a finger in his wine and very deliberately

traced the curve of her lips. Her tongue darted to lick the wine-tipped finger, and, smiling, he repeated the process, clearly enjoying the funny little game, until she suddenly sucked his finger into her mouth and closed her pearly teeth upon it. "Vixen!"

"Tell me what Lady Morris had to say."

For answer, he took a deep draught of wine and clasped her head firmly, holding the wine in his mouth as he slowly brought his lips against hers, forcing them open and filling the warm, sweet cavern of her mouth with the wine from his own. Henrietta found it the most enticing sensation, the coolness of the wine mingling with the warmth of his probing tongue, the taste of wine and Daniel so deliciously melded that she forgot all else in her utter concentration on this unusual and entrancing kiss.

When he finally took his mouth from hers, she remained perfectly motionless, as if her head were still held, face upturned, eyes closed, lips slightly parted. "More?" he asked. She nodded vigorously, still without opening her eyes, and he chuckled. "Such a sensual little thing y'are, my elf." Taking another draught of wine, he kissed her again.

"Oh!"

The startled gasp from the door brought an abrupt end to the game. Daniel looked over Harry's head to where Lizzie stood, wide-eyed.

"I thought 'twas dinnertime," she mumbled.

"It is," Henrietta said cheerfully, turning around. "There's no need to be uncomfortable, Lizzie, just because Daddy was kissing me. Married people do it all the time."

"They also prefer other people to knock upon doors before they open them," Daniel said wryly. "Try to remember that in future." A brisk pat sent the child ahead of him into the dining room. "I give you good day, Mistress Kierston."

"Good day, Sir Daniel." The governess was standing at her usual place at the table and curtsied to her employer before turning her attention to Lizzie. "You have neglected to comb your hair, Elizabeth. I do beg your pardon, Sir Daniel, but I was busy with Nan and failed to notice."

"I am certain we can overlook it today," Henrietta said. "It has been a troublesome morning and Lizzie has been most helpful, has she not, Daniel?"

"I am sure of it," he said, meeting his wife's gleaming eye. "I do not think we need worry ourselves over a little untidiness on this occasion, Mistress Kierston." He began to carve the green goose, generously heaping the governess's plate with the cuts he knew she preferred.

"Are we to have the pleasure of Julia's company, Daniel?" Henrietta inquired, passing a dish of Jerusalem artichokes to Mistress Kierston, who was finding it impossible to maintain her air of hurt disapproval under these attentions.

"Lady Morris was happy to accept the invitation for Julia," he responded. "Lizzie, do you prefer a wing or breast?"

"Both, please." Lizzie's appetite made up at dinner what it lacked at breakfast.

Henrietta helped the child to vegetables, her mind now running on another course. She must somehow let Will know of this success. He had been so wretched yesterday when he left them that she had ached for him in his unhappiness. But at that point she had not had time to formulate any plan and had had no opportunity to speak with him since. She would visit him after dinner. No, she could not do that, not with Nan still feverish. She had taken on that responsibility and would not hand it over to the governess. Daniel was bound to go out again, so would not be able to sit with the invalid. But Lizzie could take a message. The child was quite old enough to walk three streets and deliver a letter. She must take Hilde with her as escort, but that should prove no problem.

The plan proved easy to implement. Lizzie was delighted to be given such responsibility and, since Will was one of her favorite people, even happier at the prospect of visiting him. Nan had woken from a long nap, fretful and demanding that Harry read to her. Mistress Kierston had retired to her own chamber with her sewing, telling Lady Drummond that she would be happy to attend in the sickroom whenever she was required, and Daniel had gone out about the king's business.

Harry wrote a brief note to Will, telling him that she had a plan and he was to come to the house as soon as possible, explaining why she could not come to him herself.

"Now, you know the way to Will's lodging, Lizzie." She folded the paper carefully and handed it to the child. "Just tell Hilde that she is to leave her tasks for the moment and accompany you. 'Twill not take you above half an hour."

Lizzie, with an air of great importance, put the letter into the pocket of her apron.

"Wear your thick cloak," Henrietta said. "There's a bitter wind."

The child ran down to the kitchen in search of the maidservant, who was nowhere to be found. Lizzie stood thoughtfully in the empty kitchen. Hilde was presumably to be found in the attic, taking a little time to herself after her labors of the morning. It didn't seem very kind to expect her to go forth into the freezing afternoon when Lizzie was quite capable of making such a journey unaccompanied. Besides, it would be much more amusing to go alone. On which undeniable conclusion, Lizzie set off.

It was at the corner of the first street that she ran into her father.

"Where on earth are you going?" Daniel stared in astonishment at the small cloaked figure of his daughter.

"To see Will. Harry wants me to take him a message because she couldn't go herself because she was looking after Nan." The explanation poured without punctuation from her lips, but did not appear to have the reassuring effect intended.

''Henrietta sent you out to run such an errand alone?'' he demanded in disbelief.

Lizzie shuffled her feet on the cobbles. ''She said I should take Hilde, but I could not find her and 'tis not so very far.''

Daniel stood in frowning silence. Just why did Harry need to send messages to Will? Not one day could pass, it seemed, without some communication between them. And she had no right to involve Lizzie in whatever it was. If she needed an errand run, then she could have asked him. The fact that she had not done so struck Daniel as most suspicious, merely confirming his earlier conviction that his wife and Master Osbert shared a secret from which the husband was excluded. It was time to put a stop to it, that husband now decided.

''Give me the message,'' he commanded.

Lizzie looked uncertain. She had no desire to relinquish her commission. ''But 'tis Harry's message for Will,'' she ventured.

''I am not going to be obliged to repeat myself, am I?''

The consequences of further procrastination were not to be invited. Lizzie delved beneath her cloak, into the pocket of her apron, and handed over the folded paper.

''Thank you.'' Daniel slipped the document into the pocket of his doublet. ''I will deliver it for you. 'Tis not meet that you should roam the streets unaccompanied, as ye well know. Come, I will take you home.''

He escorted her back down the street to the house, saw her inside, then strode off in search of Master Osbert.

Henrietta heard the front door and emerged from the sickroom, leaning over the banister. ''That was quick, Lizzie.'' Then she saw the child's downcast expression. ''What's amiss, love? And where's Hilde?''

''Daddy has taken the message to Will.'' Lizzie climbed the stairs without her customary bounce. ''I could not find Hilde so I went alone, and I bumped into Daddy and he said it was not meet for me to be out alone so he brought me back and took the message himself.'' She paused for breath. ''He was not at all pleased. Should I not have given him the message?''

''Of course you should,'' Henrietta said promptly, hiding her dismay. Lizzie must not be allowed to imagine her stepmother held secrets from her father, or that she would advocate filial disobedience. ''Why would you think otherwise? But you should not have gone alone, you know that. You had best go to Mistress Kierston and do some sewing.'' Her tone was sharp, and Lizzie, unaccustomed to being chided by her stepmother, obeyed, unhappily but without a murmur of protest.

Henrietta returned to Nan's bedside and settled down uneasily to wait for whatever was about to transpire.

Chapter 19

Will was pacing miserably around the small chamber of his lodging, racking his brains for some solution to love's dilemma. He had walked over to the Morrises' lodging that morning, fully intending to press his suit with Julie's father yet again, and then realized that if, as was highly likely, he was again refused, then Julie would be strictly confined once more, and he would not even see her before she left for Scotland.

He would call upon Harry, he decided abruptly. She always had a bracing effect, mainly because she never accepted defeat until it was forced upon her and was not at all tolerant of moping and sighing. He picked up his beaver hat, slung his cloak about his shoulders, and marched to the door, just as the door opened to admit Sir Daniel.

"Ah, Will, it seems I am in the nick of time," Daniel observed, taking in the younger man's dress. "I do hope you can be persuaded to delay your departure for a minute."

"Aye . . . aye, of course, sir, d-delighted to see you, sir . . . 'Tis . . . 'tis an honor." He stepped back from the door and tripped over a stool. "P-pray come in. What may I offer ye? I do not keep much in the way of wine, I am afraid, sir; 'tis poor hospitality, but there's tolerable ale, or I could ask the landlady for cider, if ye'd prefer."

"Why do I make ye so nervous these days, Will?" inquired Daniel with a pleasant though puzzled smile, refusing these stumbled offers of refreshment with a wave of his hand. "At the very sight of me, you flush up as crimson as the sunset. And you don't seem to be able to put two words together anymore."

The crimson tide flooded to the red roots of Will's hair yet again, and he began to stammer a denial that in the face of the evidence was manifestly absurd. He fell silent under Daniel's steady gaze.

Daniel took the letter from his doublet pocket and tapped it thoughtfully against his palm. "I bring you a message from Harry," he said, remarking the sudden spark of interest in his young friend's eyes . . . interest, or was it hope? "Since the letter is addressed to you, I have of course not read it," he continued in a somewhat ruminative tone. "However, I do have a certain interest in what my wife might be writing to others, so perchance you will apprise me of the contents."

Will looked stricken. "Ye . . . ye could not imagine that Harry and I—"

"Nay, I do not imagine that," Daniel interrupted. "But I know my wife, Will, and I am certain she is up to mischief." He stroked his chin, continuing in the same pensive tone. "She has this habit, you see, of falling in and out of scrapes with appalling regularity . . . always from the purest of motives, of course. I would forestall this one, if possible." He held out the letter.

Will took the document with nerveless fingers. He could not possibly betray Harry. If she believed her husband would disapprove of her actions to help her friends, it was not for those friends to act traitor. The only thing they could do was refuse to implicate her further. It was all at an end now, anyway, now that Julia was going away. He opened the letter.

Harry's impulsive flowing script jumped out at him with all the eager confidence of the writer, and for a second he forgot his despondency and felt a surge of hope. She had a plan. But the hope died at birth as he looked up at his visitor, whose gaze was uncomfortably searching.

"Well?" Daniel gently prompted.

" 'Tis just that she wishes me to visit her, since she cannot come here," Will said. "I am sorry Nan is unwell, sir. I trust 'tis not serious."

Daniel shook his head. "It seems not. Might I ask why she wishes you to visit her so urgently?"

Will decided to get as close to the truth as he dared. He met the older man's look. "She is the only person I can talk to, Sir Daniel." He received a noncommittal nod and a gesture of invitation to continue. Will did so awkwardly. "I am having some difficulties . . . personal difficulties . . . and I need to have someone to talk—"

"I beg your pardon, Will." Daniel broke in swiftly. "I do not wish to pry into your affairs; they are no concern of mine. Henrietta's are, but yours are not. If she is simply your confidante in time of trouble, then that is all I need to know. Unless—" He smiled. "Unless, mayhap, I can be of some service to you myself. You should know I would stand your friend in all things, Will."

Will felt ready to sink through the floor with guilt and embarrassment. It was not as if he had lied, yet he felt as if he had committed a monumental deception in the face of the kindly concern and understanding Daniel so freely offered.

Daniel cut short Will's stammered thanks and denials with an easy gesture. "Enough said, Will. Come. If you've a mind to visit Harry, then we'll keep each other company."

It was not an offer Will could refuse, but he went with the absolute determination to call an immediate halt to Henrietta's involvement in his doomed, clandestine love affair, regardless of her planning.

Henrietta jumped at the sound of the front door. She had been expecting it, but it still sent her heart into her throat. She waited, hearing two sets of footsteps on the stairs.

Will and Daniel came into the sickroom. "I have brought Will, Harry, since you wished for him," Daniel said. ''He insisted upon visiting the invalid.'' Smiling, he came over to the bed. ''See who's come to cheer you up, Nan.''

Harry shot Will an anxious look of startled inquiry. Had he been obliged to take Daniel into his confidence? If he had, then surely her husband would not be quite so sanguine and cheerful. Will answered the look with a tiny shrug before turning his attention to the now-perky Nan.

''Where is Lizzie?'' Daniel addressed Henrietta, sounding to her apprehensive ears as relaxed and genial as ever.

''Sewing with Mistress Kierston.''

''For her sins?'' he inquired with a raised eyebrow.

Henrietta looked rueful. ''She should not have gone alone. I am sorry, Daniel.''

''There was no harm done. If you and Will wish to talk, I'll stay here and entertain this little one.''

''Will ye tell me the story of the dragon and the maiden?'' Nan demanded, her voice still a little croaky but definitely stronger.

''I don't know if I can remember it,'' he teased, sitting on the bed and taking her hand. ''Let me see, now.''

Will and Henrietta left them to it. ''Whatever happened?'' Henrietta demanded as they reached the seclusion of the parlor. ''I made sure Daniel would have questioned you about my message. He has become a little suspicious of all your visits recently.'' She crossed her arms over her breasts and rubbed her upper arms restlessly. ''Suspicious is not quite the right word, but he thinks I am up to something.''

''Which y'are,'' Will said flatly, and told her what had transpired between himself and Daniel. ''I felt the size of an ant,'' he concluded.

''Aye, I can imagine.'' She could, with no difficulty. ''And I had this wonderful plan to invite Julia to stay with me when her parents left.''

Will's face was transfigured. ''But that would be so wonderful, Harry.''

"Yes, it would," she said gloomily. "But I cannot possibly do it. You see, I asked Daniel to invite her, because that would be most likely to satisfy Lady Morris, only of course I did not tell him why. And he did ask this morning, and Lady Morris gave her permission."

"Oh, God." Will groaned, seeing the whole ghastly tangle. "You cannot deceive him, Harry. You would put him in the most abominable position. Surely you realize that."

"Yes, of course I do, *now,*" she said impatiently. "For you to conduct a clandestine liaison while Julie is under Daniel's roof and protection at his invitation would be impossible. I do not know how I could have been so stupid as to have thought of it. I do things sometimes without thinking very clearly," she added dismally. "I shall have to tell him the truth, and he will have to withdraw the invitation without explaining why. And he's going to say I have been duplicitous and unprincipled again, which I have, but I did not mean to be. And everything was going so nicely since we returned from Spain. Oh, why d'ye not just elope, Will? It would be so much simpler!"

"I would if we could find the means to do so." Will paced the parlor, pulling at his finger joints in a way that made Harry wince.

"Take Julie to your mother," she suggested. "Mistress Osbert is such a sensible person; she will scold you both most dreadfully, but then she will do what has to be done. I do not think even Lord Morris would be able to withstand her if she decided to take issue with him."

Will grinned reluctantly. He could not argue with that. His mother was more than a match for Lord and Lady Morris combined. "I do not know if Julie would be willing."

"I will ask her," Harry said. "And then I will tell you. But you cannot meet here together, at least not until I have told Daniel what has been happening."

"He will not permit it, once he knows everything," Will said. "No responsible man would."

"Oh, dear." Henrietta sighed. "Matters were proceeding so beautifully. I have been doing everything right with the girls and the house and other things—" She stopped, blushing slightly. Close though she was to Will, discussing those other delicious aspects of her marriage was not something she could do, anymore than she could tell him that she hoped soon to conceive. More than anything, Daniel's agreement to this had indicated his acceptance of her as a sensible, mature wife, and now she was about to destroy that belief by demonstrating that she was still as impulsive and reckless and irresponsible as ever.

" 'Tis my fault, not yours," Will said. "I should never have agreed to it. Let me explain it to him."

Henrietta shook her head. "I may be a thoughtless idiot, but I'm no coward, Will. But I'll talk to Julie first.'Tis only fair to prepare her. I can visit her in the morning."

Daniel found his wife in low spirits that evening, resisting all his efforts to draw her out. He delicately brought up the subject of Will and his troubles, offering again to help, suggesting she might have more success than he in persuading Will to confide in him, since it was clear the young man was wretchedly miserable.

Henrietta nearly burst into tears. She did not deserve such a husband, indeed, never had done. Everything good she tried to do turned to dross beneath her touch. What could someone so kind and considerate and loving and humorous and . . . oh, so many other wonderful things as Daniel possibly find to love in her? No one else, except for Will, had ever found anything. Perhaps those others were right and Daniel and Will were mistaken.

She went up to bed early, pleading unusual weariness, looked in on the now peacefully sleeping and relatively cool Nan, and curled miserably under the covers in her own bed, hoping she would fall asleep before Daniel came up. She did not, and he was not deceived by the pretense, but when he ran an exploratory caressing hand beneath her smock, the immediate rippling response to which he was accustomed was not forthcoming. "Harry?"

"I'm asleep," she mumbled into the pillow.

"Oh, that would explain it," he replied, waiting for the chuckle that generally greeted that particular droll tone. It was not forthcoming either. "We could at least cuddle," he suggested.

"I don't know why you would want to cuddle me," she muttered without volition. She had not intended making her confession until she had talked with Julie, but matters seemed to be running away with themselves.

The words took a minute to sink in, then Daniel sat up, twitched aside the bedcurtains and scraped flint on tinder. Candlelight flickered, then settled into a strong, steady glow.

"What have you done?" he asked with the calm of resignation.

" 'Tis not so much what I *have* done as what I was going to do. Although what I have done is bad enough if you look at it in a certain way." The balm of relief at the prospect of unburdening herself was more soothing than she would ever have imagined, and quite surpassed her apprehension as to Daniel's reaction to the tale. She rolled onto her back, shielding her eyes with the soft curve of a forearm, ostensibly from the candlelight but more because it seemed easier if she did not have to look at him.

Daniel took her arm away. "Sit up. I don't know what I am about to hear, but the sooner it is said the better."

She sat up, hugging her knees, her beribboned nightcap askew on the cascading corn silk-colored mass, and looked at him anxiously. "I think perhaps you will not wish to be married to me anymore."

He looked startled. " 'Tis not that bad, Harry, surely?"

"Worse," she said.

"God's grace!" he muttered, getting out of bed. "Well, whatever mischief y'are in this time, I can safely promise you that I will never wish such a thing." He shrugged into his warm nightgown and drew it tight against the night chill before throwing more logs on the fire, creating a roaring blaze. "Come, let us be done with this."

She told him, her voice faltering as his expression went from resignation to disbelief, and then became utterly wrathful. But the storm did not break until she had fallen silent.

He did not raise his voice and the sleeping house around them remained oblivious of the drama, but angry words buzzed around the bedchamber like the troubles released from Pandora's box. Henrietta remained huddled over her knees. Although she winced beneath the sting of his tongue-lashing, she was more conscious of relief than anything else. She had feared a repetition of that cold, silent contempt, but this was just the fury of a very angry man. He was also most eloquent in his anger, she noticed abstractedly. In her wide experience of such matters, wrath tended to render the speaker gobbling and incoherent, so he was obliged to resort to physical expression of that rage. There was no fear of that with Daniel.

She had given him the bald narrative, unadorned by excuse or explanation, and waited for the tirade to subside before venturing on either. When at last the castigation ceased and Daniel had swung away from the bed with a muttered "Hell and the devil!" she spoke up.

"I would like to say something." Her voice sounded small and subdued in the crushing silence, but there was an edge of determination in it nevertheless.

He turned and came to the foot of the bed. He braced his arms on the wooden bar that was used to smooth the surface of the feather mattress when the bed was made, and surveyed her, his black eyes thoroughly intimidating. "If you are about to tell me that you were only trying to help, I will do you a favor, Henrietta. If I ever hear that excuse for trouble on your lips again, I shall really lose my temper."

Henrietta swallowed. In the light of the last fierce minutes, that was an appalling prospect. "I was not going to say that," she denied, plucking at the coverlet pulled tight around her knees. "I was going to ask you if you thought Julia's parents have the right to prevent her marrying Will for such a stupid reason . . . or for any reason, for that matter."

Daniel frowned and snapped, "That is no more my business than it is yours."

"But I think it is," she insisted, a note of vehemence entering her voice. "They love each other deeply, and you said yourself only last night that it would be criminal to keep apart two people who really love each other."

His black eyebrows nearly met across the bridge of his nose. "Don't you dare put words into my mouth, Henrietta. That was said without thought and at a particularly susceptible moment."

"You still said it," she persisted stubbornly. "And you meant it. I refuse to accept that Lord and Lady Morris have the right to keep Will and Julia apart simply because they know nothing of Will's family and think he is not good enough. Julia has no fortune now that they are exiled. What can she bring him except love?"

"That is no excuse for your reckless and unwarranted interference! Julia is underage and her father's responsibility . . . just as you are mine, God help me!"

"You and Lord Morris and Will may all be dead in a few months," she said fiercely. "What is the point of adhering to the old rules? Why must they be denied the chance for happiness because of some outmoded convention, when the world has already fallen apart?"

She had lost the subdued mien of a scolded child; her eyes were now bright with passionate indignation, her voice strong with conviction, her back straight with purpose. Impatiently, she knelt on the bed. "I realize

I have put you in the most abominable position, Daniel, and I do most truly beg your pardon. 'Twas thoughtless beyond belief. But I will not stand aside and see Will and Julia made unhappy for no good reason. Not when there are so many good reasons for despair. Who's to say where we will all be in six months?"

Daniel could find no satisfactory answer to that question. Instead, he took off his nightgown and bent to snuff the candle. "I have had enough of this for tonight. Lie down and go to sleep. God alone knows what I am going to say to Lord Morris on the morrow."

"I said you would not wish to cuddle me," Henrietta declared, sliding down the bed and pulling the covers up to her nose.

"Mmmm," Daniel said into the darkness and made no attempt to dispute that either.

He woke first and hitched himself on one elbow to look at the sleeping face on the pillow beside him. The hair escaping from her nightcap glistened silver and gold under a finger of early sunlight. The soft curve of her mouth, the rosy flush of sleep on the high cheekbones, the pertly snubbed nose had become such a wonderfully familiar sight for his newly opened eyes. Usually, he would lean over and kiss the paper-thin, blue-veined eyelids, and the golden crescents of her eyelashes would sweep up and those big brown eyes would gaze up at him in sleepy wonderment as she came to a realization of the new day. She would reach up and put her arms around his neck, drawing him down for the first kiss of the day, and he would revel in the warm, fragrant pliancy of her sleepy skin, the languid invitation of her body, the mischievous little chuckle with which she greeted his acceptance of the invitation.

Such love and companionship was a God-given blessing, he thought, for all that she was on occasion the most exasperating creature he had ever had dealings with. He had given up believing that she would grow out of these troublesome impulses. They seemed to be a part of her nature, and he supposed one must take the rough with the smooth. The joy of her far outweighed the annoyance.

He thought of Will and Julia. They were so young, on the threshold of life—of a life that, as Henrietta had pointed out, could come to an abrupt close very soon. His could also, but he would have had much joy and love, been thrice blessed in the two women who had shared his bed and in the benediction of his children.

He accepted the likelihood of death on the battlefield; it could as easily come from the scourge of plague or smallpox, from a broken limb, or from a severe chill. Such hazards were woven into the fabric of life. But the transitory nature of existence was surely easier to accept if one had experienced the joys adult life had to offer. Henrietta had been saying that last night, offering that wisdom as the powerful, motivating force behind her actions. If only those actions did not so frequently tend to the questionable, he thought, not for the first time. And almost certainly not for the last time, either! With a wry grin, he swung out of bed, shivering in the early morning chill.

"Are ye getting up so soon?" Henrietta sounded disconsolate as she blinked dopily at him over the bedcovers. The absence of the waking kiss seemed to indicate that a night's sleep had not brought pardon.

"I have some most disagreeable business to attend to, or had you forgotten?" He kept his voice uncompromising, revealing nothing of his earlier thoughts, as he bent to mend the dying fire. "You have also a part to play, so I suggest you rise with all speed."

She sat up. "How long are you going to be vexed?"

"I have no idea. 'Tis not something I can control," he replied unhelpfully. "Now, get up and fetch my shaving water."

Henrietta pulled on her nightgown over her smock and padded barefoot to the kitchen, where Hilde was already at work, stoking the range. "Sir Daniel would like his shaving water," she said to the maidservant.

"Would you take it up to him? I wish to see how Nan is."

Nan and Lizzie were both awake, huddled together beneath the quilt. "Can I get up today?" Nan asked.

Henrietta shook her head, bending to kiss both children. "Nay, Nan, ye must rest after a fever, otherwise it might return."

"I would rather stay in bed than learn psalms," Lizzie grumbled. "And 'tis very cold, Harry. The fire has gone out."

"I'll tell Hilde to light it again when she has taken Daddy his shaving water," Henrietta promised. "You may stay in bed until then."

She returned to the bedchamber and addressed her husband's back. "Nan seems quite better, but I said she should remain in bed today."

Daniel wiped lather off his face with a damp towel. "I'll look in on them now. Mistress Kierston will have to forgo her morning's devotions, I fear, since she must take charge of them both today. Do you dress and come downstairs straightway. You have a task to perform."

Henrietta made a face. Whatever did he mean? But his present attitude did not invite questioning. Presumably Daniel would reveal all in his own good time.

She dressed with more than usual care, choosing the most demure gown of pale blue linen, a white lawn neckerchief its only adornment. The ribboned sleeves of her smock revealed by the gown's full elbow-length sleeves and the frill of her petticoat showing beneath the hem offered the only frivolity. She braided her hair and fashioned the heavy plait into a knot at the nape of her neck. A few undisciplined, feathery tendrils curled on her forehead, but they would not lie flat whatever she did. However, despite them, her appearance was as modest and unassuming as that of any Puritan on her way to church. She composed her expression to one matching her dress and went down to the dining room.

Daniel was not fooled, but he contented himself with a skeptical raised eyebrow that she had no difficulty reading. "Hilde has forgotten to bring the bread," she said. "I will fetch it. Where are Lizzie and Mistress Kierston?"

"Breakfasting abovestairs," he told her. "They are best out of the way for the moment."

It was not at all reassuring. She went into the kitchen to fetch the bread.

Breakfast was an utterly silent meal. Daniel's appetite did not seem in the least impaired by the present state of affairs, but Harry merely nibbled on a slice of barley bread and sipped a beaker of chocolate while she waited.

Finally, Daniel swallowed his last mouthful of deviled kidney, drained his ale mug, and rose from the table. "If you have sufficiently broken your fast, Henrietta, I would like you to go and fetch your friends."

"Will and Julia?" She stared in surprise. "Here?"

"That is what I said."

She stood up, plaiting her fingers in the way she had when she was uneasy. "I do not think it right for you to be horrid to them," she said slowly. " 'Tis all right for you to be so to me, because I belong to you in some sort—"

"Aye, and I have spent half the night trying to fathom what I could ever have done to deserve it," he interrupted.

Henrietta looked at him from beneath her lashes. "Oh, I expect it was because you were an exemplary little boy, a credit to your parents. I am sure ye never fibbed, or played truant from your lessons, or dug in fox holes—"

"Harry!" Daniel exclaimed, halting this revolting description of perfection. "Of course I did." Then he realized what she had done. "Y'are the most unscrupulous, duplicitous little wretch!" he pronounced savagely. "Just go and fetch them!"

She wanted to ask why, but decided she had ventured far enough for the time being and went meekly abovestairs for her cloak.

Will received the summons in gloomy resignation.

''I expect he's going to tell me how dishonorably I've behaved. 'Twould be true enough in the old days, but now, when nothing is certain, when there is so little chance for happiness, 'tis surely not wrong to seize it when one can. Oh, Harry, how can I explain how I feel?''

''I think Daniel knows how you feel,'' she said. ''I do not know what he is going to do, but I think he is going to help.'' She did not know quite why she should be so sure of that, except that she did know her husband. Last night's ferocious scolding had been entirely genuine, and she would not argue about its justice, but it was finished, for all that he was apparently still withholding pardon.

She left Will to make his own way to the house and went to fetch Julia. She had expected to find her friend relieved and happy, since presumably she knew of Daniel's invitation, but instead Julia was pale and drawn, her eyes heavily ringed. Lady Morris, however, was all affability.

''I am delighted Julia will be staying with ye, Lady Drummond. 'Twill be so much pleasanter for her than racketing around with her father and myself. Indeed, after this last news from Scotland, there's no knowing where we will be; but His Majesty has demanded my husband's presence.'' She adjusted her neck ruff and smiled with a hint of self-importance. '' 'Tis such an honor.''

''Indeed it is, madam,'' Henrietta concurred. She found herself quite unable to resist the urge to prick that purblind smugness. The woman was a fool with her obtuse preoccupation with honors and position at such a time. ''And 'tis an honor that leads to the battlefield.'' Her gaze met Lady Morris's. ''For all those embracing the king's cause.''

The older woman looked for a second both startled and annoyed at this bold and definitely challenging statement from one who, despite her married status, still owed her elders all due deference and respect. Then shadows gathered in her eyes. She sighed heavily. "Aye, 'tis so. You speak only the truth, my dear. But Julia will be a comfort to you, I trust."

Henrietta extricated herself as expeditiously as she could. If she could have withdrawn Daniel's invitation in correct and convincing fashion at this point, she would have done so, but it could only be withdrawn by the issuer. Any bumbling attempts she might make would only make matters worse for Daniel. So she simply begged Lady Morris to permit Julia to bear her company for the morning. A generally silent Julia received permission, and the two of them left.

Henrietta was too exercised with the present situation to have time to question her friend's air of utter dejection, and since she had nothing but ill news, she was hardly surprised at Julia's continued silence. "I do not know why Daniel said I must bring you," she concluded as they hurried down the street. "But Will is to be there, also. If ye would agree to an elopement, Julie, I am certain Will can arrange it. I must not take further part, you understand why not, but Will does not need help. He will take you to his mother, who will love you. She has always stood my friend, and can be a most powerful one when she chooses. Will's happiness is of the greatest importance to her."

They turned into the square, and Henrietta became aware that Julia had showed not the slightest interest in this desperate yet feasible solution to the situation. "Are ye afeard of Daniel?" She looked up at her friend. "There's no need to be, Julie. He will not consider it his place to reproach you . . . Will, mayhap, since he has known him for so long, but not you."

Tears stood out in Julia's eyes and she shook her head inarticulately. Henrietta, reflecting that Julia did not always bear up well when circumstances became a little difficult, said nothing further. As they reached the Drummonds' house, the door swung open. Will, a little pale, stood aside to let them in.

" 'Tis all right, love," he said, taking Julie's hand. "I am here." He bent to kiss her in gentle reassurance. "We will find a way out of this maze, sweetheart."

Henrietta glanced over his shoulder to where Daniel stood in the parlor door making no attempt to intervene in this illicit display of affection. She rather suspected that Will had had an uncomfortable hour of it before she and Julie had arrived, but she also knew that Daniel would credit Will for coming to him alone.

''Come into the parlor,'' Daniel said, stepping aside to let the three of them pass. He closed the door quietly and stood regarding the trio in silence for a minute. ''Well,'' he said finally, ''just what are we going to do about this scandalous pickle?''

Julia abruptly sat down on a stool and burst into sobs. ''Oh, if 'twas only that!''

''Whatever d'ye mean, Julie?'' Henrietta dropped onto her knees beside the weeping girl.

''Oh, I have been so anxious, but I kept hoping . . . I did not wish to trouble Will, but just yesterday morning, Harry, I was so sick . . . and again this morning . . . Oh, I think I am with child!'' Julie gasped through her sobs and buried her head in her hands.

''But . . . but how could that poss—'' Henrietta broke off in confusion. Her task had been simply to arrange the lovers' trysts. What went on during them was nothing to do with her. She had somehow not thought . . .

This further complication did not surprise Daniel; the intensity of Will's love for Julie had been made clear to him in the conversation they had just had. ''I hope you realize how much of this trouble falls to your hand, Henrietta,'' he declared, shaking his head wearily.

She sprang to her feet. '' 'Tis hardly my fault that Julie is with child. That is Will's doing.''

Julie's sobs became great wrenching gasps, and Will flushed crimson. He enfolded his weeping mistress in his arms and glared furiously at Henrietta. ''D'ye have to be so indelicate?''

''Well, I hardly think 'tis a delicate matter,'' she retorted. ''I do not know why ye could not have—'' Again she stopped as it occurred to her that Will had probably been as virgin as Julia, and the simple precaution Daniel took to avert conception would not have occurred to him in his ardor and innocence. Her eyes darted self-consciously toward her husband.

"Exactly so," he said, dryly comprehending. "I suggest you keep such thoughts to yourself. They are hardly helpful."

"I do not know what you must think of me, sir," Julia wailed, burying her head in Will's shoulder.

Daniel's eyebrows shot up. "What I think of your behavior, my child, is of little relevance. That is your parents' province, not mine. And I have said what I have to to both Will and Henrietta, so I suggest we turn our attention to finding a way out of this morass."

"I will take Julie to my mother in Oxfordshire," Will said shakily. "As Harry suggested—"

"Oh, did she?" Daniel broke in. "We all know that Henrietta is a hive of brilliant and invariably questionable ideas. Ye'd be well advised, Will, for once to look for a more straightforward solution."

"Like what?" Will appeared confused, even while he continued stroking Julie's hair and murmuring soft nonsense words of reassurance and comfort.

"What Daniel means is that you should try telling the truth," Henrietta informed him, her greater experience of her husband leaving her in no doubt as to his meaning.

"Y'are learning, it would seem," Daniel observed on an arid note.

"Tell madam, my mother, that I have spoiled my maidenhead?" gasped Julia. "Tell her that I am breeding a bastard? Oh, sir, she would kill me!"

"But she would not stop ye from marrying Will," Henrietta said practically. "She'd be only too happy in such an instance for the child to be born in wedlock."

"I will go and speak with them," Will said with sudden resolution. "You must stay here, love, with Harry and Sir Daniel. I will go to your parents."

"Whilst I commend your courage, Will, I think we might be able to spare Lady Morris the shock of the whole truth and thus Julia the full extent of her mother's wrath.'' Daniel bent to poke a slipping log back into place. ''Let us keep the secret of your pregnancy amongst ourselves for the present, Julia. If y'are wed without delay, before your parents leave for Scotland, no one will question the arrival of a child a few weeks short of the nine months. We will see if we cannot gain your parents' consent without the implication of coercion. If ye must play that card, then so be it.'' He brushed off his hands vigorously. ''But let us try without, first.''

''You will lend your support, Daniel?'' Henrietta asked as her husband's intent became clear.

He nodded, saying with great deliberation, ''And would have done so at the outset, if anyone had cared to take me into his confidence.''

The silence in the room was profound. Even Julia's sobs had ceased. ''A little too ordinary a solution was it, Henrietta?'' Daniel inquired in a tone of mild curiosity.

She was for the moment tongue-tied, wondering why on earth she had not thought to enlist Daniel's voice on Will's behalf. Julia's parents held him in great esteem and would assuredly have listened to him. He could have vouched for Will's family, estate, and character in the most persuasive fashion.

''It was a grave error,'' she said with some difficulty. ''I ask your pardon.''

His eyebrows lifted infinitesimally, and he turned from her to Julia. ''Go and wash your face, Julie. When y'are composed, we will see what we can do to make all right.''

They walked to the Morrises' lodging in silence, and when they were admitted to the house, Daniel took charge smoothly, forestalling the parents' angry questions as to Will's presence in company with their daughter.

He, Will, and Lord Morris disappeared into his lordship's private sanctum. Lady Morris, who at this point had no reason to accuse her daughter of wrongdoing, demanded what was happening, and when Julia burst into renewed sobs, her ladyship marched into the sanctum after the gentlemen, leaving Henrietta to do what she could for her distraught friend.

After one of the longest hours Henrietta could ever remember spending, they were joined in the parlor by the others. Will's freckles stood out prominently against the extreme pallor of his complexion, Daniel was expressionless, Lady Morris tearful, her husband grim-faced.

"So ye would be wed, would ye?" he demanded of his daughter. "And a fine way you'd go about it. I've heard the whole disgraceful story from Sir Daniel."

Henrietta's eyes shot in questioning alarm to Daniel, but he shook his head very slightly and she breathed again. "I bear the greatest responsibility, Lord Morris," she said firmly. "It would never have occurred to Julie to act in such shameful fashion had I not suggested it."

"That may be so," Morris said gruffly. "But *your* behavior is a matter for your husband, Lady Drummond."

"And I do not condone it, as I have said," Daniel put in. "But I do understand why Henrietta felt impelled to act as she did." He walked to the hearth, where the coals glowed brightly. He began to speak in a voice resonant with feeling, one that held the attention of everyone in the room. "Love is a most precious thing. And I believe it to be a rare thing, particularly in wedlock. It is, after all, in general not a consideration in the arrangement of marriages." Daniel's bright black eyes rested for a second on his wife's rapt countenance. "I have been blessed twice. There was great love between myself and my first wife, shattered only by her death." He glanced at Lady Morris, noting with satisfaction that his words were having the desired effect. A certain softness had entered her eyes.

"I did not expect," he went on with quiet deliberation, "ever to experience such joy again . . . ever to share in that way again. I did expect to wed again, but assumed that I must be satisfied with a helpmeet and a mother for my children. I certainly have that. But there is more . . . much more.''

Henrietta was aware that she was looking at him with painful intensity, that her cheeks were warm, that tears were pricking her eyes. She was also aware of Will's gaze fixed upon her.

''If anything,'' Daniel was continuing in the same steady voice, ''the love I have found this second time is even greater than the first. I would never have believed it possible, but it is so.'' He turned to Julia's parents. ''I would never deny a child of mine the possibility of such happiness . . . particularly when her heart has gone to such a one as Will Osbert. I would not hesitate to bestow the hand of a daughter upon him, and I know his parents will welcome his bride.''

He pursed his lips for a second in thought, and no one broke the moment of silence. ''I would ask you also to consider this one other thing. Will is committed to the king's cause, as are we, Morris. He will fight for that cause, and he may die for it, as may we. This is not a time to delay the pursuit of happiness when 'tis offered.''

He moved away from the hearth. ''Come, Henrietta, let us leave these good people now to manage their own business as they see fit.''

She shook herself free of the cobwebby daze enfolding her. Daniel had stood in front of these near strangers and exposed his innermost feelings to aid Will and Julia. He had declared his love for his wife in the most public fashion. And she had not even thought to confide in him and ask his help. It was a dismaying reflection.

Out in the street, she skipped a little to keep pace with his long-legged stride, and he slowed instantly. ''I do not know why I did not think to tell you,'' she said.

'' 'Twas certainly a grave oversight,'' he returned evenly.

''It was not that I do not trust you.''

''Nay, I am aware.''

They walked in silence for a few more minutes, then Henrietta asked hesitantly, "Did you truly mean what you said, Daniel, about . . . about loving me in that manner?"

"Aye, I meant it, every word. Just as I mean this: if you ever implicate me in such a disgraceful imbroglio again, all the love in the world will not protect you!"

An appropriate response failing to come to mind, she kept silent, but after a few minutes a small hand crept warmly into his.

Daniel looked down at her upturned face. Her brown eyes were laughing up at him, her soft mouth curved in that irresistibly sensual appeal. "Ramshackle creature!" he said. "I wonder if you'll ever change." He shook his head. "I wonder if I wish you to. Somehow, I do not think I do." He shook his head again at this perverse but undeniable admission.

Chapter 20

It was a night of unrelieved dark when the French fishing boat nudged the sandy shore of the little bay on the Kentish coast. Its six passengers disembarked in near silence, barely a whisper interrupting the steady slurp as waves fell and receded in rhythmic motion against the shore, causing the small craft to rock unsteadily.

"I wet my foot!" A plaintive cry rustled in the air. "There's sea in my shoe."

"Hush, Lizzie." Daniel's urgent instruction was whispered as he lifted her swiftly, swinging her away from the water's edge. "Harry, take them into the shelter of the cliff while Will and I see to the unloading."

Henrietta took the children by the hand. "Come, Julia." She moved up the beach, followed by the other woman, who walked more slowly, impeded by the bulk of her pregnant belly.

"Take your shoe off, Lizzie." In the lee of the cliff, Harry bent to unfasten the child's shoe. "Your stocking is soaked. When Daddy brings the luggage, we will find you a clean one."

" 'Tis cold," Nan whimpered. "And I am afeared."

Julia hugged the little girl reassuringly. "There's no need to be afeared, Nan." But they all knew there was.

"There, that is everything." Daniel placed his burdens on the sand, his voice still a whisper. "The boat will be beyond the headland again within half an hour."

"I wonder which one has the children's clothes in it," Henrietta muttered, peering at the oblong shapes of the leather portmanteaux. "Lizzie must change her stocking or she will catch cold."

"I want to go home," Nan whimpered again. " 'Tis dark and cold and I'm awearied."

"Why could we not stay in The Hague with Mistress Kierston?" Lizzie demanded, forgetting, as scared and exhausted children are wont to do, the delight with which she and Nan had greeted the news that this time they were not to be left behind. She sat on the sand to pull on the stocking Henrietta handed her.

"But then ye'd have had to go to church four times a day," Henrietta said in rallying tones. "Now that Mistress Kierston is enamoured of the pastor. Be of good cheer, now. Ye'll be in bed soon."

"If the messenger was able to get to Tom." Daniel stared worriedly into the darkness.

"I'll go to the cliff top," Will offered. "Perchance I'll find him above."

"Be careful, Will." Julia's voice shook slightly, and her hand cupped the mound of her belly.

Her husband turned and kissed her. "As careful as 'tis possible to be," he said simply, and loped off into the darkness.

Daniel uncorked a flask and handed it to Julia. "Take a sip; 'twill put warmth into you." She swallowed once and he handed the flask to Henrietta.

She shook her head ruefully. "Nay, 'twill only make me sick again."

He nodded, attempting to conceal his anxiety. The svelte shape showed little sign as yet of the life it carried, but her pregnancy so far was not an easy one and she had been wretchedly unwell in the tiny tossing fishing boat during the Channel crossing. Her big eyes were sunken in pale cheeks, dark circles beneath them, yet she held herself upright and her voice was cheerful, revealing nothing of the fatigue he knew she must be suffering.

She had turned to the girls and was talking to them about the shells she found on the sand, just as if this were an everyday excursion and she was imparting her knowledge of the outdoors in accustomed fashion.

"Ah, Sir Daniel, thank God y'are safe."

At the familiar gruff voice coming out of the darkness, Daniel swung around with a sigh of relief. "Tom, it does me more good than I can say to hear ye. The message got through, then?"

"Aye, the man reached me two days since, and Master Will arrived at the cliff top just as I did," Tom whispered back, clasping Sir Daniel's hand. He looked at the huddled group. "Eh, little maids, there's no need for such long faces." He patted the girls' cheeks with the familiarity of one who had known them all their lives.

"They're cold and awearied, Tom," Henrietta said.

Tom accorded Lady Drummond a long look. "Ye don't look too fit, yerself," he commented gruffly.

Henrietta smiled slightly. Tom's acceptance of Daniel's marriage to that hoity maid had been a long time coming. "Y'are not acquainted with Mistress Osbert, Tom," she said, drawing Julia forward.

Tom bobbed his head in greeting. "Seems ye've all been rather busy these past months."

Julia blushed, but the other three adults chuckled, quite used to Tom's manner.

"Let's be out of here, Tom," Daniel whispered briskly. "Ye've a cart waiting?"

"Aye." Tom hoisted Nan onto his shoulders, picked up one of the portmanteaux, and turned to the cliff path. " 'Twill take the maids and the ladies. Us'd best use our legs for now, but I've three good horses for tomorrow."

Daniel swung Lizzie onto his shoulders and took up his own share of the luggage. Will took his and gave Julia his arm. Henrietta gathered up her skirts and marched up the steep path. Daniel smiled. Four months with child, queasy and dreadfully weary, she might be, but she could manage quite well without a helping hand.

The dray and its two horses stood in the deep shadow of a bramble hedge. "The cottage is but a mile," Tom whispered, depositing his burdens on the floor of the vehicle. "I'll lead the horses."

Despite the pitchy dark, the horses moved without stumbling, heads lowered as they hauled their burden along the narrow cart track, where the mud was ridged, hard and dry after the long summer. A yellow gleam showed faint, and the beasts' step seemed to quicken as if they sensed the closeness of stable and feed.

Henrietta was sitting on the cart floor, leaning against the hard wooden side, Nan asleep in her lap, Lizzie curled against her shoulder.

"Are we here?" Julia whispered wearily. "The jolting is quite dreadful."

"Aye, 'tis so," Harry agreed, trying to adjust her stiff limbs without waking the children. "But I think that must be it." She twisted her head over the side of the cart. "Daniel?"

He came up with her immediately. "Is aught amiss, love?"

"Nay." She shook her head. "But are we close?"

"The light up yonder," he said softly. "Are ye sadly jolted?"

She grinned wearily at him. "I think you have the best of it, walking."

This was his own indomitable Harry. Ramshackle, hoity, impulsive, unscrupulous, but always courageous and ineffably lovable. He brushed a lock of hair from her forehead and smiled. "Not long now."

The cottage was bare and earthen floored, its tiny windows unglazed, but there was a fire and blankets, and a cauldron of vegetable soup over the fire. The girls barely stirred as they were tucked into blankets, and slept upon the floor as if it was the softest feather bed.

"Eat, Harry." Daniel filled a bowl with soup. She shook her head. "You need nourishment," he insisted, quiet but firm. "Ye've nothing left inside you after that voyage."

She shuddered slightly at the memory. "My stomach feels bruised and my throat aches. I don't think I could swallow."

"Y'are going to, nevertheless." He sat down on the bench beside her, dipped a spoon into the soup, and held it to her lips. "Come, do not make me annoyed, sweetheart."

She smiled faintly at that. "You wouldn't be so unkind."

"I just might. Now, open your mouth."

She did so obediently, swallowed, and felt the warmth trickle soothingly down her raw throat to curl in her stomach. She moved to take the spoon from him. "I do not need to be fed, Daniel."

"Finish every last drop."

He watched her gravely until the bowl was empty. "There, now you can sleep." Unresisting, she allowed him to wrap her in blankets, roll another one under her head for a pillow, and tuck her into a shadowy corner of the room.

"Are you not going to sleep?" she murmured against his mouth as he bent to kiss her. " 'Tis lonely under this blanket."

"Soon, but I must make plan with Tom for the morrow," he replied.

She was deep in sleep when he finally came to lie down beside her, drawing her back into his embrace as he curled his body protectively around hers, feeling the fragility of that diminutive figure. Would she have the strength to face what lay ahead? It was a question he had asked himself many times, and he still did not know the answer. But it was a question they must each ask about themselves now that the end had begun.

Cromwell's response to the crowning of King Charles at Scone had been to overrun the Scottish lowlands and advance to Perth, threatening to cut off the royal army at Stirling from its source of supplies. Royalists from all over Europe had been landing in secret throughout the spring and summer, making their way to join the king. Daniel had waited until news had come that the king, at the head of his army, had crossed the Scottish border, entered England, and was marching south. On the morrow, Daniel and Will would journey to meet them. And their wives and children, the born and the unborn, must make shift for themselves until it was finally over.

Such thoughts kept him wakeful through the tail end of the night, and dawn brought him quietly to his feet, gently disengaging himself from his sleeping wife. He went outside, breathing deeply of English air edged with the salt tang of the sea. This was his country, and whatever happened he knew that he could not continue to live in exile. He would fight once more for his king, and if he lived he would return to his home, whether the land bowed beneath the yoke of the Puritan or raised its head in acknowledgment of its sovereign.

"What are you thinking?"

He turned at the sound of Harry's voice. She came over to him, brushing her hair away from her face, knuckling the sleep from her eyes. "Solemn thoughts?"

"Aye." He put an arm around her shoulder, drawing her against him. "How d'ye feel this morning?"

"Well," she replied. "Only a little queasy."

" 'Twill pass," he said. "Nan was always sick for the first months, then it passed."

"Aye, I daresay." She shrugged slightly. " 'Tis just a nuisance at present when I would feel at my best."

"You will be at Glebe Park by this evening," he said. "Then you may take your ease and recover your strength."

"Yes," she said.

Daniel felt the first familiar prickle of unease. "Henrietta, I have told you exactly what you are to do, have I not?"

"Yes," she replied.

"Would you please repeat what I have said?" he asked carefully. "Just so that I may be certain you have fully understood."

"I am to go to Glebe Park with Julia and the girls. Julie will be brought to bed there within the next two weeks. I am to ask Frances for assistance in this and all things. On your way to join the king, Will will visit his parents and inform Mistress Osbert of his marriage and the coming child. She will, of course, make her way to Glebe Park as fast as she is able. The girls and I are to remain at Glebe Park, where news will reach us as to the outcome of the venture." She recited her lesson faultlessly, her voice flat.

"Exactly so," Daniel said. "And you are not to deviate from those instructions in the slightest. Is that perfectly understood?"

"Perfectly," she replied in the same tone. "Had we better not waken the children? The sooner we are on our way, I think, the better."

He could only agree with her, but that prickle of unease would not go away. She was composed and cheerful as they packed up their belongings again and loaded the cart.

"Y'are certain you know which road to take?" Daniel asked anxiously as he stood by the dray. Julie and Will were nowhere to be seen, presumably making their farewells in private. The children were already seated in the cart, their faces serious, eyes a little fearful. They were both well aware of the gravity of this parting, and the momentous events that were to take place. Tom, who was to go with Will and Sir Daniel, was adjusting the harness of the nearside cart horse.

"I take the road to Ashford, and then to Headcorn," Henrietta told him calmly. " 'Tis local lanes from there." Suddenly, she smiled and it was the old mischievous Harry smile. "D'ye doubt me, Daniel? There's advantages to being a ramshackle creature, you know. We may be unscrupulous and impulsive, but we are not daunted by adventures."

He took her face between his hands and kissed her, lingering long on her mouth, inhaling deeply of the scent of her skin, feeling the curve of cheek and chin under his fingers. When would he do this again? But he would not permit the question . . . could not permit the question.

He drew back at last and stood looking down at her, losing himself in the liquid velvet of her eyes. "I love you, my elf," he whispered. She did not reply, but he could read her own affirmation shining in her eyes. His hands slipped from her face, down to her shoulders, down to her waist. Then, with resolution, he lifted her into the cart.

"You will take proper care of yourself and our child that you bear," he said, putting the reins into her hands.

"I will take care of them all," she said. "Do not doubt me."

"I do not." He turned from her to his children, who were now tearful and strained and clung to him, so that he had to put them from him, swallowing his own tears as he tried to make some teasing comment in his usual style. He failed miserably.

Will, his freckles standing out against the deathly pallor of his face, helped the weeping Julia into the dray. "Look after her, Harry," he enjoined. "I cannot bear—"

"I will look after her," his friend said, leaning down to touch his face. "*You* look after yourself." Then, without a further word or a backward glance, she twitched the reins, clicked at the horses, and took them away down the lane.

Daniel stood watching until the dray had turned the far corner. His little Harry was shouldering a tremendous burden of responsibility, and he had had no choice but to lay it upon her. And she had accepted it without a murmur. The loving child who was always falling in and out of trouble in her efforts to improve matters for those she loved seemed to have disappeared under the burden, and he was filled with a great sense of loss.

It was mid-afternoon when Henrietta turned the dray between the stone gateposts of Glebe Park. She remembered her first arrival here, the children squealing with joy at their father's return from the war . . . would there be another such return? But she would not permit the question . . . could not permit it.

"Nearly home," she said cheerfully to Nan, who had clambered up onto the driving seat beside her.

"There's no smoke," Lizzie said, peering down the driveway to where the house stood, glowing under the August sun. "There's always a fire in the kitchen."

Henrietta felt the first chill of apprehension. Something was amiss. She could feel it in the air, could see it in the signs of neglect, the weeds choking the driveway, the unruly box hedges. Before they left for The Hague, Daniel's house and estate had been in good order, restored to its prewar neatness and productivity. In the two and a half years of their absence, the hand on the reins had obviously been lamentably slack. Just where was Master Herald?

She pulled in the cart at the front door and jumped down, the children scrambling after her. She turned to assist Julie while the girls ran to the front door and began hammering on the great brass knocker. The door opened to reveal a startled woman, with straggly gray hair escaping from a dirty cap and a grimy apron over an equally grubby petticoat.

" 'Tis old Jenny," Henrietta muttered. "She's been pensioned off these three years." She strode over to the door. "Where is Susan Yates?"

"Eh . . . madam . . . but she's gone to tend her sister as is sick," the woman said, backing away from this small but commanding figure.

"Then who else is here?" Henrietta marched past the woman into the hall and looked around in dismay at the thick coating of dust everywhere, the dullness of the oak paneling, the mud on the flagged floor.

Whatever would Daniel say to see his beloved home in this state of neglect?

"There's only me and old Jake, m'lady," the crone mumbled. "There's been no call to 'ave anyone else 'ere with the family all gone and no knowin' if'n they'd ever be back."

It was very clear to Henrietta what had happened. Revenues from the estate were plentiful enough to ensure its smooth running and pay the wages of the staff Daniel had left, but in the master's absence the mice had definitely gone out to play.

"Where is Master Herald?" she snapped. The bailiff was ultimately responsible, since he was Daniel's agent and representative in his absence.

Lizzie, Nan, and Julia were staring in amazement at this extraordinary Henrietta, who had started on a tour of the house, her voice rising with angry disgust, her brown eyes snapping furiously. On being informed that the bailiff had been laid up with the gout these last six weeks, she turned to Lizzie and Nan.

"Go to Master Herald's house this instant, inform him that we are back, and tell him to come up to the house straightway."

"But I wanted to—"

"Do as I say!" Henrietta interrupted Lizzie's protestation, and the children with a gasp ran off to do her bidding.

Julie sank down wearily on the window seat. "I beg pardon, Harry. I would help if I could. Perhaps if I rest a little first."

"You shall have your bed," Henrietta said firmly. She turned to the now mumbling crone. "Fetch some people to help you get this place in order. I do not mind how many or who, but I want the kitchen fires lit, the beds made, the floors scrubbed, and the furniture polished by nightfall."

"Lord, Harry," Julie said in awe when the old woman had hurried off, muttering. "Y'are a veritable terror. I would never have believed it possible."

"I'll not have Daniel robbed," she declared. "Come

upstairs and we'll see which bedchamber you would prefer. There's a very pretty one overlooking the orchard."

When Master Herald arrived, limping and leaning heavily on a cane, he was confronted by a diminutive fury who barely gave him time for excuses. Like everyone else on the estate, he had known Lady Drummond as no more than a child, unversed in the arts of housekeeping, treated by her husband rather in the manner of an indulgent guardian. This Lady Drummond bore little relation to that other. She calmed down sufficiently, however, to listen to his excuses of ill health, which had prevented his keeping a close eye on the estate.

"Well, if ye cannot perform the task yourself, Master Herald, then we must find someone who can," she said briskly. "I would do it myself, but I do not intend to be—" She stopped abruptly. Perhaps now was not a good moment to explain that she would not be remaining at Glebe Park.

The bailiff said that he thought he would be able to resume his duties now that the family was returned and then hobbled off, leaving Henrietta to turn her attention to the condition of the kitchen, the empty pantry closet, and the absence of the cook.

When Frances Ellicot arrived three days later, she found the lady of the house energetically berating the dairyman for permitting the cows to get into the field-mustard pasture, a heavily pregnant young woman sitting sewing with Frances's nieces in the parlor, and a general aura of industry about the house.

Lady Ellicot looked tired and sad, but she embraced her sister-in-law warmly. "Henrietta, my dear, I could not believe you were back when the lad came with the message."

"I was wondering if aught was amiss with ye, Frances," Henrietta said directly, certain that if James and Frances had been in good health and spirits matters would not have been permitted to deteriorate as they had done on the Drummond estate.

Frances sighed, even as she bent to embrace the girls, jumping insistently at her skirt. "James has been sick unto death with quartaine agues, and I miscarried of a child two months past." Her eyes went longingly toward Julia, who stood waiting quietly.

Henrietta made the introduction even as she realized that she would have to revise her plans in some measure. Frances and James were in no condition to take charge of Lizzie and Nan as she had intended, so she must find an alternative solution.

"Daniel has gone to the king?" Frances asked, although she guessed the answer.

"Aye, and Will, Julia's husband," Henrietta told her calmly. "When Julie is delivered, I will join them myself."

Frances looked astonished, and Julia dropped her needle. "But Sir Daniel said you were to stay here, Harry."

"Yes, but I cannot," she replied in the same calm tone.

"But . . . but y'are with child," Julia said. "Ye cannot go to the wars like ye did before."

"Y'are with child?" Frances asked.

Henrietta nodded. "Four months. But 'tis no great inconvenience at present, and will not hamper me." She went to the door. "Take your ease, Frances. I will bring refreshment. Lizzie and Nan, you may come with me and carry goblets and the apple tart Cook made this morning."

Frances took off her cloak and sat down. "What an extraordinary transformation," she said, shaking her head. "Ye've known Henrietta for long, Mistress Osbert?"

Julia explained as much of the past as she felt able. " 'Tis very hard to stop Harry when she has her mind set," she said at the end. "Only Sir Daniel seems able to do that . . . and then—"

"And then not very often," Frances finished for her.

"Well, if he knows what she is intending, he can,"

Julia offered. "But when he does not . . ." She shrugged.

Frances frowned and offered no dispute. "I was very much afraid matters would have gone awry with the house and the estate in the last months, since my husband has been unable to oversee things. But I see 'twas not the case."

"Oh, indeed, it was!" Julia exclaimed. "But Harry has hardly slept the last few days. She was most ferocious with the bailiff and the housekeeper, and she found the cook and made him come back. She says she will not permit people to steal from Sir Daniel."

Frances absorbed this and wished she could see her brother with his wife. Had that deep fondness become something else? Henrietta was certainly not the ingenuous, bristly yet appealing child she had been. And there was no question but that Daniel's daughters accepted their stepmother's authority, for all that the ease of their relationship bespoke a sisterly authority rather than parental.

However, Frances did feel that she owed her brother at least an attempt to influence his wife on this wild scheme she had settled upon. "Henrietta, I do think that you should reconsider," she began, once a goblet of warm sack had been placed in her hands. "Daniel has told you to stay here, and 'tis not seemly for a wife to defy her husband. Besides, 'tis utter craziness to go in search of the army."

Henrietta shook her head and sliced the apple tart. "Nay, 'tis no craziness, Frances. 'Tis something I must do. If Daniel is in danger, then I must be with him whatever he would say."

It was such a simple statement, one that Daniel Drummond would hear and understand with a groan of resignation. Frances was silent for a minute, then she shook her head in defeat. "Ye'll not take the girls?"

"Of course not. I shall settle them in London, at the inn with Dorcas. She will care for them as well as any could."

"I would offer, but—"

"I understand, Frances." Henrietta laid a hand over the older woman's. "I would not ask it of you, and this will do as well."

"We're to go to London!" Lizzie shrieked. "We've never been to London."

"Nay, because your father does not consider it a suitable place for children," Frances said, looking at Daniel's wife.

Henrietta shrugged. "These are not gentle times and one must do what one must."

Frances left soon after, convinced that Daniel had a wife who would do exactly as she felt she must, and no amount of persuasion or remonstrance would change her mind. In the present circumstances, perhaps no one had the right to persuade or remonstrate. If Daniel survived the closing battle of this civil war, he would deal with her defiant impulse as he saw fit, and if he did not survive, then it mattered little.

In the early hours of the next morning, Henrietta was wakened by an unearthly shriek. She shot up in the big bed, where she now slept alone. Her heart pounded as she blinked, bemused and disoriented. Then she realized what it must be. Swiftly, she pulled on her nightgown as she swung out of bed. The shriek came again as she opened the door, and she ran down the corridor to Julia's chamber.

"I cannot help it," Julia gasped. " 'Tis worse pain than you could ever imagine, Harry."

Henrietta ran to the bed, taking Julie's hand, holding it fast. "How long has it been like this?"

"Hours," Julia answered, groaning. "I did not wish to wake anyone until it was necessary. But now—" She cried out again, gripping Harry's hand until it went numb. "I am afeared, Harry."

Henrietta thought rapidly. She had some idea of the birthing process. Her stepmother had dutifully presented her lord with offspring on an annual basis and it was impossible for a curious and intelligent child not to pick up a deal of information. But she had never assisted at a delivery . . . and Will's mother was supposed to have arrived before Julia was brought to bed. Why did the best-laid plans always go awry?

She removed her hand gently from Julia's grip. "I will send someone for the midwife in the village, Julie."

"Don't go!" Julia grabbed her again, her face contorted. "I think 'tis coming . . . don't leave me, Harry!"

Henrietta swallowed hard, controlled her rising panic, and pulled aside the bedclothes. This baby was going to be born with or without her inexpert help; it would be best if it were with.

Julie cried out again and the veins stood out on her neck with the supreme effort she was making to obey the dictates of her body. Henrietta murmured encouragement and reassurance and watched in awe as a round dark head pushed its way into the world. Instinctively, she bent to help this new person in its elemental struggle, and Will and Julia's son slipped forth into her hands.

She stood looking down at the blood-streaked scrap in stunned wonder. " 'Tis a boy, Julie." The baby was lying quite inert in her hands, and she tentatively lifted him upright. At the movement, the tiny mouth opened and a squall filled the room. Henrietta breathed a sigh of relief even as she wondered what else she should do.

"Give him to me," Julie's voice was a mere thread.

Henrietta laid the baby on her breast. "Keep him warm, and I will go and fetch someone. I do not know what is to be done now."

She hurried up to the attics where the servants slept, waking old Jenny, who shrieked as she saw Henrietta's blood-stained hands but then became reassuringly competent. Henrietta watched closely as the business of birthing was brought to a tidy close, determined that in future she would know how to do it all herself. She felt a surge of envy for Julie, her labor done, a healthy son at her breast, a smile of peace and contentment on her lips. What would it be like for her, five months hence? Would the child she delivered have a father?

Would Julie's child? But such thoughts had no place in the joy of this moment. She bent to kiss her friend, to touch with a wondering finger the tiny creased forehead of the baby.

"You will stand his godmother, Harry?"

"Joyfully," she said. "I do feel I have a rather special interest in him, after all."

Julie smiled. "Will favors Robert. What d'ye think?"

"I think that if that's what his papa wishes, that's what he should be named," Harry said with a smile. "I believe he's going to have red hair."

"Is the baby born?" The excited whisper came from the door. Henrietta turned to see the two girls, in smock and nightcap, peering wide-eyed around the corner.

"Aye," she said, beckoning them in. "How did you know?"

"I heard all the noise," Lizzie said importantly. "And I remembered how 'twas when Nan was born."

"But my mother died," Nan said matter-of-factly, clambering onto the bed. "Julie isn't going to, is she, Harry?"

"No," Henrietta said firmly, adding her own private "God willing" to herself, as she watched the children exclaiming over the infant and Julie's proud presentation of her son. It was a hazardous and unpredictable business, this giving birth, and it would be a week before they could be truly certain that the mother would not fall victim to the scourge of fever.

"I think we should leave Julie to rest now," she said, lifting Nan from the bed. "You can come back later this morning." She shooed them out of the chamber and went to her own to dress. The sun was now up and she had much to accomplish before she left for London. Mistress Osbert's arrival could not be long delayed.

Chapter 21

Mistress Osbert, on her arrival the following afternoon, was much less restrained than Lady Ellicot when informed by a serenely resolute Henrietta of her intention to follow the drum.

''Do not be absurd, Henrietta,'' she said crisply, tying a capacious apron around her ample waist. ''You will stay here like a dutiful wife and await your husband's return.'' She turned to the stair. ''Now take me to my daughter-in-law and my grandson.''

''When did you see Will and Daniel?'' Henrietta did not bother to argue, but started up the staircase.

''Just two days past. I left immediately to come here. They were both well, but poor Will was in a fever of anxiety about his wife.'' Mistress Osbert strode briskly upward. ''Sir Daniel bade me tell you to be patient and of good cheer.''

''Where were they going?'' Henrietta turned to the left at the head of the staircase.

''To Worcester. His Majesty and the army were three days' journey from that town and Cromwell was marching upon it also. 'Tis to be expected that the battle will be fought there.'' Mistress Osbert gave the information in level tones. She had endured ten years of war and had reached some measure of acceptance. Her husband had retired from the battlefield, but her son had taken his place. It was the lot of women to watch and wait, patiently and in good cheer.

Worcester. Some sixty miles from Oxford . . . as far

again from London. Could she reach there in time for the battle? She would learn more in London. Henrietta flung open the door to Julia's chamber. "See who is here, Julie. Will's mother is come."

She stood aside then, watching with a smile as Mistress Osbert enfolded her new daughter in a fierce embrace, wept over her grandson, and instantly took charge. That was one responsibility she had fulfilled, Henrietta decided with a satisfied nod. Julie had no further need of her.

Lizzie and Nan were summoned to meet Mistress Osbert, who accorded them a thorough examination and pronounced them prettily behaved and a credit to their father. She turned kindly eyes upon Henrietta, noticing that the girl had an abstracted air.

"My dear child, you have done beautifully," she said. "I always knew you would not fail when you were called upon. But your husband says y'are with child, and I think 'tis time you took a care for yourself."

"I intend to, madam," Henrietta said. "I am leaving for London in the morning."

Mistress Osbert's jaw dropped. She was not in the least accustomed to being gainsaid, for all that she knew Henrietta Ashby to be a willful, unbiddable girl. A mewling cry from the crib by the window distracted her. "We will talk of this further, Henrietta." She bustled over to her grandchild.

"Come." Henrietta drew the children from the chamber. "I wish ye to gather together your belongings. You will know what you both will need, Lizzie, in the way of clothes . . . not too much because we will take only two horses. Nan may ride pillion with me."

"We are going to ride all the way to London?" Lizzie's eyes shone at the prospect of such an adventure.

"We will stop one night upon the road," Henrietta said. "But we must leave at daybreak." Left to herself, she would have set out immediately, riding through the night, but she could not do that with the children, any more than she could expect them to make the journey in one day. There was no one here with whom she could in good conscience leave them. The two Mistress Osberts would remove to Oxfordshire as soon as Julia was fit to travel, and Daniel would not wish to be beholden to Will's mother in such an instance, not when he had entrusted his daughters to their stepmother's care.

Mistress Osbert found Henrietta adamant, calm but fearsomely determined. The older woman held no authority over her. Only Daniel Drummond had the right, legal and moral, to compel his wife's obedience, and he was not here to do so. Henrietta and the girls set off for London on the first day of September, as the first gray streaks of dawn lightened the sky.

They reached the city by mid-afternoon of the following day, and Henrietta, who had not allowed herself to consider what she would do if Dorcas was not to be found in the narrow lane off Paternoster Row, felt her heart speed as they ascended Ludgate Hill. Nan was asleep, now slumped in front of her, held within the circle of her arm, Lizzie still gamely sitting her own mount, but the child's weariness was palpable. Then they were there, outside the familiar house, and the stoop gleamed as white as ever, the cobbles were swept, the brass shone, the windows winked in the afternoon sunlight. Dorcas was definitely to be found.

In a strange way, Henrietta felt as if she had come home. Dorcas, tiny and voluble as ever, bobbed, exclaimed, hugged, kissed, and brought instant relief of anxiety and fatigue. She was overjoyed to see the children, wept a little at their likeness to their mother, then recovered briskly as she remembered Henrietta, who might be uncomfortable at such an observation.

"Harry's going to find Daddy," Lizzie confided, "so we're to stay here with you."

"Where is Sir Daniel?"

"With the king," Harry said. "I would go to him, but need to be sure of the children's safety."

"I remember the last time," Dorcas said. "Sir Daniel wasn't best pleased, as I recall."

The execution of Charles Stuart. A lifetime ago. Henrietta shook her head ruefully. "Mayhap he will not be this time, Dorcas, but I must go nevertheless. There's talk of a battle to be fought at Worcester."

"Aye," Dorcas said somberly. "But 'twill take ye all of two days to reach there. Ye'd do best to stay here until there's news one way or t'other. The town criers are busy enough these days, crying the news from the rooftops . . . and gloomy enough it is, for the most part," she added. "The English militia are flocking to Cromwell, there's few who'll join a Scottish army . . . invaders, they say they are, even though it's His sainted Majesty as heads 'em."

The Royalists were going to lose this last battle. Henrietta had always known it in her heart, as she knew that Daniel had known it. But he had had to sustain his commitment until there was no possibility of doing so. Death would bring an end to that possibility . . . She could not bear his death, so it would not happen.

"Nay, I'll journey to Oxford tomorrow, Dorcas," she said. "I cannot kick my heels here, waiting for news."

She set off again at dawn, riding through the streets of London and out into the countryside, taking the Oxford road. At Henley she heard the news. Battle had been joined that day at Worcester.

She could not bear Daniel's death, so it would not happen.

She rode on, stopping in villages to discover if there was more news, but there was only the anxious buzz of speculation. Laborers leaned upon their pitchforks in the fields. Women gathered on the village greens, their menfolk outside the taverns. On more than one occasion, she came across a fanatical Puritan preaching in the open air hellfire and damnation to all those joined in the treasonous, blasphemous battle with the forces of good. The audiences muttered and shuffled, the temper of the crowd uncertain.

She rode into Oxford in the late afternoon. Crowds milled in the city streets, anxious speculation on every lip, in every eye. The city had been for the king since the long struggle had begun in 1640. The vast wealth of the university had gone to swell the king's coffers in the early days of the war. Now fear and hope hovered, trembled in the air.

She could not bear Daniel's death, so it would not happen.

Her horse was quivering with weariness after the third day's journeying. Henrietta reined in outside a small hostelry, where the sign of the Bear and Ragged Staff creaked in the chilly wind, newly sprung with the scent of autumn. Her mount hung his head and blew wretchedly through his nostrils, and she dismounted with a guilty pang.

The inn was busy, but bed space was found for this lone traveler, and stabling for the horse. If the innkeeper thought there was anything untoward in a woman of obvious rank traveling without maid or groom, he did not say so. Times were such that nothing was questionable, and the lady's coin was as good as any.

Henrietta was too tired to eat, but she forced herself to swallow soup and bread. For some reason, the nausea that had plagued her for the last two months had vanished, and it occurred to her that a body could only concentrate on one thing at once. Fear, determination, and exhaustion were quite enough to be going on with. Symptoms of pregnancy were superfluous.

She fell into a dark and dreamless sleep, undisturbed by the snores and tossings of her bedfellow, the plump wife of a local farmer journeying to assist at the confinement of her sister. Battles being fought at Worcester, some sixty miles distant, concerned the lady only insofar as they might impede her journey.

The hubbub in the street at first failed to penetrate Henrietta's stupor, and she woke only when her bedfellow sat up with a great cry of, "Mercy me, whatever is it? Is it a fire?"

Henrietta sprang from bed and ran to open the casement onto the broad thoroughfare of St. Giles. The crowds below, cloaks over their nightclothes in many instances, were surging toward Carfax. The words "Defeat . . . Great victory . . . God save His Majesty" mingled, a confused jumble drifting up to where she leaned out, straining to make some sense of the turmoil.

''There is news of the battle,'' she said tersely to her companion, dragging her gown over her head, hooking the bodice with trembling fingers, pushing her feet into her boots. Then she was out of the chamber, running down the stairs, past the innkeeper, who stood in shirt and nightcap in the open door staring at the crowds streaming past, and out into the street, joining the throng.

''What is the news?'' she demanded of the man at her side.

''The crier is at Carfax,'' he told her. ''We'll discover soon enough.''

She could not bear Daniel's death, so it would not happen.

At Carfax, the town center, where the four main thoroughfares met, the crowd jostled and eddied. On the raised dais, the crier stood ringing his bell, the sound to Henrietta's fearful ears urgent and menacing. At last, the bell ceased and he lifted his voice over the seething mass of humanity come to hear his message.

He cried of a decisive victory on September third at Worcester for Cromwell's New Model and the English militia who had fought at its side. The Scots and the Royalist forces were scattered . . . King Charles fled, a fugitive in his own land from his own subjects. Cromwell's army had taken prisoners . . . many prisoners. The hunt went on for others who had dared to take arms against the legal government of the land, and most particularly for one Charles Stuart, who, like his father, had caused so much English blood to be shed upon English soil. All honest citizens were enjoined to watch for fleeing Royalists, to apprehend them, to report any sightings to the military authorities.

The bell rang again, and again the news was cried for any who had failed to hear it the first time. Henrietta moved as if in a trance, pushing her way out of the crowd, where voices swelled in anger, in triumph, in sorrow.

She could not bear Daniel's death, so it would not happen.

But something had happened to him, she could feel it at the very core of her being. She must go to Worcester without delay. But she could not use the horse that had brought her from Glebe Park. The beast had all but foundered that afternoon. She would have to find a livery stable and see if they would be willing to provide her with a fresh mount in exchange for the mare. But she would not find a livery stable in operation at four o'clock in the morning. Thoughts and plans chased themselves through her head. She was thinking with cool dispassion, and it was the same dispassion that returned her to her bed until daylight. She was carrying Daniel's child and had promised him to take care of that responsibility. Exhausting herself was not consonant with fulfilling that promise.

Later that morning she rode to Worcester. The lanes were clogged with the jubilant members of Cromwell's army, regular soldiers and members of the various county militias, who had rallied to Parliament's call. Disbanded after the victory, they were returning to their homes, and there were many to greet them in the villages they passed through. No one took any notice of a woman on a rawboned piebald gelding.

At Evesham, she came across a disheveled group of Royalist prisoners in a tavern yard where their guards were quenching their thirst at the ale bench. She rode over to the prisoners. They were all Scots and none had news of a Sir Daniel Drummond or a Master William Osbert. She offered them money to ease their plight, but they declined, telling her with a degree of gallows humor that since they were to be detained as guests of General Cromwell what need would they have for coin.

They wished her luck with her search, and she went on, reaching Worcester at nightfall. The town was full of Parliament's soldiers, officers of the New Model, men of horse and men of foot. All, without exception, bore the triumphal mien of victors.

"I pray you, sir, where will I find General Cromwell's headquarters?'' Henrietta leaned wearily down from her horse to address a foot soldier lounging against a wall, picking his teeth.

''Eh, what's a lass like you a-wantin' with the general?'' he asked, genially enough.

''I am looking for my husband,'' she said, seeing no reason to dissemble. ''He was at the battle, and I would know if anyone has news of him.''

The soldier pushed away from the wall. ''There's been plenty on such a quest this day. 'Eadquarters 'as been busier than a bull in the cow pen.'' He pointed down the street. ''Last buildin' on the right. Can't miss it, but I wouldn't be too 'opeful. No one knows anythin' much at present. 'Tis too early.''

''Aye, well thank'ee for your help.'' She rode on. If Daniel was alive, she would be as likely to have news of him here as anywhere. A Royalist prisoner, perchance, would have seen him. If he was dead . . . But he was not dead, because she could not bear that. The conviction served as talisman, ensured that she kept hope in the forefront of her mind, gave her the strength to ignore her fatigue.

But when she reached the headquarters building and dismounted from her horse, the ground came up to meet her, and a black fog swallowed her.

Daniel Drummond sat with his back against a tall elm tree and watched the party of Roundheads, pikes at the ready, approach him. His left arm hung uselessly at his side, the wrist smashed by a heavy stave. Pain and a weariness greater than any he had ever experienced now rendered him semiconscious, but he could still feel the satisfaction of relief that Will and Tom had finally seen sense and left him, when it had become clear that he could not keep up with them. Had they had horses it might have been different, but they had all lost their mounts in the bloody fray and had fled the field on foot.

Will and Tom had made their own escape under cover of darkness, and he had stumbled on until the excruciating pain finally brought him to his knees. He had been sitting here ever since, throughout the remainder of the night and through most of this day, drifting in and out of reality as he waited for the inevitable moment of capture.

What a day of useless, bloody carnage yesterday had been! In his ears, he could still hear the moans and screams from the dying; the stench of blood was trapped in his nostrils; his eyes still held the images of writhing bodies, of the severed head that rolled under his charger's hooves the instant his horse had been shot from beneath him.

But he was alive . . . for the moment. The Roundhead soldiers were standing around him now. If they chose to make sport of him with sword tip and pike before delivering the coup de grace, it would not be the first time such savagery had crowned the savagery of the last ten years, when brother had fought brother, father had fought son. But it was done with now. Had the king escaped the field? he wondered, closing his eyes as the steel tip of a pike grazed his cheek, and someone laughed.

"Leave him be!" a curt voice ordered. "Can ye not see he wears the sword of a gentleman? They'll be wanting him in London for examination."

Daniel opened his eyes and looked into a pair of bright blue ones. They held a gleam of compassion. His savior bent to help him to his feet.

"Can ye walk, sir?"

"Aye," Daniel said. " 'Tis but my wrist."

"I must ask ye for your sword," the corporal said, moving to slide it free from its sheath hanging at Daniel's side.

"I'll give it to you," Daniel said, suddenly sharp. With his good hand, he maneuvered the weapon loose, handing it hilt first to his captor. He would never again be permitted to wear a sword in this land. Such privilege was denied one who openly contested Parliament's rule. But since he was facing examination and prison, possibly execution, such a minor indignity could presumably be borne with fortitude, he reflected with grim irony.

How soon would the news of his capture reach Glebe Park? The lists of prisoners would be posted in all the towns soon enough. And Tom would make all speed, he knew. He would bring Henrietta to London. She would perhaps be permitted to visit him . . . if he was in fit condition to receive visitors after examination.

As he walked as straight as he could in the midst of his captors, he wondered in bitter self-knowledge what had been the point of this final futility on the battlefield at Worcester. Henrietta had been right. Honor and principle made unsatisfactory substitutes for love.

A group of prisoners stood beside a couple of carts laden with wounded. Roundhead soldiers offered apparently desultory guard, but their muskets were primed, the pikes at hand. Daniel searched the faces of his fellow prisoners but saw none he recognized. They exchanged nods as he joined them, cradling his injured wrist.

"Ye'll be better riding, sir." The compassionate corporal who had saved him from torment gestured toward the cart. "There'll be a chirurgeon at Worcester to look to your arm."

"My thanks, but I'll walk," Daniel said.

The corporal shrugged, gave an order, and the sad procession moved off toward Worcester.

Henrietta choked as the brandy was forced between her lips, trickling down her chin.

"Easy now, mistress," a voice said. "Sit ye up a bit." She was lifted against a broad shoulder and the flagon of brandy was again presented to her lips. This time she swallowed and felt a measure of strength return to her limbs.

"What . . . what happened?"

"Why, ye swooned dead away," the same voice said. "Right in front of headquarters."

She struggled to sit up alone and looked around. A circle of concerned faces peered at her . . . soldiers every one, and Roundhead soldiers at that. "Ye've been most kind," she managed to say, shaking her head in an effort to clear it of the muzz. " 'Tis mayhap because I am with child."

The concern became vocal. "Why, mistress, ye should never be riding in such a case."

"I wish to see General Cromwell," she said.

For some reason, that made them laugh. "The general's on his way to London, mistress . . . and even if he weren't, he's a mighty busy man."

Henrietta gave herself time to absorb this piece of information and to formulate some kind of strategy. She wanted information and had come to the horse's mouth for it. But she doubted that these rough yet kindly men would be able to tell her of the fate of Sir Daniel Drummond. Mayhap, she would do better to bide her time, keep her eyes and ears open. If she offered neither nuisance nor threat, perchance they would permit her to remain in headquarters for a spell. She would hear much, and some of it might be useful.

"My man," she said, closing her eyes as if exhausted, "he's in the Kentish militia, came to join the New Model, but I would know what has befallen him."

"Eh, now, mistress, you give us 'is name, then, and we'll see what we can do." They patted her hand in friendly fashion.

"Jake Green," she improvised. "Oh, I do feel poorly."

"Ye just rest quiet 'ere, Mistress Green. The night draws in and ye'll not find lodgings in the town. Is it a bite of supper ye'd be glad of?"

Henrietta realized that she was famished, not having eaten since the previous evening, and found herself accepting Parliament's hospitality with voracious appetite. Her enthusiasm for bread, meat, and buttermilk was regarded with approval by her caretakers, and she found she felt not a pang of guilt at this particular deception.

Someone had gone in search of information about the mythical Jake Green of the Kentish militia . . .

'Twas to be hoped he *was* mythical, she thought, as she was encouraged to a seat alongside the fire and told to take her ease and sleep awhile if she could.

With faintly whispered gratitude, Henrietta settled down to watch through half-closed eyes and listen with wide-open ears . . . something at which she had long been skilled.

It was near midnight when they brought the latest batch of prisoners into headquarters. The carts rolled to a halt on the cobbles outside and shouted instructions broke the somnolent peace. The men in the guard chamber rose to their feet, buttoning tunics, grumbling at this disturbance, and went outside, leaving the apparently still slumbering Mistress Green alone at the fireside.

Henrietta sprang to her feet, hurried to the door, which stood ajar on the corridor, and stood just behind it, peering through the crack between door and frame. They were carrying in those too severely wounded to walk even with support, then came the halt and the lame, gray and bloodless, drawn with pain and the despair of defeat.

She saw Daniel. He swayed slightly but scorned the offer of a supporting arm. His left arm was cradled against his chest. She saw the blood, the jagged edge of bone jutting through the skin. There was a moment when that black fog threatened again, but it receded under the blinding light of relief and purpose. He was alive, and so long as the wound was attended to rapidly it would surely not become mortified. How were they to get out of this place?

Not for one minute did it occur to her that they would fail to do so. It was simply a matter of hitting upon the right plan.

She left the guardroom, a search for the privy her excuse should she be questioned, and, hugging the shadows, followed the procession of guards and prisoners. They went outside at the rear of the building and into a barn. Voices were raised in greeting as the new arrivals entered. The barn door was left open, two guards sitting on either side of it, muskets between their feet. The only way of escape was back through the headquarters building riddled with armed soldiers, so why should they concern themselves with the possibility of a runaway?

Henrietta hastened back to the guardroom, regaining her fireside seat before her kindly companions returned, all unaware of her journey. She kept her eyes closed. Sleep would not ordinarily have been hard to feign, but the need to go to Daniel, to tend his hurt, to touch him with the hand of love, threatened to obscure all caution, and she could feel her muscles twitching.

"D'ye have the names of those newly brought in?" The question served to concentrate her mind most wonderfully.

"Nay, 'twill do in the morning." A yawn accompanied the statement. "We're to make lists of all prisoners by noon tomorrow. The gentlemen among 'em are to be taken direct to London for examination."

There was no time to waste. Henrietta stirred deliberately, stretched, blinked around the room.

"D'ye have need of summat, mistress?"

"The privy, sir," she said, rising. "I do not know how to thank ye for your kindness."

"Nay, think nothin' of it. We still wait for news from the Kent men. They were stationed on the left flank of the field, and none have reported 'ere as yet. 'Tis possible they were already disbanded."

"If 'tis so, then I had best return home," she said. "If ye'd direct me to the privy, sir."

"To the right of the courtyard, mistress. Go down the passageway and through the door at the end."

With a smile of thanks, she left them. The courtyard was empty of all but the guards sitting at the open barn door. A thrust of candlelight from the barn made a narrow path across the cobbles. Soft voices and an occasional, swiftly stifled moan murmured in the night air.

Moving into the shadows, she bent to lift her skirt, took her petticoat between both hands, and ripped it into strips. Holding these prominently, she stepped boldly across the courtyard. "Ye've a wounded man in there. I've orders to dress his injury. He's wanted fit for examination in London."

No one could be here without proper business. The guards regarded her with scant interest, one observing, "There's plenty wounded, mistress."

"Aye, but this is an arm wound, and I have description of the prisoner."

They waved her through the door. She stepped within, stood looking around at the huddled figures stretched upon the straw. Most were asleep. What did they have to stay awake for but pain? Pain of the spirit if not of the body.

Daniel was sitting propped against the far wall, legs stretched out before him, arm held against his chest. His eyes were closed as he drifted between sleeping and waking, preferring sleep because it brought relief from pain, offering instead the image of Harry . . . Harry at her most exasperating, her most loving, her most determined, her most helpful. His lips curved at the memories even as pain stabbed fiercely and he opened his eyes. Henrietta knelt at his side.

"I am come to be with you," she said with customary simplicity.

He closed his eyes for a long moment to dispel the hallucination. Then he opened them again. She was still there, her head on one side, her expression the one she wore when she thought she might be skating on thin ice.

"I am come to be with you," she repeated.

He smiled, murmured, "Aye, you would be of help, I daresay." What absurd conversation was this? Yet, it seemed perfectly right and natural. He must be in the grip of nightmare turned dream.

"Yes, I would." She brushed his lips with her own, a featherlight touch as if she were afraid any pressure might add to his hurts. "Do not mock, Daniel, 'tis far too serious a matter." She looked at the shattered wrist and shook out her makeshift bandages. "I would bind it for you, love. But I am afeared it will pain you most dreadfully."

"No more than it does already, elf." He fought to bring his mind into focus. This was no vision dredged from the depths of agonized exhaustion and despair. *But what the hell did she think she was doing here?* "Where are the children?"

"With Dorcas," she said, biting her lip in fierce concentration as she draped the bandage over the exposed bone. "Ye need not fear. I left them safe."

"And Julie?" He tore his mind from the agony as she began to twist the material around his wrist, her fingers delicately, but in terror, attempting to readjust the bone, to remove shards.

"Brought to bed of a fine son," she said. "I delivered him, Daniel. 'Twas the most wonderful thing." Holding his forearm, she twisted the bandage as tightly as she dared. "Will's mother is with her now. What of Will?"

"Escaped, I trust. He and Tom were well on their way to Wheatley before yesterday daybreak."

"They left you?" She stared, incredulous.

"At my insistence, elf. I was endangering them, and there was no point losing three of us. They have families."

"As do you," she said, fastening the bandage with an ungainly but efficient knot. "I have a plan to contrive your escape."

Daniel rested his head on the wooden partition at his back. "Sweetheart, there is no sense in such thought. Even were I to succeed in escape, they would arrest me at home. I will not again go into exile. Glebe Park is to be my children's home. This is their country, whether it be ruled by King or Parliament."

"But if they do not know who y'are, they cannot arrest you at home," she said practically. "And they have not yet taken names."

Daniel forced himself to focus on this statement. It was quite correct; no one had yet demanded his identity.

"God's grace, Harry! How d'ye know these things? How did you get in here?"

"I fell into a faint outside headquarters," she explained. "I think 'twas because I had not eaten and I was very tired. The soldiers were most kind to me. I've been sitting in the guardroom all night, listening."

"You swooned?" Daniel found his fatigue fade under a wash of anger at this cheerful admission. "How *dare* you not take care of yourself at this time!"

She regarded him with a stubborn turn to her mouth. "Y'are not strong enough to be vexed."

He closed his eyes. "Just wait until I am!"

"Daniel, I had to come," she said. "I could not know you were in such danger and not be there."

"We seem to have had this discussion on some other occasion," he murmured wearily. "But y'are right, I've not the strength to take you to task for it, and am in no position to enforce my commands. I can only beg that you will behave with circumspection."

She chewed her lip for a minute. "I must return to the guardroom. They will wonder what has happened to me. 'Tis an unconscionable long time to spend in the privy."

Daniel's lips curved involuntarily. "That's where y'are supposed to be, is it, my elf?"

She nodded. "Listen to me, Daniel. When they ask for your name, you must give them a false one. Ye can be Daniel Bolt again." She saw prideful refusal on his face and spoke with angry intensity. "You *must* do as I say! I will not have this child born without knowing a father. Either they will execute you or you will die in prison, if not of examination! D'ye think I do not know what will happen to you? You owe it to all of us to take this one chance for escape."

He did, for all that he knew the chance to be minuscule. But he could be no worse off, and when he was recaptured his pregnant wife would be excused her attempts to save him. It would be accepted as a brave example of wifely duty. "Very well."

"Look for me on the road," she whispered, her eyes

shining with relief. "I will be riding a piebald gelding. I will come up with the march."

"And then what?" Some of her enthusiasm and vigor spilled over to him, and he felt stronger, no longer gripped by the sapping quality of helpless resignation.

"You will see." She kissed him again, but this time with much less hesitation. Then she was gone, slipping amongst the recumbent forms of his fellow unfortunates, offering an insouciant wave to the guards, returning to the guardroom and her preparations.

Chapter 22

A surgeon came into the barn at dawn. Harry's makeshift bandaging had afforded Daniel some relief during the remainder of the night, but he welcomed the more expert attentions. They were not offered with much gentleness, it was true to say, but his wrist was splinted, rebandaged, and a sling provided. Once he had recovered from the faintness engendered by this care, he found he could view the day with a degree of composure.

There was breakfast, also; a meager offering of dry bread and weak beer, but it brought renewed strength as he realized that it was the first time he had broken his fast in two days. He lay back against the wall of the barn and closed his eyes. Just what did Harry have in mind? He knew her to be ingenious and determined in her planning, but even if she could succeed in spiriting him away from the line of marching prisoners, how did she think a wounded man was going to elude capture between here and London, when the entire countryside was crawling with search parties?

He must have slept a little, because the sun was high when a foot nudged his thigh and he looked up into the face of a Roundhead officer, holding quill and parchment. "Your name?" the officer demanded.

Daniel Drummond, Baronet, of Glebe Park, in the village of Cranston, in the county of Kent; His Majesty's most loyal servant.

"Daniel Bolt, Esquire, of Lichfield," he replied heavily. The officer scrawled on the parchment and moved along the line.

An hour later, they were herded out into the sunny courtyard. Daniel blinked in the brightness and wondered if he could endure the humiliation of being bound on this long march to imprisonment. But the officer directed him to one side of the yard, where were gathered the walking wounded. The able-bodied were roped together, but presumably it was assumed that the wounds of the others would have a sufficiently prohibitive effect.

It would certainly make Harry's task easier, Daniel reflected, and it further lifted his spirits. They were marched out into the street. He looked around, for the moment stunned at the scene. There were hundreds of prisoners gathered for the walk to London, Scots and English, in torn clothing, some without shoes, some still bloodied, all grim-faced with the despair of defeat. Many of them would already have marched from Scotland with the king, he knew. Exhausted by that journey, by the depredations of battle, and now another forced march, how many of them would fall by the wayside?

There was much milling around, much shouting and arguing amongst the military authorities, and the lines of prisoners stood under the sun, weary and resigned. But at last the order came to move out. Daniel offered his good arm to his neighbor, who hobbled from a pike wound in his thigh.

People came out of their houses to watch them as they passed. They stood in doorways and lined the streets. One or two ran up to them with cups of water and milk, hunks of bread and cheese. There were many words of comfort and loud calls of encouragement. Not everyone in this land was happy to accept Parliament's rule, and many wept for the king, whose whereabouts were still unknown. He had fled the field, but had he reached the safety of one of the Channel ports?

The presence of a young woman on a rawboned piebald gelding caused no remark. She was just part of the crowd. At sunset the order came to halt the march. Bivouacs were made in a cornfield, prisoners and escorts sank down with relief, but the prisoners were dependent for their supper upon the kindness of the countryfolk. The young woman, no longer mounted, moved amongst the men with a basket of apples, bright chatter upon her lips; she was one of many.

Daniel took a crisp green apple. "My thanks, mistress." Her eyes raked his face, took in the lines of fatigue and pain sharp etched around his eyes and mouth. She looked around the busy field. The setting sun threw long shadows.

"Soldier . . . your pardon, sir." She called to one of the soldiers escorting Daniel's party. He strolled over to her.

"Aye, mistress?"

"Sir, I know this man," she said. "His name is Bolt. He is a friend of my brother's. I wonder . . . I wonder . . . since he is wounded, if I could offer him hospitality in my house for the night. 'Tis but a step down the road. He'll be better for a mattress and a good supper. And you, of course, sir, since he'll need escort."

The soldier considered this. The prospect of a decent night's lodging and a good supper was tempting, and he had nothing against the prisoner, who was a gentleman after all. "Well, I take that most kind in ye, mistress," he said. "I'll just inform the captain." He loped off in the direction of the officers' bivouac.

"Ye'll find it easier to walk with the aid of a stick," Henrietta said evenly, handing Daniel a heavy blackthorn that she had concealed in the folds of her skirt.

So, it presumably fell to his hand to dispose of the escort, Daniel reflected, hoping that he still maintained sufficient vigor in his right arm to wield the blackthorn usefully. He leaned heavily upon the stick and tried to look as if he were drawing upon his last vestige of strength. It must have been convincing. When the soldier came back with permission for the visit, he looked with great sympathy at the prisoner and made no objection to the walking stick.

"Eh, sir, ye'll be much better for a decent bed this night."

"Aye, he will that," Harry said. "Follow me, if ye will." She set off across the field, leading them away from the camp. " 'Tis quicker cross-country," she called cheerfully over her shoulder as she dived through a gap in the far hedge.

Her companions followed more slowly, since Daniel did not think he could convincingly increase his speed whilst leaning on a stick. Harry, in her enthusiasm, had clearly lost sight of this.

"Just along this field and then over the stile," she said, pausing to wait for them. "The house is on the other side of the lane."

"I thought ye said it was but a step," grumbled the soldier, looking behind him at the distance they had traversed.

"A big step." She offered him a ravishing smile, then set off toward the stile, where again she waited for them.

Her eyes flicked toward Daniel. "Perhaps ye'd better go first, sir." So it was to be here. His hand tightened around the blackthorn, then with genuine awkwardness he clambered over the obstacle.

Henrietta gathered up her skirt, climbed onto the first step, swung her leg over the top rung, teetered, then half jumped, half fell, landing in a heap on the grassy verge. Her cry was but barely issued when the soldier sprung across the stile to her assistance.

"Eh, mistress, be you hurt?" He bent over her.

Daniel raised the blackthorn, brought it down, and the soldier tumbled inert beside Henrietta.

She scrambled to her feet. " 'Tis a great shame. He is such a nice man. Ye've not killed him, d'ye think?"

"I trust not," Daniel said, bending to lay a finger against the artery in the soldier's neck. "Nay, the pulse beats strongly. He may not be out for long."

"Then let us make haste. The piebald is tethered in that spinney." She set off at a run toward a clump of trees at the far side of the field.

Daniel tossed aside the blackthorn and followed, catching her easily. The exhilaration of the escape combined with the sharp spur of danger to banish his exhaustion, at least for the time being.

Henrietta looked up at him and grinned. "I told you I had a plan."

"Aye, so you did." He touched the tip of her nose with his forefinger and returned the grin.

They plunged into the dark seclusion of the spinney and Daniel breathed a little more easily, although he knew the illusion of safety was just that. The unconscious soldier could be discovered at any moment and the hue and cry would begin. They were far too close to the camp for any real security.

"Here we are." Henrietta stopped in a clearing, where the piebald grazed placidly. She leaned against a tree trunk and closed her eyes for a minute.

"Henrietta, are you feeling all right?" Daniel caught her chin with his good hand, lifting her face.

She nodded. "Quite all right. 'Twas just the excitement."

He examined her upturned face and exclaimed in worried frustration, "God's grace, but I wish you'd stayed at home as I told you to! This is no proper business for a pregnant woman."

"I do not think 'tis proper business for anyone," she retorted. "But you would go to war again, so what else was I to do?" She pulled free of his hold. "Come, we must change our clothes."

He was obliged to accept that recriminations were both futile and time-wasting in the circumstances. "What have you in mind?"

She shot him a look both mischievous and uneasy, her moment of dizziness forgotten. "Well, it seemed to me that they will be looking for a woman and a wounded man, not for a lad and his old granny." She pulled a package from the saddlebag. "See, these are for you."

Daniel's jaw fell and he stared aghast. She was holding out a voluminous print gown with a calico petticoat, and a heavy, hooded cloak. "You are not serious?" he said slowly.

"Oh, do not be so prideful," Henrietta snapped, having expected this reaction. "Y'are not going to start talking of the honor of the Drummonds, are you? You are fleeing for your life, Daniel! 'Tis no time to consider your dignity. D'ye think the king is?" She shoved the garments into his arms and turned back to the saddle-bag, pulling out a smaller package.

"Hell and the devil!" Protest made, Daniel shook out the gown, regarding it with revulsion. "Where did you acquire these, Harry?"

"Off a washing line, very early this morning," she informed him. "I did feel a little guilty at stealing them, but there did not seem any alternative."

"No, I suppose there wasn't," murmured Daniel, watching as she began to take off her own gown and petticoat. She shivered in her smock, yanking on a pair of woolen britches, her head bent as she struggled with the hooks at the waist.

"This is absurd," she exclaimed in chagrin. "I seem to be getting fat. I made sure they would fit me, but I cannot do them up."

"Your shape is changing," he reminded her evenly, struggling one-handed out of his doublet. "Leave the hooks undone."

"I suppose I must. I will leave the shirt hanging outside to cover the muddle." She suited action to words, then moved to help Daniel, dropping the petticoat over his head, fastening the tie at his waist. "I trust your britches will not show beneath. D'ye think you should take them off?"

"No, I do not!" he declared forcefully. "I am not racketing around the countryside in my drawers!"

"Oh, I think y'are ridiculous!" She dropped the gown over his head, gently maneuvering his wounded arm into the sleeve and hooking up the bodice. "There, what a splendid granny you make." Laughter bubbled in her voice, sparkled in her eyes, and despite the desperate predicament Daniel could not help his own reluctant amusement as he imagined the picture he must present.

"For God's sake give me the cloak," he said. "At least I may hide my shame beneath that."

"You must keep the hood over your face and walk bent over," she instructed, pulling the hood over his head. "With luck, ye'll not have to do much walking. But you must ride sidesaddle." She pulled on a rough woolen jacket, tucked her hair beneath a close-fitting knitted cap, and bent to grab a handful of mud from the ground at her feet.

"Smear my face with this. 'Twill make me look more like an urchin."

"You are an urchin, you ramshackle creature." He took the mud and spread it liberally across her cheeks, dabbed a smudge on the end of her nose, and then bent to kiss her. "I trust that at some point in the not-too-distant future, I'll have the time and opportunity to do that properly."

"Well, you will not if you waste precious time grumbling at my plans." But her voice caught, and the smile trembling on her lips held both promise and regret. "Can you mount one-handed?"

"If I were not hampered by petticoats, I could do so with ease." He managed nevertheless and stretched down his sound hand to Harry. "Put your foot on my boot."

She did so, his fingers clasped hers tightly, and she sprang upward, swinging astride the saddle in front of him. "The horse is quite fresh and should carry us to Oxford. I will take him back to the livery stable there and reclaim the mare, who will carry us to London. We should reach Oxford by daybreak and can be in London by the evening."

"We are going to Wheatley," Daniel said.

"But that is not what I planned."

"Maybe not," he calmly replied, "but that is what *I* have planned."

"But surely it makes sense to make all speed to London. The longer we linger over the journey, the greater the danger. I do not see why you should take over the planning when I have done so well so far.'' She sounded greatly injured.

''If you think I am going to permit you to ride all night and all day, you must think again, madam wife,'' Daniel returned, still perfectly calm. ''You had no sleep last night, fainted once already with fatigue, and enough is enough. Even if you were not with child, I would not permit it. We go to the Osberts, and if y'are going to argue with me, just remember that I still have one strong hand.''

She twisted her head to look at him over her shoulder. There was laughter in her brown eyes, glowing in her dirty face, but it could not hide their tiredness. ''You are *so* ungrateful!''

''Nay, elf, never that,'' he said, suddenly soft. ''Come now, let us be on our way. I would have you tucked up in bed as soon as possible.''

''I trust you'll be tucked up with me,'' she said, leaning against him for a moment, before she shook the reins and the piebald moved out of the spinney, carrying its double burden.

The banter was but disguise for the very real fear Daniel felt for her. He held her securely with his one arm. It would look to anyone as if the old woman riding pillion was hanging on to the youth for support, but they both knew the reverse to be the case. His own exhaustion he had dismissed by an effort of will and now concentrated on relieving the slight body in front of him of the need to hold herself upright, or to do anything but guide the gelding through the night.

They steered clear of the roads, where they might run into a troop of Parliament's soldiers on the lookout for any suspicious traveler. An old woman and a lad riding at night would be certain to draw attention, although not as much as a wounded man and a young woman. But fortune smiled upon them, and the closest they came to a dangerous encounter was chancing upon a troop of soldiers camping in a field. They managed to see the troop in time to turn back and skirt the field unnoticed, but the incident left them both with sweating palms and fast-beating hearts.

Daniel's anxiety grew apace as dawn streaked the sky and they circled Oxford. They would need to take the open road from this point and Henrietta was slumped against him, barely conscious. He now held the reins himself in one hand, the arm in its sling concealed beneath his cloak.

"Sweetheart," he whispered, "you must sit up and take the reins while we are on the lanes, in case we are stopped."

She struggled upright. "I beg your pardon. Did I fall asleep?" She stiffened as they rounded a corner. A troop of soldiers were striding ahead of them.

"Ride straight through them," he instructed softly. "We are on our way to assist at a birthing in Headington. I think 'tis the next village."

Her back straightened, her head came up. She pulled the knitted cap lower over her brow and pressed her knees against the gelding's flanks, urging the weary beast into a trot. Daniel hunched forward, his hood concealing his face, and adjusted his skirts so that they completely covered his boots.

They came up with the soldiers.

"I give ye good day, good sirs," Harry called down, her voice strong and cheerful.

"Where be you off to at such an hour?" demanded a trooper.

"Why to a birthin' in Headington," she responded. " 'Tis a breech, and old granny 'ere is the best midwife fer miles."

The trooper raised a hand in acceptance and he and his fellows stood aside to let the gelding through.

" 'Tis to be hoped they do not realize how the horse is flagging," she muttered, kicking the animal into a canter until they were out of sight. "In another couple of miles, we can take a shortcut over Shotover Hill. Perchance there'll be no one but poachers abroad there at this hour."

She sounded relatively robust, Daniel noted with relief, even as he summoned up his own last reserves of strength. Twice more they were hailed by soldiers and Harry produced the same explanation for their dawn journey. A cheeky, begrimed urchin and a silent, shrouded old woman on such an errand gave rise to no suspicions, and at last they were able to turn off the lane and onto the common land of Shotover. The horse stumbled in a rabbit hole, but recovered, whinnying unhappily, laboring up the bracken-covered slope. They crested the rise, and Harry suddenly sighed, her shoulders sagging.

"There is Osbert Court." She gestured toward a stone gatepost. "We are here." She slumped against him, finally defeated.

Daniel tightened his supporting arm around her waist and simply took the reins again, guiding the horse through the gateposts. As if he sensed journey's end, the gelding lifted his drooping head and stepped out along the driveway to the long, low, thatched house at its end.

"They'll still be abed," Harry murmured weakly. "Go around the back to the stables."

But as he turned the horse, the front door swung open. "God's grace, Harry, but I thought 'twas you from the window, although I could not credit it." Will, in his nightgown, ran out. "The messenger brought news of my son from my mother. But, oh, Harry, I do not know how to tell ye of the battle . . . I have not been able to sleep, worrying . . . " Then his voice died as he took in Harry's extraordinary companion. "Sir Daniel . . . Can it be . . . ?"

"One of Harry's brighter ideas," Daniel said dryly, resigned to the inevitable reception. He shook back the hood of the cloak and slid to the ground. "Lift her off, Will. I cannot with one arm, and she's too fatigued to manage alone."

Will's beam would have melted the Arctic snows. "I cannot believe y'are safe. Tom and I were to leave this morning for Kent. We thought it safe enough, since we've not been disturbed by troops here, and there's none to suspect we've been at the battle. Tom has been so wretched. Oh, Harry, how did ye contrive it?'' He lifted her down gently. ''Come within.''

Esquire Osbert, summoned from his bed, arrived in the parlor just as Sir Daniel Drummond, with Will's help, was divesting himself of a voluminous print gown and calico petticoat.

''Good God!'' he ejaculated.

''Quite so, Osbert,'' Daniel said with a tired grin, holding out his good hand. ''We must impose upon your hospitality for a short while, I fear.''

''For as long as ye care to. We've had no visits from Parliament's men and no reason to expect any, so the house is safe enough.'' The squire, taking the hand, looked from the grubby urchin slumped on the settle to the wounded man. ''But I understood ye to be taken prisoner, Drummond . . . Henrietta?''

''Aye,'' Daniel affirmed, and his smile shone with pride and tenderness. ''Henrietta . . . reckless as ever upon her errands of mercy . . . contrived my escape. I owe her my life.'' He bent to brush her forehead with his lips. Then he returned briskly to the matter uppermost in his mind. ''She's to be put to bed immediately. D'ye have a woman who could assist her?'' He gestured to his useless arm. ''I would do so myself, but, as you see . . .''

''I will fetch old Nurse,'' Will said promptly. ''She has known Harry since we were children.''

''I do not need to be put to bed.'' Henrietta spoke up, her voice sounding strangely stiff and distant. ''And I do not care to be spoken of as if I were not here. When do we start for London?''

''*You* are going nowhere, my elf,'' her husband said firmly.

''Eh, Sir Daniel . . . eh, but I can't believe my eyes!'' Tom's voice, hushed with astonished wonder, came from the doorway. ''I was sure ye'd be a prisoner by now.''

''So he was,'' Henrietta said. ''Until I came along.''

Tom stared. "Well, I never. I said you was a wild hoity maid when we took you off the field at Preston."

Daniel laughed softly. "That good deed has brought me more blessings than one man in one lifetime is entitled to, Tom." He turned back to the still figure on the settle. "Sweetheart, I want you in bed, *now.*"

"But I shall be fit directly I have had something to eat," she enunciated, frowning hard in concentration as she picked her words. "Then we can go to London to the girls. I have been thinking that we could borrow a cart. 'Twould be easier for your arm. You can keep your granny disguise and I will drive the cart. If we fill it with produce, then we will draw no attention, and once we are in London no one will ever question us."

Her plan was received in disbelieving silence, a silence broken by the arrival of an elderly woman in cap and apron who seemed to find nothing untoward at this strange gathering in the early morning. "Well, now, Miss Henrietta, what have you been up to this time?" She bustled across the room. "Fair peaky, ye looks, even under all that dirt."

"But are we not to go to London?" Henrietta looked at Daniel with the enormous, desperate eyes of one pushed beyond the limit of endurance. "Do not leave me here . . . Please do not leave me again, Daniel."

He was sitting beside her, her head clasped to his breast, almost before the forlorn plea had left her lips. "Dearest love, I do not intend leaving you ever again, not for so much as a minute," he promised with instant comprehension. His wife was at breaking point. The fear and desperation subsumed for so long under the need to plan and to act was now taking its toll, rendering her more vulnerable than he could ever remember seeing her. "Tom will go to London and bring the children here."

"Aye, that I will, Lady Drummond," Tom agreed hastily. "I'll be off within the hour and bring the little maids to ye. Now don't ye worry about a thing," he added awkwardly, scratching his head before turning and stomping out of the parlor.

"Come, elf, I will take you abovestairs, and Nurse will put you to bed."

" 'Tis a peppermint caudle she'll be needing, I shouldn't wonder," the woman said. "Always was partial to them, was Miss Henrietta. Come along, m'dear. Master Will says y'are with child. Ye've more than yourself to take care of, these days."

Henrietta yielded the dikes of self-determination. She was aware of being undressed, of warm water laving her skin, of soft linen covering her body, of sweet-smelling sheets and the deep embrace of a feather mattress, of hot, thin, wine-spiced gruel spooned into her obediently opened mouth. And all the while, she was aware of Daniel, who never moved out of her line of vision, who spoke gently to her, caressed her cheek with his finger, brushed her mouth with his, held her hand until she slipped into merciful, healing oblivion.

Daniel gazed upon his sleeping wife and wondered how such a wondrous, magical creature had been shaped, how such a loving and giving spirit could have emerged from the arid soil of her childhood. And he wondered what he had done to deserve the gift of her love, the immeasurable joy of her self to inform his life.

"Did Daddy really dress up as a lady, Harry?"

"Most definitely not a lady, Lizzie. A veritable crone in print and calico." Laughing, Daniel came into the sunny bedchamber, where his wife lay propped upon pillows in the big bed and his daughters were sprawled in most indecorous fashion across the quilt.

"What an adventure," Lizzie said wistfully. "I wish I could have an adventure."

"I don't," Nan said, clambering off the bed and going to hug her father's knees. "Daddy was wounded, and he hasn't let Harry get out of bed for a week. I do not think adventures are at all nice things."

Daniel bent to hitch her up onto his hip, awkward because of his one sound hand. "I think ye have the right of it, Nan. I have certainly had enough of adventuring. Mistress Osbert and Julie and the babe are arrived. Why d'ye not go and greet them?''

''You just want to be alone with Harry,'' Lizzie observed, sliding off the bed.

''Impertinent minx,'' her father said, but there was a chuckle in his voice. ''Off with you!'' He set Nan on her feet, pointing with an imperative finger to the door. The girls followed its direction, Lizzie casting both adults a mischievous grin over her shoulder.

''Do you think that child is taking shameless advantage of my reduced mobility?'' Daniel inquired, mildly curious, as he turned the key in the door.

''I shouldn't be at all surprised,'' Henrietta replied, smiling.

''Mmmm . . . well, she's going to be in for a shock one of these fine days,'' he said amiably, sitting on the bed. ''I must find them another governess. Unbutton my shirt, will you, love. 'Twill be quicker if you do it.''

Henrietta chuckled in mischievous comprehension and her fingers moved nimbly, pushing the shirt off his shoulders, easing it over his bandaged arm. ''Am I to understand that matters between us are now to return to normal, husband?''

''You are,'' he answered with a complacent smile. ''I have been restrained quite long enough. 'Tis time you resumed your conjugal duties, madam wife.''

''Anyone would think I had been neglecting them through choice,'' she murmured, aggrieved, lying back on the pillows and kicking the bedcovers aside. ''I thought 'twas your wound causing the difficulty.''

''I do not make love with my arm.''

That was certainly true, reflected Henrietta some considerable time later, stroking the dark head resting against her breast. ''Will we go home now, love?''

''Aye,'' Daniel said, pressing his lips into the soft curve of her bosom. '' 'Tis time for the peace of surrender, my elf. The world we knew is defeated. We must fashion a new one from the materials given us. England is still for Englishmen, be she a Puritan commonwealth or no.''

"And a man can still tend his land, care for his children, enjoy his wife," she said with that same mischievous chuckle. "And this wife would like to be enjoyed again, if you please."